# The Journey

## William Burdett

The Journey
Copyright © 2007 William Burdett
All Right Reserved.

ISBN 978-1-4303-2333-4

# ACKNOWLEDGMENTS

As with all creative endeavors the support and assistance of friends is always desired and greatly appreciated. For their kindness in offering technical advice to improve this novel, the author wishes to thank Joseph Kramer and Rose Hozjan.

# Chapter 1

## Sunday morning 5:00 am

*R*ain soaked darkness gripped the night at this five am hour, the intermittent traffic and the fact it was a Sunday made for easy going. Occasionally lights from passing eighteen wheeled trucks enhanced the illumination generated by my pickup truck headlight beams. I had been making very good time on this thousand plus mile trip back to Chicago, having left my mother's home in Massachusetts at nine the previous morning. Strapped safely in the truck's bed was my dead brother's prized Harley Davidson. Having ridden motorcycles ever since I could remember, I had decided a few years earlier to give it up and be content with my fond memories, Of course age, aches, pains and according to my wife a little wisdom, made the decision easy for me. Then my brother Steve died and I promised Candace his widow I would buy it from her. At least I kept my promise. I often wonder if he was keeping tabs on the situation and if I failed to honor my promise, would I be in for an earful when and if we met again? So, figuring better safe than sorry, and against my wife's better judgment, I followed through and bought the beast.

A green sign advising Chicago was a scant forty miles distant loomed into view, followed closely by blinking yellow warning lights and caution signs letting me know the final Indiana toll booth was a mere two miles distant. Moving my left thumb the fraction of an inch necessary to find the speed control switch, I pressed the "off" button. Almost immediately, the steady pull of the engine subsided and the speedometer began its slow descent. If I timed this right, I should just coast into the toll booth. Yet another game played on this entirely boring trip from the east coast. Rounding a slight bend in the road, the flashing yellow lights of the tollbooth came into view. Normally, I would have maintained cruising speed through the tollbooth using the I-PASS lanes allowing the RF reader to capture my bar code number and have the database automatically deduct the toll amount from my self-loading account. Unfortunately, the Illinois and the Indiana databases had not yet become intimate and willing to share my hard earned currency. Gently applying the brakes for the final fifty feet, I came to a stop at the booth's window. The attendant, a middle-aged or perhaps very tired less-than-middle-aged woman glanced toward the back of the truck I assume looking for trailer in tow before taking my toll slip and advising the financial impact of the past hundred miles or so.

"That will be Twelve-Eighty" she said, boredom evident in each word. I nodded as I handed her a ten and a five. "Can you tell me how far to the next rest area?"

Her reply carried a degree of unspoken sarcasm; she jerked her hand westward and said. "Read the sign Sir."

"Sorry, I guess I'm more tired than I thought." My words no doubt sounded a little weak and her knowing smile only reinforced this thought.

"Just over the Illinois line sir, about five miles, can't miss it, bright lights, a gas station, even has a restaurant and gift shop." She paused for a moment. "You have a safe drive sir and come back to see us soon."

Her sarcasm was not lost on me and in spite of, or perhaps because of fatigue, I couldn't stop myself from laughing and saying "You betcha by golly, I'll put that on my things to do list," my foot depressing the gas pedal at the same time. I don't know if she heard or understood, but it sure felt good to have matched her sarcasm.

I definitely needed to stop for a cup of coffee and perhaps a sandwich. As I was ahead of schedule maybe I could even contemplate dozing off for an hour or two. Even with the Torrance Avenue roadwork fiasco ahead, I would still be home for the noon kickoff of the Bears game. Besides, at this rate I would get home too early and would wake the wife and THAT was not a pleasant thought. The last time that happened she called the police about an intruder.

As promised, the rest area came into view, or I should say the bluish-white glare of parking lot lights were visible well in advance of the off ramp. Again shutting off the cruise control, I allowed the truck to coast off the highway and onto the ramp. There were not many cars or trucks at this hour, so finding a parking spot just outside the circles of light emanating from the halogen light poles was not a problem. A little darkness would probably make for easier dozing. Stepping from the truck, I walked slowly around the bed checking the straps that secured the bike in place. This had become a habit since my first stop when I discovered one of the straps had come loose somehow. A blue tarp, new the day before, still covered half of the bike, the other half was covered only by blue plastic threads. This the wind effect of driving nine-hundred plus miles, consistently exceeding the speed limit. Occasional blue threads from the tarp protruded from pinch points on the bikes frame and I could only hope it had not messed up the paint. Satisfied the straps were secure. I started the short walk toward the building holding the promise of coffee and food. The gift shop would most certainly be closed at this hour. Too bad, a package of "antacids" would probably be needed soon.

Perhaps it was the fatigue, or maybe the thought of hot coffee and food which distracted me, but I never heard the two men approaching from behind. My first sense of trouble came when a hand grabbed my shoulder and pulled me around and down towards the ground. As I fell I caught a glint of light reflecting from what appeared to be a gun.

"Give me your money" a harsh voice demanded from one of the two dark shapes standing over me.

"It's in my coat pocket." My hand instinctively reached into my coat to retrieve it.

"He's got a gun!" a second voice yelled just as I heard an explosion and simultaneously I saw stars, followed by the deep darkness of unconsciousness.

# Chapter 2

## **Sunday morning 6:45 am**

*D*amn! Where was he? It was only a fifteen-minute ride from his apartment. Standing in the doorway, she watched as headlights slowly approached hoping it was Andrew. He needed to get here before the police did.

She knew instinctively something was wrong when the telephone rang so early in the morning. She knew Bill would not call that early and while she knew he would be home sometime in the morning, she also knew he would probably stop for a few hours so as to not disturb the household: two cats, a lizard, and herself. He was funny that way.

The toneless voice on the telephone served only to heighten her fear. A male voice, obviously not Bill simply asked if this was the Reynolds residence and if she was the wife or daughter of one William Reynolds.

The caller id indicated the caller's number was being "withheld", something telemarketers often did, but even they would not call this early. Unsure of the caller's intent, she asked. "Whom am I speaking with?" The voice answered that he could divulge no further information unless he was in fact speaking to the wife of one William Reynolds. Sensing this to be no time for telephone games she replied. "Yes, this is Mrs. Reynolds. Now who are you?"

The voice then identified himself as a dispatch officer from the Illinois State Police. Hearing this, she felt the proverbial knot beginning to form in her stomach. Something had happened. The voice went on to say that there had been an incident involving her husband and that it was necessary for her to get to the Saint Jude Hospital in Calumet City as soon as possible.

Her demands to know what had happened and how serious the

4

"incident" was were to no avail. The officer claiming to be only a dispatch officer did not have the details but again emphasized that her presence was required immediately. He went on to advise her that a patrol car would be dispatched to pick her up and would provide transportation to the hospital. This only confirmed to her the situation was as bad as, or even worse than she was imagining. "How long before the car will arrive?"

"At least forty-five minutes." The officer went on to add, "Is there anybody else you can bring with you?"

"Yes I have two sons and will see if I can contact them." She knew Andrew would be home. Whether or not she could rouse him from sleep was a different question altogether.

"Very well Mrs. Reynolds, I will dispatch the car right away. Please make sure your sons are there when the car arrives, the officer will not be able to wait for them." The phone went silent as he hung up.

Surprisingly, Andrew was already awake. While Andrew and his father had their problems as all teenage boys did, she knew beyond any doubt that he respected his father and loved him very much. Even though she knew he would never outwardly convey this to his father, she could see it in his mannerisms and behavior. He unknowingly emulated his father in virtually every aspect including his nutty sense of humor.

When the phone rang he answered rather cautiously. "Not even seven in the morning, this must be important." He knew "Mom" calling this early could only mean there was a problem. She of all people would be worried that she would be "disturbing" him.

"Yes! I am afraid so! Something has happened to your father." She went on to relate the details of the call from the State Police including the fact she needed to get to the hospital in Calumet City as soon as possible.

"I can drive you there. I'll throw on some clothes and leave right away." His mind raced with all kinds of thoughts, few of them positive. What had dad gotten into now? His dad was the type of person every kid wanted for a father. He was always there when you needed him and sometimes even when you didn't. He was the type who was usually getting into, or was in some way contributing, to some sort of juvenile behavior, yet almost always in a constructive way. He remembered with a smile the paint-ball excursions he and his brother Eric had put the old man through. They were not surprised that dad was the type who thought paint ball was cool and often went to great lengths to make sure they shot each other multiple times. When they wanted a go-kart it was dad who sided with them over mom's objections. That episode resulted in his having to replace all of the sod on the front lawn to get rid of the oval track the tires had made. When Eric went crazy about fishing, it was dad who made sure he had all the right equipment. He even bought a "summer cottage" so he could fish to his heart's content. The fact that dad liked to fish as much as Eric resulted in the two becoming fishing buddies of the first order. More than once mom was heard to say, that she had three children not two. At the same time, he was the epitome of responsibility, even when his job took him to the farthest corners of the earth, he always came home with something for each of them, as if to reinforce to them that he was always thinking of them. Yes, he was a good father. Even when they argued, that could not be questioned.

"That won't be necessary, the State Police are sending a car for me, and they should be here in forty-five minutes. But I would like you to go with me; can you be here before they get here?"

"I'll be there in twenty minutes, don't leave without me." While it was only a fifteen-minute ride he would need to stop for gas, he was running on fumes. In fact, he was mildly surprised he had made it home the previous evening. He smiled to himself, remembering the many times mom told him "fill the tank when it gets to the halfway point. You wouldn't want to run out at a bad time." And now certainly qualified as a bad time.

"Good, you better hurry. The officer said they will not be able to wait for you. In the meantime, I'll try to get in touch with Eric." Eric had spent the night at a friend's house as he usually did on the weekends.

"No problem, I'll be there." he clicked the "end call" button and went searching for a clean shirt and trousers.

The police car pulled into the driveway a few minutes after Andrew arrived.

Craig!

Thank you for purchasing my work! I hope you enjoy reading it as much as I did writing it.

Bill
William Burdett
July 24, 2008

www.lulu.com -

# Chapter 3

## <u>Sunday morning 7:20 am</u>

$S$ergeant Harridy slowed the car as he read the house numbers. As he was southbound, number 807 should be on his left. The thirty-four year veteran did not mind the "taxi" duty. It was better than pulling over drunk drivers on the interstate. He had done his time in that capacity and on other duties of a far worse nature. Another year and he would take early retirement, probably sell his house, and move to his summer cottage on the lake in Wisconsin.

The house was a white raised ranch with juniper bushes surrounding the front exterior. Obviously these people didn't realize the disadvantages of growing bushes that close to the house. Aside from the inherent damage caused by the expanding root system they also provide security and cover for would be bad guys. The front door stood open and a woman in her mid-forties followed closely by a young man in his early twenties came down the stone stairs as he came to a stop in front of the house.

Exiting the patrol car he smiled at them. "Mrs. Reynolds?"

"Yes, I'm Mrs. Reynolds. This is my son Andrew," stress was clearly evident in her voice.

"Good morning, my name is Tom Harridy; I'm here to escort you to Saint Jude Hospital in Calumet City. Do you know how to get there?"

"No but I can follow you if that would be all right."

It was obvious to Harridy, she was in no condition to drive and the son did not look much better. "Perhaps it would be better if you just rode with me." It would probably be faster and certainly safer. He knew well the risks involved in allowing a civilian vehicle to follow his car at what would be a higher than normal rate of speed.

"How would we get back if we did that?" The young man

asked.

Looking at the young man he smiled. "I understand your father was driving a pickup truck." Harridy knew this was the case from the crime scene information collected.

"Yes, he was on his way home from visiting his mother in Boston."

"Well, from what I understand, the truck was not part of the immediate crime scene and should be available for you to bring home. If you like, I can arrange for you to be brought to the truck when you're done at the hospital."

Andrew nodded then looked at his mother. "Mom do you have the spare set of keys?

"Yes, they're hanging on the dog." The dog was the key holder where their vehicle keys were hung when not in use. This was the result of years of shifting vehicles in the driveway to suit different schedules.

"Okay I'll get them, you get in the car." Andrew turned to go back into the house.

Harridy opened the driver side rear door and motioned for her to enter. Andrew followed a few minutes later.

"We'll have you there in no time." Harridy tapped the computer console sitting on the passenger side and activated the overhead cruiser lights. He didn't think the siren should not be needed.

"Can you tell us what happened?" Andrew voiced the question he knew his mother wanted to ask but could not.

"What did they tell you when they called you?" Harridy did not have all the details.

"They told me there had been an incident, involving my husband." Mrs. Reynolds replied quietly.

"Well ma'am, from what I have been told, there was a robbery at the rest stop near Calumet City and your husband was injured." Harridy watched her reaction in the rear view mirror.

"How bad is it?" Her voice strained.

"I don't know ma'am. I know that when the medical technicians reached him, his vital signs were good and he was transported to the hospital in stable condition. But evidently he did

9

sustain a wound to the head which knocked him unconscious." Harridy did not really know much more, except that two suspects were apprehended after making a u-turn across the highway median. The two were now in the barracks holding cell.

"Did they catch the robber?" Andrew asked as if reading Harridys mind.

"We think so." Harridy could not say anything more, as the investigation was still underway but added. "A .32 caliber pistol had been recovered from the highway median, but not yet tied to the suspects."

They were quiet for the remainder of the trip watching as the car moved easily through traffic. All other cars moved to the right allowing their car to speed on.

# Chapter 4

## Sunday morning 5:48 am

*I* don't know how long I was out. Light at first dim but slowly getting brighter, began to seep into my vision. I could hear distant voices growing louder with each passing moment.

"I need more light" a male voice. "What is his heart rate?"

"Vitals are steady doctor!" a woman's voice.

"How is the EEG?" the first voice again.

"We certainly have activity. I've never seen this before, he is spiking every other cycle" yet another female voice.

"What do you mean spiking? Let me see!" He must be a doctor.

"Think he'll make it?" A new voice, not heard so much as sensed.

"Does it matter?" Again sensed not heard.

"Of course it matters. He's my charge, remember?"

What the hell was going on? I pulled myself into a seated position, a feat in and of itself a bizarre experience given the doctor still stood over me applying sutures to my head. The actual act of sitting however seemed effortless and I could have sworn I passed right through the doctor in doing so.

Feeling disoriented, I looked around. The room was evidently an emergency room and was brightly lit. Several nurses bustled around as a Doctor worked to repair a bloody gash on my head.

Wait a minute, how could they have been working on me, if I was here? Was I dead? I had read of people who had died and then been revived and claiming to have seen their bodies as if from above as I apparently was.

I looked in the direction from where the other "voices" I had heard seemed to come from. Two shapes were standing at the end of the bed.  From their clothing, it was obvious they were not part of the hospital staff, it must be their conversation I was hearing, or should I say, "thought" I was hearing.

"Excuse me, but who are you and what the hell are you doing here?"  My voice, or should I say my thought projected voice, appeared to take them by surprise.

The taller figure glanced in my direction then looked at the other. "Did you hear that? Did he just say something?"

The smaller figure, with an equally shocked expression, merely nodded in response.

"How can that be?" The taller of the two figures was clearly confused. "He has not separated, yet he knows we are here?"

Judging from their reactions, I knew they had heard me. I asked again. "Excuse me, who are you, what are you doing here and what do you mean by separated?" My disembodied voice sounded strange, this was more than a little spooky.

"I have heard of this happening, the smaller figure said" ignoring me completely.

"What do you mean?" the larger of the two was still staring at me in amazement.

The smaller of the two continued. "Times when the Bio is still alive but capable of seeing and even speaking, with their companions. The Bio's call it a near death experience, and of course, there are also cases where contact has been made as the result of higher level meditation and sometimes from the use of hallucinogenic drugs."

Not liking the fact I was being ignored, I again interrupted them. "Excuse me, I do not wish to be rude but who are you? Why are you here?  Am I dead?" Obviously that wasn't the case or the Doctor would not be working to repair the hole in my head, and the monitors would not be showing my heart rate and blood pressure.

Still ignoring me, the taller of the two spoke as if to no one in particular. "Okay! Give me a full systems check."

Still another voice, "Station two reporting, all functions operating within acceptable parameters, no sign of Sleepers yet. We should be okay, as long as they don't administer anesthesia."

"Roger that station two.  Keep me advised.  Station three, report"

"All systems are on line." The smaller figure, although present, responded.

"Station five what is your status?"

"We're a little busy. Can we get back to you?"

"Affirmative five," then almost as an afterthought he said. "Five, be sure to check the northern region for anomalies and advise." The tall figure turned back to face me.

Still looking confused, the larger figure updated the smaller one. "Two reported acceptable levels of activity but we'll have to wait for five's report. They are pretty busy right now supporting the northern area."

"What do we do about him?" The smaller figure glanced in my direction. "It's obvious he can see and hear us. We can't just ignore him."

The larger figure looked at me again. "Not much we can do until five reports in." The truth was he did not know what to do. "Let's assume this situation is temporary and it will resolve itself when he wakes up." He paused and looked at the smaller figure. "You could be right, this would not be the first time a Bio managed to tune into us. Fortunately, when he wakes up, we will be only a memory and probably a pretty hazy one at that."

"Let's ignore him for now." The larger figure again looked at me.

The smaller of the two frowned. "I don't think that's an option, it's obvious he is "tuned" into us as much as we are into him." the smaller figure paused. "I would be surprised if he wasn't listening to us now."

Inching myself slowly off of the bed. I positioned myself between the figures. Glancing back, I could see myself lying inert on the bed, cables attached to my chest, legs and head. An intravenous line ran from my arm to a plastic drip bag. Monitors beeped and chirped in tune with my pulse. The EEG printout showing a spiked pattern that looked inconsistent, or perhaps too consistent, as it seemed to spike every time I spoke to the figures.

The Doctor, a young resident, finished applying the final sutures to the lacerated scalp. This was his first gunshot wound and he was thankful it was only a grazing wound. While bloody, it was not as bad as it looked. "That should do it." He took a final survey of his handiwork. "Probably have a scar, but it's the best I could do, keep someone with him until he wakes up." he paused. "Any word yet on who he is, or his family?"

One of the nurses, a heavy-set woman in pale hospital greens answered. "His name is William Reynolds, the State Police found his truck keys and cell phone in his pocket. They called the last dialed number and got his mother. She gave them the number of his wife and they are trying to contact her. I'll check with them as soon as we're done here."

"Okay, keep me posted on his condition. I'm going to get some coffee." The doctor peeled off the plastic surgical gloves and dropped them in the "bio-hazard container.

"What about these EEG readings? They are still spiking?" The nurse wanted her concern to be noted if only for the record.

The doctor looked at the monitor and shrugged. "There isn't much we can do without the right equipment. For now monitor them, I suspect they'll stabilize when he wakes up." He paused. "Worst case, we send him to the "Neuro" at the Loyola Medical Center," he entered the final notes in the patient's log before he closing the file and placing it on the clipboard at the foot of the bed. "Let me know when his family gets here."

# Chapter 5

## <u>Sunday morning 8:00 am</u>

*H*arridy eased the cruiser into the emergency room parking spot reserved for official vehicles. Except for their initial conversation very little else was said during the thirty-five minute ride. He had been pleasantly surprised at how smooth the trip had been, especially through the work-zone at the Torrance Avenue exit. The annual road maintenance had reduced the traffic flow to one functional lane and the shoulder.

Harridy turned to face his passengers. "The emergency room is through the double doors on the right." Seeing the tentative expression on her face he added. "Would you like me to come with you?" Doing so would allow him to make arrangements for them to retrieve the truck.

"That would be great if you have the time." Mrs. Reynolds responded, her face pale in the morning light.

"No problem ma'am." He found himself hoping she would be okay. He turned off the engine and stepped from the cruiser before opening the rear passenger door. This could only be done from the exterior of the vehicle. It was a custom feature on all patrol cars that the rear doors could only be opened from the outside.

Mrs. Reynolds, flanked by Andrew and Harridy, with each supporting an elbow entered the hospital emergency room. Harridy stopped a passing nurse and inquired as to the location of a patient named William Reynolds. The nurse, a middle aged woman with soft brown eyes directed them to a desk sitting outside the closed emergency room doors.

The receptionist, one Emma Pearlman checked the computer. "He is in the last bed on the right." She paused and looked at the computer screen. "Before you go in, we need some information. You know medical history, insurance information and such."

Harridy, stunned by her insensitivity turning to face her, his face a mottled red, he was clearly struggling to maintain his composure. "Emma! It is Emma isn't it?" He was looking at her nametag. "I think the paperwork can wait for a few minutes, why don't we just bring Mrs. Reynolds to see her husband?"

Emma, oblivious to the subtle rebuke just shook her head. Clearly she felt her needs should come first. "I'm sorry but we really do need this information before we can proceed, hospital rules you know, besides the Doctor asked to be advised when his family arrived, so while were waiting for him we can do the paperwork, okay?"

Harridy, his face now a bright red, grasped the arm of Andrew and his mother, directing them toward the last bed on the right. "I think we will just do the right thing, Emma, if you have a problem, feel free to call whomever you like."

"What's going on here?" The nurse who initially spoke to Harridy stood blocking their way.

Emma, glaring at Harridy replied. "They're refusing to provide insurance information and are insisting on going to the patient's bed without the Doctor."

The nurse, one "Georgia Renault" based on her name tag immediately grasped the true situation. Emma while diligent in performing her tasks was young and was sometimes insensitive to the needs of others. She would have to talk with her about this.

"Emma, I think it would be okay for them to go back. We can take care of the information later. "She turned to look at the trio. "You will stop before you leave and complete the forms won't you?"

Mary smiled. "Yes, of course, we don't want to cause any problems. We are just concerned about my husband."

"I understand." Looking back at the receptionist, Georgia nodded. "Emma, why don't you escort them to the correct bed."

Emma glared at the older nurse. "The Doctor wanted to see them first." She was clearly unhappy by this turn of events.

"I'll get the Doctor. He can meet them at the bed. Now please do as I have asked." She paused then added. "And when you're done come see me. We have a few things to discuss." Georgia smiled, knowing well Emma had caught her meaning.

"I'm just trying to follow procedures and if anyone says anything, I'll tell them you're responsible." Emma walked briskly away in the direction of the last bed on the right.

"I'm sorry she's young, and can be a bit insensitive. I'll have a talk with her shortly." Turning aside, she indicated they should follow Emma.

"Thanks, Georgia. I was beginning to think things were going to get a little out of hand, and given where we are." He spread his hands indicating the room. "That probably would not have been good for any of us." Harridy placed his hand on Mrs. Reynolds's elbow and guided her in the direction Emma had gone.

The bed, surrounded by various pieces of chirping and beeping equipment, was in a horizontal position. The patient was apparently sleeping and seemed oblivious to the tubes and wires linking him to the machines. Were it not for the large bandage wrapped around his skull, one might think he was merely sleeping, not recovering from a medical procedure.

Footsteps, preceded by the squeaking sounds made on linoleum floors, could be heard approaching the bed.

A young man in surgical green clothes approached and extended his hand. "Hello, I am Doctor Turner. I assume you are Mrs. Reynolds?"

Taking his hand, she was comforted by his firm handshake. "Yes I am, please call me Mary. This is my son Andrew." She glanced at the prone figure of her husband. "How is he?"

The doctor acknowledged Andrew with a nod of his head. "He is stable for now but he did lose a lot of blood, were giving him a plasma transfusion." He pointed at the intravenous drip. "As you can see he is still unconscious and we've done all we can until he wakes up."

"What do you mean unconscious? He looks like he's just sleeping." Mary looked at her husband.

"He has been as you see him, since they brought him in. We sutured the wound on his head and scalp, now all we can do now is wait, please try not to worry. It's not unusual for a person who has experienced trauma to the head to be unconscious for several hours. I assure you he is in no pain or immediate danger, and I think it best to just let him come out of it on his own." The doctor really didn't have much else to add. "While we wait, I was hoping you might help me with his medical history, that is if you're up to it."

"Can I stay with him while we do?"

"Of course we can do it right here." Turner reached for the patient's chart hanging on the end of the bed. "Okay then, does your husband have any pre-existing medical conditions?"

"Yes, he has had two heart attacks. The first was in nineteen eighty-six, and the last in nineteen ninety-nine. The last time, they put stents in two of his arteries."

Turner busily updated the medical chart. Nineteen Eighty-Six, according to his license he was only fifty-three years old. That would mean his first heart attack was at thirty-three, very young. He must have other contributing factors of a hereditary nature.

"Does he have a Primary Care Physician?"

"Yes, Doctor Brangeel, he runs the family medical clinic in our town, and his cardiologist is Doctor Tomkowicz. His office is in the Sherman Hospital."

"Good!" Turner looked at the nurse. "Contact Dr. Brangeel and let me know when you have him on the line."

He turned his attention back to Mary. "Does your husband have any allergies?"

"Yes he is allergic to penicillin."

Turner hastily wrote this into the log. "Do you know when he had his last physical?" He could get that from Brangeel but saw no harm in asking.

"Yes, he had a physical three months ago and a stress test last month." She smiled to herself remembering how much he hated that particular test. He invariably complained for days about the aches and pains resulting from such a strenuous workout.

"Okay good! Can you think of any other conditions we should know about?"

"No, that's all I can think of right now."

"Great, I'll contact Dr Brangeel and bring him up to speed on this situation. More than likely, he will want to transfer your husband to a hospital closer to home. I will have a transport standing by just in case." Turner closed the file, hanging it again on the end of the bed.

18

"Do you have any more questions for me?"

"Yes. Was there any brain damage?" Mary looked uncomfortable asking and dreaded the reply.

"It really is too soon to say. The damage to the front right of the head was superficial, a grazing wound that opened the scalp but there is no visible evidence of a fracture or bone damage." Turner paused. "There was, however, a significant contusion on the right rear of his head in the occipital lobe region, which could explain his being unconscious, and more than likely he has also suffered a concussion." Seeing the concern on her face he continued. "Again, I want to stress he is in no danger at the moment, but, we will not know the full extent of his injuries until he wakes up." He looked at the EEG monitor and frowned. "We do not have the equipment here to perform a complete diagnosis but if for some reason he does not wake up in a few hours I will recommend transport to the Loyola Medical Center. They have a world class neurologist's staff and are much better equipped for that type of testing." Turner hoped he was succeeding in masking his real concern, the elevated and erratic EEG readings. They were unlike anything he had seen before. Clearly there was something unusual going on in the patient's brain, and that was always a reason to be concerned.

"Thank you Doctor." She paused again looking at her husband. "Can we stay with him?"

"Yes of course. If you need me for anything just ask the duty nurse to page me." Turner smiled and grasped her arm. "Listen to me. Everything will be okay. Just relax and be with your husband." He turned to leave, his beeper chirping a demanding sound.

Harridy stood listening to the conversation between Turner and Mary. "Mrs. Reynolds, why don't I take your son to get your truck? I'll take him to it and escort him back. We should only be gone a half hour or so." He glanced at Andrew, indicating his support would be needed.

Andrew nodded saying to his mother. "Dad looks like he's okay for now. I'll go with the Officer and be back in a flash." He touched his mother's arm lightly. "Dad is in good hands. Why don't you stay here in case he wakes up, I'll try not to be gone long?"

She nodded absently. "Okay, turn your cell phone on and I'll call you if there's any change." They had turned the phones off when they entered the hospital.

"I will as soon as I get outside. I'll be right back." Andrew nodded his head toward Harridy and moved toward the door.

# Chapter 6

## **Sunday morning 8:00 am**

*T*he two figures standing at the end of the bed watched and listened as the Doctor explained to Mary the condition of her husband, I also watched wanting to gauge my family's reactions, especially Andrew's. I had always tried to remain calm in times of crisis and hoped doing so would set a standard for my children. Overall, I thought Andrew was handling the situation well, although I did not think leaving his mother alone was a good idea. But at least he was doing something positive. Clearly they would need the truck to get home.

My new companions stood silently watching the situation and although they did not outwardly express any thoughts or opinions directly to me, I could still hear their thoughts. The taller of the two was apparently communicating with the "others", the ones I had yet to see. I could sense the smaller one reaching out towards Mary, as if trying to support her in some way.

The taller one, having finished his dialog with the "others", turned to the smaller one. "Five just reported the Bio is performing as designed and is healing itself." He paused before continuing. "He said there is some type of abnormal neuron activity in the northern region; one he is not sure what to do about it. When I asked if he could fix it, he gave a strange reply."

"What did he say?" The smaller figure directed her attention to him but glanced at me to see if I was hearing the conversation.

"He said the activity, while abnormal, is by design, as a result, the Bio does not consider it a problem and is not attempting to correct the condition." He had heard stories passed down through the ages that at one time human beings, what they now referred to as "Bio units" or "Bios" had possessed powers far greater than their current capabilities. According to the stories, they had at one time used a much greater proportion of their brain than they did now. However, as he was not at a sufficient level of the hierarchy to have the intimate details of that time period to him, they were just stories.

The smaller figure shrugged almost imperceptibly "That could explain why he can see and hear us, what do we do if it continues?" She knew they were in uncharted territory, she knew as well, that in the many known instances of "Bios" tuning into the higher sphere, few had successfully been able to maintain contact. Fewer still remembered much when they eventually returned to consciousness. The few who did retain memories often did so out of context, much the same as with dreams. However this seemed different. This one was clearly capable of sustaining himself in both realms and there was no way to tell how much he would actually retain. Regardless, her role as the recorder for the Bio left her no option but to record everything and hope the others would be able to suppress his memories.

The larger of the two, sensing her thoughts, simply replied. "Let's wait and see what happens. It may be temporary and will go away when he wakes up." Yet even as he said this, he knew that it was already too late, his charge had already been tuned in far too long to forget all he had heard and seen. "Maybe we'll get lucky and he will think it was all just a dream."

As I listened and read their thoughts, it occurred to me that they had still not responded to my presence. "Excuse me, but would one of you kindly tell me what's going on? Who are you and quit ignoring me. You can't anyway, so why try?" I knew they heard me based on the pause in their movements.

The taller of the two looked directly at me. "We are your companions."

I nodded. "How many of you are there, who are you to me, and what do you want?" At least they were acknowledging my presence.

"There are some things you simply would not understand." The taller figure spoke even though his thoughts said otherwise. He always knew that at some point, the Bios would be able to tune into their presence. He just thought it wouldn't be for several more centuries, assuming they survived that long.

"I may not understand, but would still like an answer." Deciding to press the issue, I continued. "You can tell me directly, or I can simply tune into your thoughts until I find out for myself. I doubt you can hide it from me for long." It was obvious to me that the only way for them to tune me out of their thoughts, would be to shut down their own thinking processes, and quite frankly, I doubted they could do that and still function.

The smaller figure looked at her companion. "He's right, we can't just shut down. He is tuned into us and we won't be able to keep him from knowing our every thought. Perhaps you should just answer him." She paused looking at me. "Besides, what's the harm? More than likely he will forget most of this when he returns to his Bio state."

"And what if he doesn't forget, what then?" The larger figure said this knowing he had little choice.

"What if he does? Maybe this is supposed to happen. You've heard the same stories as I how some Bios have actually used the knowledge to benefit mankind. In fact in some cases the knowledge was used to actually accelerate the process."

The taller figure was thinking this over and I could hear his thoughts clearly. "Perhaps you're right. One thing is certain; we cannot function properly and block him at the same time." Turning to me he nodded. "Okay Bill, ask your questions and within reason, I will answer them." He still had doubts, but would do his best to answer, hopefully at the same time still controlling the information provided.

"Okay. First who or what are you? Do you have names? Where do you come from?"

He smiled for the first time. "Let's do one at a time, okay? As I said, we are your companions. We have been with you since the beginning, these others help me." He glanced at the smaller figure. "But I am the one responsible for you, and I might add, accountable for you."

"What do you mean accountable?"

"It is my job to help you become what you can be. If you fail, I fail."

"I don't understand; help me become "what?" How do you help me? Do you make my decisions for me?" The prospect of being someone's puppet was disconcerting to say the least.

The larger figure grinned at my thoughts. "No, I do not make your decisions for you, only you can do that. In fact, just for the record I am not allowed to make decisions. But I do try to influence you into making the right ones."

"How do you do that?"

"There are a number of means at my disposal. For example, I know you have heard your inner voice, well I am that voice. I also know you do not always listen, and that's you."

I knew what he said was true. I have always believed that each person had an inner voice along with an innate understanding of right and wrong. This was something I always tried to make my children recognize.

"That's you?"

"Yes that's me! And there are other means at my disposal. For instance, your "Bio" is subject to physical stimuli. Sometimes you need to feel pain to learn a lesson. I admit it doesn't make the Doc very happy, but sometimes that's the price you pay."

"Who is the Doc?"

"Remember I said that there are others who also support you? Counting yourself there are a total of seven. The Doc is the one who keeps your body physically healthy. A job I might add that you make exceedingly difficult at times."

"Who else is there?

"Well there's "Three", he glanced at the smaller figure. Her job is to record everything that happens to you, as well as what you think, say, feel or do. And during the evaluation process, she recalls this information for all to see."

"What evaluation process?"

"When your Bio unit ceases to function due to age or trauma, your essence or spirit, or whatever you want to call it, returns to the evaluation center. If appropriate, it is recycled into a new Bio. In this manner it continues its evolution."

"You mean reincarnated?" I always wondered what happened when we died.

"Yes, it is sometimes referred to as reincarnation."

I smiled at him. "Just out of curiosity, I have always thought that if the goal of reincarnation is to evolve, wouldn't it be best if we reincarnate with the knowledge gained in our previous lives? It seems to me, we would evolve much faster if we retained that knowledge." This was one of those questions I always asked when I found myself in pointless discussions with people who supported the reincarnation theory.

The taller figure thought for a moment before continuing. "Much of the knowledge does accompany the essence into the new Bio. However, this knowledge fades into the recesses of the mind as the Bio acquires new experiences. Even so, aspects of this knowledge are retained and passed on at the genetic level by virtue of what your scientists call morphic fields. Over time, this "morphic" aspect does reduce the empirical learning curve, thereby increasing the overall state of a species understanding." He paused as if sensing my confusion. "Let me put it another way, all cells of the Bio retain knowledge. This knowledge is passed on to each succeeding generation, and if properly nurtured, assists in the evolution process."

Still confused, I pressed on. "You said there were seven, who else is there?"

"Well, there is myself, I am your "Seven". Then we have your "Two", he is responsible for maintaining your Bio functions at the subconscious level. "Four" is probably the most valuable in terms of your Bio coping with the external reality. His role is to take the wants and desires of the "One", that is you, and then working with your "Two" they try to develop solutions to help satisfy those wants or desires. Then there is "Five", who as I mentioned, is in charge of the Bio's med lab so to speak, kind of a resident Doctor. When your body begins to degenerate, "Five" makes sure the regenerative process works to replace old cells with new ones. Unfortunately, over time his capacity to regenerate the body becomes diminished. And eventually he cannot keep pace with the decay process; at that point the Bio ceases to function properly and dies. Then there is your "Six", this companion is, for lack of a better description, the scientist in you. He is the one who often makes the relational links that you refer to as intuition." Seven paused. "How many times have you intuitively known the answer or the "right thing to do"? That is your "Six" at work."

I shook my head. "That's just a bit confusing. Don't you have names? I was already struggling to keep them separate in my mind.

Seven smiled. "No, but if it would help you could make up names for us."

I did not answer, deciding instead to pursue the train of thought. "You didn't tell me what you do." I got the sense he was the one in charge.

"Actually I did, I am (for lack of a better term) your "Primary companion." It is my job to coordinate the rest of your support unit and of course to guide you through life's processes. At some point your essence will separate from the Bio unit, when it does "Three" and I accompany it and stand witness to your life during the evaluation process. "Three" will play back all of the records for review. If you have done well, you are assigned to a new Bio. Hopefully, at some point you will evolve to the level where further reincarnation is no longer necessary. When that happens we will return to be reassigned."

"And where do you come from?"

Seven paused before answering. He had often asked himself the same question, since the beginning, he had known and accepted his role in the process, knowing the role served the process of human evolution, but not why. "I do not know where I come from, only that I am what your species has always referred to as a guardian Angel." He disliked using that analogy and did so only because they were terms he knew the Bio could understand.

Sensing an opportunity, I decided to press this line of thinking. "So you're an "Angel?" Does that mean there is a Heaven and for that matter a Hell?"

Seven was quiet; he pondered these questions and more importantly tried to think how to answer. The concepts of Heaven and Hell had been woven into the very fabric of the human social and psychological structures. Given it was possible for this Bio to return with this knowledge. He knew his answer had the potential of undoing centuries of effort.

Finally he said. "Tell me about this Heaven, what is your definition of Heaven?"

I had little difficulty answering this, having spent a good portion of my youth studying the various ideological beliefs. "We are taught that at the end of our lives if we have lived well and believed in a higher power, we would be rewarded and sent to a place we call Heaven. In this place, we would be able to find and be with loved ones who have already died, assuming of course they went there as well. It is a place free of worry and of eternal peace."

Seven listened intently. He had always found it interesting that throughout time people had diverse ideas of what the afterlife would be like. Ideas while different in context all contained the common theme of peace and contentment. He found it ironic that if the evolutionary process he supported could be realized, the very state they referred to as Heaven, could actually exist in the physical realm. "I can only say there are two conditions, there is life and energy, and there is decay and the absence of energy." Seven knew well his response would be unsatisfactory. He had after all nurtured this one through many lives and knew well such an answer would not go without challenge.

Not to be put off so easily, I pressed the issue. "Okay, let me ask it differently. Many people have claimed to have near death experiences where they reported going through a tunnel into a bright light. While there, they claim to have seen others who had already died. They report feeling happy and without burden, is this true?"

"Yes, it is partially true. The sensation of not being burdened is the result of the essence no longer residing within the confines of a Bio unit. The bright light is a good description of the place where the essence returns for evaluation and recycling. The others are no doubt memories taken from their own record."

I pondered this before replying. "Then is there a Hell?"

Seven almost smiled at this unexpected question. "Not in the classical sense." He paused, thinking of how to best answer. "When the essence and the Bio unit separate, they must be prepared to accept the separation, this is not always the case, there are instances when the essence has not been properly prepared for the separation from their Biological unit or the life they had led. Consequently, when their Bio unit fails, they have difficulty letting go and as a result the "essence" ends up in a state of "between." Generally, this occurs in cases where the Bio failure is the result of trauma where the support unit has not had the opportunity to prepare the essence for separation. This is very similar to what almost happened to you today."

"What is this state of "in between" and what happens to the support unit?"

Seven was quiet for a moment before answering. "The between state is just what it sounds like. The essence clings to the physical realm although it can no longer interact with it, when this happens it does not complete the process of evaluation and recycling. This can be very frustrating as you can imagine. The "Three" and "Seven", because they are assigned and accountable for the essence, stay with it until the evaluation process is eventually completed."

If this was "Hell", was there no penalty for breaking the rules? "So if a person kills another person there is no penalty, no eternal damnation? Again the spiritual leaders or what I call the "ism" addicts had it wrong.

Seven smiled, obviously sensing my thoughts on the "isms". "Again in the classical sense no. However, there are conditions much worse than your classical concept of Hell. Setting aside the anguish experienced if you are stuck in the "between" state there is also the evaluation process to consider. If an essence, while in the Bio state, kills another Bio, they are held accountable during the evaluation process. In most instances it would not be possible for that essence to evolve to the next level during the reincarnation process. In fact, in the case of murder, the reincarnation process would no doubt be to a regressed state."

# Chapter 7

## **<u>Sunday morning 9:00 am</u>**

*A*ndrew returned to the emergency room with Emma escorting him to his father's bed. Evidently Georgia had a conversation with her because her new demeanor was almost sweet. Approaching the bed he looked first at his mom then at his dad. "I'm back. Any change?"

Mary nodded. "No, there is no change. The Doctor said it might take a few hours." Doctor Brangeel had made the trip to the hospital and had taken personal charge of the case. He and Bill were the same age, and he often said Bill was his first patient when he initially started his practice. Whatever the reason, she was glad to see him. He had already reviewed the charts and graphs and was overseeing the transport to the Loyola Medical Center. Although he didn't directly say it, she knew he was concerned by the still erratic and spiking EEG readings.

Andrew sensing his mother's level of stress asked. "Let me buy you breakfast?" He doubted it would help but thought getting her away from here for a few minutes would be the best thing for her.

"I'm not really hungry, maybe just a coffee." She stood up and smiled, appreciating what he was trying to do, we did raise him right. "Just give me a minute to tell the nurse where to find us if there is a change."

Andrew with a final glance at his dad said. "I'll come with you."

# Chapter 8

## **Sunday morning 9:00 am**

$S$even watched Bill intently. Although he had been honest with his answers, he had not given all of the information needed to fully answer the questions, especially regarding the concepts of Heaven and Hell. While it was true they were "instilled" concepts designed for social control of Bio behavior, they also adequately described two of the possible outcomes. Should humans continue the path they were on, it was more than possible their physical reality would literally go up in the smoke and flames they associated with their concept of Hell. And while it was equally possible, it was much less probable they would evolve quickly enough to recognize their own self-destructive tendencies and take the necessary steps to avoid this calamity. It was intriguing to him that the classical portrayal of their destructive end always involved fire. Fire was perhaps the only thing from which life could not recover. Floods and other calamities, while devastating, rarely destroyed the fundamental building blocks of life as fire did. It was his job and others like him to provide guidance to insure their survival. As guardians they were not of the physical world and were therefore immune to physical influences, but they would be affected by the end result.

In spite of his reservations about providing this information, he also knew that even if this Bio were able to retain the knowledge, it would probably not change anything. Human history was replete with examples of how the powers that controlled the physical world viewed those with radical ideas. They would certainly view him as a threat, and as they had throughout history, would take steps to discredit or perhaps even destroy him. If his charge did manage to return and try to use the knowledge, he could minimally expect to be locked up forever, perhaps even eliminate.

I could not sense the thoughts of my Seven, I was struggling to sort through and catalog into memory the information he had already provided, some of which was mind boggling in their own rights. Information which if true, could result in a complete reassessment of the concepts currently espoused by the many "isms". Many years before, I had concluded that all religions of the world were right in some ways, yet in many ways also very wrong. Every religion, Taoism, Hinduism, Buddhism, Islam, Christianity, Judaism and even Paganism all possessed the common theme of the existence of a power so great as to be unknowable to man. Invariably, each also offered the reward of a happy and contented afterlife. Every "ism" also had their set of rules defining acceptable behavior, rules that promised eternal rewards if adhered to, and of course, severe penalties if they were not. Unfortunately, as had been repeatedly demonstrated throughout recorded history, these same rules of appropriate behavior (while pure of intent) usually became the justification for unacceptable behavior by the "isms" themselves in terms of war, and to a large degree the types of socio and political structures created for control. To now realize, that the world was in fact nothing more than a great recycling machine, would certainly upset the established order.

I turned my attention back to "Seven". "So let me understand this. Based upon what you have said, everything I have been taught and believed is a lie. There is no Heaven or Hell. My existence is nothing more that a series of reincarnations designed to help me evolve." Evolve to what? I wondered.

Seven smiled. "As I said before, there is no Heaven or Hell in the classical sense. Such concepts were necessary to sustain your kind and to insure they did not simply destroy themselves. Because your kind is susceptible to the needs of the flesh, some form of punishment and reward system was necessary or your uncontrolled physical urges would have led to the annihilation of all but the strongest groups. I might also add that even with these controls your religions and governments still found creative ways to justify their excesses and atrocities on each other. I mean, think for a moment. They would have you believe that killing for the sake of ideological beliefs or nationalism is acceptable and doing so exempts you from any retribution in the next life. I can assure you this is not the case. All life is sacred and to be responsible for any death goes against the very nature of your being. Our goal and yours should be to promote the well being of your kind and of the physical world that supports them. To do otherwise is counter to all that is natural."

I knew what "Seven" said was correct. There were too many instances in history where the behavior of man ran counter to the rules of behavior deemed appropriate by the "isms". It had always baffled me how killing in the name of nationalism, or for the sake of ideology, could be deemed acceptable, in fact, often rewarded. To my way of thinking, killing should be unacceptable under any circumstance. "There is logic in what you say, but it still leaves me with the fundamental question of why, to what end and where does it stop?" Surely, there must be an ultimate goal, a point where evolution is no longer required.

Seven had often asked the same question during the thousands of years and hundreds of lifetimes he witnessed. No one knew for sure, their best guess came from stories passed down from generation to generation, stories of a time when humans had lived in harmony with each other and their natural environment. Of a time before the great separation, perhaps the goal was to evolve again to that point, he did not know. Just as he did not know how the Bio's had become the beings he had served these thousands of years.

"I wish I knew. All I know is what I have already told you."

As I tuned into their thought process, I sensed I was not being told everything.

"Surely there must be a reason for this besides evolution. What about you and the support unit? How did you become as you call yourselves, my companions?"

Seven clearly frustrated, shrugged his shoulders. "I have told you all I can tell you. I do not know why, or how, just that it is what it is."

"There has to be more than this?" The thought of endless reincarnations without purpose offended my sensibilities. Logic dictated there had to be a greater purpose.

"Is there no one who can answer me? Surely there must be someone with the answers, or some way to get to them."

Seven was quiet for a moment contemplating the question before answering. "Please understand this is highly unusual for me. In all of your past lives, your Bio degraded to the point of separation or was traumatized to the point where your essence was released. At that point, I simply facilitated the process necessary to evaluate and reincarnate it to the next Bio." He stopped, unsure whether to continue. "However, there may be a way for you to get the answers you seek."

"How?"

"As I said earlier when the Bio and Essence separate, the Essence is brought to the place of evaluation. Those which cannot or do not accept the separation find themselves "stuck" in a state between the physical realm and the energy realm, or what we call the "between state". If and when they come to terms with their separation, they proceed through the evaluation and the subsequent recycling process. You understand me?"

"Yes, I understand you so far."

Seven continued. "Very early in your history, Bios did not live as long as they do now. Disease, war and famine were common and quite frankly, the intellectual level of the Bio unit was primitive compared with today. As a result, a very high proportion of the essence population found themselves in this "between state"." He paused watching to make sure I understood what he was saying.

"The fundamental property of your "Essence" is in fact energy and it is not unlimited. In fact, the continuation of your kind is totally dependent upon what you refer to as recycling. "Essences" in the "between state" do not recycle in a timely manner and this limits your ability to continue the evolutionary process." Seven paused watching me intently. "Are you still with me?"

"Yes, I'm still with you." So far everything made sense.

He continued. "In an effort alleviate this problem, we decided to create a process to assist the "between Essences" to come to terms with their separation and to continue the recycling process. To facilitate this, we created what we call the "Hall of Understanding". This is a place designed to help the essence understand what they are and the role they play in the overall scheme of things."

He paused looking in my direction. "Do you have any questions?"

"Yes, first, is this "Hall of Understanding" required for all of the "between" essences as you call them and second, you mentioned an overall scheme, what is that scheme?"

"To the first question, the answer is no. Until the moment of evaluation, the essence has what you refer to as "free will". It cannot be required to go into the Hall. In fact, I suspect more than a few of the essences in the between state choose to stay there rather than face the evaluation process. These are typically those who carry a heavy guilt associated with their actions while in the physical plane. As to your second question, yes, there is an overall scheme but my knowledge of it is limited and I would prefer to not comment on it or risk of giving you wrong information. Now, as I was saying, it may be possible for you to enter this "Hall of Understanding". I say possible because you have not actually separated from your Bio and assuming you did gain access, I do not know what would happen should your Bio wake up while you are in the Hall." Seven paused before continuing. "Because the essences which go into the Hall of Understanding are already separated, the ONLY way out is through the evaluation process, or, back to the "between" state. Therefore, should you be in the Hall when your Bio wakes, it may not be possible for you to return to it. If that happens, your Bio will simply deteriorate and will eventually cease to function."

I looked at my physical body lying inert on the bed, monitors chirping away. "What about you? If I go into this "Hall of Understanding", will you go with me and be my guide so to speak? I am assuming of course, you have been there before." Perhaps the answers I wanted could be found in this "Hall".

Seven thought for a moment before replying. "No, I have never been in the Hall, it was never necessary. Those times when your essence could not accept the separation process we stayed in the "between state" until you reconciled your separation issues. And no, it would not be possible for me to accompany you. As your Bio and essence have not separated, I must stay here and continue to support and protect your Bio."

"Protect it? Protect it from what?" Looking again at my body lying on the bed I knew it was safe from harm.

Seven glanced at "Three" before responding. "There are other factions at work here, and while their goals are the same as ours, but their methods are radically different than those we use. Just as I am here to guide and support you through the evolution process, they would try to lead you astray, to keep you from evolving along the same path. Just as I try to advise and influence you, so do they. We call them "Sleepers" because they are most influential while the Bio is sleeping, or as in this case, unconscious." Seven paused, obviously sensing my confusion. "When you are awake and your conscious mind is active, they cannot succeed in taking control without your consent, and of course, we are always there to assist you. However, when you are asleep or as in this case unconscious, we are solely responsible for keeping them away."

"I don't understand how they can hurt me, if all they can do is guide me, wouldn't I still make my own decisions, you know free will and all." I now knew without a doubt, there was more to this than I had been told. Any doubts I had about visiting this "Hall of Understanding" were gone.

"Yes, the concept of free will applies even to them. However, your ability to exercise that free will is generally indisposed while you are sleeping or unconscious."

Seven paused. "Let me give you a simple example of how it works." He looked at the floor before continuing. "Let's say you are walking down the street and see a bag of valuables lying on the ground. One side of you says *"Take it and find its rightful owner"* that would be me of course. The other side says. *"Keep it for yourself, you found it, its yours."* that would be them, "the sleepers". In the end, you must make the decision to act or not act. Do you see what I mean?"

In spite of the crude example, I caught the gist of what he was saying. "So let me understand this, conflicting self points of view are the two factions trying to guide me?"

"Yes, but again this was a simple example. Apply the same concept to how you interact with others. Have you ever been so angry with someone that you have entertained the thought of killing that person?" He knew the answer. After all, he had been my companion every moment of every day. "And have you not done so because the voice of reason has stopped you? The "Sleepers" presented you with that option. So yes they are a threat. Even now, while you are lying there in a comatose state, you are vulnerable to them. "Two" and rest of your support unit are doing all they can to prevent them from influencing and altering your consciousness. We cannot let them influence you in such a way, as to place at risk, your next level of reincarnation." He did not add that he also shared the risk. After all, he had no desire to mentor a rock for the next ten thousand years.

"But what do they want, if their goals are the same as yours, what do they gain by doing this. I don't understand." I always knew there were "*voices*" with different points of view pulling at me and probably every other person who ever lived. The "ism's" ascribed them to be the embodiments of good and evil, evidently there was a grain of truth in that.

"I do not know what their true motivations are. I only know their methods are different than ours. Perhaps you can find the answer in the Hall of Understanding as well. But again, I must caution you, should you pursue going into the Hall, the sleepers will more than likely use it as an opportunity to influence you. You see unlike us, they are not required to stay with your Bio and can follow you there as well."

Undeterred I looked at him. "How do I get to this hall? Can you take to me there?" I was going with or without a guide. The limited information "Seven" had provided left too many unanswered questions. There must be a purpose beyond what "Seven" had said and I was determined to find it.

Seven hesitated. "Yes I can take you there. Are you sure you want to do this?"

"No." I replied. "But I don't really have a choice, I have to know."

"Okay, come with me." Seven turned and strode into what appeared to be a tunnel.

# Chapter 9

## **Sunday morning 10:30 am**

$M$ary and Andrew watched silently as the portable gurney was loaded into the transport ambulance for the trip to the Loyola Medical Center. Doctors Turner and Brangeel oversaw the process, each immersed in their own silent thoughts.

Turner extended his hand to Brangeel. "Let me know if there is anything else I can do.

Taking the extended hand, Brangeel shook it. "You've done a fine job Doctor, thank you."

Andrew, Mary and Brangeel started toward the exit only to be stopped by Turner's voice.

"Dr. Brangeel. I wonder if it would be possible for you to let me know what the neurologists at Loyola find." The EEG readings had captured his interest as well.

Brangeel smiled. "Yes of course, I'll call you as soon as I have the results."

"Many thanks." Giving a slight wave to Andrew and Mary, he turned and walked into the emergency room.

# Chapter 10

## **<u>Sunday morning 10:30 am</u>**

*T*he tunnel was darker than any night I had ever witnessed. With each step I felt increasing pressure pulling me back toward the room where we had entered. Seven, feeling the same pull, stopped and again asked if this was really what I wanted.

"What is that pulling sensation?" I thought I knew, but decided to ask anyway.

"You have not separated from your Bio. Each step away from it is weakening the ability of the essence and Bio to remain together." On one hand, he wished the ethereal bond would break. This meant the Bio had succumbed, thereby presenting them immediately to the evaluation and recycling process. On the other hand he also wanted to know the answers to the questions.

"Is my Bio in danger?" I had not planned on this possibility.

"It is possible, yes. Do you want to go back?"

To me, going back was not an option. The answers I sought made the risk of separation an acceptable one. Besides, if "Seven" was right, the worst case scenario was no answers and a reincarnation to another Bio. "No, keep going."

The darkness in the tunnel began to slowly dissipate similar to the light just before dawn. As we rounded a corner the tunnel suddenly became vibrant with a light brighter than any I had ever experienced. Seven, raising his hand, pointed to the right. Straining my eyes I could just make out the dim form of another tunnel branching off into the distance.

"This is where I must leave you." Seven turned, facing me again. "Go into that tunnel and good luck. I'll see you when you return." With that, he walked briskly back in the direction we had come.

The tunnel, only dimly lit from the reflective glow of the recycling center, opened into a broad expanse of a room. Although at first appearing empty, I was aware of the low buzzing of voices and of intermittent flashes of light. Stepping into the room, I could make out the shapes of others each time the lights flashed on. The light appeared to emanate from all sides and it took several seconds before I realized the entire room from one end to the other was projecting images similar to a television but far more expansive. If there was something comparable to "surround sound", a "vision surround" this was it. The image being flashed appeared to be that of a flower pushing out of the ground, followed by a moment of darkness causing the image to disappear. In the next instant, the image returned. The flower was unfolding and blooming. Again, there was darkness, followed by a new image of the flower spewing forth pollen. Small brilliant flashes of light exploded on the screen as the pollen fell to the earth. Then, more darkness and again, there was the flower now wilting and falling to the ground, followed yet again by brilliant flashes of light. This image, now gone, was followed by a bright flash not unlike an old fashioned camera flashbulb followed by the image of sprouts again leaping from the ground. Around me, I could see there were others also watching this collage of images. Some stood mouths open, gaping in wonder. Yet another was speaking animatedly to the person or persons standing with them. As I stepped further into the room, the projected image changed, this time to one of a woman giving birth. Then darkness followed by the image of the baby, apparently now a toddler. More darkness was followed by the image of a young man in his mid twenties making love to a young woman. Brilliant bursts of light surrounded them, again darkness preceding the image of an old man lying in a casket surrounded by a brilliant light. This last image burst upon the screen with such clarity it caused me to instinctively step back. As I did, the image reverted once again that of the flower wilting and falling to the ground. Stepping forward, the scene changed back to that of the human, now middle aged, followed by darkness and a new image of the old man lying peacefully in a casket. It was evident the images depended upon where you were standing.

"Amazing, is it not?" The voice came from my left. I turned to see a kindly looking man who looked to be in his forties.

"Yes it is." "I have never seen anything like it before. What is it?"

"It is a holographic projection unit designed to emanate radial images. As you step further into the Hall, the images change to further reinforce the message we are trying to deliver." He paused, looking at me intently, realizing for the first time that I was alone.

"Where is your Seven?"

"Not here. He couldn't make it. Had another engagement I think." My attempt at humor was clearly lost to him

"That's not possible. How did you get here?"

"My Seven brought me, but couldn't stay." No more humor for this guy.

"Where did he go?" My new-found friend was clearly getting more agitated by the moment.

"You cannot be here unescorted." The strobe like effect of the lights gave his features a surreal aspect.

"Why?" I hoped this guy didn't throw me out.

"Why? Why? It is not allowed, that's why." This had never happened to him before. "Step over here, would you?" Taking my arm, he gently pulled me off to the side. The images stopped, leaving us standing in a somewhat normal yet subdued light.

Not willing to be put off lightly, I decided to challenge him. "Who says it's not allowed? My Seven said I should come here to get answers to the questions I have been asking, and now you're telling me I cannot be here?"

"Look! Whoever, you are."

"My name is Bill."

"Thank you. Bill, I don't think you understand"

"Well, what is your name?"

"I am called Jonathan."

"Okay Jonathan, my Seven could not answer my questions and thought perhaps if I came to this place, I might find the answers. He brought me here but had to return to support my Bio unit."

"You mean you have not separated yet?" Jonathan had heard of this happening but had never actually witnessed it. Others had been assigned deal with that issue.

"No, my Bio unit, as you call it, is alive. It's simply not conscious. If all goes well, I hope to return to it as soon as I have my answers." From the look on his face, it was clear Jonathan was confused.

"Look Bill, I don't know what you're "Seven" told you or what answers you seek, but this facility is intended to be used to help SEPARATED essences accept the evaluation and reincarnation process. And if as you say, you have not separated from your Bio, I am not sure you should be here."

Having come this far, I was not going to be put off easily. At the same time I did not want to be too confrontational. "Tell you what Jonathan, why don't I wait here while you find out? I promise I will not interfere in any way."

"Fine, but I will have to ask one of my associates to stay with you." Jonathan could not allow him to wander around unescorted and it would be better if one of his staff provided escort rather than one of the sleepers.

Relieved at not being thrown out I replied with a smile. "Sure. No problem!" Perhaps this associate would be more forthcoming and could help me better understand this place.

As if on cue, a younger man appeared on my right. Looking at Jonathan he nodded his head then turned offering his hand to me. "My name is Thomas. I will be your escort while you are here."

Releasing his hand, I smiled, hoping to set the right impression. "Hello Thomas my name is Bill. Can you show me around?"

Thomas looked in the direction of Jonathan, whose almost imperceptible shrug was not lost on me. Clearly Jonathan was of a higher rank than Thomas. "Yes, of course. If you would follow me we can get started. Is there anything specific you would like me to show you?"

Jonathan had indicated the images were designed to deliver a message to the essences and I wondered what that message was. "What if we start at the beginning, what is this place and how does it work?"

Thomas hesitated. "What do you know about the Bio-Essence relationship?"

"My Seven explained all of that to me and I think I have a pretty good grasp. Every Bio, as you call them, has an associated essence or energy and a support team whose role is to help the person maintain their physical and emotional state of well-being. He also told me that when the Bio unit fails, the essence or energy undergoes a transition process which involves an evaluation and a reincarnation process. He also told me that in some cases, especially when the separation process does not happen naturally, that the essence gets stuck in a "between" state where it cannot move on. He said this place was created to assist them so they could move on."

Thomas, listening closely, nodded his head. "Good summary. It is true that those who come through here are the ones having difficulty adjusting to the separation process. In most cases, their Seven is able to persuade them that this is the best way to get out of the "between state" as you call it." Thomas paused. "You see, under normal circumstances, the support unit for the Bio has adequate time to prepare the Bio and Essence for the inevitable separation process. However, in cases where the separation was either unexpected or in the situation where the Bio's attachment to the physical world is too strong, they are unable to cope with leaving it."

Thomas looked at me. I assume trying to gauge my comprehension.

"Yeah, as I said, my Seven filled me in on that. Perhaps you can tell how your process works. How do you know when or if it is successful? I saw your holographic projection on my way in. How does it work? What role does that play in the process?"

"You saw that huh? Great, isn't it? As you may or may not know, the mind processes information via images. In fact, one might say imagery is the universal language. So we use image projection to communicate our message. And I can assure you, it beats the old-fashioned method of individual counseling."

"How many of you are there?"

"Actually, there aren't that many of us. We are fortunate that in most cases the "Seven" serves as the primary counselor. We merely support them as needed."

"Do all who come here succeed?" I recalled the comment my Seven had made about some coming here to get out of the "between" state, yet still avoiding the next step.

Thomas, as if sensing the real motive for my question, merely smiled, "Time here is not the same as in the physical realm. Therefore, it would be difficult to answer in terms you would understand, and yes, there are some who have been here a long time. However, for the most part, the process works well and the essences move on fairly quickly. But, as you have alluded, some do stay longer than others. To control this we conduct periodic evaluations and generally can tell if the process is being abused."

"What happens if you determine the process is being abused? What do you do?"

"In most cases, the essence is given the opportunity to be tested and hopefully move on in the process. If they are unwilling to be tested, or if the testing shows they are trying to manipulate the results, they are returned to the "between" state. However, I must stress that this is rare. The majority choose to move on." Thomas smiled briefly. "The "between" state is not very pleasant. Coming from the physical realm, to one where you can still see and hear, but not directly interact with the living must be difficult." Thomas grimaced as if to reinforce the purported pain. "Lets get started, shall we?"

Following Thomas, I returned to the room where the holographic images continued their unceasing sequences. "What are these images? What are they supposed to represent?"

Thomas paused before answering, as if formulating the best way to describe the process. "The majority of those who come here do so because they cannot cope with their separation from the physical realm. These images are an attempt to help them understand what has happened to them and hopefully what they can expect."

"So, if I watch all of these images will I understand? Will I then go through the evaluation process?"

"Well, not exactly. Just watching the images is not sufficient. Understanding the lessons innate to the images is of greater importance."

"How do you know when they understand? Is there a test or an exam?" Let's see how humor works with this one.

Thomas smiled, evidently catching my attempt at humor. "For the most part, the essence simply moves on to the evaluation process.

More specifically, when they finally accept their separation and understand these lessons they simply disappear. For those who do not, there is a test on the four key points of understanding that must be mastered to move to the next step. In fact, until you understand all four concepts, your Seven will not allow your essence to move on. If this were to happen, there is a high probability the essence would enter the next cycle incomplete and the new Bio would be negatively affected."

"What do you mean by negatively affected?"

"The essence of a Bio is that which makes it function properly. While ninety-nine point nine percent of the Bio is organic, the remaining one-tenth of one-percent is, for lack of a better term, "energy". This energy is the manifestation of your essence. If the essence is incomplete, the energy needed for the Bio unit to properly function, will be inadequate."

My face must have reflected my confusion, causing Thomas to stop.

"Let me give you a simple example. What happens when a Bio sticks his hand into a fire?" He looked at me waiting for an answer.

Having had first-hand experience in this, I immediately answered. "They hurt themselves and feel pain." In my case, I should have added, learned not to do it again.

Smiling, Thomas went on. "So the biological structure is damaged and they feel pain, correct?"

"Yes." I wasn't sure where he was going with this.

"I see. So how is it is possible for a Bio to walk through burning embers without damaging his physical body or for that matter feel any pain?"

Thomas smiled, seeing the images I had conjured up in my mind. Images I had watched on television of people walking through hot coals, yet experiencing no pain or physical effects. He continued. "The fact is the physical unit is totally controlled by thought. If one thinks one is hurt, the physical body behaves in a manner suitable to the pain in question. On the other hand, if one controls the thought process, it is then possible to walk through burning embers without impacting the body at all." Thomas paused before continuing. "You see, thoughts are nothing more than a manifestation of energy and this energy is derived from your essence."

"You're talking about mind over matter right?"

"Yes, you could put it that way. Now, as I was saying, if an essence were to return to the physical world in an incomplete state, it is possible the Bio unit will suffer emotionally and physically."

Although still little confused, I was not ready to give up. "So the essence is the mind? And the mind controls the Bio or body as it relates to the physical world?"

Sensing my confusion, Thomas smiled. "Yes something like that. Let's move on shall we?"

A thought occurred to me. "When we're finished here, can I be tested on these four concepts you mentioned? Would that be possible?" One way to make sure I understood was to see if I could pass their tests.

Thomas smiled. He had anticipated this question. "Well, Jonathan would need to agree, but yes, as far as I am concerned, you could, in fact, you should." When Jonathan returned, he could intervene and stop the process if he disagreed.

"Good, how do we start?"

"I suggest you simply follow the process like everyone else. I will stay with you and try to answer any questions you may have."

"Great, let's go."

Moving past the projected images of the flower and the human child, I found myself staring at the image of a large tree, following the same format as the other scenes. I watched as the tree erupted in a thousand little balls of brilliant light just as the buds sprouted on the branches. In the next scene, the buds had turned into leaves. Eventually the leaves turned color and fell to the ground. As the leaves came into contact with the ground, more brilliant lights flashed again. This process repeated itself over and over. Taking another step forward, the image changed again, I found myself staring at the globe of the earth, as if from outer space. As I watched, the crust of the earth shifted ninety-degrees causing the oceans and continents to shift and in some cases merge. Momentary darkness gave way to the image of the new earth, different, yet in some ways, the same. New oceans and continents appeared before me. The new earth, although barren, sparkled with brilliant flashes of light. New plant life emerged from the soil. An effervescent glow encompassed the globe. Darkness, indicating a scene change returned. The image of a new earth, now lush and green appeared. Yet, even as I watched, I saw a shadow creeping slowly across the scene, clearly indicating advancing decay. I watched the glow diminish as it left in its wake an emptiness one could only surmise was death. Fascinated, I watched as the cycle repeated itself again in its entirety. Feeling Thomas pulling lightly on my arm, I stepped to my left, off of the main path. As the holographic imagery disappeared, I found myself standing again in a dimly lit room.

Thomas watched me as I tried to cope with what I had seen. "What have you learned?"

Still sorting through the images and their sequence, I remained silent.

Thomas continued. "What can you tell me about what you have seen?"

"I think I understand. Each scene appears to represent a birth through death cycle. A flower sprouts forth from the earth. It blooms, pollinates then wilts and dies. A child being born, it grows, then ages and dies. A tree comes out of winter dormancy. It buds and turns into leaves, then they wither and die as the tree goes back into dormancy. The last scenes looked like the earth being reborn, life beginning, growing and dying again." This was a simple test, and anybody who had spent any time reflecting on nature would have seen this cycle first hand.

"Good, what else did you see?" Thomas looked at me intently, as if trying to gauge my depth of understanding.

I thought for a moment before answering. "In each scenario, I saw brilliant flashes of light. In the case of the flower, it occurred when the pollen came into contact with the ground and then again after the flower died and fell to the ground. In the case of the human, it occurred when he was making love to the woman and again after he died. In the case of the tree, just before the buds sprouted and as its withered leaves hit the ground. In the earth scenario, just before I saw new plant life."

"What do you think was happening?" This was a critical step in understanding.

"I think the brilliant lights were moments of creation, of life beginning." It was the only possible thing it could mean.

"Good, what else did you notice"? This, the final seed of understanding was one critical to the next set of lessons that had to be learned. Thomas waited patiently for a response.

"What do you mean? I told you all that I saw and what I thought it meant. What did I miss?" I had obviously missed something.

Thomas was silent. Normally at this point, the Seven would assist the essence. In this case there was no Seven to provide that support. Thomas was unsure if he should play this surrogate role, but decided it would do no harm.

"Tell me about the sequences. For each scenario, how many images were there?" Perhaps the best approach was by asking questions since he could not simply provide the answers.

I thought again of each set of images. The flower sequence began by sprouting from the ground, blossoming, pollinating, then wilting and dying. The child was born, grew, made love to the woman, and then was old and lying in a casket. The tree scenario began with brilliant lights and buds sprouting, leaves appearing, aging, then falling off. The earth sequence had first changed, life had begun again, blossomed, and then began to decay. Each scenario had four images.

"I think each contained four images." I looked at Thomas knowing this was the correct answer. But was it a complete answer? I somehow doubted it.

As if to reinforce this thought Thomas continued. "Good! Now can you tell me the significance of that?"

I knew the answer had to be fairly obvious, I just needed to think. Each scenario contained a scene representing birth, a scene indicating growth, a scene for aging, and finally a scene representing death and rebirth. Could this be the answer? Seeing the look on Thomas's face and knowing he was reading my thoughts, assured me I was right. "Each of the scenes represented a stage in the life cycle. There were two associated with growth, and two associated with decay or aging and death."

"Thomas smiled. "Good, now summarize what you have learned, then we'll move on to the next lesson."

Choosing my words carefully, I began to summarize my thoughts. "In all things, there is a natural cycle consisting of birth, growth, decay and eventually death and subsequent rebirth. This cycle is continuously repeated in all aspects of the physical realm." I paused, realizing for the first time, that the aspect of the cycle repeating itself meant that in fact there was no permanent death. The life cycle merely begins again, although perhaps in a different form.

Sensing my understanding, Thomas interjected. "Nothing every truly dies. The wilted flower, the human body, the dead leaves which fall to the ground merely becomes something else. They become part of the next cycle of life just in a different form. Do you understand?"

Of course! The concept of recycling logically would apply to all aspects of reality, not just at the essence level. So it's true you never really die! You just become another aspect of the physical reality. "Yes, I think I understand. Just as all Biological matter recycles itself so does the essence. Nothing every really dies. It simply transforms into another form of matter."

"In most cases, yes, that is the way of the natural order. However, there are exceptions when this order is not maintained. But that's a lesson for another time. Shall we move on?"

Moving again onto the path, the holographic images returned. I watched as the light-dark sequences unfolded around me. The first image was of a male figure followed by that of a female figure. Moving forward, the scene changed to the image of woman again giving birth, followed by the old man in the casket. Now, I saw a new image that of the noon sun blazing in brilliant light. This was followed by an image of a moon in the dark sky. The message of these images was intuitively clear. Each represented opposite sides of each other. The male was opposite to the female. The sun was opposite to the moon. Birth was opposite to death.

Thomas smiled, knowing I understood the message. "I see you understand these images."

"Yes, it would be hard not to understand. Each image represents the opposite of each other." Although I understood the superficial meaning of the images, I was equally sure it was not that simple. Surely there was another meaning, one I was not grasping. With his response, Thomas did not disappoint me.

"You are correct in that they do represent the opposites to each other. What else do you think they represent?"

Yes, they were opposites. But what else could they represent, what was I missing?

Thomas, obviously sensing my confusion continued after a brief pause. "What do they have in common?"

"They have nothing in common. They are opposites. Except that they both exist." I had barely spoken the words when the realization hit me. "I get it; they exist, are opposites, and as a result cannot exist without each other. You cannot have light without dark, male without female, death without birth."

"Good. You are correct. In all that exists, there is a fundamental duality. You cannot have light without dark, death without birth, land without seas, cold without warmth, and so. But, of equal importance, is the understanding that the two states must always be in a state of relative balance. Do you understand?"

"What do you mean relative balance?" I had not picked that up in the images at all.

Thomas hesitated before answering. "What would happen if a flower got too much sun?"

"It would die."

"Good! Now, what would happen if the same flower did not receive enough sunshine?"

"It would die."

Thomas continued. "Yes, now expand that concept to every other facet of the physical realm. In all instances, a significant or even insignificant imbalance would have a negative effect. In fact, even those instances which you consider good would be detrimental if carried to an extreme." Thomas stopped trying to think of an example. "Consider this, if everything made you happy, you could not realize you were happy, since there is no corresponding opposite or unhappy."

"That makes sense."

Thomas continued. "Do you remember the phases from the first set of images?"

"Yes." I replied.

Thomas nodded. "There were four, two of them represented birth and growth, and two represented decay and death. So you see even then we had symmetry or balance."

I pondered this for a moment. If there is an inherent duality to all that existed in the physical realm, is that also the case in this realm? "Can I assume the same duality exists here in this realm as well?"

Thomas was quiet for a moment. This was always the most difficult of the concepts to understand. "As there is a physical realm, and the concept of duality is true, then does it not make sense there must be a corresponding "non-physical" realm?"

I continued. "So in the beginning, there "was" and there "was not"?"

"Yes."

"And they were in proportion to each other?"

Thomas smiled in response. "Yes, relatively speaking. In reality, there is always a small degree of imbalance; perfect symmetry would leave no room for growth."

I paused. The ramifications of this concept of duality and balance, while self evident, left many possibilities my mind only now began to consider. I was also unsure if Thomas had truly understood my question. I was not asking if there was a "non-physical" realm corresponding to the Physical realm. The fact that I was here and having this discussion answered that question. "Yes, I understand there is a "non-physical" realm. That was not my question. What I am asking, is "within" this "non-physical" realm, does the concept of duality apply as it does in the physical world?"

"Yes, even here the concept applies."

"So, assuming you are a positive energy, there is a corresponding negative energy?"

Thomas shook his head in agreement. "The duality applies to everything including energy."

Intrigued, I pressed the issue. "Yet can you see this negative energy?"

"No, you can't, however, I would point out that while you are in the physical state, you cannot see the non-physical realm either. Does that mean it does not exist?"

"But it is possible to see the Physical realm from the "non-physical" realm? That doesn't seem balanced to me."

Thomas smiled again, knowing well his next response would

utterly confuse me. "Actually *that* is the balance."

"I don't understand! How do you figure that?"

"Well, we can, and you cannot. Is this not a form of symmetry? Has not balance been achieved? If both *could* see, there would be no difference or opposite position."

I knew instinctively what Thomas was saying was true. Just because we could not see, measure and catalog something, did not mean it did not exist. Scientists were continuously finding new and improved methods of viewing our reality.

As if reading my thoughts, Thomas smiled. "Your scientists have achieved great success in understanding the physical world, but to truly understand it, they need to also understand the non-physical aspect as well. They need not only to understand what is, but equally, what is not. By limiting their scope to the physical realm, more specifically to the cause and effect relationships, they can at best, only understand half of the whole. The fact is your scientists disallow the study of anything which cannot be measured." Thomas stopped as if musing to himself. He had always found it fascinating when scientists came through here and were shown the true nature of reality. All of them fundamentally understood there was "something" which could not be measured, but were compelled to ignore its existence by the dogmatic rules they applied in their methodologies.

"So what is the point of all of this? I understand this place and the purpose it serves, but still want to understand the higher purpose. Simply recycling the energy or essence, cannot be the ultimate goal. When does it stop?" I was really no closer to answers than when I had arrived in the Hall.

Thomas did not smile this time. In fact, if anything, he looked confused.

"So, how are your two getting on?" The distinctive voice of Jonathan approached from behind. "Have you found what you were looking for?" Jonathan returning from meeting with his superiors was still uncomfortable with the situation, but had been advised to provide whatever assistance he could, within certain defined limits. His superiors had been as surprised as he had been to learn that a non-separated essence had come to the hall. Surprised enough, to have had a side-meeting, one to which Jonathan had not been invited. After the meeting, Jonathan was simply told that although rare, it was not the first time such a thing had happened. It was recommended, that the best course of action, was to "provide whatever assistance he could" but only in the area of understanding the Hall and its purpose. They also advised him, that more than likely, the knowledge given would be lost or forgotten when the Bio unit awoke. Or, if necessary, it would be removed from memory during the next reincarnation process.

Noticing the change in Jonathan's demeanor, I knew the opportunity for further inquiry had presented itself. "We're doing just fine. Thomas has been very helpful in providing me with an understanding of this place and its purpose. He is a good teacher."

"Good, I'm glad we could help. Can I assume you have found what you were looking for and will be returning to your Seven?" Jonathan could only hope this to be the case.

"Actually, I do still have a few questions." Pausing, I could not help noticing the look of consternation pass across his face.

I continued, not waiting for a response. "While I understand the purpose of this place and certainly appreciate its role, I still do not understand the overall purpose of the entire process. I understand the evaluation and reincarnation process as a method of recycling the essence or energy back into the Physical realm, but I am still unclear as to the ultimate goal. Surely, simply re-constituting the energy over and over again is a means of achieving some higher purpose. What is that purpose?"

"I just can't wait to hear this." A new voice came from behind me.

Jonathan turned toward the voice and looked as if he had been punched in the face. "What are you doing here?" While he did not know the name of the voice, he recognized the dark hue surrounding her. She was a "Sleeper".

"Why don't you answer the question? Better yet, why don't they?" She nodded past Jonathan to the figures in the shadows behind him. "I'm here because of him." She nodded her head in my direction. "It is not everyday a non-separated essence comes to visit. Are you going to introduce us?" Clearly she enjoyed needling him.

Jonathan, clearly frustrated by her presence, seemed unsure of what to do or how to respond. Looking at me, he said. "This Bio is called. "Bill". He came here to learn about the Hall of Understanding and was just leaving to rejoin his Seven." He paused before turning to face me. "Bill, this is what we call a Sleeper and you would do well to be wary of her."

I did not hear the rest of Jonathan's statement as a sudden jolting shock not unlike an electrical current coursed through me. I felt an intense pulling sensation and the Hall of Understanding disappeared.

# Chapter 11

## Sunday morning 11:00 am

*T*he ambulance ride from St. Jude's Hospital to the Loyola Medical Center was faster than expected. Evidently Sergeant Harridy had arranged for a police escort, even though the situation was not life threatening. By doing so, he had probably broken a few rules. Andrew followed behind the ambulance, struggling to keep up and hoping not to be pulled over for speeding. Inside the ambulance, Mary sat quietly. Her gaze moved between the portable machines attached to her husband and the face of the EMT. It was clear he was concerned about the insistent beeping of one of the devices. Speaking into his shoulder microphone, he urged the driver to make haste, while at the same time, trying to look positive for her benefit.

"Is everything all right?" Mary's voice sounded weak, even to herself.

"Yes, we're doing fine, but I want to transfer him as soon as possible." He didn't share with her his concern about the EEG readings alternately spiking then flat-lining. There was definitely some strange brain activity going on, unlike anything he had seen in his seventeen years as an EMT.

The Loyola emergency entrance had been cleared for their arrival. A Doctor, or perhaps a resident, stood with Dr. Brangeel watching as the EMT's unloaded the portable gurney. Brangeel spent a few minutes studying the EEG printouts provided by the EMT, before turning and advising the young resident to immediately move the patient to the fourth floor. Dr. Wong, head of the Loyola Neuro Department would, be waiting for the patient.

Dr. Brangeel turned toward Mary and Andrew, who had just arrived from the remote parking lot. "We're taking him up to the Neuro floor now. They have a room set up for him and Dr. Wong is

54

standing by. In the meantime, you will need to go to the in-patient receiving area and complete some forms. When you're done, have the receptionist page me and I will take you to Bill's room." Brangeel, seeing the obvious stress on Mary's face, patted her arm reassuringly. "Relax; he's in the best possible hands. He will be just fine."

Mary, unable to speak, merely shook her head. Andrew took her arm. "Can you show us the way to in-patient receiving Doc?"

Dr. Brangeel smiled, recalling the time when Andrew was a little tyke, hiding under a chair in the examination room to avoid getting a shot. His father should be proud, he turned out well. "Down the hall your first door on the right."

"Thanks Doc, see you soon." With that, he led his mother down the corridor. While he was as shaken by the ordeal as was his mom, he was determined not to show it. He knew one thing for certain; his dad would not give up. It just wasn't his way.

Dr. Brangeel must have "run interference" for them as the in-patient receptionist was expecting them. She had completed all the forms required and they simply needed to sign them. With signatures intact, she paged Dr. Brangeel who arrived a few minutes later.

"Ready?"

The receptionist nodded and then turned to Mary. She squeezed her hand, whispering to her not to worry, that her husband was in the best of hands.

"Good. Follow me." Dr. Brangeel led them to the elevator and pushed the number four on the panel. "He is in his room, and Dr. Wong is with him as we speak."

"Can we see him?" Andrew asked the question so his mother would not have to.

"Yes, of course." Brangeel smiled inwardly. "But I should warn you there are a lot of pieces of equipment hooked up to him, and it looks more serious than it is. Don't let them worry you. They are just machines which allow Dr. Wong to see at a diagnostic level of what is happening. Okay?"

"Sure Doc! Would it be possible to get a printout? We've always wondered what was going on in his brain. Maybe this will help." Andrew's attempt at humor was clearly designed to relieve the tension.

Dr. Brangeel chuckled, appreciating the attempt. "Sure, but what if it's blank?"

Even Mary smiled at that, "It would only confirm what I have thought since I met him."

Dr. Tai Chen Wong sat studying the EEG printouts provided by the EMT, occasionally glancing at the charts updating in real time on the computer screen over the bed. As a practicing neurologist, he was certainly qualified for this case. As head of the Neuro department, he could easily have assigned another Doctor. He would have, except when the call was first received along with facsimiles of charts from St. Jude, he was intrigued by what the charts indicated, he immediately decided to handle this case himself. In fifteen years of practice that followed ten of medical school and residency, he had never seen charts with such abnormal activity in the brain, specifically in the Occipital and Frontal Cortex regions. More specifically, he had never seen the level of activity between the two. Of greater interest to him, were the patterns of the synapse charges crossing between the left and right sides of the brain and the Cortex and Cerebral Hemispheres. Normally, this synaptic exchange only occurred when the subject was under extreme duress, and even then, in a non-continuous, non-repeating manner. Yet, these charges were repeating exactly with only the duration or sustentation period changing. To his knowledge, this level of synapse activity had never been reported before, or for that matter, seen in any of the test conditions he had tried to simulate. He wondered to himself, what was happening in the patient's brain.

The door to the room opened quietly as Dr. Brangeel, Mary and Andrew entered. Mary was surprised to see the middle-aged man sitting in a wheelchair. The name tag on his starched white coat confirmed he was Dr. Wong. As if reading her thoughts, Dr. Brangeel introduced them.

"Mary, Andrew, I would like you to meet Dr. Wong." He paused, trying to gauge Mary's expression. "Dr. Wong is the head of the Neuro Department here at Loyola, and will be managing Bill's case."

Dr. Wong looked up and gave her a reassuring smile. "Sorry for not getting up." An ill-fated round of golf, in a sudden mid-western electrical storm when he was fifteen, had permanently damaged the portion of his brain which managed the motor functions of his lower body and legs. The specialists told him the surge of current through his body had overloaded his neurological system, and the damage was irreparable. That was the moment he decided Neurology would be his field of research. He firmly believed, that the damage could be repaired, if they could only understand the brain functions well enough. He had since devoted his life to acquiring that knowledge.

Mary was, in fact, wondering to herself how this handicapped Doctor was going to care for her husband. Yet at the same time, she trusted Dr. Brangeel and if he said Dr. Wong was the best person, she believed him. "How is he?" she asked.

"I have only begun my evaluation, but based upon the initial physical examination and the first pass diagnostic results, I can definitely say two things. First, your husband is NOT in a coma, and second, there does appear to be buildup of pressure from the fluids around his brain."

"If he is not in a coma, why doesn't he wake up?" Andrew spoke for the first time.

"I'm sorry, who are you?" Dr. Wong looked at Andrew inquiringly.

Dr. Brangeel interceded. "This is the patient's son Andrew."

Dr. Wong paused before answering. "I cannot definitively answer your question. But I can tell you; based upon the diagnostics the level of brain activity does not in any way resemble a person in a comatose state." Dr. Wong paused before continuing. "It could be that his body has simply chosen this state as the most appropriate one for this moment. Let me also add, that were he to be awake, he would probably be feeling a moderate-to-high level of pain, most certainly a severe headache."

"Is there anything you can do to relieve the swelling and pressure on his brain? I mean, if that is the major issue, wouldn't that help?" Mary asked, her voice barely a whisper.

"Yes, there are several possible methods available if that is the course we must take, but in this instance, as he is not in pain and not in jeopardy, I think the best course of action is to wait and simply allow nature to take its course." Dr. Wong looked again at the monitors.

"We will of course, keep a very close eye on him and intervene if necessary."

Andrew, listening quietly to one side, wanted to know more. "You said there were several methods of treatment available. Are they dangerous?" He was envisioning brain surgery.

"Dr. Wong, sensing the real question replied. "There is a non-invasive method available, where we try to reduce the swelling using chemicals. Should that fail, we could perform a more invasive procedure to physically drain the fluids thereby relieving the pressure. However, I think for now, the best course of action is to do nothing. I suspect he will wake on his own and in his own time."

"You mean drill holes in head?" Mary's voice rose well above a whisper. "I do not think he would want us to do that." She turned to Dr. Brangeel looking for support.

Dr. Brangeel took her hand and gave it a gentle squeeze. "We can cross that bridge when come to it. As Dr. Wong said, that would be a procedure of last resort and one we will discuss in detail before it is performed."

# Chapter 12

## <u>Reynolds Support Unit.</u>

My Seven and Three stood silently watching and listening to the Doctors. Seven merely observed while "Three" busily transcribed the words and actions into the memory recorder. Evidently, even though I was not conscious and would probably not remember any of this, they still needed it to be recorded just like every other detail of my existence.

"What happened? Why am I back here?" The last thing I remembered was a jolt and a strong pulling sensation. I was upset. I had asked the question I most wanted an answer to only to be pulled back before the answer was given. And who did that new voice belong to? It was female and Jonathan said she was a sleeper. Who was she and what did she want with me?

Seven glanced in my direction and answered in a matter of fact tone. "I brought you back. I sensed there was a sleeper nearby and did not want you to be near one without your support unit." He paused before continuing. "As I told you before, "Sleepers" can cause serious harm unless properly controlled."

Still frustrated at being denied my answer, I mentally chastised him. "Jonathan and Thomas were there. Couldn't they have protected me? Besides, she didn't look or sound dangerous to me." I was infuriated.

Seven merely shrugged. "I don't know if Jonathan or Thomas COULD or WOULD have protected you. What I do know is, YOU are our responsibility, and it is OUR job to protect you. I did what needed to be done."

Still angry, I looked at the hospital scene before responding. "I was close to finding out what I wanted to know and you stopped me."

The room was, as would be expected, small and brightly lit.

The bank of monitors and the snakelike cords attached to my body, gave it the look of a high-tech science fiction movie. I recognized Dr. Brangeel, Mary, and Andrew, but the other three people in the room were new to me. "Where am I, and who are they?" My question was directed at no one in particular.

"They have moved you to the Loyola Medical Center. More specifically, you're in the Neuro ward. The Bio in the wheelchair is Dr. Tai Chen Wong, a neurologist. The female Bio to your right is an RN named Charlene White. And the last, is a resident Doctor named John Blake."

"What's going on?" I could see myself lying on the bed, and still found it to be a little disconcerting.

Seven, still focused on the scene before him replied. "They were just explaining to your wife and son, that you are not in a coma, but there is a significant fluid buildup in your head, which is applying pressure on your brain."

"Sounds serious, is the Bio unit in danger?" Clearly, I needed to pay more attention to what was happening. I was not feeling anything at all.

"According to "Five", aside from the cut on your head, your Bio is in excellent shape. In fact, it is working at a higher capacity than ever before."

"Then why am I still unconscious?"

Seven shrugged. "I think maybe you wish to be here, rather than there."

Was that true? Was it possible that I was putting my family through this ordeal to satisfy my own need for understanding? "You mean I can go back at any time?" All this time, I had been under the impression I was simply allowing events to transpire. It had never occurred to me that I was in control of the situation.

Seven, looking intently at me, simply replied. "You can do whatever you want to, we are simply your support unit. Only you can decide to stay or return."

"How do I get back?" I motioned in the direction of the hospital room.

"Simply decide to wake up."

"You mean just think of waking and I will?"

Seven shrugged. "Try."

Looking again at the room, I thought to myself that I needed to return to my family to let them know I was okay. Almost instantly, my eyes opened and I found myself staring into the soft green eyes of a middle-aged woman I knew to be the RN, Charlene White. Looking around, I saw Dr. Wong sitting in his chair with Mary, Andrew and Dr. Brangeel standing a few feet behind him. Yet even while seeing this, I was also aware that there were others in the room. In fact, there were many more figures in the room. More than I had seen while with my support unit. Focusing on these figures, I recognized them immediately. I was seeing the support units of the other people in the room. A blend of voices provided the background noise interrupted by the continuous beeping of the machines.

"Doctor, I think he's awake."

My eyes focused on the RN. As I did so, I could hear her "Seven" speaking to her. His words were distinct and clear. "You should let Melissa go on the trip. She will be fine."

Dr. Wong glanced in my direction. "So, you decided to rejoin us? Do you recognize anyone here?" The question was obviously intended to assess my cognitive abilities.

The resident Doctor, whose name-tag said Dr. Blake, leaned over me causing me to look in his direction. I could hear the conversation of his support unit. His "Five" was imploring his "Seven" to send a warning signal that the Bio unit was in danger of a life-threatening heart-attack. I could hear this in my mind, as if I were the one thinking the thoughts.

Ignoring Dr. Wong's question, I looked at Charlene, who was watching my face intently. "Charlene, you should let Melissa go." Turning to the resident Doctor, I said to him. "You need to see a Cardiologist soon."

Charlene, a moment earlier focused on my condition, was now thinking of her daughter Melissa. Melissa was sixteen-years old and had been invited to take a trip to France by her best friend. In spite of the fact it would be fully paid for by the friend's family, she was understandably torn about letting her go. How did he know? He couldn't know! Yet he did.

Blake, the resident Doctor was having similar thoughts. Of

late, he had been more fatigued than normal, but had chalked it up to the long hours of his work. He had not considered the possibility of a heart condition. Now that he was thinking in that direction, he supposed the symptoms could be early warning signals.

I moved my head looking for Mary in the crowd of images. Catching her eye, I mouthed to her. "No surgery!"

Dr. Wong reached his hand through the side rail of the bed, intending to take my hand. As his hand came into contact with mine, a jolt of energy coursed through my body into his, causing an almost instantaneous paralysis, not unlike one caused by an electrical shock. His body absorbed the energy and began to spasm violently.

Dr. Brangeel, while not understanding the events unfolding before him, instinctively forced his body between Dr. Wong and the bed thereby breaking the energy connection. Yet even for this brief moment, he also felt the jolt of energy.

Dr. Wong, dazed by the jolt, sat in his chair, his legs and arms convulsing with uncontrolled spasms.

"We have a "Code Blue." Dr. Brangeel yelled while simultaneously pushing the emergency button on the control panel, at the same time pulling Dr. Wong to the floor. Even as he did so, Wong's eyes fluttered open, and the convulsive spasms began to subside.

"What happened?" Dr. Wong, still a little groggy, slowly regained control.

"I don't know. When you touched him, you received some sort of shock." Brangeel leaned over his friend. "Just relax for a minute." Turning to Charlene, he instructed her to cancel the emergency call.

Shaken myself, I opened my eyes and was surprised to again find myself viewing the room from above. My Bio appeared once again to be sleeping.

"What happened?" Even here, I felt somehow drained.

Seven and Three, looking somewhat haggard, stood mouths agape. For the first time, "Three" was not recording into her machine.

"I don't know." Seven, for the first time in thousands of years, had been surprised. The return of this essence was unexpected to say the least. "Somehow, when the Doctor touched you, there was a transference of energy from you to him, or perhaps I should say, from us through you to him."

I was beginning to feel more like myself, as each moment passed. Or more accurately, my energy-self seemed to be reconstituting itself. "Did I hurt him?"

Seven, watching the scene in the room, did not immediately respond. "I don't think so, look."

Looking at the room, I could see Dr. Wong being helped into his chair by Brangeel. Occasional spasms still caused his feet to jerk involuntarily. From the look of excitement on Wong's face, I sensed something good might actually have happened.

A familiar voice coming from behind me caused me to take my eyes off the room.

"What happened here?" Jonathan and the "Sleeper" from Hall of Understanding stood watching us. An energy-spike, unlike any observed in thousands of years, had been felt throughout the non-physical realm.

Seven ignored the question and completely focused his attention on the "Sleeper". "What do you want?" His team busily re-focused their efforts into a defensive mode.

The "Sleeper", unperturbed by these actions, spoke in a soft yet clear voice. "We also felt the disturbance." This was the same essence she had observed in the Hall of Understanding.

My support team, now prepared for any trickery, waited patiently for the "Sleeper" to make a move toward their charge. Seven was comfortable that any attempt to influence his charge would be easily defended. "You are not welcome here, please leave immediately."

The "Sleeper" merely shrugged. "I have as much right to be here as you." My Seven did not respond, so she continued. "In spite of what you think, I intend him no harm. I have been sent to investigate the disturbance and have no other agenda."

"Why should we believe you? ˙ Your kind, are masters at deception and trickery." My Seven was obviously not going to let his guard down for a moment.

Jonathan focused his gaze on the support team. "Relax; she will not interfere with your charge unless he chooses to allow it." Turning to the "Sleeper" he received her nod of agreement.

My energy level was by now fully restored, and I was intrigued by the scene playing out before me. "Excuse me, but can someone please tell me what this is all about?" I directed my gaze toward Jonathan and the "Sleeper". It was becoming evident, that Jonathan carried more weight than I had originally thought.

Taking his eyes off my support team, Jonathan turned to face me. "A short time ago we observed an energy disturbance emanating from here. A disturbance large enough to upset the balance maintained between the Physical and non-Physical realms. Although not serious to the overall dynamics, it was decided that an investigation was in order." He paused before continuing. "In keeping with the rules, I was sent. As was this "Sleeper".

"What rules?" Obviously, my earlier assessment of greater purpose was right on the mark. Furthermore, it was evident that this little episode had in some way concerned them.

The "Sleeper" spoke to me for the first time. "You would not understand, and quite frankly, it is not important. What IS important is to understand what has happened here, and more importantly, how and why."

Turning toward her, I decided that admonishing her for deciding what was important to me could wait. "Who are you? Do you have a name? My Seven says you are dangerous to me. Is that true?"

The Sleeper nodded. "Those are fair questions. First, my name is Christie, and I am a form of energy just like your support unit. I might also add I am no more dangerous to you than they are." She nodded in the direction of my support unit.

"Then why do they say you are? What is your purpose? What do you want with me?" I understood the roles played by my support team and thought understanding her role was only fair.

Christie thought for a moment before responding. "My role and the role of others like me, is to ensure that you and your kind, receive appropriate guidance from them." She nodded again in the direction of Jonathan and my support team.

"Wouldn't it be easier if you simply became part of the support unit?" To my way of thinking, this would have been more logical than assuming an opposing role.

Christie smiled. "One would think so, but the fact is, there are far fewer of us and unlike them, we did not have to dilute ourselves as they were required to." She paused. "I know this does not fully satisfy your question, but you must believe me. I cannot be more specific without being guilty of unwarranted influence on you."

I sensed she was speaking the truth, and in spite of the comments made earlier by my support unit, I believed her. But, what were they not telling me? Turning to Jonathan, I was determined to again ask the question I had posed to him, before being pulled from the Hall of Understanding.

"Jonathan, earlier in the Hall of Understanding, I asked you what the greater purpose was. Clearly, simply recycling energy is not the long-term goal. I ask you again, what is the overall purpose of all of this?"

Jonathan, clearly uncomfortable, looked first at Christie than at me. "As Christie said, there are limits to what we can tell you, without violating the "rules." Quite frankly, we are not permitted to answer."

It only now occurred to me, that I was unable to sense or read their thoughts as I could with my support unit. Obviously, they were different, or at the least, had abilities the support unit did not. What were these rules they referenced? What had I done that had frightened them to the extent that they set aside their own agendas, to work together now? One thing was certain. I would not get the answers I sought from them, yet at least now I knew there were answers to be had.

"So, let me understand the larger picture." I decided a recap of what I had learned was in order. "There are two realms, one physical the other non-physical. These realms co-exist in a state of balance, and in fact, logically cannot exist in the absence of each other. While every aspect of the physical realm is subject to the natural processes of generation, growth, decay and death, in the non-physical realm, this natural cycle does not apply. Furthermore, in order to maintain the physical realm, and correspondingly, the non-physical realm, energy is continuously recycled using a process of re-incarnation." I paused, but only for a moment. "The fact that the Hall of Understanding was created in the first place, leads me to believe that failure to ensure recycling, would have a negative affect in both realms. Additionally, based upon my earlier conversations with Thomas, a balance between the two must be maintained in all aspect of these realms." I stopped trying to gauge their reactions. "I also now believe, that based upon what is happening with support units, and with "Sleepers" in the "non-physical" realm, dualities also exist here comprised of opposing, yet I assume, balanced energies. One group professes to be dedicated to maintaining the well-being of the biological-essences, and the other claims to be an oversight group of the other."

The glance shared between Jonathan and Christie confirmed to me that my understanding was greater than they had thought. I continued, not waiting for a response. "Now, *I* come along, and for some reason, am capable of participating in both realms. Something I did, or am capable of doing, has you worried. I am assuming of course, you would not be investigating in a cooperative manner were this not the case." I stopped my summary at this point and allowed them to absorb what I had said.

"While your insights are correct, they are also incomplete." Christie's voice interrupted the silence. "Perhaps if we can work through the immediate issue, we can help fill in some of the missing pieces later." She looked inquiringly in Jonathan's direction.

Jonathan, still looking uncomfortable, merely nodded his assent.

"What do you want to know?" To my thinking, at least the door was open for future dialog.

"What do you remember?"

"Why don't you ask my Three, she records everything?" I was not trying to be uncooperative, but even I would not recall every detail.

"Good suggestion." Turning to my Seven she asked. "Would that be acceptable to you?"

Seven, disturbed by this turn of events, looked thoughtful for a moment. "You know full well, that the data record access is only permitted during the evaluation process."

"That is unless Bill agrees." Jonathan knew the memory logs opened during the evaluation process, were done so only with the consent of the essence. Under normal circumstances, this was not an issue, as by then, the essence had already separated from its Bio and wanted to move on. In this case, he was making an assumption that if the essence agreed, it could be viewed in the same manner and therefore would not be a violation of the rules. Besides, given the downside risk potential, he was willing to take a chance.

Seven glared at Jonathan and shrugged. "It's your call, but for the record, I oppose." He turning to face "Three", nodding in my direction. "If he agrees, show them the record from the moment he woke up, until he returned here."

All eyes turned to me. "If I agree, do I have your word that we can have further discussion on my other questions?" I knew I had to agree, if only because I also wanted to know what had happened. At the same time, I was not willing to let the opportunity for more understanding and knowledge get away.

"Yes, within the boundaries set for us, we will help you." Christie chose her words carefully. Although she could not violate the rules, she was also aware that there had been others in the past that had sought understanding, others who had been given far more than what had been given to me, so there was a little room for movement.

"Fine, you have my permission." I had noted her guarded response but, instinctively knew, it was the best I would get.

Almost immediately, an image similar to the holographic images from the Hall of Understanding appeared. This image, however, appeared to be three-dimensional, giving it the look and feel as if you were participating first hand. As we watched, I saw the eyes of my Bio open and heard for the first time, my words (or should I say my thoughts) as the Bio had not yet spoken.

What green eyes! My Bio was looking at Charlene, the RN. I watched the eyes shift away from Charlene, bringing Dr. Wong into focus with Andrew, Mary and Dr. Brangeel standing a little behind him. Equally important, I was aware of the presence of others. I remembered thinking the room was very crowded. I heard the combined voices of the others Bio's support units. Charlene's voice interrupted my thoughts. "Doctor, I think he's awake." I watched as my Bio re-focused on Charlene and could clearly hear her "Seven" talking to her. "You should let Melissa go on the trip. She will be fine."

"Stop the playback." Jonathan instructed my "Three".

Looking in my direction he had a puzzled look on his face. "You *saw* and *heard* the support units of the other Bios?" This was virtually unprecedented. Even the support units were incapable of seeing or communicating with each other. By design, such communication was blocked by the Bio's electro-magnetic field.

Christie appeared to be equally excited by this revelation and chimed in. "It's almost as it was in the beginning."

Jonathan shot her a warning glance. "Let's continue."

The image resumed. In it, I saw Dr. Blake lean over my Bio and once again I was aware of another conversation taking place *within* his support unit. His "Five" was imploring his "Seven", to send warning signals regarding an impending health issue. I saw myself looking at Mary, and heard myself telling her "no surgery". As I watched, I heard Dr. Wong's voice welcome me back to land of the conscious, and could sense his hand reaching toward me. As his hand came into contact with mine, I could feel my energy flowing outward into him. Even now, watching after the fact, the sensation was almost overwhelming. The record ended with the image of my Bio being viewed as if from above. I had returned to the presence of my support unit.

There was silence for a moment. I looked at Jonathan and Christie, trying to sense their thoughts. Unlike my support unit, I was not "tuned" into them, and could not hear their thoughts.

"That's amazing." Jonathan spoke to no one in particular. To me he asked. "What did you feel when the doctor touched you?"

"I felt a surge of power or energy leaving me and going into him." I was beginning to understand the source of their concern. His surprise at my being able to see and hear other support units was a clear indication that something extraordinary had happened. The energy transference to Dr. Wong was the cause that had prompted this investigation.

"Do you remember anything else?"

"No, just the surge of energy, and I was back here."

Jonathan looked away, obviously deep in thought. While there had been instances throughout history of a Bio harnessing energy and to a limited degree transferring that energy to others, only once had the Bio also been "tuned" into the support units of other Bios. Could this be the first step of the long awaited journey home?

Christie, immersed in her own thoughts, had similar questions. Was this a sample of what was? Is this the beginning of the transformation? One thing was certain, she had to find a way to keep this one from going back to his Bio, at least until she was sure of what was actually happening. The problem was how? Even under these extraordinary circumstances, she could not break the rules by directly intervening. The decision to stay had to be his alone. Although the rules did allow both sides to serve advisory roles, the final decision had to be his.

"Is there anything else?" Seven spoke aloud. In spite of Jonathan's assurances, he was still wary of Christie's presence. She was after all, a "sleeper" and the sooner she left the better.

"I would like to make a suggestion." Christie sensed this was her opportunity. Perhaps providing the opportunity to gain more knowledge was the best approach. What she had in mind would almost certainly delay his returning to the Bio. "Bill, earlier we promised to help you better find your answers. To do so, I would like to suggest we take you to the Hall of Knowledge."

"Hold on, you can't do that." Jonathan had not been prepared for this suggestion. "I would suggest to you doing so could be construed as direct intervention, and I might add, a clear violation of the rules."

Christie gave him a sharp look. "Of course we can. You know full well, we have allowed many visitors in the past. As for being construed as direct intervention and a violation of the rule, please note, I made this offer only as a suggestion. It is his choice whether to go or not." Christie smiled. She knew that posing it as a suggestion was within the operating guidelines. "Besides, you should welcome this opportunity, as this will also give you time to properly assess this situation."

In spite of his immediate reaction, he knew she was right. He was equally concerned about this essence returning to the Bio unit, at least until they better understood what was happening, and the "Hall of Knowledge" would certainly provide that time.

Not sensing their true motivations, I asked. "What is this "Hall of Knowledge? I have already been to the "Hall of Understanding".

Is this different?"

Jonathan, still looking at Christie shook his head. "This is very different than what you have already seen. The "Hall of Understanding" serves the purpose of helping "essences in the between state" with the transition process. The "Hall of Knowledge" serves a different purpose."

Not to be put off, I pressed the issue. "What purpose is that?"

Christie turned to face me. "It would be best for you to see for yourself. This way, you can form your own opinions without undue influence from us." She nodded in Jonathan's direction. "I can assure you, that my definition of its purpose would be much different than his."

"Can "Seven" accompany me?"

"No! Your Seven needs to stay with your Bio. But I promise, if there is a need for you to return, he will pull you back just as he did from the Hall of Understanding." Jonathan was beginning to like the idea. The Hall of Knowledge was immense, and one with such an appetite for answers would be there for some time. Most certainly, enough time for him to understand what was happening.

"Will either of you be with me?"

"I will accompany you, and provide whatever assistance I can." Christie knew by doing so, Jonathan would be forced to provide a similar service. "What about it, Jonathan? Surely you will be coming as well?"

Jonathan, obviously deep in thought, merely shook his head. "No! But I will send Thomas in my place." He needed to digest what was happening, and to review it with the others.

"Three", still watching and recording the events in the hospital room, interrupted. "Maybe you should take a look at this."

All including myself, turned to view the scene.

The room, though still brightly lit, was quiet. The incessant beeping of the equipment had ceased, as had the displays on all of the monitors. Dr. Wong, having been helped to his chair, sat as if mesmerized, watching his left leg and foot spasm every few seconds. To no one in particular, he said. "This is amazing. I can feel a tingling sensation like little pins." He had not felt anything below his waist in decades. Fortunately, not wanting his muscles and tendons to

70

shrivel up, he had continued daily regimens of physical therapy.

Dr. Brangeel, standing by his side, shook his head. They had been friends since medical school, and he had long-silently-wished success for his friend in his research. Turning to Dr. Blake, he nodded in the direction of the bed. "How is the patient? Find out what happened to the monitors."

Blake reached instinctively for the patient, only stopping his hand a moment before coming into contact. "Do you think it is safe?" Having witnessed what had happened to Dr. Wong, he was in no hurry to come into physical contact.

Andrew, standing with his mother at the end of the bed, glared at the resident doctor before reaching his hand out and touching his father's leg. "Look, its perfectly safe. Now, is he okay or not?"

A sheepish Blake tentatively reached out taking the patient's wrist. "Pulse is strong, maybe a little fast." He looked at Charlene and said. "Get a blood pressure reading. I will look into getting new monitors." He then looked in the direction of Andrew and his mother. "His vital signs are good, and once we get new equipment, we will do a full diagnostic." He smiled at Andrew. "That took courage kid, I'm sorry I didn't have it."

Andrew again demonstrated his maturity. "Not your fault Doctor, given what happened to Dr. Wong, I can't say I blame you". He paused. "Somebody had to do it, and I figured he would not hurt me."

Dr. Blake paused. "You're assuming that what happened was intentional. Did it ever occur to you that it was not?" With that, he went off in search of new equipment.

Brangeel, satisfied that the patient was not in danger, again turned his attention Dr. Wong. "How are you feeling? Still getting the tingling sensation?"

Wong nodded, yes a little. "What do you think happened here?" Aside from the seeming miracle, he was only now allowing his mind to process the events, and the possible implications. Somehow, the unusual brain activity he had been observing had manifested itself into a form of healing energy. Instances of psychic healing were documented throughout history, and he had always suspected the human brain possessed such capabilities. He further hoped that with his research and perhaps another hundred years, it could be proven. Perhaps, even used as a medical tool.

Brangeel looked pensive and replied. "I don't know my friend, but I think it may be prudent for everyone involved to keep this "low-profile" until we have had an opportunity to discuss it." He did not add his concern that their excitement was potentially premature. He would not want to take that hope from his friend.

"Wong looked at the patient, and shook his head in agreement. "You're right, of course. Let's not jump to conclusions." He turned to Charlene. "Charlene, please find Doctor Blake. I would like to have both of you in my office in fifteen-minutes." He looked at Andrew standing with his mother and said. "I would appreciate if both of you would join us as well."

"What about him?" Andrew nodded in the direction of his father. "Will he be all right?"

Wong shook his head. "He will be fine. They will bring in new equipment, and as Dr. Blake said, will perform a complete set of tests." He paused before continuing. "It will be a few minutes until they are ready, certainly time enough for us to meet." Nodding to the nurse, he wheeled himself out of the room. Brangeel, Mary, and Andrew followed not far behind.

My companions were silent, listening intently to the conversation from the room. Finally Jonathan spoke. "What? I did not see anything unusual."

Christie, still watching the room, spoke softly. "Don't you understand? What if the Bio named Wong has been cured? How did it happen? How do you think that will be received by his peers?" She knew the answer already. Throughout the past ten-thousand years, there had been a few who had possessed such capabilities. Invariably, they were sought after by every person with an illness. More frightening, he would be sought after by the controlling powers, and if they did not get what they wanted, the person with the power was deemed a threat and subsequently eliminated.

Seven, having seen this during his long tenure as a guardian, had also been witness to the ignorance of the Bios. "What can we do? If he chooses to return and demonstrates this ability again, he will be sought after until his cycle is complete."

Jonathan, finally comprehending, interceded. "Wait a moment! We do not even know if the Bio called Wong IS cured. And if he is, whether it was because of him." Jonathan nodded in my direction. "What if what he did was involuntary? What if he has no control over it?" To him he thought, Reynolds was able to see and hear the other Bio's support units, and now has the healing power. What next?

"Can one of you explain to me what the issue is?" I had picked up on the thoughts of my Seven, and had heard the dialog between Jonathan and Christie. Could I really be in danger?

Seven did not wait for the others to respond. "There have been instances throughout history, of the Bio-essence combination having the ability to heal sickness through energy transference. As you might imagine, these Bios were viewed as very powerful and sought after not only by the sick and infirmed, but also by the controlling powers. Invariably, the "powers" either retained the services of the Bio-essence, or had it destroyed out of fear." He paused before continuing. "In all but one instance, the Bio-essence learned to control his ability and hid it from his captors. In some instances, they were released, but more often than not, they were terminated."

"You said, in all but one instance, what was that one?" I could certainly understand how such a being would be coveted and feared. If I did possess such power, would I be able to control it?

Christie, not wanting the Seven to respond interrupted. "Perhaps, that is one of the answers you should seek in the "Hall of Knowledge".

Jonathan, also wanting to redirect the conversation was quick to agree. "Rather than hearing our version, perhaps it would be best for you to observe and decide for yourself. I will say, however, that one person forever changed the human psyche."

It was evident I was not going to get an answer. "I had better learn how the others controlled this power. Can you tell me what they did?"

"According to the records, they were able to control it using their minds." Jonathan knew this was one question they needed to answer.

"Are you saying they simply decided not to use it?" How do you think not to use something?"

"Yes, in a sense! Each created their own method of redirecting their thoughts to prevent the inadvertent use of the power. Some even created a secondary magnetic field which blocked any transference due to incidental contact with other Bios."

"And, if they wanted to use their abilities, were they able to?" How do you create a secondary magnetic field? Would I be able to?

Jonathan seemed to be enjoying his current status as mentor and teacher. "From what the records tell us, they created combinations of words known only to themselves which when spoken, allowed the energy transference to pass through the magnetic fields. So yes, they were able to exercise their powers."

"So, it was some form of spell or incantation? So that's where witch's spells had originated."

"Yes, to those who did not understand, it would appear as some form of magic had been used." Jonathan was beginning to feel uncomfortable with this line of questioning. He knew what was coming next, and also knew he could say very little more.

"What is this power? Where did it come from?" The enormity of it was beginning to set in. Do all Bios have this capability? What happened to me, that I now have use of it?

Christie, in full agreement with Jonathan, knew that to answer would be a violation of the rules. Only Eldred, the keeper of records, was permitted to give such information. Only he could determine if the time was right for the dissemination of such knowledge. "We cannot answer any more questions in this area without violating the rules. However, Eldred can provide you these answers."

"Who is this Eldred? When can I meet him?" My list of questions was growing longer, not shorter.

Jonathan answered, not waiting for Christie's approval. "Eldred, is the keeper of records in the Hall of Knowledge. He is the only one who can give you the answers you seek. But I must warn you, he will not just give them to you. I suspect he will require you to derive them yourself, at least to the extent the records exist. At that point, he may or may not give you further information." Even Eldred had rules to follow, less stringent, but rules nonetheless.

"When can we go to this "Hall of Knowledge"? I was more determined to find answers. If this "Eldred" was the key, I would go to him.

Christie exchanged a quick glance with Jonathan. "We can go now if you wish." She looked at Jonathan. "Is Thomas ready?"

Almost as if on cue, Thomas appeared from behind Jonathan. "I'm ready." He nodded in my direction. "We meet again."

# Chapter 13

## **Loyola Medical Center 11:30 am.**

$W$ong's office could have easily accommodated several times the number of occupants now seated around the large conference table. Dr. Blake sitting to Wong's right, appeared deep in thought. Charlene sat next to Mrs. Reynolds with Andrew on her other side. Brangeel still standing, brought the meeting to order.

"How are they doing with the new equipment?" the question was directed at Blake.

They should be ready in ten minutes." Blake had arranged to move the patient to a new room, rather than try to find all the equipment. "There is a vacant room with everything we need, and I am having the patient moved as we speak."

Dr. Wong, listening to the conversation, looked intently at Blake. "That is not what I asked you to do." The last thing he wanted was to have the patient wake again and to have a similar effect on others.

Blake, who had anticipated this, replied. "I instructed the staff moving him to wear protective gloves and clothing."

"Great! Now everyone will want to know why." Wong clearly displeased.

Brangeel sensed his friend's frustration and interceded. "Let's not overreact. We can tell them something later to dispel questions. Right now, I think we need to review what happened." he paused. "Who wants to go first?"

Charlene, unaccustomed to such meetings, raised her hand. "What exactly are we trying to do?"

Dr. Wong regained his composure and spoke quietly to the group. "We have witnessed some sort of event with a patient. At this point, we have no idea what it was, what caused it, or what affect it will have." He paused briefly. "I propose that as a group, we pool our observations and develop an understanding of the event more clearly." The headache in its infancy earlier was beginning to become a distraction. In fact, sitting here, he was sure his eyesight was starting to be affected, as he was seeing shadows around the others.

Brangeel watched his friend rub his temples and sensed something was amiss. "Are you okay?"

Wong shook his head. "Yes, just a bit of a headache. I'll take some aspirin, let's continue."

Dr. Blake decided to take the leadership role. "I was standing next to the patient's bed when he opened his eyes. The patient was looking at her." he nodded at Charlene. "He turned towards me, looked at me for a moment then looked back at her. He said something to her, then looked at me, and told me I needed to see a cardiologist. It was about this time, when you tried to touch him and got some sort of shock or something."

Brangeel listened intently and turned to Charlene. "Did the patient speak to you?"

"Yes! He told me I should let Melissa go on the trip, that she would be fine." She still did not understand how he knew Melissa, or about the trip.

"Who is Melissa?" Brangeel could see the look of bewilderment on Charlene's face.

"My daughter, she is sixteen and has been trying to convince me to let her go on a trip to France with one of her friends and their family."

"Do you know the patient? Does your daughter know him?" Brangeel knew there had to be some rational explanation.

"No, I've never set eyes on him until today, and even if Melissa did know him, how would he know I was Melissa's mother?" She had been asking these same questions ever since he had spoken to her.

Brangeel turned to Blake. "What about you? What did he say to you?

Blake shook his head. He remembered clearly the intense blue eyes, staring as if looking through him. "He simply said I should see my Cardiologist soon."

"Are you having a problem with your heart?"

"Not that I know of, although lately I have been feeling a little fatigued, but I don't think it is heart related." Even as he spoke, he remembered his initial thoughts when the patient first suggested it to him.

Brangeel nodded and looked at Wong. "What do you remember?"

Wong's headache was beginning to subside from the aspirin. He gazed at the table as if trying to visually recreate the moment. "I was looking at the charts when Charlene said the patient was awake. When I looked at him, he was looking at Mary." He paused. "I remember seeing him mouth the words "no surgery" to her. At this point, I grabbed his wrist to take his pulse when I felt a surge of energy almost electric in nature jolt me. I can tell you from experience, it was electric. It literally froze every nerve in my body. I had absolutely no control." He stopped as if feeling it over again. "The next thing I knew, I was on the floor and you were standing over me." He glanced at Brangeel.

Brangeel knew it was his turn. "I remember Charlene saying the patient was awake, and I remember looking at the monitors looking for changes. The next instant there was a bright light, and the monitors went blank, and you were being electrocuted or something. I forced myself between you and the bed and you were thrown to the floor."

The others were silent for a moment before Wong spoke. "I guess I should also tell you that ever since the "shock", I have been feeling a tingling sensation in my lower body and legs." He paused and did not know how to proceed. "I bring this up because as you know, I have not been able to feel anything in my lower extremities for decades. Now, I can feel strength in them that should not be there." Wong paused again. "In fact, other than this headache and a little blurry vision, I feel better than I have in many years."

Brangeel looked in Mary and Andrew's direction. "Do you have anything to add?"

Andrew looked briefly at his mother shook his head. "No, he did not speak to me, and Dr. Wong already said what he said to my mother."

"Okay. Where do we go from here?" Brangeel asked the

question, already knowing what they needed to do. He received no response and continued. "I would like to suggest the following. Firstly, I think we need to re-assess the patient's condition, and compare the EEG readings to new ones. Secondly, I think we should take steps to prove or disprove the adequacy of his statements."

Blake interrupted. "What do you mean prove the adequacy of his "statements"? Surely, you're not serious." Even as he said it, he knew Brangeel was serious.

Brangeel looked at him. "Yes, I am serious. And quite frankly, we have nothing to lose, and a great deal to gain. If he is right about your heart condition, he may have just saved your life." He turned to Wong and said. "I think we need a full EEG scan from you as well. Let's see what, if any, changes have taken place." He paused then asked. "I assume you have EEG charts we can use for comparison?"

Wong nodded. "Yes, I have them. In fact, I have a recent set as well." He had over the years re-tested himself, hoping for some change. None had been observed, but he still continued with the periodic testing.

"What about me? What can I do?" Charlene did not want to be left out. She had already decided she was going to allow Melissa to go to France.

Brangeel looked at her and smiled. "Maybe you should let Melissa go."

Charlene smiled back at him. "I have already decided to let her go, although I must admit it wasn't until after he spoke to me. I was more referring to the overall situation. How can I help? What do you need me to do?"

Adopting a more serious countenance, Brangeel looked thoughtfully at the table. "Now that you mention it, I think we should all keep quiet about what has happened." He paused before continuing. "At least until we know more."

Blake was clearly frustrated. "Keep what quiet? We don't know anything." He had already described what had happened to the duty-nurse while searching for a new room.

Brangeel, having years of experience with patients who were less-than-forthcoming, sensed immediately that it was too late. Even so, they should try. "Who did you tell?"

Blake looked down at the table. "When I asked the duty nurse for a new room, she asked why, and I told her what had happened." Blake knew the duty nurse and there was no doubt in his mind it was already on the hospital grapevine. "I'm sorry, I wasn't thinking."

Wong interjected his thoughts. "Don't worry about it, if I am right, the EEG will show I have been partially, if not fully healed, and the first time I decide to get out of this chair, they are going to know anyway." And he WAS going to get out of his chair.

Andrew listened to this and raised his hand. "Why the secrecy, Doc? What are you worried about?"

Brangeel, only days before, saw a news clip from Mexico showing thousands of people flocking to the site of a supposed shadow of the Virgin Mary. As the clip ran on the global news network, he could only assume it had been aired worldwide. He could only imagine how people would respond, if what had happened here was real.

Wong answered for Brangeel. "People would think of this as a miracle, especially if all his statements prove to be true. I mean, think about it. He seems to be able to read minds, can diagnose illness, and as in my case, potentially reverse a condition that our leading doctors said could not be reversed."

Brangeel nodded his head in agreement. "You can be sure of one thing, our patient, your father, would be headline news worldwide by this time tomorrow. And I'm afraid that would only be the beginning. Everybody, from the leaders of nations, to the person with a common cold will be trying to get to him". He stopped. He could not bring himself to add that the interest would not be one of a benign nature. Scientists would want to study him, and the governments would want to use him for their own purposes. Those governments that could not get him would most certainly want him removed as a potential threat. No, only bad things could come from this. He turned to Blake. "Will you agree to see a cardiologist?"

"Yes, of course, I will schedule as soon as possible." While he still believed there was nothing wrong with his heart, it would not hurt to have a professional assessment. Besides, if the tests prove negative, it would prove this patient was not responsible for the events they had been witness to and this would all die down.

Brangeel nodded his approval. "Good! Make it today! I think Dr. Ambrose is in today. I will call him and set it up for this afternoon." Ambrose, the staff cardiologist owed him a favor and it was time to collect.

"What about us? What should we do?" Mary spoke for the first time.

Wong turned to her and smiled. "At this point, there is not much you can do, but trust us and trust we have your husband's welfare in mind. Keep quiet about what you have seen for the time being, at least until we have had time to complete our testing. Perhaps then we can decide the next steps." The ringing of Wong's telephone interrupted him. Wong reached for the phone. "Hello!" he paused listening into the phone. "Very well, we will be there in a moment. In the meantime have them post a security guard outside the room. Nobody is to be allowed in without my approval." He replaced the phone back in its cradle and looked at the small group. "Well, it's begun. There are reporters on their way to his room." He looked at Blake. "Blake, schedule your test for this afternoon. In the meantime, I want you to run the EEG on both our patient and on me. Let's find out what's going on."

"Yes sir." Blake sensing the urgency nodded. "I'm ready when you are.

# Chapter 14

# **The Hall of Knowledge**

The trip to the Hall was similar to the one taken earlier. Thomas and Christie walked beside me toward the bright light of what I thought was the evaluation center. This time, however, instead of turning before the light, we continued past the light into the shadowy recess beyond. We stepped through an arched doorway and I found my self in a room not unlike a library. The room was large, with lines of what looked like bookcases unlike any I had ever seen before. The shelves were transparent, as clear as glass. But unlike a tiered bookshelf, this one had only one row. It was about waist high, and extended away from me as far as I could see. Where you would expect to see a book sat a shiny ring. The ring itself was contained in a translucent case similar to the cases used for compact discs. The cases trailed away, giving the appearance of a line of silver, as I watched, the rings closest to the aisle lit up, flashing on and off intermittently. Similar shelves extended to the left and right. They curved until almost a full circle was formed. I looked around and felt the sensation of standing in a field of silver. Occasional shapes could be seen at the end of some of the rows. Evidently, the library had patrons.

"What is this place?" I voiced this question to no one in particular. From the look on Thomas's face, he was equally awed.

"This is the Hall of Knowledge." Christie replied. She had been here many times, in fact, it was her home base.

"More accurately, it is the Hall of Records." This answer came from behind us.

I turned and saw three figures approaching. An elderly man was accompanied by a younger man and woman.

"Hello, my name is Eldred. These are my assistants Anne and

Franklin." The older figure spoke softly, yet his voice contained a note of firmness. He nodded to Christie. "Hello, I haven't seen you for awhile."

"Hello Eldred, it's good to see you again. Christie smiled at the elderly man. "I have been a little busy, as you can imagine."

"Yes, yes I'm sure." He turned to Thomas and said. "And you must be Thomas! This is your first time here isn't it?"

"Yes it is." Thomas had spent all of his time in the Hall of Understanding. He had heard whispers of this place, but never thought he would actually see it.

"And you must be Bill. I must say you have caused quite a commotion." Eldred peered at me curiously.

Feeling inadequate, I simply nodded.

"Welcome to my library. What can we do for you?" Visitors were not a new occurrence for them. Since the time the hall had been created, many had come seeking answers, most arriving as a result of meditation. And there had been others arriving through the use of various drugs. And always, as in this case, all were in the company of a Sleeper.

"I was told I could find the answers to my questions here." I was still overwhelmed by the spectacle in front of me and was sure my voice sounded weak.

Eldred nodded. He had heard this response countless times and knew most didn't mean it. The typical search for knowledge invariably migrated to the question of what the future held. Only once had a visitor really wanted to know about the past. Which was this one? He certainly arrived here by an unconventional route. "What answers do you seek?"

Without hesitation, I answered. "I have been to the Hall of Understanding and understand the concepts of the natural cycle and of balance and harmony." I know there is a process of evaluation and reincarnation." I paused, trying to decide how to best phrase my questions. I decided to be direct. "What I do not understand is, why? There must be a greater purpose to this whole process than simply recycling."

"Why do you feel there must be a greater purpose? Is not the continuation of your kind enough?" Eldred had known this time would come, when one would come asking not what, but why and how.

"Of course that is important, but unless you are the source of life, I suspect that would happen without your assistance." I do not know why I said this, but knew intuitively it was true. Not waiting for a reply, I pressed on.

"And, what of my support unit, and for that matter, these Sleepers as you call them. Who are they, and what is their purpose? For that matter, who are you and what purpose do you serve?" I looked around and continued. "What is this place? How does it fit into the overall picture?"

Eldred smiled, this one was different. Whereas others had come with pre-defined opinions searching for validation, this one appeared to have an open mind. "My, you do have a lot of questions. Perhaps we can help you find the answers. But tell me, why do you wish this knowledge? What would you do with it if you had it?"

I had not really thought of this. Until this moment, I simply wanted the answers to satisfy my own curiosity. "I don't know, I guess that would depend on the knowledge and I suppose what I could do with it."

Eldred listened, a slight frown on his face. "Throughout time, others have come seeking knowledge. Most professed a desire to use that knowledge to better the human condition, to change the future for the better. Is this not your goal as well?" Could it be true he had no agenda?

I was surprised at the revelation that others had seen what I was seeing, so I decided to again be direct. "Others have been here before me?"

"Yes, in fact, if you look over there, you will see a few of them now." Eldred pointed in the direction of a cluster of figures several shelves to my left.

Glancing in their direction, I found myself responding without knowing the source of my words. "If others have come as I have, they have not succeeded. Nothing has changed, we are still in this endless loop, and the true purpose is still not known."

Christie took exception to my statement and was quick to respond. "How can you say that without knowing where you were

84

relative to where you are now?"

Eldred raised his hand as if to stop a developing dispute. "Christie is correct. Perhaps it would be best if you spent some time studying your past. After that, we can talk some more."

I continued to look at Christie, and desperately wanted to respond. I knew they were right. I did not know enough to support my own argument, regardless of how right it felt. "Very well, since this is the "Hall of Knowledge", or as you say "Library of Records", help me understand."

A relieved Eldred nodded. "Anne and Franklin will help you as will Christie and Thomas. You are welcome to stay as long as you wish, and should you have questions they cannot answer, feel free to ask for me." With a curt nod to Anne and Franklin, he turned and strode away.

I turned to Anne. "I'm all yours, how do we begin?"

Anne glanced first at Christie, then at me before answering. "Let start with a tour of the library. I will explain how the system works, and we can go from there."

"Okay, lead on." I found myself mesmerized by her melodic voice.

As if she sensed my thoughts, she smiled. "Good, first, this is where all records related to your kind are kept. Every event affecting your species since the beginning, are contained in these rings."

I again looked at this sea of rings. "Where do the records come from? Does someone here create them? Are they just significant events? Who or what determines significance?" While my mind grasped the concept, I was having difficulty understanding how such a feat could be accomplished.

Franklin, silent until now, spoke in an effort to clarify what Anne had said. "Perhaps "event" is not the correct term. These records include every thought and memory of every Bio who has gone through the evaluation process. They are only used as individual records to evaluate the Bio's life. However, we also construct data rings at a higher-level based upon significant events, which resulted in a change to the overall development of your species. Those data rings are maintained in a separate section of the library."

Anne nodded to Franklin and picked up where she left off. "As I said, a record of every event is contained within these rings. And as Franklin said, there are other data rings maintained by our group that pertain to specific events of importance. As Franklin indicated, the original data is derived from the memory recorders, which are maintained by the "Three" of each Bio's support unit." She paused before she continued. "As you know, every thought, every action, every word, or deed experienced by a Bio is recorded for use during the evaluation process. When the evaluation process is completed, the records are brought here and added to these."

The magnitude of what she said was only beginning to occur to me. "You mean each of these rings is an individual life? There must be billions of them! Why are some of them lighting up, flashing on and off?"

"Yes!" Anne smiled. "There are a significant number. The rings you see flashing, are data rings of evaluated essences that are being remembered by a living Bio, or perhaps, as part of the transition process of an essence undergoing evaluation."

A thought occurred to me, if these were the records of past lives, and reincarnation was the means of perpetuation, was it possible for me to see my past lives? "So, these records are the memories of every person that ever lived?"

Anne nodded. "Yes, since we began keeping the records."

I looked at the sea of rings surrounding me in every direction, and almost missed the qualifying statement. "So, if re-incarnation is the means of continuation, I should have data rings from my previous lives?"

Franklin, as if he had read my mind spoke again. "Yes, if you lived a prior life, there is an associated data ring. But no, you would not be able to find it. You see, each Bio cycle is unique. In other words, YOU as you are now in the Bio state will never be exactly replicated. However, your essence or energy IS repeated. So, to answer your questions NO, you cannot find your previous Bio lives, but yes, it may be possible for you to trace your essence migration through your strand."

Anne either sensed, saw or read my mind. She knew I was struggling to comprehend what Franklin had said. "Let me try to explain. Imagine you are standing in the forest, and all around you on the ground, are leaves that have fallen from the many trees. If you pick up a single leaf, you understand that this leaf had its own natural cycle of creation, growth, decay and finally death." She paused. "Will the next leaf on the original tree be that same leaf?

"No, that leaf has already lived its cycle." I thought that I was beginning to understand.

Anne continued. "Good! Look at the leaf, is it possible for you to identify which specific tree it came from?"

"Well, yes, I suppose you could do that through some sort of DNA analysis." I had read somewhere that every living organism had a unique DNA sequencing which would provide such results.

Anne continued. "If that leaf, acorn or nut were to propagate and become the next generation tree, will that new tree have the exact same leaf, or for that matter, the exact biological characteristics as the original tree?"

I was beginning to understand! "No, it would probably be different in some ways, yet still retain characteristics of the original tree. It is still an Oak tree, just not exactly the same as the original."

Franklin nodded. "So, you see, while each Bio has characteristics which make it unique, it still retains a thread from its biological source."

This made sense, but still left lingering questions. "So, if I understand correctly my biological factors are passed on to my children, and theirs to their children, but they are different as each generation is a blend from other biological contributors."

Anne nodded. "Yes, as a result, no two Bios are exactly the same." She paused then added. "However, your energy or essence is different. It is separate from the biological unit, as it is a form of energy. This energy is what is recycled after the evaluation process."

I was still confused, and was having difficulty separating the essence and Bio relationship. "So, at the point of reincarnation, it is the essence that is recycled. When it is recycled, does it return to the same Bio strand or simply recycled back into the general pool?"

Christie, until now just listening, answered for them. "Just as there is a unique strand linking the biological, there is also one which links the essence or energy. During the recycling process, your energy or essence is returned to its paternal source, and used to strengthen that strand."

Still unclear but less confused, I pushed for clarification. "So, the essence which is part of me today is unique to a single source or strand, and it is returned to this "paternal" source for use in the next cycle? Just for my understanding, what is this paternal source?"

"Yes, the essence is returned to the paternal source, or in other words to the dominant strand in the Bio relationship." Anne stopped, sensing I still did not understand. "The procreation process results in the merging or combining of several different biological strands. This assumes of course, that the merged strands are not related biologically. One strand is from the mother, and one strand if from the father. However, in the case or your energy or essence, the strand is derived solely from the father. After the evaluation process, it is returned to the father's source strand."

"There must be millions of strands out there." I looked at the sea of data rings, and this seemed obvious.

Franklin smiled. "Actually, there aren't that many. Let's use the tree example again, assume there is one tree, and that tree creates thousands of leaves. Each leaf contains the biological and energy signatures of the source tree, yet at the same time, each leaf has a unique biological signature. The energy or essence however is common, and has the same signature for all the leaves. So you see, from the one strand of essence came many unique biological strands." He paused, raising his hand toward the sea of rings. "So, if you think of each data ring as a leaf of a tree, it's not difficult to imagine there are fewer source strands."

"I see. So how many source strands are there? My mind still envisioned millions.

"Actually, there are only one-hundred and forty-four thousand source strands." Anne knew the exact number.

Incredulous, I replied. "How can that be? There are six-billion people on the planet. Are you telling me each energy strand is supporting over four hundred-thousand Bios? Surely, there is a limit to what a single strand can support."

Thomas, silent until now, seized the opportunity. "Now, you understand the importance of the Hall of Understanding. Each essence MUST be recycled to support the continuation of your kind."

88

Anne ignored the outburst from Thomas and continued. "Yes, that is a concern to us as well. While we do not know the precise limits, we do know that when that limit is reached, the process tends to stabilize itself."

This was confusing to me, yet somehow not unexpected. "Stabilize how?"

Franklin picked up where Anne left off. "Let's return to our tree example. "At what point does a tree stop growing?"

I thought in terms of the natural cycle and replied. "More than likely during the decay phase."

Franklin smiled "Yes, of course. But even before the decay phase, the tree reaches a point where the upper branches are weak, and cannot support continued growth. Although the tree is healthy, it simply cannot provide enough nutrients to its furthermost points to support continued growth. Well, the essence source strand is similar to that tree. As each new Bio is created, a part of the essence is taken to support it. In doing so, the source strand is proportionally weakened. If unregulated, at some point, the source becomes depleted to the point where it can no longer sustain growth. Fortunately, as each Bio cycle is completed, the essence or energy is returned to the source strand, thereby strengthening it again."

Christie watched me struggle with these concepts and laughed out loud. "It can be a lot to absorb. Perhaps as we go on it will become less confusing."

While I did not necessarily like her laughing at my difficulty, even I was grateful for the interlude. "You're right, let's move on." While this new information had helped clarify essential facts about the process, it had done little to help me get the answers I was seeking.

"Very well, follow me." Anne led the group to a small alcove which contained what appeared to be a small box hovering without visible support about waist high. The box itself had no distinguishing features other than an opening on one side and a monitor of sorts above it.

"Put your hand in the box." Anne said as she smiled. "Do not worry, it will not hurt you." She did not add that in my present state, physical feeling was not possible.

I stuck my hand into the box. "What does this do?"

Anne watched the monitor and replied. "This will determine your source energy signature. With that, we can find the correct essence strand." She smiled and added. "You may recall, I said earlier there were one-hundred and forty-four thousand strands. Finding yours would take some time without this device."

As if on cue, the monitor flashed a series of numbers. Section twelve row one-thousand and thirty-three. "Good, we found it." Anne saw the look on my face, and just smiled.

"What now? Do we go to section twelve?" I looked around and saw nothing to indicate where I was, let alone what defined a section.

Franklin pointed to our right and said. "No, just step over here". He was pointing at a small alcove I had not seen before.

The alcove was empty save for a monitor, suspended apparently in midair. On the screen were two characters or figures. The first character was shaped in the form of a box, the second a triangle.

Franklin looked at me, pointed at the characters, and said. "You need to choose one of these."

I looked for some way of determining the meaning of the symbols, and found nothing. "What do they represent?"

"The symbol you select, will determine how the data is presented to you. Franklin pointed at the box-like character, selecting this one will present the data in a two-dimensional format. Not unlike your television. The other will present data in holographic mode, where you are immersed in the scenes."

"Which is better?" I liked the holographic idea.

"I like the holographic mode myself. It gives me the sense that I am part of the action." Anne smiled. "Of course, you may be more comfortable with the two-dimensional format. It can be a little overwhelming otherwise."

"Can we sample both and then decide?"

Franklin agreed. "Good idea, now if you would select a symbol, we will get started."

"How do I select?"

"Simply touch the symbol you want."

I reached toward the screen and selected the symbol shaped like a box. Instantly, the screen was changed. Now in place of the symbols, there were boxes containing data rings. The boxes reminded me of the desktop icons I see on my computer. At the bottom of the screen, was a red arrow pointing down. I assumed I was supposed to select one of the boxes. "Should I select one?" There were no identifying marks indicating the data type or source.

"Yes, simply touch one of them." Franklin waited for the question he knew was coming.

"How do I know which is which? They all look the same. Are there names or dates or something to help me?"

Anne gave Franklin a reproving look and stepped forward, standing next to me. "Each box is a data ring, or in other words, the memory data of an evaluated Bio. The most recent in this is in the top left corner. Moving to the right is the next most recent and so on and so forth. When you reach the bottom of the page, you can select this arrow. Doing so will bring the next series or page onto the screen."

It was just like my computer. "Is there any way to tell who the data ring belonged to or for that matter, even a time period?" Surely, there must be some method of indexing.

Anne smiled. "No I am sorry there isn't. Although I suppose a relative time could be assumed from the position of the icon selected, the first being the most recent. Of course even that could have been a long time ago. We never thought to catalog the rings, once the evaluation process is complete and the data has been reviewed by our staff, it is of no value to us. We simply store it."

"If it is of no value, why keep it at all? Why not simply discard it?" This made little sense to me.

Unperturbed, Anne went on. "While I said "We" have no further use for it, there may be a need for the original data at some point, so we file it. Besides, it seems to me that discarding it would be the greater waste. After all, it is the life of a Bio we are talking about."

Franklin interrupted. "Do you recall earlier there were other visitors here? Without this data they would not be able to complete their research. Just like you, as a matter of fact."

I knew they were right and simply shrugged. "How does it work?"

Anne pointed at the data ring boxes. "Select one."

I reached to the screen and touched the first box. Again, the screen changed. The many boxes had been replaced by the single box I had selected. The Ring shaped circle now filled entire the screen. What had appeared to be a circle now looked like the capital letter "Q", only with the tail pointing to the left not to the right.

Thomas, until now a passive observer, looked surprised. He excitedly exclaimed. "It is the circle of life. Or what we refer to as the natural cycle."

Christie was amused at Thomas's reaction and smiled. "Yes it is. Now if you recall, the cycle of life is divided into four groups. Do you know what they are?"

Thomas, glad to participate instantly replied. "Yes, they are the birth or creation phase, the growth phase, the decay phase, and finally the death phase."

"Good! Now! What do you think this little extension is?" Christie pointed at the reversed tail on the "Q"."

I intuitively knew this. "It is the beginning of the next cycle for the Bio." While I did not know exactly where the tail led, I knew it had to be the beginning point of another type of life cycle.

"Correct! The process of life is, by its natural design, a transition process. For example, a chicken lays an egg, when you look at this egg you say to yourself "this is an egg". As time passes, the egg changes, eventually it hatches and a new chicken is born. Is it still an egg? No! The egg's cycle has been completed, and it has become something completely different. If however, you look at the life cycle of the chicken that laid the egg, you see that the creation of the egg is nothing more than the result of its procreation phase. The original chicken is already working through its natural cycle." She paused. "If you look at your natural surroundings, you will see this process taking place in all things. In fact, in some cases, you can see the migrations of life cycles completing. For example, the silkworm starts as an egg, becomes a silkworm, becomes a cocoon and then a butterfly." Christie paused trying to gauge my understanding.

While I understood what Christie was saying, it was unclear as to why she was bringing this up. "Christie, I think I understand what you are saying, but why are you bringing this up now?"

Anne nodded to Christie then looked at me. "The cycle changes can sometimes be very violent and I think what Christie is trying to do is to prepare you for the possibility of seeing things which could in some way damage you unless you keep in mind that it is history and cannot directly harm you. You must understand that most of our visitors are like you, they are in some way still connected to their Bio units. Consequently, when they return to their Bio state of consciousness, what they see here returns with them, very similar to your dreams. After all, you are seeing a life-cycle and possibly images that are difficult to accept at the rational level. To carry these memories back to the Bio state could affect you at the psychological level. We can only hope you will also carry this warning message as well"

I had seen and been through a lot in my life and did not think this would be a problem. But I did understand their concerns. "I understand! How do we get started?"

Franklin pointed at the screen. "Simply touch the area of the circle where you would like to begin viewing."

"Does it matter where?" I had an idea that it was similar to a clock, except in this case, six o'clock represented the beginning point and the nine, twelve and three positions represented phase changes. I pointed at the nine o clock position and asked. "If I select here, will I be somewhere near the middle of the person's cycle of life?"

Franklin shrugged. "It would depend on the overall life cycle of the Bio. If the Bio lived a long life, that would be the case. There is really no way to tell."

"Let's take a look and see." With that, I reached to touch the screen at the nine o'clock position.

# Chapter 15

## **Loyola Medical Center 11:45 am.**

*H*arridy had to weave his patrol car slowly through the maze of television vans lining the entrance to the Medical Center. Reporters and camera men stood in clusters, most simply standing, one or two recording some tidbit of information that may or may not make the evening news. It would seem the newshounds had heard the same rumors as he. Word had made its way through the radio signals his earlier charge had performed some sort of miracle. According to the report, he had somehow healed a Doctor. Harridy was a realist and did not place credence in the report. During his thirty-plus years of service he had heard a lot of strange rumors, most if not all, invariably turned out to be misunderstandings hyped for the purpose of providing news to the public. As he got out of the patrol car, he made his way through the knot of reporters and into the lobby. As he approached the information desk, he flashed his badge and credentials to the harried receptionist.

"Good afternoon, could you tell me the room number for a William Reynolds?"

The receptionist looked at the credentials and did not need to search the computer for the answer. It seemed as if every person in the lobby wanted that information. "Are you here on official business?" If not, he would be given the same response given to the others.

"Yes, I am." Harridy needed to complete the felony incident report, and with any luck be able to have the two suspects now in custody identified. The patrol net had managed to capture the two suspects, but a search of the vehicle had not yielded any evidence linking the two to the crime. The gun found in the highway median could not be definitively linked with them either. However if a positive ID could be made, the two would be charged. If not, they would have to be released.

The receptionist nodded. "Doctor Wong has left instructions that the patient is not to be disturbed without his approval. If you wish, I will leave a message for him advising him of your request." She paused then added. "You may want to take a seat, this may take awhile."

Harridy, knowing the receptionist was simply following orders nodded. "I think I will just visit the Doctor myself, his office is on the fourth floor isn't it?" He knew well that because he had indicated his presence as an "official business visit", the receptionist could not prevent him from doing so.

"Harridy, What are you doing here?" The voice came from behind him.

Harridy did not need to turn around to identify the source of the voice. He had heard it enough over the last thirty years to recognize it. Without turning, he simply replied. "Hello Harold! Just here on business." While Harold was probably one of the few decent reporters left in Chicago, he knew well enough to guard his words carefully.

Harold smiled. He had known Harridy since he was a rookie officer and he a young beat reporter. While they had never become "friends", they worked well together on a number of occasions and developed a mutual, yet unspoken agreement to respect each other's often opposing positions. "I overheard you asking about Reynolds. What's your interest in him?" Harold already knew this, but in keeping with their mutual understanding, would play the game by the rules.

Harridy also knew the game. "Just finishing up the paperwork on an incident report from this morning." If he knew Harold, the morning incident and the related facts were already known.

"Yeah, I heard about that. Do you think Reynolds will be able to ID the suspects?" Word had it that the police had the suspects, but no direct evidence to tie them to the robbery attempt.

While no official statement had been released by the department, Harridy was not surprised that Harold knew the situation for what it was. The veteran reporters, especially those with a reputation for being fair, had their own unofficial inroads to information well before the rest of the media. Regardless, he knew well enough to not become an official source. "Harold, you know I can't comment on an ongoing investigation." He knew his response would be interpreted correctly for what it was.

Harold smiled. "Understood! Now, off the record, what's the scoop? Word has it that Reynolds woke up for a few seconds, and in that time diagnosed one Doctor as having a heart condition, and he actually healed another who could not walk."

Harridy looked at his old friend and merely shrugged. "Who knows? I've not seen anything to support the rumors. And quite frankly, I'm not interested. I must say though, I am a little surprised that you would place credence in them at all." More often than not, a story like this back-fired on reporters when the facts eventually came out. More than one had seen their career go south as a result. Harold was not a fool. If he was here, there had to be something to it.

Harold chose his words carefully and smiled. He knew the risks Harridy was alluding to. Ordinarily he would have deferred this assignment to one of the younger, less experienced (and expendable) reporters. A reporter that was still building a reputation, and was willing to take the risk, but the fact was, he was desperate. Angelina, his wife of thirty-years, had recently been diagnosed with a non-operable tumor at the base of her brain. The doctors said it was eventually going kill her. If there was ANY truth to these rumors, he was going to find a way to meet this Reynolds guy. "The cardiologist's receptionist is married to my neighbors' son, Tom. It seems the Doctor Reynolds told to see the cardiologist, a guy named Blake, had a series of impromptu tests done and sure enough, he was diagnosed with a serious heart condition. In fact, "Blake" is scheduled to undergo a triple-bypass this afternoon."

"You're kidding!" Harridy was surprised.

"No, it's true. I verified it through "other" sources, and it is true." Harold waited a moment trying to decide if he should take the next step. In all of the years he had never taken advantage of his friendship with Harridy, and was reluctant to do so now. "Harridy, I need to ask a favor from you." He did not wait for a response before continuing. "I need to meet this Reynolds guy, it is important to me personally. Trust me when I say that. Although I am here as a reporter, I have a greater need than just getting a story."

Harridy looked intently at his old friend, and sensed the struggle going on Harold's mind. To ask directly for a favor from him was a violation of unspoken rules. Prior exchanges had always been made by way of innuendos, and read between-the-line suppositions. This method allowed both to assume the unofficial positions necessary to maintain a viable working relationship. "What's the problem Harold? You wouldn't ask this without a good reason." He paused before continuing. "If I'm going to help you, I need to know why." He already knew he was going to help if he could. He was past the point in his career where he really cared what the department thought. The only thing he would not do was to break the law, or in this case, allow Reynolds's rights to be violated.

Harold looked directly into Harridy's eyes, trying to gauge the sincerity of his words. "It's Angelina. She is very sick. The doctors say she is terminal." His voice broke slightly as he said this. "I know I am grasping at straws, but I thought if this guy Reynolds was for real, maybe he could, well, you know."

"Sergeant Harridy". Andrew came rushing toward him, his mother in tow.

"Andrew, don't be rude, can't you see he's busy?" Mary looked at Harridy. "I am sorry. It seems someone needs to work on his manners." She shot a reproving look at Andrew.

"Hello Andrew, Mrs. Reynolds. There is no need to apologize; you're not interrupting anything at all." Harridy gestured in Harold's direction. "Let me introduce my friend Harold Rhodes. Harold, this is Mrs. Reynolds and her son Andrew."

"The" Harold Rhodes, the reporter?" Andrew's father had read Rhodes articles and commentaries for years and had considered him one of the best "unbiased" reporters left in the otherwise good-for-nothing "cesspool" of egocentric idiots.

Harold, always uncomfortable with what he considered undeserved acclaim, laughed aloud and reached out to shake Andrew's hand. "If the "THE" you used is meant positively, I thank you. If not, just give me a thirty-second head-start."

"No, No, it's positive, believe me. My dad says you're the greatest. He looks for, and reads your stories and column every day."

"How is your dad doing? I heard he had quite an incident this morning." While he would have asked the same question under any circumstance, he felt ill at ease asking, especially knowing his own hidden agenda.

"We were just on our way to see him. Last time we checked, he was sleeping." Andrew remembered Doctor Brangeels admonishment to keep the other activities quiet and said nothing more.

"Well, I'm sure he will be fine." He turned to Harridy and nodded. "I should let you do your job, just think about what I asked." The pleading look in his eyes reinforced the desperation he was feeling.

Harridy shook his hand and nodded. "I will call you this evening." While he did not personally believe in miracles, he found himself hoping that just this once it could be true, and both Angelina and Harold would be okay.

Harridy turned back to the receptionist and looked inquiringly at her. "Were you able to contact the Doctor?"

"I am sorry, evidently the doctor is in but not taking calls. I left a message with his administrative assistant who said she would call me as soon as the Doctor was available."

"I see." Harridy returned his attention to Mary and Andrew. "It seems I am going to be here for awhile. Can I get you something to eat?" Perhaps they would share what they knew with him. Given that he was being stone-walled by a Doctor, it was apparent to him something unusual was happening,

"We were just coming back from the cafeteria when we saw you." Mary replied. "But I am glad we ran into you. I wanted to thank you for all you did for us today. Your kindness made a difficult day a little easier to handle."

Harridy smiled. "It was my pleasure or I should say just part of my job. In either case, I am glad I could help."

"What are you here for? Are you waiting to talk to my dad?" Andrew felt a little uncomfortable asking a policeman these questions, but decided Harridy would not take offense. Besides, if it affected his dad, he figured he had a right to know.

"Actually, yes I am. I need to take his statement as to what happened this morning, and of course, see if he can provide a description of his assailants."

"So, did you catch them?" In the excitement of the day, it was only now he was thinking of what had happened.

Harridy knew he should not respond until the case was closed, but again decided to break protocol. "Actually, yes, we have two suspects in custody. Unfortunately, there is no physical evidence linking them to the incident and without firm evidence, we will not be able to charge them. We were hoping your father could identify them."

Silent for a moment, Andrew looked at his mother before turning again to Harridy. "How can we help?" If there was anything he could do to catch the ones responsible, he was willing to help.

Harridy smiled. "Well, I have been trying to get in to see your dad, but am being told the Doctor has issued instructions limiting access without his approval. As I cannot seem to get the doctor myself, perhaps you could speak to him for me and get it cleared."

Andrew looked at Harridy, a grin on his face. "I'll get you to Dr. Wong's office, but it will be his decision if my dad should have visitors." Andrew turned to his mother and took her by the arm. "I think it's time to check in on dad, maybe he is awake by now." Looking at Harridy, he said. "Could you help me bring my mom up to his room?" He smiled to the receptionist and smugly said. "He is with me." The receptionist had little choice but to pass them through the security checkpoint.

# Chapter 16

## **Loyola Medical Center 12:10 pm.**

*F*ollowing the meeting, Wong, accompanied by Charlene and the Reynolds's, worked their way through the throng of reporters and camera-men crowding the fourth floor hallway. A security guard blocked the entrance to the room. As his wheelchair approached, the reporters descended upon them. Questions were thrown at them from all directions. "Is it true? Were you healed? Did he really read your mind?" This last directed toward Charlene. Wong raising his hands, waited for the noise to subside. "Before I answer your questions, I would like to remind you, that this is a hospital, and I would appreciate it if you would exercise a little constraint" Wong paused, allowing his words o sink in. "If you cannot, or will not, I will have you removed. I will answer your questions, but please have a little consideration for the other patients." He pointed at the closest reporter. "What is your question?" The reporter, a young female he recognized from one of the local television channels, lost no time in getting to the point. "We heard that one of your patients, a "Mr. Reynolds", was able to read her thoughts," she gestured toward Charlene. "Also, that through some sort of energy-transference healed your condition. Is this true?"

Wong tapped the arm of his wheelchair and gave her a look that by itself answered the question. "Well, as you can see, I am still in my chair. As for reading someone's mind, I can only say that if he did, it should not be considered an unusual event. In fact, I would venture to say that every person here at some point or another, has been able to sense another person's thoughts simply by virtue of the circumstances, their body language and yes, in rare instances, through intuitive insight. The human brain has many capabilities, and the degree of use is unique to each person. Only Charlene can say what she was thinking at the time, and whether what the patient said was in fact, what she was thinking." He paused before continuing. "Let me sum it up for you. At this point, there is nothing. Let me repeat that, "nothing". No evidence that I can see which justifies your being here, disrupting this hospital and disturbing the patients." Wong paused again. "Now, if there are no more questions, I would ask that you leave this floor immediately." Silence, broken only by the whirring of camera's followed his statement. "Doctor, you said "at this time", does that mean something has happened, but you do not have "evidence" to support it came from Reynolds?" This question coming from an older reporter, a guy named Rhodes.

Wong smiled. "Astute question, but no, that is not what I meant." He was going to have a lot of explaining to do in the very near future. "Now, if all of you would please leave the floor, I am sure the staff and patients would appreciate it." With that said, Wong wheeled his chair through the now less crowded hallway, past the security guard and into the patients room, Charlene and the Reynolds's followed.

Having checked the new test results, Wong was satisfied the patient's condition had not been adversely affected by the power-surge or whatever it was. The new monitors and printouts reflected the current, still abnormal activity, was consistent with the earlier results. The patient still appeared to be sleeping, although the rapid eye movement clearly supported the chart data, indicating a very high-level of activity in the brain. The analysis of his own EEG had been much more surprising, at least to Blake. The new charts showed significant synapse activity in his brain where the prior charts had shown none. Wong was not surprised. He knew this would be the case even before the tests were conducted. He had been "feeling" sensations in his knees and feet, that had been foreign to him since childhood. Having completed the EEG testing, Blake kept his appointment with Dr. Ambrose, the staff Cardio specialist. An hour later, Wong received the news. Blake's tests had indeed come back positive, indicating a serious heart condition, one which would require an immediate triple-bypass operation. Wong, now sitting in his office, pondered the events of the day. While he could not understand the how, or why, of the situation, he knew that everything Reynolds had said had been true. His own physical considerations were evidence that something far beyond medical science had in some way intervened in his life. The only question remaining was whether he had the courage to try? He knew what the next step had to be. While he was not afraid of failure, of not being able to stand or walk, he feared that he was wrong, that his hope had been misplaced. Yes, he knew what he had to do. Calling his administrative assistant, he sent her to the cafeteria ostensibly to bring back lunch. He knew he had at least ten minutes before she returned; the first three were spent here working up the nerve to try. Damn! Let's just do this, and get it over with. Grasping the edge of his desk, he pulled himself slowly out of the chair. Relieved of his weight, the chair slid slowly away banging with a clang into the metal bookcase near the wall. His weight was now fully supported by his arms and back. Slowly, he allowed the weight to shift onto his legs. This was the true test. He would either collapse, or he would stand. Hearing the office door open, Wong looked up to see the door frame almost completely filled by the shape of an Illinois State Police officer.

# Chapter 17

# **Hall of Understanding**

$J$onathan, having left Thomas with the Sleeper and the Bio essence, decided to pay a visit to the support unit of the Bio called Wong. Wong's support unit was not surprised by his visit. The "Five" had reported the Bios condition was undergoing significant changes. The changes, while normal in most Bios, should not have been happening to this one. The new biological regenerative demands were consuming all of his capacity to support the regeneration of previously dead cells. To make matters more interesting, the "Seven" had also reported that for a brief moment, the "thoughts" of the Bio unit, indicated he had been able to see the support units of the other Bios present in the room. Although the observation had been a fleeting one, it was dutifully logged by the units "Three". As they were prohibited from replaying the memory data without the Bio's consent, Jonathan could only assume the observation was true.

Leaving the support unit, Jonathan returned to the Hall of Understanding. On arrival, he requested an immediate meeting with the others. The meeting, underway for some time, had reached an impasse. The general consensus of the group was that the events, while potentially troublesome, were inconsequential to their longer-term goals. And short of a miraculous specie-wide change of attitude and culture, the end result would not be affected. There were however, a few who shared Jonathan's concern that there was more happening than what appeared on the surface. There were too many coincidences for this to not be a planned design. Having two Bios, with the capability of seeing other support units, was improbable at best. Having the second acquire that capability after coming into contact with the first, elevated it into the realm of more than just mere coincidence.

Jonathan, standing across from the leadership, decided to pose the questions nagging his thoughts. "While I am not of a level to fully understand the overall plan, I must tell, you these events have me more than a little concerned. Is it possible, this is a designed effort to upset the processes we have worked so hard to install?" he paused before continuing. "From what I understand, this would not be the first time they have tried to circumvent our efforts." He stopped, trying to gauge their reactions. "The fact Christie is involved, also makes me think this is more than a coincidence." It was common knowledge Christie was a member of the opposing council, not just a foot-soldier. There had been many instances through the expanse of time, when they had suspected her of influencing or intervening directly in the affairs of the human's. As one might expect given her skills at deception, there was never any direct evidence of rule violations. Still, they knew she had managed to influence the human evolutionary process. Jonathan also knew his side was equally guilty of manipulation and influence, also, with the same degree subtlety.

Arinon, leader of the meeting, frowned and said. "You have a valid point. We would be remiss to overlook the possibility that this is more than interesting coincidences." He paused and looked across at Peter. "What do we know about these bios, Reynolds and Wong? Is there any history to suggest they are players?" Although he had not voiced his opinions, Arinon shared the view that there was more to what was happening than could normally be expected. He had also dealt with what they jokingly called "the Christie effect" on other occasions, and knew her to be a very capable adversary. Jonathan was correct in one observation, if she was involved, it was important.

Peter, the Director of Operations, glanced up from his notes. "I can tell you with certainty; we have no active operations involving either of them. However, I have dispatched several agents to research their lineage at the Library". Peter was quiet for a moment. "It is possible they were used in operations from the other side. However, at this point, there is nothing to suggest they are players." He did not expect them to find anything. He knew every major operation that had ever been initiated by both sides and would have remembered if they had been involved. Still it was clear they were in some way, involved in the game. Was it possible Eldred was opening a new front?

Arinon nodded. "Keep me apprised of what you find." He

turned to Jonathan. "You say Christie showed up here, and then as well, directly to the Bios support unit? That's a bit unusual, don't you think? Were you able to get any sense of her involvement?"

Jonathan, replaying back in his mind the two meetings, suddenly realized, that Christie had seemed as surprised as he, especially when the memory record was played back. Of course, being a "Sleeper" and one of their best, she could have easily been masking her true feelings. Even so, he could not shake the feeling that she was as much in the dark as he. "Given she is a sleeper, and a master at deception it is difficult to know for sure. But, in retrospect, based upon her reactions, I think she was as surprised by these events as I." Jonathan paused. "Of one thing I think we can be certain, just as we are, you can be sure, she is also looking for a way to "manage" these events."

Peter, listening carefully, put into words what he knew the others were thinking. "Is it possible we have another player in the game? I mean, if it is true that Christie WAS surprised, and this is not one of their operations, and it is clearly not one of ours, whose is it? Where is it coming from?" He did not add that there had been other times in the past when he had observed other unexplained effects. He had always simply assumed the "Sleepers" were somehow responsible. Now, he was not so sure. He made a mental note to review them again, this time with the possibility of a subtle third party being involved.

Arinon, gazing thoughtfully at the others, shook his head. "Peter, look into that possibility, but I must say, I do not think there is another player. It is unreasonable that we would not have noticed another player long ago. No. Assuming this is not an active operation from Eldred's side, I think we can safely conclude these events are just coincidences. If that is the case, neither our current operations, nor the ultimate end will be affected." Looking at Peter he continued. "However, if this IS an active operation from the other side, we need a much better understanding of what they are doing, and how it affects us." He turned again to Jonathan and said. "How sure are you that this Bio "Wong" can actually see other support units? Your report only indicated a brief instance, have there been any further reports of this?"

"No, the Seven indicated it was a single possible instance

based upon the thoughts of the Bio.  His three did log it into memory, but as you know, we cannot view the memory data until the evaluation process."  Initially, Jonathan had reservations about even mentioning this possible instance, but had decided to report it in the off chance it was important.

"I see.  I think it would be prudent to have both support units provide regular reports, at least until we understand what, if anything, is actually happening."  Arinon knew it was not uncommon during energy surges for the electro-magnetic fields surrounding the Bios to go "out of phase" for brief moments before readjusting.  During those moments, it is possible a Bio would be able to see the shapes of other support teams.  Perhaps, this was what had happened, and in fact, the Bio called Wong had returned to normal.

"I will see to it."  Jonathan, knowing he was being dismissed, slowly walked toward the entrance of the Hall.

# Chapter 18

## **Hall of Knowledge.**

*C*hristie watched as the essence called Reynolds hesitantly touched the nine o'clock position of the circle. This had been an event-filled day, one which she was still trying to understand. The memory playback by his "Three" convinced her that something unusual was indeed taking place, something she had not witnessed in two-thousand years. The difference in this case was that she was not responsible. Nor based upon Jonathan's reaction, was it an operation from the other side. Although she would not put it past Peter to conduct an operation well above Jonathan's grade, this did not feel like a "Peter" operation. She was also sure the other side would not run the risk of providing such capabilities to a Bio, or for that matter, to its essence. She would meet with Eldred as soon she could break away from this current activity. Eldred had resources, still unknown to her, that somehow kept him ahead of all the plays and players in the game. As she watched, the screen changed.

I had selected a point on the circle where I thought mid-life would be. I watched, as the image changed from the circle, to a scene of an automobile speeding down a dirt road. Clouds of dust billowed in its wake. The road was just wide enough to accommodate the vehicle. Trees flashed by, giving the sensation of speed. A young woman, seated in the passenger seat, was admonishing the driver to slow down. "George, you slow this car down, your going to fast, and it's scaring me." Looking in the direction of the driver, a young man in his mid-twenties, I could see his Seven beside him. I could hear his Seven also advising him to slow down. "That good advice George, you should slow down before you crash." A third voice, one of a more mechanical nature, said. "I've got it under control."

Stepping away from the screen, I looked at Franklin. "I

assume, this is the data record of the guy named George!" I had arrived at this conclusion having heard the Seven clearly speaking to him, and of course, the woman could be seen talking to him. Where is the third voice coming from?"

Franklin, looking at the screen nodded. "That is the data record of his memories and thoughts at that moment."

I turned back to the screen, and watched the image unfold as if it were a movie. The car, a 1957 Chevy, looked new. "I don't think I will be able to keep all of these separate, maybe I should try the other mode. How do we switch to it?"

Anne pointed at the icon at the bottom left of the screen. "You can change the mode there. But before you do, I want to show you some of the features. You see the woman in the car with George?" Not waiting for my response, she went on. "Touch her image on the screen."

I reached out and touched the screen where the image of the woman was still screaming at the driver to slow down. Almost instantly, the screen view changed, I was now looking at the driver as if viewing him from the perspective of the woman. I could hear her Seven telling her to make George slow down. "What happened? I thought we were in "George's" data record?"

Anne smiled. "We were! When you touched the image of the woman, the perspective of the moment changed to that of the woman, at that exact point in time." Anne touched the screen again causing the image to disappear, and once again, I found myself looking at the original data ring.

"I don't understand!"

Franklin smiled. "Let me try to clarify! You originally entered the data ring of the deceased Bio, evidently his name was George. The moment in time that you selected was presented in a two dimensional format, at that moment, George was as you saw him, as well as, I assume his Seven. The woman was also part of that memory so she was also presented doing exactly what was recorded by the "George's" "Three". When you touched the image of the woman, you in fact, changed or linked to the essence of the woman." He paused before going on. "I realize this is a little confusing, but what Anne was trying to show you, was that at any time in a Data record, you can in effect, switch to a different data source. In this case the woman. Now, listen carefully to what I am going to say, as it will help you in your search. If that woman had completed her life cycle, you would have been automatically taken into her data ring, at the same point in time you saw her on the screen. In this case, however, there is no data ring as she has not yet completed her cycle, or gone through the evaluation process. In other words, for all practical purposes, you became her, at that moment in time."

Strange as it seems, I thought I almost understood what Franklin was saying. "Let me see if I understand what you are saying. While I was in the data ring of George, who is, I assume deceased, I was able to switch to the essence of the woman, who is still alive. When I did this, I was no longer in the data ring of George, but was seeing as "her", at that instant in time."

"Correct!" Anne, evidently pleased that I grasped the concept so readily was beaming. "Not only that, but when you switched to her, you also had access to all of her active thoughts and feelings, at that moment in time. Because she is still alive, it is not possible for you to access her memories directly, however, had she for some reason decided to think of her grandfather, you would have been able to see that memory and attach yourself to his image, and subsequently to his essence, or if he is deceased to his data ring. Using this technique it is possible for you to "piggy-back" memories backwards in time."

I had not thought of that, not that I should have, given all of this was completely new to me. "In the case of "George" would I have been able to do the same?"

"Yes, you could have, in fact, the process is even easier. In the case of the woman, you were dependent upon her recalling the memory of her grandfather. In the case of George, you could have simply selected a point on the data ring where there would be a high probability of his father or grandfather being actively involved in his life. At that point, you would simply link to them there." So, as you view "Georges" data record, the point in time you select, in some ways provides access to the past."

I was getting excited about these new capabilities and the possibilities they presented. If I could select a point on the data ring early enough in the Bio's cycle, I could attach myself to another life cycle data ring, all the way back in time. The only question was how to find my own family lineage in this sea of data rings. "I think I would like to try that again, this time in the holographic mode." I reached again for the screen, intending to activate the symbol for the new mode.

Stepping forward, Anne placed herself between me and the screen. "Before you do, we need to take steps to protect you, or perhaps I should say, prepare you."

"Prepare me for what? You already warned me about graphic images, memory retention, and all that stuff. I think I can handle it."

Looking serious, Anne simply said. "This is different. The holographic mode is much more interactive. In fact, in many ways, it will seem as if you are actually part of the action." She paused. "As I said earlier, you are still linked with your Bio, and yes, there is the issue of possible memory retention. However, in this case, there is an even greater danger to your Bio."

"What danger?" My physical body was in a completely different realm. The "me" here at this point in time, was essentially pure energy. How could anything I do affect the other realm.

Without hesitating, she continued. "To understand what I am saying, you must first understand the relationship between your essence and your Bio unit. While it is true, you are here in energy form, the greater part of your essence still resides within your Bio unit. The Bio unit is by design, controlled by your mind, which is a manifestation of your energy or essence. Consequently, even while here, it is possible that your mind can influence the physical state of your Bio unit."

My earlier conversation with Thomas regarding the minds ability to control pain came back to me. "So, what your saying is, I need to be careful to not let the images and "action" affect me to the point where it will affect my physical being?"

Anne, still looking somber, nodded her head. "I can tell you from experience, it happens. We have had some visitors, who upon entering the holographic data record, did so in times of a significant crisis occurring at that point in the life cycle. More than a few have experienced extreme anxiety. Some actually went into cardiac arrest and succumbed."

"What do you suggest?" While I was confident I could manage extreme circumstances, it would not hurt to have a plan.

"My suggestion is for you to always keep foremost in your mind, that what you see and hear has already happened. You are simply an observer." She did not add that this was not always an easy thing to do. "Also, remember you are in control. You have the ability to leave the scene at any point, by simply "thinking" your way back to this point."

"Thinking my way back to this point? How does that work?" I figured getting back here was something I probably needed to do regardless of the circumstances. Getting lost in the memories of a billion people did not sound like something I wanted to do.

Franklin pointed at the screen where the symbols patiently waited to be selected. "The symbol you did not select will still appear even in the holographic mode, you can simply touch it. This will switch you automatically to the two dimensional mode. At that point, you will find yourself standing here, just as we are now. If, for some reason you cannot do this, you can also simply say the words "stop data display", this will also stop the process."

"Okay, I think I understand. When can we get started?" I was eager to begin.

Anne, still looking unsure, replied. "As soon as you select a data ring, we will go to holographic mode."

"The same ring?" A thought had just occurred to me, something Anne had said about linking to images.

"Yes, unless you would like to select another." she was wondering if he had picked up on her earlier suggestion. While it would have been easier to simply tell him directly, it would have been a violation of the rules.

I stared at the screen, thinking of the best way to formulate my question. "Anne, you said earlier, it was possible for me to attach or link myself to images from other persons in the Bio data record."

"Yes! That is possible."

I continued. "I have a brother who recently died. I have his image in my mind, could I attach to that image as a starting point?"

Christie, pleased with the direction this appeared to be going, answered for Anne. "As your data ring or record, is not yet part of the library, we could only do what you are asking by accessing the memory files maintained by your "Three"."

Hearing this, Thomas immediately objected. "You cannot do that, it is a violation."

Looking at Thomas, a coy smile on her face, Christie nodded her head. "Jonathan has taught you well, but, not well enough. The agreement states, that no one can access those files without first obtaining the agreement of the file owner. That would be you". She looked at me. To Thomas, she added. "Furthermore, before you bring it up as another issue, I realize we are not permitted to tell the file owner to allow such access. To that end, please note, that I have not told him to allow access to the memory data. I have only "suggested" it as a possible way of getting him what he is asking for."

I remembered the earlier discussion on this same issue and decided I needed to better understand why this access was so tightly controlled. "Look, I do not know anything about the "rules" or any "agreements", but one thing is clear to me, for some reason, these memory data records and access to them, seems very important. Would somebody please tell me why?"

Thomas, perhaps due to his inexperience, answered apparently to the chagrin of the others. "Because those data records are used during the evaluation process, if access is allowed before the evaluation process, there is a risk of tampering with the data."

"Why would anyone want to tamper or change the records? I mean really, if the record is of the Bio's life cycle, what do you care what it says? That life cycle is completed." Even as I asked this, I was remembering an earlier "thought" picked up from my Seven, something about coming back as a support unit for a rock. It suddenly occurred to me. The evaluation process affected the support units as well. They were also recycled, and massaging the record to insure a positive result could have been the source of the "rule". Yet, even while thinking this, I intuitively knew there was more to it. If that was the case, why would the rule apply to non-support entities, such as Jonathan or Christie? My list of questions was growing.

# Chapter 19

## <u>Hall of Knowledge.</u>

$E$ldred left the group in the care of Anne and Franklin and immediately called for a meeting of the council. It was clear to him that the problem developing with the essence called Reynolds, had the potential of radically changing the outcome of the project. To make matters worse, he didn't know what the source of the problem was.

The council, consisting of experts in all aspects of human affairs, did not meet often. They relied instead, on the process of maintaining the "macro" data rings. These data rings, taken from the individual Bio data rings, contained information related to changes and events within their particular fields of endeavor. Eldred often reviewed these rings, and had frequently surprised the council with integration aspects they had not observed from their own individual perspectives.

Joan, the council's expert in the area of human sociology, stood listening as Henry, the council's geologist, described the most recent changes to the world's polar ice fields. Henry, always the doomsayer, was in the process of predicting a polar meltdown when Eldred made his appearance.

Nodding to the council members, Eldred assumed the lead position. "I have asked you to come here because I need your input to a potentially serious problem." He paused. "As you may have heard, there is a situation developing, which is to say the least, unexpected." He paused and allowed the members to settle into their chairs. "At this moment, there is a Bio in the library with Anne and Franklin. This Bio appears to be searching for answers to questions related to his origin, the support units, us, and of course, the overall project."

James, the council's resident historian, raised his hand. "This is not unusual. We have visitors all the time. What makes this one so special?"

Eldred shrugged his shoulders. "I'm not sure if he is special." He paused before continuing. "At this point, all I know is what I have been told by Christie. According to her report, this Bio has not separated, yet managed to get into the Hall of Understanding. Additionally, it would also appear that he is capable of interacting with his support unit directly, and has shown he can see and hear the support units of other Bios as well." Eldred paused, knowing his next statement would get their full attention. "And most importantly, he also appears to have the healing power." While these capabilities were not unique and had been observed before, they had rarely been collectively possessed by a single Bio.

Each member of the council understood the source of Eldred's concern. They had all witnessed the only other time this had happened. It was perhaps the only time when all of them had incorporated the same event as significant in their respective data rings.

Joan, the sociologist had been affected to a greater extent than any of them. The effects on the social fabric were still being felt two-thousand years later. "Are you suggesting this Bio is an Independent?" While she knew there were no true "Independents" left, she knew the possibility existed that their descendants did. Fortunately, these descendants rarely managed to harness their true powers.

James, the historian looked bemused. "Surely you don't believe that, do you? I mean, even if this Bio is a descendant of an "Independent", he couldn't possibly possess the same power." As the historian, he had witnessed the appearance of many descendants. In fact, in the early times, it was quite common. The original "Independents" were biological, and as a result eventually died. Those who managed to procreate did so with the hybrids. While their children were still powerful, they were no longer truly independent. As the years passed, continued breeding with hybrids eventually led to the loss of their powers, or least, the knowledge of how to harness their powers. However, on occasion, a Bio would appear with some extraordinary power, but it was usually singular in type and rarely controlled.

114

Eldred listened to this exchange and raised his hands, requesting their attention. "As I said, I don't know what to think at this point. I would ask each of you to review your data rings to see if this Bio is in any way associated with Arinons group. And yes, perhaps he's a descendant from an "Independent"." While he did not believe this to be the case, it would not hurt to check. More than likely, Arinon and his followers were behind this. If that was the case, he needed to know what they were up to. Eldred continued. "In the meantime, I think it is likely this Bio will be visiting each of you, looking for answers to his questions. I suggest you be supportive to the extent the agreement permits." He paused before he continued. "I will ask Christie to stay close to this Bio, at least until we better understand the situation."

The council, having had many visitors, understood well what Eldred was saying. The agreement allowed them to share their knowledge of the recorded data, as long as they did so without influencing the visitor. There were a few, who felt that even sharing the knowledge was a form of influence. But Eldred, as the project leader, decided that as long as they presented only the facts, and the decision to use or not use the data remained with the visitor, there was no violation of the agreement.

The room was silent, and footsteps could be heard approaching. The main door opened as Sean, the Director of Operations, entered. As the counterpart to "Peter", he was responsible for the coordination of all activities needed to offset the plans and actions of Arinon's group. Approaching the podium, he whispered into Eldred's ear. Based upon Eldred's reaction, the council knew it was not good news.

Eldred, his face ashen, turned to the group. "It would appear as if the situation is more serious than we thought." He paused. "We have just intercepted a report, and it appears the Bio called Reynolds has taken control of two of his support unit's functions. The report says the "Two and Five" are no longer able to function." This said Eldred strode through the door and out of the meeting. Any question as to whether this Bio was special had now been answered.

# Chapter 20

## O'Hare Airport, Chicago Illinois, 2:30 pm.

*T*he plane banked sharply as the pilot aligned it for the final approach into O'Hare's traffic pattern. The two hour flight from Washington's Dulles Airport had allowed him the opportunity to review the situation reports handed to him before departure. Closing the file, he removed his glasses and rubbed his eyes to relieve the strain. Dr. Tom Ryan would rather have stayed home to watch the Redskins versus Cowboys football game, but fate it seemed, was not a football fan. As assistant to the Presidents Senior Science Advisor and the only "staffer" with graduate degrees in Physics and Electrical Engineering, he was the most qualified for the current assignment. The file, handed to him by a homeland security agent, contained a series of magnetic field flow charts assimilated from the six orbiting W-star satellites. A two page risk assessment, representing the Office of Homeland Security concern was also included. The W-star satellites, in geo-synchronous orbit, had originally been used to spy on the Soviet nuclear program. And, of course, as far as the general public knowledge, to track severe weather. With the advent of more precise spy satellites, the W-stars had outlived their usefulness and were subsequently leased under government control to the scientists studying electro-magnetic field modulations. Under the terms of this lend lease arrangement, the National Security Agency, and now, the Homeland Security Agency, still received live data feed from the satellites. That was the data he now possessed. Several hours earlier in the day, the satellites had detected a disturbance or anomaly in the magnetic flow fields significant enough to set off the built in alarms. The magnetic flow charts reflected the anomaly, something they did daily without fail. Disturbances in the flow fields were not unusual. Scientists had already determined there were magnetic hot spots, and for that matter weak spots, that followed the curvature of the earth. These disturbances generally occurred in the same relative grid locations, those locations dependent upon the varying gravitational effects of other planets and, of course, the sun. However, in this case, what had triggered the alarm was the location of the anomaly. This disturbance occurred "outside" the expected grid. The attached risk analysis had naturally reflected the "terrorist" paranoia gripping the current administration. The concern of the security force was simple. Had this "disturbance" been a prelude, or possibly a dry-run, of an impending terror attack using electro-magnetic pulse weaponry? While Ryan knew such weaponry was available within the world's military establishments, he also understood the limitations of such weapons. Short of a nuclear blast, even the largest EMP weapon developed would only have a localized effect, no more than a mile in diameter. Even then, if detonated above the world's largest financial district, the disaster recovery processes of the financial institutions would preserve the data to the penny. However, if such a blast occurred near a nuclear or hydroelectric power generator the consequences would be serious enough to adversely affect the basic infrastructure, and certainly, the day-to-day living habits of millions. While he personally thought these scenarios unlikely but did agree that it wasn't the physical effect the terrorists wanted, it was the psychological one. Just being capable of pulling off an attack of this nature would send shock waves throughout the world.

Ryan stood as the plane came to a halt at the gate. According to the file, an agent from the Chicago Counter Terrorist Unit would meet him on arrival.

Agent Samuel Costa, formerly of the FBI's Chicago office, stood watching the plane taxi to the gantry. He had a picture of Ryan in the file under his arm and knew who to look for. His team had already completed the preliminary investigation and had found nothing to support the theory of an EMP device being used. Still, his superiors wanted a professional assessment, or as he called it, "a cover-your-butt assessment". He saw Ryan emerge from the gantry and stepped forward extending his hand. "Dr. Ryan?"

"Yes?" Ryan took the extended hand and gave it a firm shake.

"I am Agent Costa, Office of Homeland Security." He flashed

his badge and credentials. "If you would come with me sir, I have a car waiting."

Ryan slung his overnight bag over his shoulder and smiled. "I'm pleased to meet you." He followed, as Costa walked past the security checkpoint.

The car, a black late-model Suburban, was in the "official car" parking zone. The driver, a young man sporting a wispy beard and shoulder length hair, sat reading the sports pages of a newspaper. The radio was on too loudly and the announcer excitedly declared a touchdown for the "Bears".

Costa opened the passenger side rear door and gestured for Ryan to get in. "Dr. Ryan, this is Agent Dougherty. He will be your driver for the duration of your stay." He did not express his thoughts that the stay would be a short one.

"I'm pleased to meet you, Agent Dougherty." Ryan extended his hand.

Dougherty turned the radio off, and shook the outstretched hand. "It's a pleasure, Dr. Ryan."

Dougherty looked at Costa and asked. "Where to boss?" He turned the key and the engine roared to life.

"Let's go to the office." The team should be back by now and a debriefing would be the first step. He turned to Ryan and asked. "What do you know about this operation?" He had been told Ryan had been briefed.

"Only that an electro-magnetic disturbance had been recorded coming from this area, and there was some concern it might have been "terror" related." Ryan did not share his personal opinion on the matter.

Costa shook his head. "We sent a team to investigate. They should be done by now, and will meet us at the office." As a trained observer of behavior, Costa could see that Ryan shared his own opinion that this was a wild goose chase.

The thirty-minute drive to the office was uneventful. Dougherty stopped the car in front of the building and allowed Costa and Ryan to exit before he pulled into the parking garage. Costa led the way, slashing his id card through the card reader and passed through the security checkpoint unchallenged. Ryan presented his credentials manually to the security officer and subjected himself to the mandated electronic wand search.

"Please sign in here sir." The security officer pointed to the log book lying on the counter. "We'll have a visitors badge for you in a moment."

Ryan dutifully signed the log, intentionally listing himself as a consultant in the box, asking for the Company represented. He took the visitors badge, and nodded to the security officer. "Thank you, I will return it when I leave."

Costa smiled at him and said. "Sorry, but protocols must be followed."

"No problem." Ryan would have been disappointed if he had been simply passed through.

"Follow me." Costa turned and walked toward a bank of elevators. He pressed the "up" button, and they waited for the elevator to make its appearance. Dougherty had parked the car and joined them.

The office was on the tenth floor. Glass or Plexiglas partitions separated the room from what looked to be a computerized command center. Consoles and screens formed a series of concentric circles which filled the main room. Armed security officers wore maroon shirts and walked in pairs around the perimeter of the circle. Flashing red dots indicated video surveillance cameras were also actively used. The office itself was large. A rectangular glass table occupied the center area, computer terminals and an overhead LCD display unit rested on it. Six men and two women sat in chairs talking quietly.

Costa, as lead investigator brought the meeting to order. "Okay, let's get this meeting going." He turned and extended his hand toward Ryan. "This is Doctor Ryan. The head office sent him to assist in this investigation."

Ryan nodded. "Anything I can do to help." He could sense they were not overly pleased to have him.

"Dr. Ryan, let me introduce the team." Costa turned toward the table. "Starting from your left, you've met Dougherty. He is our driver and also our Crpto specialist. To his right is Mary Schofield, our electronics expert. Then we have Jeanine Narcon, our chemical and biological expert. Sam Delaney is our computer analyst. Tom

Berringer is our explosives expert. James Buchannon is the tactical team leader. Bill Thomas is our inter-agency liaison."

"Okay, let's get started." He turned to Buchannon. "What do we know so far?"

Buchannon stood and faced the only solid wall of the room. He picked up the remote and activated the LCD projector. The image of a preliminary investigation report flashed onto the screen.

"At approximately 11:45 am this morning, we were advised by central command that some type of electro-magnetic disturbance had been detected at these coordinates." The numbers flashed on the screen were longitude and latitude coordinates. "The precise location was identified as the Loyola Medical Center." Buchannon paused allowing the image to return to the preliminary report. "As per protocol, we immediately initiated a level three response team." He gestured toward the group. "We also notified the local authorities and the State Police. Our team arrived at the Center at approximately 12:20 pm, where we met with John Larsen, the Center's Chief of Security. According to Mr. Larsen, at approximately 11:30 this morning, a situation occurred on the fourth floor, in the Neuro ward. Evidently, they experienced some type of "short" in one of the patient's rooms. The short circuit affected only the one room, and as of this moment, the cause has not been determined."

Ryan listened closely, and then leaned back in his chair. Interrupting the dissertation, he said. "I do not think a "short circuit" would create the electro-magnetic disturbance we saw."

Buchannon nodded. "That's what our resident expert said as well." He paused and looked in Costa's direction. "At our request, Mr. Larsen arranged to have all of the equipment from that room placed under our control. Our technicians are performing diagnostic tests as we speak."

Ryan again interrupted. "What type of diagnostic testing are they doing?"

Buchannon smiled. "If the overload was due to an energy spike or surge, the circuits may be fused. That would tell us the event was triggered by an external factor, perhaps one of a mechanical nature. On the other hand if, the circuits are not fused, the event had to have been triggered internally. And as yet, we do not have a

120

scenario to account for that possibility."

Ryan nodded and asked. "What type of equipment are we talking about." He doubted the circuits would be fused as most electronic equipment manufactured today had overload features that simply shut the units down.

"EEG, EKG, Blood pressure and chemical analysis equipment." Buchannon did not know the exact equipment terminology.

"I see." Ryan was familiar with most of these devices. With the exception of the blood pressure equipment, all of the devices had a built in "closed loop" monitoring computer. This computer allowed the equipment manufacturers to download performance data, which was used to ensure the devices were working properly. The fact that the data could be used to ward off unwarranted liability claims was equally important to them. If a "short circuit" was the source of the problem, only the electronic features of the devices would have been affected, but not the computer hard drive. If on the other hand the drives were empty, the possibility of a magnetic influence should be considered. "Mr. Buchannon, I would like to suggest your computer expert also look at these devices. I would like to suggest you contact the manufacturers for their assistance."

Mary, the electronics expert of the group, immediately understood what Ryan was saying. "You're right, if the hard drives are empty, it could not be from an overload condition."

Buchannon nodded in agreement. "Good idea, thank you Doctor." He turned to Sam Delaney, their computer expert. "Sam, contact the manufacturers. I want them here within the hour."

Costa, so far silent, looked at Buchannon. "What else do we know?"

Buchannon turned back to the LCD projector and pushed the next slide button on the remote. "Hospital security provided the security tapes, and we are currently digitizing the    images and running them through the face recognition analysis program." The "face recognition" program compared the faces of all known terrorists to those digitized from the video surveillance tapes. "So far, no matches have been found." Buchannon continued. "Additionally, we have completed the preliminary background checks on all of the persons who were present in the room during the event." He pushed the remote keys to change the screen image again. "There were six people in the room at the time, seven counting the patient." The screen now showed the pictures of the seven people.

Buchannon highlighted the first face. "The patient, William Reynolds, is fifty-three, married with two children. Mr. Reynolds appears to be your run-of-the-mill middle-aged, bowl twice a week citizen. Pays his taxes and has no criminal history. Military records indicate he served a couple of tours in Vietnam, and then went to college. After that, he started a software company, which he sold in April 2004. Currently he is unemployed. At approximately Five o'clock this morning, he was the victim of a robbery attempt. He was shot once in the head and, with the exception of a few moments this morning, has been in what appears to be a coma. I would also add that the few moments during which he was awake, coincided with the event we are investigating."

Buchannon paused. He used the highlighter and pointed at the next face. "Dr. Tai Chen Wong, age 42. He heads the Neurological Unit at Loyola Medical Center. Doctor Wong is an American citizen, born in Chicago in 1962. Graduated from the University of Chicago in 1984. Medical school at Harvard graduating in 1988. Served his residency at Loyola and has been there his entire career. Dr. Wong was the victim of a lightening strike at the age of fifteen. Since then he has been restricted to a wheelchair and according to his Primary Care Physician he will never regain the use of his legs." Buchannon decided to withhold the most recent rumors until later in the presentation. "Dr. Wong's father and grandfather immigrated to America in 1947. The grandfather, also a doctor, served with the American volunteer Air force in Burma, fighting the Japanese during WWII. His wife, grandmother of Dr. Wong, was killed during the Japanese occupation of Shanghai. The records are a bit sketchy, but they think she was used as a guinea pig for the Japanese biological program. Wong's father was ten years old at the time. He also became a doctor and is now retired, living in the northwest suburbs."

Costa raised his hand. "Is there any record of the older Wong's being affiliated with their homeland?" He knew that during the fifties and sixties, immigrants from the communist countries were often "monitored". If they were, there should be an FBI file they could review.

Buchannon shook his head. "There was a file maintained on the grandfather. We have reviewed it but there is nothing that warrants further attention. When they came here, it appears as if they completely severed ties with their homeland."

Buchannon continued and selected the image of Doctor Brangeel. "Doctor Thomas Brangeel, age 53, married, two children. Doctor Brangeel runs a Family Medical Center in a local suburb, and has been the patient's Primary Care Physician since 1987. Brangeel also graduated from the University of Chicago. Harvard Medical School, class of 1982 as well."

The next face belonged to Charlene White. "Charlene White age 36, Registered nurse, single mother, one daughter, Melissa, age sixteen. No significant history. Appears to be what she is, a hard working middle class citizen."

The litany of faces continued. "Doctor Blake, age 29, in his final month of residency. Graduated University of Chicago 2001. Medical school in 2005. Parents are dead, killed in an automobile accident in 1996, raised by his grandmother in Indiana. No criminal record or known affiliation with "radical" groups."

Buchannon selected the next face, that of Mary Reynolds.

Costa, sensing more of the same interrupted. "Is it safe to say the rest of these people are also "clean"?"

"Yes sir, they are. There is nothing to indicate they should be viewed as anything but what they are, ordinary people." Buchannon also felt this was a waste of time. However he wanted to make sure they had not missed anything in their analysis.

"Good. Please summarize your team's assessment." Costa did not want to appear uninterested, but also suspected there was more than what had been presented.

Buchannon shut off the LCD unit and took his seat at the table. This next part was not one he would do standing up. He looked around and received imperceptible nods from the rest of his team. As he looked at Costa and Ryan, he had the sinking sensation what he was about to say would probably end his career. "I know this is going to sound crazy, but we," he paused and stretched his hands toward the team, "think there is more going on here, than we can prove."

Costa, as a former field agent, understood Buchannon's discomfort. There had been many times when his instincts told him one thing, while the evidence pointed elsewhere. To have the support of his full team also impressed upon him the need to give them some latitude. "Go on," he then added. "Jim, the best investigators follow their gut instincts. Whatever you have to say, let's get it on the table."

Buchannon, visibly relieved and appreciated the show of support. He wasted no time. "On our way to the Medical Center we heard news reports about something happening there. The reports seemed to indicate that some sort of miracle had taken place. We thought this was very coincidental, given that was our target location." He paused before going on. "When we arrived, there were news reporters and video trucks all over the place. Not long afterwards, they left. According to them, it had all been a misunderstanding."

"What kind of miracle?" Costa had also heard the reports, but had simply dismissed them.

"According to the reports, the patient Reynolds woke up for a few minutes and while awake spoke to White and Blake. We do not know precisely what he said to White, but we know he advised Blake to see a cardiologist." Buchannon paused. The tough one was next. "It was also reported, that while Reynolds was awake, Dr. Wong touched him. When he did, some sort of electrical charge was generated that knocked Wong to the floor. After he revived, he claimed to have feeling in his legs."

Ryan, until now a passive listener, interrupted. "Let me get this straight, you think this guy Reynolds, the LEAST capable of all the people present, is responsible for this?"

A knock on the door saved Buchannon for the moment. A security guard entered and handed Costa a sheet of paper. Costa glanced at the paper, looked up then passed the note to Ryan. "It seems we need to pay Dr. Wong and this guy Reynolds a visit."

Ryan looked at the note, and could not believe what he was reading. It was from the Loyola Medical Center Chief of Security, John Larsen. Evidently, Dr. Blake had just gone into surgery for a triple bypass operation.

# Chapter 21

## <u>Loyola Medical Center.</u>

*H*arridy, having reached the fourth floor with Andrew and his mother, set off in the direction of Wong's office, while they proceeded to the patient's room. Harridy expected to be met by the receptionist, but found the office empty. He glanced at the closed inner office door that he knew had to be Wong's office, but resisted the urge to knock. As he turned to leave, he was stopped by the unmistakable sound of a bang coming from the inner office. Worried that the Doctor may have fallen, he opened the door. As he looked into the room he saw the shape of a man standing, or perhaps trying to stand, next to a large desk. A wheelchair, obviously the source of the bang, rested against a metal bookcase a few feet behind him. As he watched, the figure slowly began to fall. Harridy crossed the space between them in three steps and caught the falling man under the arms, easily absorbing his weight. He hooked the now empty wheelchair with his foot and pulled it into a position which allowed him to gently lower the man into it.

Wong, sweating profusely, looked at Harridy. "Thanks, I guess I should be more careful."

Harridy nodded in agreement. "I assume you are Doctor Wong." So the rumors were true.

"Yes, I am Wong. What can I do for you officer."

"My name is Harridy."

"Yes of course, Officer Harridy". He paused. "How can I help you?" Wong was grateful for Harridy's timely intervention, but he would rather have fallen. He had years of practice, and would have easily been able to get back into his chair unassisted.

Harridy, as if he sensed Wong's thoughts, decided to take the initiative. "Well? Were you successful?" He knew Wong understood the real question.

Wong looked at Harridy. He knew the officer understood what he was really trying to do. He could only hope the officer would keep it quiet. "Well, as you see, I am still in my chair." In reality Wong was ecstatic, he HAD stood. It had been for a few seconds, but it was enough to convince him he was right. He now knew without doubt he would eventually regain the use of his lower body. It was just a matter of time, and of course, therapy.

Harridy, not fooled by Wong's answer, smiled. "From what I saw, you're on your way to being out of that chair for good." He did not understand Wong's desire to keep this a secret, but he played along with the charade. "I was told I needed your authorization to visit your patient Reynolds. I need to speak with him regarding the events from this morning."

"I see." Wong paused before he continued. "I would like to help, but at this point he is either sleeping or unconscious. In either case, he is not ready for visitors, and certainly not available to answer any questions."

Harridy do not want to appear too callous. He stopped himself from asking if waking the patient was an option. "Any idea how long it will be before I will be able to talk with him?" He knew the answer, even as he asked the question.

Wong gave him a sharp look. "No, it could be in minutes, maybe hours, even days. It's not something that can be predicted. If you leave a contact number, I will make sure you are notified when he does wake up."

The shrill chirp of Wong's beeper interrupted, before Harridy could respond. Wong looked at the beeper and frowned. "I'm sorry, but I need to go. Please leave your contact information with my receptionist. I will make sure you are notified when the patient is available." This said, Wong wheeled his chair toward the door and left Harridy standing there.

Harridy watched as Wong maneuvered his chair through the doorway. He opened his wallet and extracted his business card. He dropped it on the receptionist's desk and followed the doctor into the hall. As he approached the elevator he could see Andrew standing with his mother outside of one of the rooms. The security guard, a big beefy fellow, was holding the boy at arm's length. Andrew struggled unsuccessfully to get past him into the room. "You can't keep me out of there, he's my father." Harridy could see that Andrew's mother was crying. She pulled on her son's arm, trying to get him away from the security officer. "Andrew, stop."

Harridy moved quickly for a big man, and grabbed the security officer's arms, forcing him to break contact with Andrew. "What's going on here?" Harridy looked at Mary, then at Andrew.

Andrew was visibly upset and glared at the security guard. "He won't let us in."

The guard did not like the fact the officer had interfered with him, but nonetheless was glad he had. The security guard seemed to regain his composure. To Harridy, he replied. "I'm sorry, but the doctor requested the room to be cleared of all unnecessary personnel."

"Doctor Wong?" Harridy posed the question.

Mary took Andrew's arm and answered. "No, Doctor Brangeel. He is my husband's Primary Care Physician." She paused, and then added. "Doctor Wong just went in."

Harridy knew that the doctor would not request this without a good reason asked. "Did something happen?" He looked again at Mary.

"I don't know. One minute that nurse, I think her name is Charlene White, was changing the bandage on Bill's head. She must have seen something and told Doctor Brangeel. The next thing I knew, they were paging Doctor Wong and escorting us out of the room." Mary paused. "I want to go back in there. Can you help?"

Harridy looked at the security guard. He knew forcing entrance into the room would be a serious breach of conduct. At the same time, he knew that if he were in the Reynolds family's position, he would certainly want to go in. He looked at the security guard and said. "We're going in."

The guard knew that he would not be held responsible, smiled. "I would if I were you." With that, he stepped away from the doorway.

Andrew did not waste a moment he turned the knob and pushed the door open. His mother and Harridy followed him into the room.

Brangeel heard the door open and turned toward them. "I thought I said I wanted this room cleared." His eyes were focused on the security officer.

The guard defiantly stared back and shrugged. He motioned in Harridys direction. "He outranks me." With that, the guard closed the door and resumed his position on the outside of the room.

Harridy had initially assumed the clearing of the room was because of an emergency with the patient. Yet as he stood there, it was evident that was not the case at all. The Doctors were not performing CPR, or any other life saving techniques. They were simply standing to one side in quiet conversation. The nurse stood at the head of the bed, bloody bandages on a tray in front of her.

Doctor Wong fixed his eyes on Harridy. "I thought I told you to leave your card. You have no right to be here, and you certainly do not have the authority to bypass hospital security."

Andrew heard this and replied angrily to the Doctor. "I asked him to come in." He paused and glanced at his mother. "And what right do you have to force us out? He is my father and we have every right to be here."

Brangeel answered. "That was my decision. If you need to vent your anger, do so at me."

Mary, knowing Andrew would escalate the situation interceded. "Why? Why did you have us removed? Is there something wrong with Bill?" Except for the absence of the bandages, she could see no difference in her husband's condition.

Brangeel looked at Wong who gave him a nod. How do you tell someone that something good had happened, yet at the same time, tell them that what had happened was potentially bad? "Perhaps you should look for yourself." He motioned for her to approach the patient. Charlene moved aside and allowed Mary to take her place.

Mary approached the bed unsure of what to expect. The old bandages, encrusted with dried blood, were lying on the table next to the bed. The bandages had not yet been replaced and she was expecting to see the laceration and the sutures on her husband's head. What she saw left her speechless. The sutures were there, but there was no sign of any cut or laceration. It was as if nothing had happened to him. "I don't understand, what happened to his cut?" She looked at Brangeel, confusion clearly evident on her face.

Brangeel shook his head. "Exactly! When Charlene removed

the bandages this is what she found. When I saw it, I asked the room to be cleared."

"But why? Isn't this a good thing?" Andrew was as confused as his mother.

Wong who had been quiet until now, answered. "Yes of course it is a good thing." He paused, unsure how to continue. "But at the same time, we have to consider the possibility that it is not good at all."

Strange as it seemed, Harridy understood the Doctors' concerns. Since they could not explain what had caused it, protocol required them to implement immediate quarantine procedures. That was why the room had been cleared. Now, because of his intervention, he had unwittingly exposed the Reynolds family, as well as himself, to whatever had caused this. "I'm sorry; I didn't realize what was happening." Harridy knew his apology did not change anything, but felt the need to say it anyway.

Brangeel gave him a reproving look and shrugged. "It's too late now." He relaxed and smiled. "Look at the bright side. If whatever caused this is a virus or contaminate, it's certainly one of the better ones we have seen." He then looked at Wong and added. "I also think if there was a risk of contamination, they," he motioned at Mary and Andrew, "are already infected. The question we need to answer now is whether to round up all of the others who have come into contact with him." Established CDC protocol dictated this as the appropriate next step, but he was not convinced it was necessary. He and Wong were discussing that topic when Harridy and company barged into the room.

Wong and Brangeel had reviewed all of the available data in the patients file. Test results of his blood analysis, urine analysis, and toxic screening. All of the biological tests showed nothing unusual. For all practical purposes, the patient was as normal as any other person. Neither of them thought placing him in quarantine, although procedurally appropriate, would yield any further data. Even if the contaminate or virus was of the airborne type, both knew it would have still required an organic base. According to the test results this base did not exist.

A knock at the door interrupted their discussion. They glanced up and saw the security guard's face through the door opening.

Brangeel approached the door. "Yes, what is it?"

The guard, having been bullied once, was standing firm against the new visitors, even though their credentials exceeded even those of the State Police, he personally did not like their attitude of superiority, and was enjoyed the opportunity to stand in their way. "You have visitors, sir. They are from the Office of Homeland Security."

Wong looked at Brangeel. "How could they know? We just found out, and nobody has left the room."

Brangeel nodded thoughtfully. "They don't know." He paused and tried to decide what to do. He turned toward the door and told the guard. "Tell them we will be out in a moment." He looked at Charlene and said. "Put fresh bandages on his head."

Andrew was obviously confused and looked at Brangeel. "Why put new bandages on?" There was nothing that required a bandage.

Brangeel was unperturbed and smiled. "Trust me, Andrew. Just trust me. I will explain later." With that he opened the door.

# Chapter 22

# Hall of Understanding.

*A*rinon had just returned from his meeting with the others and had the foreboding sense that things were about to go terribly wrong. This episode with the Bio called Reynolds had taken him and the others by surprise. While the events had disturbed him, the fact that they had happened without warning, concerned him even more. As the leader of the support units, he had spent considerable time and resources creating an environment that would ensure anomalies such as this would become apparent very quickly. Although the support units were blocked from communicating with each other in the physical realm, those limitations did not apply in the non-physical one. As a result, an ethereal communication network allowed him, and the other administrators to have access to virtually real-time information. The good news was that the process had worked as designed. This situation had certainly become evident in a very short period of time. The problem was they had no idea where it had come from. Peter, his Director of Operations, had been adamant. He knew, without doubt, that whatever had happened was not part of any of their current operations. At the same time, he was equally confident Eldred and his group, were also not responsible.

A quiet knock interrupted his thoughts. As he glanced up, he saw Jonathan standing a few feet away. "Jonathan, that was quick." Based upon the expression on Jonathan's face, Arinon suspected he was not the bearer of good news.

Jonathan wasted no time. "You asked to be appraised of any changes in the Bios Reynolds and Wong." He hesitated before going on. "It seems there has been a development with the support unit for Reynolds." Jonathan was glad Arinon was sitting. "His Seven just reported that units "Two" and "Five" are no longer functional."

Arinon stared at Jonathan. "You know that's not possible. The Bio unit cannot survive without them." Maybe this was good news after all. If the Bio unit failed, the Essence would be introduced again to the evaluation and recycling process and all of this nonsense would stop.

Jonathan nodded. "Yes, but it seems the Bio unit is not being affected at all." He also thought as Arinon did. The Bio unit's "Two" was responsible for maintaining all of the bodily functions without the conscious knowledge of the Bio. The unit's "Five" supported these efforts by ensuring the continued good health of the Bio through its regenerative functions. Normally, the failure of either of these critical functions resulted in the demise of the Biological unit. Yet, the Bio unit appeared to be functioning without them.

"I see, what is the status on Wong?" If he was correct in his assessment, the Bio called Wong would also become problematic.

Jonathan hesitated before responding. "According to the last report from his "Seven", his "Five" is reporting significant regeneration activity in areas where it should not be occurring. His estimation is the Bio Wong will be fully functional within a matter of hours." Jonathan quickly added. "However, there have been no further reports of his seeing other support units."

Arinon listened as Jonathan gave his report. There was no longer any doubt the events between the two Bios were related. It was equally apparent steps would need to be taken to deal with the issue. "Thank you Jonathan, I will review this with Peter and the others. In the meantime, I want you and Thomas to stay with these Bios, especially Reynolds. Keep me informed of any further developments."

Peter arrived in time to hear these last instructions and simply nodded to Jonathan. "I will keep you apprised from this end." He waited until Jonathan left the room before turning his attention to Arinon; he already knew what Arinon was thinking.

Arinon did not disappoint him. "I thought they were all gone. When was the last time we saw one?"

Peter expected this question and had already searched his archives. "They ARE all gone. The last one disappeared one-hundred and fifty-thousand cycles ago." His records of the event indicated this last one, who they called Croatian, had disappeared over four-hundred years earlier. Other support units of the time, mostly Indians from the mainland, had reported that Croatoan was angered by settlers encroaching on her island. In a fit of rage she had sent the settlers along with herself, to the "other" side. Their whereabouts was still a mystery, even to Peter. Since that time, there had been no other reports or sightings of any "Independents", as they called them.

Arinon looked at Peter. "So, you do not think he is an "Independent"? He paused. "Is it possible he is a descendant of one?" There had been other occasions, when a Bio had seemed to possess some of their original powers. On every occasion, it was found the Bio was a descendant of an "Independent". Fortunately, as they were hybrids, these Bios still required the use of their support units. As a result, they had little difficulty blocking them from fully understanding, or learning to control their powers. To now have a Bio, with the potential of having this power and one who did not need his support unit, was not a scenario Eldred wanted to consider.

Peter shook his head. "We have found no linkage to any of the known descendants." He had always understood the threat the independents posed. Early in the process he had created a group whose sole responsibility was to keep track of known descendants. While he could not preclude the possibility of a non-linear culmination, the probability of such a genetic pooling was incalculable. "No, I am sure he is not related to an "Independent."

"Do you still think this is coming from Eldred and his group?" Arinon for the first time hoped that was the case. He had not forgotten the events from two thousand years before, when another Bio seemed to possess these same capabilities. Christie saw it as an opportunity and had "suggested" to the Bio, that his power should be used to right the wrongs in the world. Only Peter's masterful manipulation of the political and social events of the time stopped him. Even so, the effects of that episode were still being felt in this time.

Peter merely shrugged his shoulders. "We are still assessing that possibility, but at this time we have not uncovered any operation involving this Bio." He continued. "No, I am still of the opinion this is a random event, clearly one we could not have foreseen." He paused before adding. "I should also tell you, I have initiated an operation to put a stop to this before it gets worse." As the Director of Operations, he was within his rights to do so, even without Arinons approval.

Arinon had expected this to be the case. "What operation?" The most expeditious way, although rarely used, would be to send word to the Bios support units instructing them to "restrict" the level of support provided. This restriction was best accomplished using the "Two or the "Five", as loss of either meant the Bio unit would cease to function. This method, however, was not without risk. The "restrictions" had to be such that during the evaluation process the "failure" could not be definitively tied back to them. That would not be easy, and although the typical Bio had enough negative external physical influences to easily mask their lack of effort, it was still a risk. To Arinon this was academic. If the reports were true, that approach could not be used as those two elements of Reynolds's support unit were no longer functional. This time they would need to utilize external resources.

Peter smiled. "Without going into great detail, let's just say that steps are being taken to neutralize this Bio." Peter had direct control of every bio support unit in existence. As such, it was relatively easy for him to influence events in the physical reality. However, doing so without leaving any trace required cunning and skill. This was a skill he had mastered early in the game. Eldred's foolish acceptance of the agreement that allowed the use of suggestions had provided him a great deal of latitude. Consequently, regardless of the events that transpired, he was only concerned that the decisions that would eventually lead to the events were not traceable to his group.

# Chapter 23

## **Hall of Knowledge.**

*A*s I looked at the screen and the "circle" I knew to be "George's" data ring, I thought about what Christie had said. According to her, it was possible for me to find my brother's data ring if I would allow access to the records maintained by my "Three." Yet in doing so I risked having the data ring contents altered in some way. While I still did not fathom why anyone would want to change them, I knew the restrictions served some purpose or they would not exist.

Christie, along with the rest of the group, stood waiting patiently. She hoped that the Bio would grasp the underlying message she had tried to convey. Thomas was right. She was treading a fine line between suggestion and instruction. However, if her instincts were right about this Bio, he would intuitively understand what she was "not" saying.

I looked at Christie. "You said I would need to access the records maintained by my "Three"."

"Yes," Christie nodded. "That is one way."

"But my "Three" is not here." I had an idea, but did not know if it would work. I decided to pose the question anyway. "Because I am still "alive", wouldn't I have access to all of my memories without having my "Three" present?"

Christie smiled. He had not disappointed her. The rational link had been made. "I don't know, Thomas what do you think?" This question removed any culpability she would have assumed, if the actual data record had been opened by the "Three".

Thomas realized he had been outwitted and simply nodded. "Yes, active memory recall without opening the data records is permitted." Jonathan was right. Christie was cunning.

I looking at Franklin and asked. "So all I need to do is

remember my brother, and from that memory, we can find the correct data ring?" I hoped my visual memory was accurate.

Franklin nodded. "Yes, it's possible we could find his data ring that way."

"Okay, what do I do?"

Franklin reached out and touched the monitor. The screen immediately changed to the one containing the larger list of data rings. Do you remember asking about the data rings which were lighting up?" He did not wait for a response, and continued. "When you remember your brother, his ring will also light up. Now, close your eyes and try to remember as clearly as you can the image of your brother. If we are successful, his data ring will light up. When it does, I will select it for you."

A thought occurred to me. "What happens if someone else remembers somebody else, at the same time? Wouldn't that ring also light up?"

"Yes, that is a possibility. But unless you want to open your "Three's" records, this is the only way." Franklin was also worried about this happening but he had a plan in case it did.

"Okay, I'm ready." I closed my eyes and tried to recall the last memory of my brother. Not surprisingly, it was the memory of him lying in his casket at the funeral home.

Franklin watched the screen and saw several rings light up. He watched and waited to see if they blinked off again. Eventually, only one ring remained lit for the full time. He ignored the others he reached out and touched the one ring. "You can open your eyes now."

I opened my eyes and saw that the screen had once again changed. It now held the image of only one ring. "Were we successful?"

Franklin nodded. "I think so. We'll know in a minute. Are you ready?" He was equally curious to know if they had selected the correct ring.

I took a deep breath and nodded. "Yes I think so." As I looked at the ring it occurred to me for the first time that I was no longer a passive observer. In the case of "George", I had been simply watching for lack of a better term, a television show about a stranger. This was different. This was my brother. I knew him, or thought I did. Now, I was about to see his life from a whole new perspective, and was also sure my memory of him would be forever changed.

Anne seemed to sense my thoughts. She an empathetic look on her face and in her soft melodic voice, she asked. "Are you sure you want to do this?"

As I looked at her, I could not help but see her inner beauty. "Yes, I need to understand."

She patted my arm and smiled. "Perhaps it would be best if you entered the data ring at a very early time. Those memories should not impact you as much as the more recent ones. If you can find and link to another image quickly, you would not have to run the risk of having the memories of your brother impacted. And try to remember to not touch anyone except the one you want to link to."

I nodded. "Thanks for the advice." I reached out and selected a point on the ring near the seven o'clock position. I hoped that I had selected a point very early in Steve's life.

Almost immediately, I found myself standing in a room that looked like a child's bedroom. The furniture included a crib, a playpen and a changing table. A small child I knew to be Steve sat in the playpen. What I recognized as a "Lincoln log" grasped firmly in his chubby fist. There were three other children, five or six years older playing nearby on the floor. As I watched, the girl began to cry. At the same time she threw what appeared to be two pieces of her doll onto the floor. "You killed my baby." Her anger appeared to be directed at one of the two boys playing nearby. "I'm telling mom." This said, her crying immediately escalated into a loud wail. I remembered this. My brother "Bob" had torn the head off her doll in retribution for her breaking apart his log cabin.

I also knew what was about to happen, and it was NOT going to be a pleasant experience for any of us. Unfortunately for us, my mother was not at home, she was shopping for groceries. This meant we were under the dreaded supervision of my father, who although a wonderful man in his later years, was notorious for having very little patience with screaming children. As I watched, the door to the room opened and the looming and even now, scary, figure of my father filled the doorframe. When I saw him I walked forward and reached out to touch his image. This caused the holographic image to stop, and once again I was standing in front of the monitor. A new circle sat on the screen waiting to be accessed. My timing was impeccable. Had I entered Steve's data ring five minutes later, I would have arrived in time to feel the spanking I knew was coming.

Anne still held my arm and smiled. "Good timing on that one."

I looked at the new ring and realized it belonged to my father. This only served to increase my trepidation. "Do you think as I go farther back, to people I did not really know, it will get easier?" The question was not directed to anyone in particular.

Franklin nodded. "It should."

I reached toward the screen again hoping to again select a point early in my father's life but was stopped by the voice of Eldred.

"How are you doing? Have you found your answers yet?" Eldred knew that no answers had been forthcoming. From the earlier conversation, he was of the opinion that the Bio, while curious, did not really know what he was looking for. And while "piggy-backing" back into time following his energy strand might provide a familial understanding, it would not lead to the answers he was seeking.

I watched as Eldred approached the small group. "No. I was just getting started."

Eldred looked at Christie. "Christie, if I might have a word please." To the others he said. "I know you're in the middle of something and I apologize for the interruption." He paused and looked in the direction of the Bio. "But right now I am afraid your guest is needed elsewhere. You can pick up where you left off when he returns."

I looked at Eldred. "Where am I needed that takes precedence over what I am doing?" I had only begun my search and now I had to leave.

Eldred nodded. "Unfortunately yes, you need to leave. Your Bio unit needs you." Eldred looked at Thomas. "Please bring him back to his support unit now." This said, he turned and walked away. Christie followed close behind.

As they reached the room beyond the main library, Eldred turned and watched as Thomas led the Bio away. As he looked at Christie, his demeanor changed to one of concern. "It seems things have changed dramatically in the time you were in there." He nodded in the direction of the library.

Christie noted Eldred's serious countenance and knew enough to wait for more information. "What's happened?" In the time she had known Eldred, she had only seen him express this level of concern on a few occasions.

As he cast his eyes to the floor, Eldred replied. "It would seem this "Reynolds" is more than he appears." He went on to tell her the few details he possessed as well as the consensus of the council.

Christie was astounded by what Eldred had said and immediately grasped what he had just told her. "You think he is an "Independent?"

Eldred shook his head and at the same time shrugged his shoulders. "We don't know. So far he has only fully demonstrated one of the powers. A second one, if you count his apparent telepathic abilities. And perhaps a third if he has managed to assume the activities maintained by his support unit. That is part of what we need to determine." The original "Independents" had possessed five basic powers.

"Why would you send him back to his Bio?" To her way of thinking this was the last thing they should have done.

"As long as he is unconscious he is vulnerable." Although Eldred shared her concern, he also knew the Bio needed to protect itself. And while his group could have done the same, doing so would have been a violation of the agreement.

"Do you think Peter is already mounting an operation?" She could well imagine the turmoil Arinon and Peter were facing.

"Yes I do. In fact knowing him as I do, I am sure of it." If Reynolds did possess these powers and was learning to use them, Peter would have no choice but to try to stop him.

Christie shrugged. "Why do you let Peter continue to do these things?" They had known for a long time Peter's goals were contrary to his assigned task.

Eldred gazed into the distance and simply smiled. "We have an agreement. Unless you can bring me positive proof he has broken that agreement, I cannot act." In the end, it would not really matter if there was proof, Peter would get his due.

"What do you need me to do?" Christie was accustomed to

receiving unusual assignments, and looked forward to them.

"I want you to take Anne and Franklin and stay close to Reynolds. If Peter does have an operation planned, you're the best person to find out what it is." Eldred paused before he added. "Use Anne and Franklin to keep in touch with me. You stay with Reynolds and advise him as best you can, but under no circumstance are you to violate the agreement." He added this last remembering the last time similar events had transpired.

Christie noted the twinkle in Eldred's eyes and smiled to herself. Although his official position was one of neutrality, she also knew he did not approve of the tactics employed by Arinon and Peter. Still, if she were to violate the agreement, he would have little choice but to follow its terms and conditions. "You realize Reynolds is going to want to come back here. He has only begun his search."

Eldred nodded. "Test him. Find out if he possesses the other abilities. Equally important, find out where his heart lies. If in your opinion he is worthy, bring him back. But before you do, make him understand what he is looking for cannot be found by searching his energy strand." He knew she understood what he was implying.

Christie nodded. "Have you advised the council?"

"Yes they are expecting him."

# Chapter 24

## **Reynolds Support unit.**

$W$e left the Hall of Knowledge in the company of Thomas and made our way back to my support unit. My "Seven" and "Three" had been joined by Jonathan and several others I had not yet met.

"Welcome back. Did you find the answers you were seeking?" Jonathan asked this with a knowing grin on his face.

I ignored him and turned to my "Seven". "I was told my Bio needed me. What's going on, and who are they?" I nodded in the direction of the two newcomers.

Seven glanced first at the newcomers then at the hospital room scene and replied. "The one on the right is your "Two" and the other is your "Five". As for your Bio needing you, I don't know why. I did not summon you.

I looked at the newcomers and asked "Shouldn't they be with my Bio?" I looked at my "Seven" and pointed in their direction. "Why are they here and not there?" I pointed at my Bio.

"Seven" shrugged. "It seems your Bio no longer requires their services, so they came here." He did not understand either. This was just another unprecedented event, something he had slowly become accustomed to.

I turned to Jonathan and Thomas. "Why would Eldred tell me my Bio needed me?"

Jonathan raised his hands as if indicating he had no answer. "They are "Sleepers". Who knows what they are planning or doing? "We tried to warn you." Was it true? Did he really not know about the "Two and Five"?

"Sure, just blame the "Sleepers"." Christie's voice preceded her entrance.

I watched as Christie, Anne, and Franklin emerged from the

tunnel joining my ever expanding group. My support unit, as expected, moved closer together, assuming a defensive posture. Jonathan was correct. It was a "Sleeper" who told me to return. I focused on Christie and pressed the issue. "For once I think they are right. Why did Eldred tell me to return to my Bio?"

"Perhaps your Bio needs you and they" she nodded in the direction of Jonathan and Thomas. "Simply aren't telling you."

On hearing this, "Seven", his jaw muscles tight, replied angrily. "We would never do that. If he was needed we would be the first to tell him."

Jonathan was equally confused, why had Eldred sent him back? Earlier, it was Christie who had convinced him they needed to make sure this essence did not return to his Bio. Now Eldred was sending him back. Why? And why did he send three "Sleepers"? Looking at Christie he asked. "Yes why did Eldred send him back? I can assure you the support unit would have brought him back if there was a need to do so. And while we're asking questions, why are you three here?"

Christie did not want to overstep her authority and merely smiled. "Does anyone ever really know what Eldred is thinking? Perhaps Eldred feels Reynolds needs to return to his Bio for reasons we do not understand. As for us," she glanced at Franklin and Anne. "We are just like you, simply following orders"

As I stood there and listened to this "chess game" of words it became apparent that no further benefit would be gained by my staying. Perhaps I did need to return to my physical state, if only to care for my family.

I raised my hands and decided it was time. "Stop, both of you. I have decided to return to my family." I glanced in the direction of the scene containing my family. "However, before I do I want to thank all of you for your assistance during my stay. While I still have many questions, you can be assured I learned a great deal from you." I paused and hoped that what I was about to say would be taken in a constructive manner. "If possible I would like to return at some point and continue my search. But at the same time, I must tell you I am not an "object", and quite frankly do not like being treated as one. Your two groups remind me of two children fighting over a favorite toy." I stopped trying to gauge their reactions to what I had said.

"Seven" simply smiled. "Do you remember how to get back?"

I looked at him. I could sense he had enjoyed my little outburst. "Yes, I simply decide to wake up."

"Correct." He paused then added. "We will be here for you, and I will keep your "Two" and "Five" on standby in case you need them."

I looked at him and for the first time realized my support unit had proven to be the only group that did not have any agenda except my well being. "I'm counting on that." With that I focused my thoughts on the scene before me, the thought of needing to wake up, paramount on my mind.

# Chapter 25

## __Loyola Medical Center.__

*B*rangeel waited for Charlene to apply sufficient bandages to cover the now absent wounds on the patient's head. As he opened the door, he nodded to the security guard. "Thanks. You can let them in now." He waited as the three new visitors entered the room then closed the door.

Costa entered first, followed by Ryan, then Dougherty. As he looked in the direction of the bed, he noted that the patient appeared to be sleeping. He turned toward Brangeel and extended his right hand. His left held his credentials, as he was sure they would be needed. "My name is Costa." He gestured in the direction of Ryan and Dougherty and continued. "This is Dr. Ryan and Agent Dougherty."

As he took the offered hand, Brangeel nodded at Ryan and Dougherty. "Good afternoon Agent Costa. To what do we owe this pleasure?" He took the offered credentials and handed them to Harridy.

Brangeel pointed at Wong. "This is Dr. Wong. He is the head of the Neuro Department here at Loyola." He turned to Mary and Andrew and continued. "This is Mrs. Reynolds, the patient's wife and his son Andrew. This is Charlene White, the nurse assigned to this floor."

Costa eyed Harrridy curiously and wondered why a State Police officer was there. "We're following up on an incident reported this morning. Perhaps you are familiar with it?" Their response to this open ended question would tell him more than any answer they could give to a direct question.

Wong was not fooled by this approach and responded. "I assume you're referring to our miracle boy here?" He gestured toward the bed. "If so I am afraid you've wasted a trip. As I already told the

144

reporters it was simply a misunderstanding."

Costa wasted no time. "Tell me, how is Dr. Blake doing?"

Wong was not surprised they knew about Blake. "Dr. Blake is currently undergoing surgery and will not be available for sometime. Is there something we can help you with?"

Ryan had until now been a passive observer. He stepped forward and offered his hand to Wong. "Dr. Wong, my name is Tom Ryan. I am here at the request of the President's Senior Science advisor. Earlier this morning a magnetic anomaly was detected and was subsequently determined to have originated in a room near here. We are trying to ascertain the origin of the anomaly and thought perhaps you could help."

Wong took the offered hand. "I assume you are also a scientist?"

Ryan smiled. "Yes. I have a Doctorate in Physics and a Masters in Electrical Engineering." He paused, and then continued. "As you might imagine, the boys from Homeland Security" he nodded in the direction of the two agents. "Are also interested, but I can assure you not necessarily from a scientific point of view."

Brangeel laughed. "Let me see if I understand this. Some sort of magnetic anomaly occurred and you people think we are responsible? Has it occurred to you how much power it would take to create an anomaly large enough to be detected" He paused. "Let me guess, detected from orbiting satellites?" Although he was not an expert in the field, he did know the level of power required for satellite detection could not possibly be found in a hospital room.

Ryan smiled. "Actually, Doctor, I do know. And ordinarily I would agree with you. But as these charts show, it did happen and we do need to understand how." He handed the magnetic flow field charts to Wong. When he saw Costas reaction, he shrugged. "Calm down, the documents are not classified."

Wong looked briefly at the charts and asked. "So what exactly do you want to know? Surely you do not think this anomaly is related to our activities?"

Costa resumed the lead role. "I understand there was some kind of an incident involving your patient this morning. An incident which coincided with the complete loss of power to the equipment used to monitor him?"

"Yes, that did happen. But I can assure it is unrelated to the patient. He was only conscious for a few minutes at best. More than likely it was a power surge or fluctuation. I'm told the equipment is being checked out as we speak."

"Yes, we have just been advised the equipment has been checked and the electronics are fine." Costa paused. "However, they did find the hard drives were somehow erased." Ryan watched Wong's face uncertain if he understood the implication.

Wong had understood. "So you think this magnetic anomaly erased the hard drives?" That would make sense, as a sudden increase in the magnetic field density could cause erasure of magnetically coded data.

Ryan nodded. "Yes, we think there is a relationship between the magnetic flow field anomaly and what happened to your equipment. But we do not yet know the source of the disturbance."

Wong continuing his thought process audibly. "Is it possible the disturbance on these charts could simply be the result of restarting our MRI scanner? The hospital's MRI scanner was located on the third floor and would have been shut down for routine maintenance checks and of course the "topping off" of the Helium coolant. This weekly maintenance procedure was scheduled for Sunday mornings.

Ryan looked thoughtful and agreed. "Of course that's possible, but quite frankly, not very probable. The changes we saw in the magnetic field flow density would have required at least a magnitude of five teslas, certainly more than the single tesla generated by your MRI scanner. But rest assured we will take that into consideration."   .

Wong smiled. "What would happen if two superconductors were to operate within close proximity at the same time?"

Ryan nodded before responding. "That would depend on how close they were to each other. If the two magnetic fields were in close proximity with each other, it was possible that an electrical charge could have been generated between them as their magnetic fields tried to repel each other. Although he thought this scenario unlikely, it was theoretically possible that the resulting electrical charge could have caused a spike in the magnetic field density. "Why, do you have two super-conductors located here?"

146

Wong smiled. "Well, as a matter of fact we do. There is a low temperature MRI scanner on the third floor and we are currently beta-testing a newer high temperature super-conductor on the fifth floor. We hope that this new MRI scanner will replace the less efficient existing MRI scanner." While Wong did not understand the technical differences between High and Low temperature superconductors, he had been told that the operational costs of the new one were a fraction of the old. It had something to do with the availability and cost of the Helium coolant, as opposed to the newer Nitrogen coolant.

Ryan nodded. "We will certainly look into that possibility. Thank you."

Costa did not understand the technical aspects of the conversation and used the time to mentally assess the others in the room. He knew their backgrounds, and could not imagine any scenario that could account for the disturbance they were investigating. Aside from the fact none of them could have access to the highly secured weaponry, he was hard pressed to think of a motive. And even if one of them did have the means, it was improbable to think that the act could have been carried out without the knowledge of the others. While it was possible they were co-conspirators, he knew it was also improbable. Nevertheless, his instincts told him that they knew more than they were saying. He turned to Brangeel and asked. "So how is he doing?"

Brangeel, glanced first at the monitors and then at the patient before answering. "He is doing fine. Right now he is sleeping."

Costa looked again in the direction of the bed and asked. "Sleeping? Can you wake him?" If the patient could be awakened, it would save him a return trip.

Even as he said this, the patient's eyes opened. The reaction of Charlene, the nurse, was equally surprising. The instant she knew he was awake, she instinctively pulled her hands away, as if she had come into contact with a hot pan. Costa remembered the story of what had happened earlier, and now knew there was some truth in it.

As I opened my eyes, I looked around. "What's going on?" The room once again seemed to be overly crowded.

Wong heard his patient's voice and immediately turned away from Ryan. "Excuse me but I need to tend to my patient." As he approached the bed, he was careful to avoid direct contact and hoped his efforts were not obvious. He picked up the patients chart and looked at the monitors, trying hard to give the impression everything was normal. "How are you feeling?"

As I lay there and watched as the Doctor picked up the charts. I could hear his "Seven" talking to him. I could hear him advising his Wong to act naturally and to react as he would with any other patient. "I heard myself answer, the words coming automatically. "I feel fine." I could hear other voices and conversations taking place all around me. The sheer number of them was beginning to overwhelm my ability to focus. I focused my thoughts on Wong and his "Seven". The others, while still present, seemed to recede into the background.

Wong looked at the charts and nodded. "Good." He held up two fingers and asked. "How many fingers do you see?" He had expected the EEG charts to resume their normal patterns when the patient woke up. However, the monitors still reflected the same degree of abnormal activity as seen earlier.

I looked at the fingers and answered "Two."

"Good." Wong began to move his fingers in a circular motion. "Can you tell me which direction they are moving?"

His "Seven" laughed at this and told Wong. "You forgot to give him a perspective position."

I smiled. I heard his Seven's comment and answered. "From my perspective clockwise, counter-clockwise to you." On hearing my response, his "Seven" looked at me. I could hear his thoughts. "Can *he hear me"?*

Without stopping to think I answered. "Yes I can see and hear you."

Wong smiled and jokingly replied. "Well that is good news." He was pleased. The patient's response to the finger movement had answered several questions for him. His ability to recognize not only the motion but also the directional aspect told him the patient was capable of deductive reasoning.

I looked around and saw the nurse I knew to be Charlene with Brangeel standing beside her. I looked in the other direction and saw Mary and Andrew standing next to the State Police officer Harrridy. At the end of the bed there were three faces I did not recognize, surrounded by five others I did. Christie, Anne, and Franklin stood to the right of the three newcomers. Jonathan and Thomas were to their left. Jonathan appeared to be having an animated conversation with one of their Sevens. I focused my attention on Jonathan and managed to catch his final words. *"He's lying."* Angered that they had followed me and I lashed out at Jonathan. "I thought I told you to leave me alone." While I had intended this as a thought projection to the five unwanted companions, the reaction of the three newcomers told me I had spoken aloud.

Costa a trained observer of behavior, had noted Charlene's involuntary reaction to the patient, he also noted the fact that neither of the Doctors nor, for that matter, the patient's family had as yet come into contact with him. What were they afraid of? He approached the bed and extended his hand. "Mr. Reynolds, my name is Costa. I am with the Office of Homeland Security. If it is okay with you, I would like to ask you a few questions."

The surreal aspect of listening to Costa's words, while at the same time listening to his "Seven", was proving to be a difficult task. While I did not fully catch every word from his "Seven", I had heard enough to know Costa was using this opportunity to determine if the stories he had heard about the earlier events were true. I remembered my earlier discussion with Jonathan and Christie about learning to control my power. I focused my thoughts on "not" using my power. I only hoped it would be enough. I reached out and shook the extended hand, relieved to see the look of disappointment in Costa's eyes. "Office of Homeland Security? What happened? Did I commit some type of terrorist act while I was sleeping?" Inwardly, I was ecstatic. My thought control attempt had worked, now all I had to do was to learn to control it without having to focus on it.

Costa smiled. "How are you feeling?"

"I feel fine. A little bit of a headache, but otherwise okay." Even as I said this, I was aware of the unspoken dialog within his support unit, his "Six" was advising his "Seven" that there was something more going on. The "Six", as the rational and intuitive aspect of the support unit had sensed there was something more they could not see.

Costa continued. "Are you up to answering a few questions?"

He did not know how he was going to ask the questions without appearing to be foolish, but knew that they had to be asked.

"Sure, fire away. How can I help you?" I could not help but notice Jonathan and Christie glance at each other. I wondered what was worrying them.

Jonathan stepped toward me, a look of concern on his face. "I would suggest you be careful what you say. They will not understand."

Christie, for once, seemed to agree with Jonathan. "If you tell them what you know, they will think you are mentally unbalanced, by the same token if they believe you, they will consider you to be a threat. In either case you will lose." Of the two options, she much preferred the former. If they thought he was crazy they might leave him alone. On the other hand if they believed him, he would no doubt become the subject of an intense and potentially dangerous study.

Ryan, who until now had been watching and listening, could not help but notice that the patient's eyes glanced randomly in directions away from the room's participants. Equally puzzling, the patient almost seemed to be listening when no words were spoken. "Mr. Reynolds, my name is Thomas Ryan. I am here with Agents Costa and Dougherty." Ryan paused and waited for the patient to focus on him. "I understand earlier today you woke up for a few minutes?"

"Yes I remember that."

"Do you remember what happened during the time you were awake?"

"I remember seeing her." I glanced at the nurse. "Dr. Brangeel and my family were also here." I hesitated before going on. "And there was somebody named Blake."

Ryan nodded. "Do you remember anything else? Did something happen?"

I looked at Ryan. I could see his support unit as well. His "Seven" was advising him to ask about the diagnosis of Blake. "Not really, I seem to remember some sort of electrical disturbance. I think there may have been a power failure or something." Jonathan and Christie apparently relieved by my answers and were smiling.

Costa again took the lead and asked. "Do you recall talking to anyone while you were awake?" His "Seven" was also pushing for answers about Blake.

I knew where the conversation would go if I answered truthfully, and decided the best course was to claim ignorance. I tried to give the impression of trying to remember and waited a few seconds before answering. "Not really. It's all pretty fuzzy right now." For added emphasis I raised my hand and rubbed my forehead. "Why, did I say something I shouldn't have?"

Wong saw me rub my forehead and seized the opportunity to end the interrogation. He wheeled his chair between the bed and Costa and in his best professional tone said. "I think we should end this discussion and allow Mr. Reynolds time to rest. So unless you have further questions for either me or Dr. Brangeel, this meeting is over."

Costa looked at Wong and replied. "Of course, we should allow him to rest." He paused then added. "I would like to ask how you are feeling." He glanced at Wong's chair. Although he did not believe the stories, a tickling in the back of his mind made him ask. The look in Wong's eyes told him he had scored.

"I'm feeling fine, thank you for asking." Wong sensed, more than knew, that Costa had discovered his secret.

Costa smiled and nodded. "I'm glad to hear that Doctor." He turned to his companions and added. "We should go now and let Mr. Reynolds rest."

Brangeel was relieved that they were leaving and opened the door. "I hope we have been of assistance." Somehow he knew this would not be the last time they would meet.

As I lay on the bed and watched Ryan and Dougherty exit. I could hear Costa's "Seven" admonishing him to stay and ask more questions. I knew this would not be the last conversation we would have.

Costa nodded to Brangeel. "You've been of great help. If we have more questions we will contact you." With a curt nod he followed his companions through the door.

The rhythmic beeping of the monitors provided the only sounds in an otherwise silent room. As I lay there I could hear the intermingled thoughts of the others. I focused my attention on Mary and listened as her "Seven" told her to remain calm. At the same time I could hear Christie advising her to take me home. I turned my attention back to Wong and listened as his "Seven" advised him to take steps to further study what was happening to me. I heard Andrew's voice and turned in his direction.

"How are you feeling dad?"

"I'm fine Andrew. I'm ready to go home."

Mary glanced at Brangeel and asked. "Can we take him home?"

Brangeel looked first at the patient and then at Wong before he shrugged his shoulders. "I think it would be better for him to stay here for a day or two. He turned to Wong and asked, what do you think?"

Wong glanced at the monitors and nodded in agreement. "I would prefer that he stay for a few more days of observation." He paused then added. "I'm still concerned about the cranial fluid buildup. If it continues the pressure could still pose a problem." In reality he wanted to keep the patient for further study.

Mary with a look of concern on her face, nodded. "Maybe that would be best." Yet even as she said this some part of her knew it was not the best.

As I lay there watching Mary, I was partially listening to Christie who was still trying to speak to her, Mary's Seven appeared highly agitated, as he tried to block her. "He needs to get away from here, take him home." It occurred to me it was the first time I had seen Christie conversing with anyone other than myself or one of her kind. I couldn't help but remember the comments my "Seven" had made about "Sleepers" using deception and trickery. Was this a trick of some sort? I wondered to myself why she would want me away from here. What could she gain by my going home?

Andrew listened patiently to the discussion between his mother and the Doctors before interrupting them. He turned to Wong and asked. "Is my father in any danger?" If his father wanted to go home, he was going to take him there regardless of what the Doctors said.

Wong looked in Andrew's direction and nodded. "It's possible. If the pressure builds too much he could have a stroke." He paused before he added. "If that happens we would have a much better chance of treating him in a timely manner."

Andrew looked at his father then said to his mother. "Maybe it would be best if he did stay a few more days. On the other hand, I think it's his decision not ours."

Harridy, who had been silently listening, looked at Wong. "A short while ago you were thinking he was a threat, a virus or contaminate. Can I assume that is no longer the case?" While he personally did not think there was a risk, he felt obligated to ask. After all, his job was to protect the public.

Brangeel appreciating Harridy's concern shook his head before responding. "We have no evidence to warrant a quarantine protocol." He paused, then with a wry smile added. "Except of course, for the missing wound on his head." He stopped and thought how ludicrous that sounded.

Wong agreed with Brangeels assessment. "I do not think quarantine is justified given the absence of any biological causal factors." He silently wished there were, as that would have provided him the time needed to further study the patient.

I heard this talk of quarantine and it occurred to me that I had no idea what they were talking about. "Why would you want to quarantine me?"

Harridy looked at me, evidently surprised by my question. "You don't know?"

"No! If I did I would not have asked." I looked at Brangeel. "What are they talking about? What happened? And why were the Homeland Security people here?"

"You don't remember?"

"I remember getting shot, and going to some sort of clinic where a Doctor Turner worked on me. I remember waking up earlier. But I don't remember anything about being quarantined." Even as I said this, I knew I had said too much.

Brangeel, with a confused look on his face nodded to Charlene. "Remove the bandages." How was this possible? He had been unconscious, how could he have possibly have remembered the clinic.

Charlene, still uncomfortable with the thought of touching the patient removed the bandages, making a conscious effort to avoid coming into contact with him.

Brangeel nodded. He picked up a mirror and handed it to the

patient. "You remember being shot in the head?"

"Yes."

Brangeel motioned at the mirror. "Look."

I took the mirror and raised it to an angle where I could see the side of my head. The image in the mirror showed a portion of my scalp had been shaved and black sutures above the ear extended back for about two inches. At the same time I realized there was no wound. "I don't understand. What happened?"

Brangeel nodded. "We don't know." He paused. "It is physically impossible for that type of wound to heal that quickly, and then, to do so without leaving a scar. Yet as you can see, there is no scar, no evidence of a wound, except of course for the stitches."

"And that is why you were thinking of putting me in quarantine?" This must have happened while I was in the Hall of Knowledge. I certainly did not remember it.

Wong reached out and took the mirror placing it carefully on the table next to the bed. "Yes, while your miraculous healing is good, the fact we do not know how it happened does concern us."

As I lay there I focused on Wong, I heard his "Seven" chiding him. "He healed you, didn't he? Do you think he could not heal himself just as easily?" I looked at Brangeel then at Wong. "I'm going home."

Brangeel smiled. "I thought as much. You never were a good patient." He glanced at Wong and nodded. "Let's take those sutures out before he leaves, it's obvious he doesn't need them." He turned to Mary and grinned. "I'm going to want him in back here in three days for a follow-up, and I'm sure Doctor Wong would like see him as well."

Wong was disappointed but knew that Brangeel, as the patients Primary Care Physician had the final say in the patient's care. "Yes I would like to also do a follow-up." He turned to Charlene and pointed at the sutures. "Get me a removal kit." He had noticed her reluctance to come into contact with the patient and would not force her to do so. He lowered the bed into the horizontal position, one which would allow him to reach the patient from his wheelchair. He turned toward Harridy and nodded. "The patient is available if you want to ask your questions now."

Harridy took a step closer to the bed. At the same time he removed a small notebook from his breast pocket. "Mr. Reynolds, I need to ask you a few questions. That is if you're up to it."

I glanced at Harridy, then at Mary and Andrew. "Sure, what can I tell you?" I could hear his "Seven" trying to help him formulate the questions.

Harridy looked at his notebook and nodded. "What do you remember about the robbery attempt this morning?"

"Not much actually, I remember checking the tie down straps on my bike, then being pulled to the ground." I paused trying to recall the events. "I remember a voice demanding money, a loud explosion and then I blacked out."

Did you manage to get a look at your assailants?" This was what he really needed to know.

I thought back and I realized I had not been able to see their faces. "No, it was all very sudden. All I saw were two dark shapes."

"I see." Harridy busily wrote in the notebook. "Is there anything you can tell me about them? Anything that might help identify them?"

"No. I'm sorry, I really don't remember." I hesitated then asked. "Did you catch them?"

Harridy nodded. "We think so. We have an eye witness account of their vehicle, and we found a weapon not far from where they were stopped. We also found a shell casing at the scene we think will tie to the gun. It's all circumstantial, but it is enough for us to hold them." He did not share his opinion that it would not be enough and the two suspects were probably going to be freed.

"I'm sorry I cannot tell you more, but I really don't remember."

Harridy closed his notebook and placed it in his pocket. "I understand completely. I did not really expect you to, but I had to ask. You never know, we might have gotten lucky." Harridy nodded in the direction of Mary and Andrew. "Can you find your way home from here?" He had developed a fondness for the two in the short time they had spent together. "If you like, I can lead you there."

Mary smiled. "Thank you for the offer, but I'm sure you have more important things to do than baby sit us. Besides you have already done more than enough." She could always follow Brangeel if necessary.

I watched as Harridy picked up his hat from the chair and turned to leave. It occurred to me I had not thanked him for helping my family far beyond what his duty required. "Harridy! Before you leave I want to thank you for all the help you have given to my family, especially bringing Andrew to get the truck, I know you did not have to do that."

Harridy, in the act of reaching for the door, stopped. How did Reynolds know he took Andrew to get the truck? He was unconscious at the clinic, and unless it was a topic of discussion during the brief time he was awake this morning, he doubted anyone had told him. Maybe Rhodes was right about this guy. Based upon what he saw in Wong's office, it was obvious Wong thought he was healed. With the gunshot wound having healed so quickly, and the involvement of the Homeland Security people, it all added up to one thing. There was something extraordinary was going on.

As I lay there and listened to these thoughts run through Harridys mind, I decided to really have fun with him. I raised my hand and waved him closer. I hesitated, waiting until I had his full attention. "Tell Rhodes I will talk with him. In fact, why don't you pick him up and bring him to my house?"

Harridy stepped back, a look of confusion on his face. How could Reynolds know about Rhodes? Harridy had not mentioned him. Was Reynolds reading his mind? "I'm sure Rhodes would appreciate that." Then as an afterthought, added. "When would be a good time?" Harridy thought for a moment. He needed to finish his report, and wanted to change clothes. But also knew he wanted to see where this was going.

I looked at the Doctors. "How long will it take for me to be released?"

Wong looked at his watch and shrugged. "Well, to clean you up, get you dressed, and signed out, maybe an hour. Not much more than that."

"And it's an hour's ride home, why don't we plan to meet in three hours. That will give us time to off load the bike and get ready for dinner." I paused and looked at Harridy. "Is three hours enough time for you to find Rhodes?"

Harridy nodded. Contacting Rhodes would not be a problem. He knew about Rhodes desire to meet Reynolds, and had the feeling he was probably already close by. "Three hours should be plenty of time." He paused then added. "If you wait for me to get there, I will help you get the bike off of the truck."

Andrew smiled. "Thanks, but our neighbors have a ramp and will help us get it off, but it was nice of you to offer." He was also pleased his father had invited Harridy for dinner. It was the least they could do to repay him for the help he had given them. He knew his mother felt the same.

Harridy turned to leave. "I'll see you in three hours then." He nodded to the others and quietly closed the door as he left.

Wong finished removing the sutures and handed the removal kit to Charlene for disposal. He raised the bed to a sitting position and turned to Mary and Andrew, Why don't you go with Charlene to the duty desk? She will help you complete the required release forms. We'll be finished here in a moment, after your dad gets dressed he will meet you at the desk." Wong wanted a moment alone with the patient.

Wong waited until the door had closed behind them before turning his attention back to the patient. He nodded to Brangeel before grabbing the patient retention bar on the side of the bed. He pulled himself slowly out of the chair. He gently allowed his weight to shift from his arms to his back and legs, until at last he was standing at the side of the bed. Although he wavered slightly, he focused his attention on removing the adhesive strips which held the monitor leads in place. One by one the beeps and chirps of the equipment diminished. "Can you tell me what happened here today?"

Brangeel was astonished to see old friend standing unassisted. He fought the urge to rush to his side. "Well! This is surprise."

Christie, Anne and Franklin were standing with Jonathan and Thomas at the end of the bed. Anne, Franklin and Thomas not knowing Wong's history, did not seem surprised. But Christie and Jonathan, who did know, were clearly excited.

"He did it." Christie was smiling. She now knew for certain he had the power. Eldred would need to be told. She turned to Anne and said. "Tell Eldred the healing power is genuine."

Jonathan was equally excited but less surprised. They already knew the Bio had the power. His "Seven" had already confirmed it.

I looked at Wong for a few moments before I replied. "No I don't think I could." While the obvious answer was that he had been healed, the way in which it happened was not apparent. I knew I had somehow come into possession of a great ability or power, but I had no idea where it came from, or for that matter how it worked. And although I was happy for Wong, I also remembered the conversation between Christie and Jonathan about what had happened to others with similar "gifts".

Wong nodded. "I wish you would stay here and let me study you. Perhaps the answers can be found."

"I'm sorry but I cannot let that happen." I paused before I added the words I knew would not be received well by the Doctor. "In fact I need to ask you for a favor."

Wong chuckled. The man who had virtually given him his life back was asking him for a favor. "I owe you a debt I can never repay. Whatever you ask, I will do my best."

From the corner of my eye I glimpsed Christie looking inquiringly at Jonathan, who looked equally puzzled. He merely shrugged his shoulders.

I looked down at the bed sheet which still covered me. I felt terrible knowing the words I was about to say. "Doctor, perhaps you should sit down." I waited as Wong again found his chair. "I know you want to get out of that chair, and to never return to it. However, I am going to ask you to remain in the chair until I ask you to leave it." I paused then added. "And I promise you, I will ask you to." I looked at Brangeel. "I would also ask that you also keep these events quiet, at least until I ask Wong to give up his chair."

Wong with a shocked look on his face sat quietly listening. "I don't understand. I've spent the better part of my life waiting for this moment, and now that it is here, you want me to wait. Why?"

I didn't fully understand why I was asking this of him, I had no reason, no plan. Yet I sensed it was the right thing to do. Just as "I knew" to not ask, would have disastrous consequences. "I'm sorry Doctor, I know what I am asking is a lot. But, not an hour ago we had visitors from Homeland Security. I suspect if word of this reached them, they will come back, and while I am happy for you, I do not think either of us could provide an acceptable explanation for what has happened." I paused, my heart torn by the look of resignation on his face. "With any luck in a few days they will forget about this and you will be free to walk again. But please honor my request and wait for me to say when."

Brangeel, sensed his friend's frustration, looked at Wong and nodded. "You know, he's right. It would be impossible to explain what has happened to you. And you have to think about him. What do you think will happen if this gets out?" Even as he said this, he knew it would be just a matter of time. Wong would eventually get out of his chair, and when he did, Reynolds would never know another moment of peace, or for that matter, freedom. At best, this request would only delay the inevitable.

Wong looking dejected nodded. "You're right of course." He paused briefly then looked at Reynolds. "Please, don't take too long." That said, he removed the last electrical lead and slumped again into his chair.

As I lay there I could feel the emotional struggle within Wong. I could hear as his "Seven" and Jonathan tried to help him rationalize his decision. At the same time, I could hear Christie as she took an opposing position, suggesting to him that he should take advantage of his once lost abilities. As I looked at her, I could not help asking. "Why would you tell him to do that? I thought your role was to oversee them." I nodded in the direction of Jonathan and Thomas.

Christie smiled and turned to face me. "There are greater issues at stake here than just the Doctor." She paused then added. "Beside it would not serve their purpose for this to become public. Until it does they can still stop you." While she did not know Jonathan's intentions, she knew Peter and his methods. He was almost certainly going to view this as an opportunity to further his own agenda. Going public now would limit his options, something she desperately wanted to do.

Wong and Brangeel exchanged puzzled looks. Neither had spoken and as such did not understand the question. Finally, Brangeel took a small flashlight from his pocket and placed his hand on the forehead of his patient. He shone the light into one of the patient's eyes and he asked. "I don't understand, oversee who?" His concern of a concussion was alleviated by the papillary response.

Once again I chastised myself for speaking audibly. I really needed to control that or they were going to lock me up for good. I looked at Brangeel and smiled. "Sorry, I was just thinking out loud Doc." I watched his face, and at the same time saw Jonathan laughing, I knew he did not believe me. "Where are my clothes? I want to get out of here." I reached down and tossing the sheets to one side swung my legs over the side of the bed.

Brangeel put the small flashlight back into his pocket then walked to the small closet, he returned with a small white bag. The words "St. Jude's Hospital" were printed in big blue letters on its side. "I'm afraid they are a little wrinkled." This said he dumped the contents of the bag on the bed.

I looked at the pile of rumpled, dirty, and blood encrusted clothing, I had the fleeting thought of my overnight bag sitting in the truck. I looked at Brangeel and toyed with the idea of asking him to have Andrew retrieve it for me.

Brangeel looked at the pile of clothing and spoke aloud as if he had read my thoughts. "I'm going to ask Andrew to get your overnight bag from the truck." This said, he turned and left the room in search of Andrew.

Alone now with me, Wong wheeled his chair into a position facing me. "We only have a few minutes and I need to ask you something." He paused as if unsure how to continue, finally decided to come directly to the point. He nodded in the direction of Christie and the others he asked. "Can you see them?" Ever since the episode earlier in the day, he had been seeing shadowy figures, at first lacking definition, but now becoming more apparent. He had initially attributed this to a severe headache, but after watching me speaking in their direction, he knew it was much more than that.

I looked at the Doctor and smiled. "Can you hear them as well?"

Wong cocked his head as if trying to listen finally shaking his head. "Not really. I hear a buzzing sound, but nothing I can make out. Why, can you?"

For a brief moment there was silence in the room. Even

Christie and the others were quiet. Obviously they were as surprised as I.

I nodded and turned my attention back to Wong. "Yes I can, clearly, as a matter-of-fact." I paused and tried to think of the best way to explain this. "Doc, I suspect you will also be able to hear them soon. When you can, call me, we will need to talk." What was happening here? I looked in the direction of my companions, Jonathan appeared confused while Christie only smiled what appeared to be a knowing smile.

Wong nodded. "Of course, but what's going on? Do you know? Do you understand?" He was confused and in fact a little afraid.

"Not completely. But a little bit. Let's talk about it later." I sensed that telling him what I knew now would be wasted effort. Perhaps after he had time to see and hear the others as I could, he would be better prepared to accept what I would say.

The door to the room opened and Brangeel a puzzled look on his face entered. "Andrew will be here in a moment." He had found Mary at the duty desk but Andrew had already left. According to Mary, he had gone to get a change of clothes for his father. When he heard this, he was stunned. It was only then that he realized that his own efforts, and now those of Andrew, had taken place without being requested; in fact he had not even known Reynolds had an overnight bag in the truck. Reynolds had not asked him to find Andrew, and how did Andrew know his father needed a change of clothing?

A light knock at the door was followed by the face of the security guard as he peered into the room. I noticed that the guard had an ear piece similar to those used for radios. I wondered to myself if he could get the "Bears" football game.

The guard opened the door wider and allowed Andrew with my overnight bag in tow, to pass by him into the room. With a curt nod to Wong, the security guard smiled at me. "Bears won 13-10. They recovered a fumble with twenty seconds left and kicked a last second field goal for the win." The door closed silently behind him as he resumed his position outside of the room.

I smiled to myself knowing I was the only one present who knew what had prompted this announcement. "Well that's some good news." I said this to no one in particular. I took the overnight bag from Andrew, removed a clean set of clothes, and dressed to leave.

# Chapter 26

## <u>Loyola Medical Center.</u>

*H*arridy found Rhodes and it proved to be even easier than he had imagined. When Harridy left Reynolds's room he had almost collided with him getting on the elevator. Harridy took Rhodes arm and redirected him back into the elevator. He pushed the button for the Lobby floor before turning to look at his friend. He knew it was pointless to ask him what he was doing. "I thought I told you I would talk to Reynolds and call you later. What were you doing?"

Rhodes smiled. "Actually I wasn't going to see Reynolds. I was going to talk to the security guard." The guard in question was one of Rhode's confidential sources regarding hospital related issues. It was he who had heard the Cardiologists assistant talking about what had happened with Blake.

Harridy nodded. "Why did you want to see him?"

Rhodes paused before answering. He had already decided to tell Harridy what had happened, and besides Harridy was probably present at the time. "After I left you in the lobby, I went to see how "Blake" was doing, and to see if there was anything I could do to help."

Harridy smiled. "So now you're a doctor? Help with what?"

Rhodes, a look of hurt crossing his face replied. "No I'm not a doctor, but I thought perhaps I could help get his family here." He paused then added. "Of late I have had a special affinity for the families of people facing life threatening issues, I thought I could help."

Harridy nodded. "I see, and you thought maybe they were on Reynolds's floor?"

Rhodes smiled. "No, but when I returned to the lobby from the Cardio unit I saw Costa from Homeland Security getting off of the elevator. I put two and two together and figured they were here because of Reynolds. I was going to confirm it with the security guard." He paused then added. "And yes, the guard does get a bonus for his assistance."

Neither man spoke again until the elevator lurched to a stop at the lobby floor. Finally Rhodes spoke. "Were you able to talk to Reynolds?"

"Yes, we spoke." Harridy paused trying to decide how long to make Rhodes wait. He was still mulling over Rhodes' explanation. "How do you know Costa?" Harridy although an officer of the law, was also a citizen and knew well that the different levels of government had varying ideas on individual rights and freedoms. He was of the opinion most of these agencies had surpassed, even trampled the rights of the individual. And to his way of thinking, that was a crime in itself. If Rhodes was working with them or for them in some capacity, Harridy would have second thoughts about helping his friend.

Rhodes sensed Harridys motivation and was quick to dispel these thoughts. "I was appointed by the paper to be the contact point for the Homeland Security Office. As you know, they try to use us as a source for leads on terrorism and other crimes. Costa is my official contact." He paused before he continued. "When I saw him and the other two getting off the elevator I figured something had happened and thought I would look into it."

Harridy was well aware that the various law enforcement agencies had well-established relationships with the primary news groups of every type. The same could be said for his own police organization. "And what were you planning to do with the information?"

Rhodes knew it was Harridys nature to be cynical and suspicious of everyone and everything was getting angry. "Officially speaking I would do nothing. I just figured if they were involved there must be something to the stories we heard earlier." Rhodes paused then continued. "I told you earlier if Reynolds could in some way help Angelina I was going to find out."

Harridy silently thought through Rhodes statement, a process second nature to him after years of note taking in his official capacity.

"I met Reynolds and spoke to him briefly." He paused before adding. "He seems like a nice guy." Harridy did not add that in his opinion, Reynolds was definitely hiding something.

"Did you tell him about my situation?" Rhodes watched Harridys face closely; half hoping his demeanor would betray his thoughts.

Harridy could feel Rhode's eyes boring into him. "No, actually I didn't have the opportunity. Besides, there were too many people in the room and bringing you up would have been awkward to say the least." Harridy sensed more than saw the look of disappointment on Rhode's face. "However, he did say he would meet with you." Harridy smiled to himself.

Rhodes shook his head. "I don't understand. I thought you said you didn't talk to him about my situation."

"I didn't! He just seemed to know about it." Harridy paused. "Or should I say he knew about you. Angelina was never brought up in the conversation."

"But how could he know about me? Is it possible his wife or son mentioned meeting me?"

Harridy shrugged. He had been asking himself the same questions for the past half hour. "I doubt it. When I got to his room, Reynolds was still sleeping and the Doctors said he had been that way for hours. I was there the entire time and don't remember your name being brought up at all. In fact, except for a brief second, even I didn't think of you." Was it possible in that brief second Reynolds had read his mind? No that couldn't be, nobody could read another person's mind. Could they?

Rhodes sat quietly and thought of what Harridy had said. "Is it possible Reynolds somehow picked up your thoughts?" Maybe there was something to the stories. "What exactly did he say?"

Harridy shrugged. "I don't know anything about mind reading. I guess it's possible he picked up on my thoughts. He simply said "Tell Rhodes I will meet with him and even suggested we meet at his house for dinner."

"What did you say?" Rhodes was excited. This was even more than he had hoped for.

Harridy pushed open the lobby door and motioned for Rhodes

to proceed outside. "I told him we would be there in three hours." Harridy allowed the door to close before he turned back to face Rhodes. "I assume three hours is good for you?"

Rhodes, ecstatic, smiled broadly. "Two would have been better. Does that mean they're releasing him from here?" He motioned towards the lobby. "What's his address? Are you coming?" He would need to arrange for the nurse to stay with Angelina longer than planned, but did not think that would be a problem.

Harridy smiled. Finally something good was happening in an otherwise stressful day. "Yes. I will be going. In fact, I thought perhaps we could go together." Given the events of the day, he wanted to see for himself how things worked out. "I need to go to the barracks to file my report, and I want to change into civilian clothes. How about I pick you up at "Sam and Ella's" bar around five o'clock."

Rhodes nodded. "Sam and Ella's" originally a family restaurant bearing the name of the founder and his wife, had been converted into a sports bar in the early nineties. The conversion was the result of an outbreak of salmonella poisoning hundreds of miles away. Regardless, given the restaurant's name, the economic consequences forced them to change to a sports bar. And a relatively successful one, it had become a popular hangout for off duty police officers and low to medium level businessmen. "I'll be there." As an afterthought, he suggested to Harridy. "Perhaps we should take my car. I'm sure the Reynolds's would rather not have your squad car parked outside their home for the entire evening."

Harridy nodded. "Okay, I'll meet you here at five o'clock and we'll take your car." He was going to suggest they take Rhodes car and was glad Rhodes had offered. "See you then." Harridy turned and walked to his patrol car.

# Chapter 27

## <u>Sam and Ella's Sports Bar.</u>

*T*he evening crowd slowly filtered into Sam and Ella's. At four-forty-five p.m., it was still a little early for the main throng to arrive. In another hour this place would be packed with football patrons waiting for the Sunday night game. Harridy sat at the bar, a half full glass of draft beer in front of him. Ordinarily Harridy would not have been drinking, but since Rhodes was driving, he decided one would not hurt. Harridy stared at the small notebook lying open in front of him. After leaving the hospital, he had returned to the barracks and had dutifully filed his daily report. The report had been accurate in terms of facts, the victim had not able to provide a viable description of his assailants. He had driven Reynolds's wife and son to the clinic and had released the truck to the family. What the report did not contain were these notes. These were his questions regarding the events of the day. Questions like. What happened in the patient's room when he first came out of his coma? Did Reynolds really diagnose Blake's condition? What about Doctor Wong? Clearly he was hiding the fact that he was getting better, more likely already cured. And how was Reynolds able to remember people and events from the clinic? Harridy was certain Reynolds was unconscious the entire time he had been there. And what about the now healed wound? And then there was the Homeland Security involvement. While they were a suspicious bunch by nature, the administrative controls would certainly have precluded their involvement unless somebody thought something was going on. And then there was Rhodes. He had known Harold for thirty years and knew him to be as cynical as he was, cynical but honest. Rhodes had good instincts, and equally important he had the intestinal fortitude to publish the truth, regardless of the personal impact they may have had. He clearly believed this guy

Reynolds was special. And how did Reynolds know about Rhodes? Harridy was ninety-nine percent positive Rhode's name had not come up in any discussion with Reynolds. Yet Reynolds knew Harold wanted to see him.

"Still working?" Rhodes slid onto the stool adjacent to the one occupied by Harridy. "I'm not late am I?" Rhodes signaled to Ella, who was minding the bar. "Ella! Can I get a cup of coffee when you get a minute?"

Harridy glanced at Rhodes. "Hello Harold. Not really work, just gathering my thoughts about this Reynolds guy." He paused then closed the notebook and returned it to his shirt pocket. "What about you? How are you doing?" Harold's usually rumpled suit had been replaced by a turtleneck shirt and sweater ensemble. Harridy was feeling better about his own attire, a flannel shirt and jeans. "I take it you didn't have any problem getting the nurse to stay with Angelina for the evening?"

Rhodes stirred his coffee thoughtfully. "No! At a hundred bucks an hour she was happy to oblige." Having said this he immediately felt guilty. The money wasn't the issue. He would have gladly paid ten times that amount to avoid having to bear witness to the pain Angelina was going through. At the same time, his sense of guilt almost overwhelmed him. He knew he was being selfish, Angelina wanted more than anything for him to be with her. "I just pray this guy Reynolds is for real."

Harridy lifted his glass slowly and took a sip of beer. He could see Harold's pain and didn't know how to respond. Having never married he could only imagine the sense of hopelessness and loneliness that his friend must be feeling. "Harold, I don't know whether Reynolds is real or not, at least in the way you wish him to be, but I do know he has some kind of extraordinary capabilities, and if anyone can help it will be him." Saying this Harridy immediately wished he could take it back. The last thing he wanted was to increase the level of disappointment for his friend if things did not work out. "I'll tell you what. On the way to Reynolds's house I'll use you as a sounding board for my questions. Maybe between the two of us we can figure this out." Harridy hoped this would help Harold keep his expectations under control, or at the very least, his mind off his problems. Harold was an educated astute person, one who might be able to provide valuable insight to his questions, perhaps based upon things he had seen during his time as a reporter.

Rhodes nodded. He knew Harridy was trying to help in his own way and appreciated the effort. "Thanks Tom. Do you think we should go now?" Harold's watch beeper was emitting a shrill beeping sound. It was five o'clock.

Rhodes buckled his seatbelt, something he rarely did because he felt it was too restrictive. Angelina had always questioned his wisdom on the matter, especially given the number of accidents he had covered as a reporter. Accidents where the victims had been thrown through windshields and sometimes even side windows. Still, he remembered the one or two times where the use of the seatbelt had actually caused the death of the users. In his heart he knew she was right, hopefully the current problems would work out and their perpetual disagreement would continue for many more years. Harold watched as Harridy again opened his notebook. "Okay Tom, what's so perplexing?"

Harridy smiled. He was glad to see Harold had regained his composure. "I don't know where to start. There are so many incongruities." Harridy paused then added. "What makes you think Reynolds can actually heal people?" Harridy was hoping getting Harold to start the conversation might help him focus on the issues.

Harold flipped the turn signal lever down. At the same time he twisted his head to the left to verify it was safe to change lanes. After resuming his normal position he replied. "When I was in college I did a little research on the subject as part of my philosophy studies. At the time there was a priest, or I should say a mystic, in India who people claimed had the power to heal all types of illnesses. That in itself is not unusual, most eastern cultures have similar beliefs. Unfortunately there are few actual historical records to support their claims. Even so I was amazed by the number of people who believed in this mystic." He paused then added. "The few people we were able to interview who claimed to have been healed by the mystic, reported feeling energy similar to a mild electric current pass through them when the mystic touched them. The pre and post medical records that we reviewed did support their claims that the illness or whatever was ailing them, had simply disappeared." Rhodes paused then added. "Even without those records the sheer number of people who believe in it make me inclined to think there is, or was, some solid foundation to support the possibility."

Harridy having sat quietly listening to Harold finally spoke. "What did you find in the case of the Indian mystic?"

Rhodes shrugged. "We made a number of inquiries but never heard back." He paused, a frown on his face. "About a year later we received a letter from one of his students saying that the "Doctor" had moved on to a higher plane and could no longer be contacted." Harold shook his head. "We never again heard about him, or for that matter heard of any other healings where he was involved."

"What did they mean by "higher plane"? Is that academic talk for died?" Harridy had a sense of what was meant, having investigated a mid-western cult in the seventies.

Rhodes leaned his head to one side, a pensive look on his face. This was another of those philosophical arguments from so long ago. "There are those who believe that our "being" or "consciousness" evolves from lower planes to ever higher ones as wisdom is achieved. They say the goal is to transcend the need for the physical body, to become a state of energy or spiritual purity." He paused, before continuing. "I've studied enough philosophy to become an agnostic and don't place much credence in the various doctrines."

Harridy looked at Harold. "What does that have to do with the healing power?" Harridy stopped then added. "In any case I am reasonably sure Reynolds is not a practitioner of some remote far eastern religion."

Rhodes shrugged. "You asked me about the various planes of existence and I answered. Although some of the religious practices, like meditation, may allow a person to access these abilities, I personally don't think the healing power is the result of a religious doctrine. That being said, it naturally follows that this healing ability must already reside within us. Or in this case in Reynolds. Scientists, even our Doctor Wong, will tell you that humans use only a fraction of their brains. Some believe we are capable of using many powers, including that of being able to heal. The real question is, did whatever happened to Reynolds somehow allow him to access those aspects of his brain?"

Harridy quietly digested what Harold had said. He remembered the EEG monitors and Wong's comments about unusual electrical synaptic activity taking place in Reynolds's brain. Was it possible the gunshot had in some way "re-routed" his wiring, reopened pathways to these capabilities? Harridy made a notation in his notebook to remind himself to follow this line of reasoning with Wong. He turned his attention back to Rhodes. "Harold something else happened that I don't understand." He paused then continued. "Before he left the hospital, Reynolds was able to describe the events that took place at the St. Jude's Medical center. He described the procedure and even the name of the Doctor who worked on him." Harridy paused before adding. "I was there and I know for a fact he was unconscious the entire time. How could he have known?"

Rhodes looked in Harridys direction. "You're joking! He was able to do that?" He saw the look on Harridy's face and knew it was not a joke. Rhodes shrugged his shoulders. "Same answer as before!" He paused before adding. "There are many documented cases where people in life-threatening situations have reported what is commonly referred to as "out of body experiences". Generally those involved had nearly died, and were then brought back at the last moment." Rhodes looked at Harridy. "I didn't know Reynolds had been that close to death."

"He wasn't. According to Doctor Turner Reynolds was never in real danger of dying." Harridy made another note to re-check this with Turner. "I don't suppose this is another one of those "super-powers" like the healing one?"

Rhodes shrugged. "I do not think anyone knows what latent abilities we have. I guess it's possible." This was getting interesting. In a few short minutes Harridy had confirmed his suspicions. Reynolds had somehow managed to tap into abilities scientists had only theorized existed within the brain. He remembered Harridy's earlier comment about Reynolds having agreed to meet with him and knew what the next subject. "Let me guess. The next question is related to Reynolds seeming to be able to read minds?" The look on Harridy's face told him he had scored.

Harridy nodded. "Yes, there were a few times when he seemed

to know what people were thinking. It was almost like he anticipated their thoughts." Harridy thoughtfully added. "Take yourself for example. I did not bring you up during the conversation, but, I did think to myself that maybe you were right about Reynolds healing Wong. Maybe that was when he "picked up" on your name." Harridy was uncomfortable with the thought that someone else had the ability to know what he was thinking. Although in his line of work this capability would be a nice tool to have. "I suppose this also fits the "latent" capability scenario?"

Rhodes smiled and nodded. "Yes I suppose it does." This just kept getting better, if the events were real Reynolds appeared to have the power to heal, but also the power of telepathy. "I'm surprised Wong allowed him to leave the hospital. It seems to me he would want to keep Reynolds to further study him."

Harridy looked out the window and watched as their exit came into sight. "Wong did not want him to be released, but he had no choice. Reynolds decided to check himself out." Harridy found himself thinking about the Homeland Security guys. Did they suspect what he and Rhodes did? As he thought through it, he decided they couldn't know. They were not present when most of these intangible events took place. Still, they must have some suspicions. Harridy knew their type. He knew as well that they weren't done investigating.

Rhodes exited the Elgin-O'Hare expressway heading west into the village. Another five minutes and they would be at Reynolds's home. As he made the final turn to the Reynolds's street, he was forced to swing wide to avoid a dark van parked three or four houses down from Reynolds's house. "Somebody should ticket that guy. He's blocking the road."

Harridy also saw the van, but immediately knew it would not be ticketed. The rear bumper of the van had a bright orange sticker with an American flag emblazoned on it. Harridy recognized it from the monthly briefing books. This month that decal identified this as a law enforcement vehicle. No policeman would approach the vehicle for fear of disrupting a surveillance operation. He motioned for Rhodes to continue. "It would seem the Homeland Security guys are keeping an eye on Reynolds as well."

Rhodes looked at Harridy. "You mean the van is theirs?" He wondered how they knew Reynolds was here, and then grinned at his own naiveté. Of course, they had probably had him in their sights even at the hospital. He smiled to himself as he pictured their expressions when he and Harridy made their appearance.

Harridy nodded. "Yes, the orange sticker on the bumper is this month's code for official vehicles. They do that to make sure their operation is recognized by the local police."

Rhodes eased the car to the side of the street and parked it one house away from the Reynolds home. He recognized Reynolds's wife immediately and assumed the man standing with her to be her husband, although the man did not have bandages as he had expected. "Is that him?"

Harridy glanced at Reynolds. "Yes. And that is his wife Mary standing next to him." The pickup truck with a ramp now attached was in front of the driveway. Harridy could see Andrew standing in the truck loosening the straps that held a motorcycle in place. A man in his forties and two younger men stood by the ramp waiting for Andrew to roll the bike back to them.

Rhodes continued to look at Reynolds. "Where are his bandages?" Given he had been shot in the head he had expected him to be heavily bandaged.

Harridy grinned. "Oh yeah, I forgot to tell you. He is also completely healed. In fact there is no evidence to suggest he had even been shot." He paused and with a short laugh added. That is except for the really bad haircut." Harridy had not had time to prepare Rhodes for this revelation. He also knew that doing so would only bolster Rhodes expectations, and as well his level of disappointment if things did not work. Harridy opened the car door and exited onto the sidewalk. Rhodes joined him a few seconds later.

Mary watched as a car came to a stop in front of their neighbor's house. She saw Harridy unfold himself from the car and grinned and waved to him, she recognized Rhodes from the earlier meeting in the hospital lobby, she gently pulled her husband toward the newcomers. "Bill, this is Harold Rhodes. And of course you know Sergeant Harridy."

I glanced at Harridy and Rhodes and nodded hello. "Hi! I'll

be right with you. I need to keep an eye on those yahoos." I looked back in the direction of the truck where the older man had positioned himself at the front of the ramp. One of his sons was behind him and the third person, one of Andrew's friends, stood to the right of the ramp, waiting. Andrew, astride the motorcycle, used his feet to propel it backward onto the ramp. Apparently Andrew was planning to ride the bike down the ramp while the other three supported him. I knew this process was risky and decided to intervene before somebody got hurt. "Andrew! Don't ride that thing down, it's too heavy." I was not exaggerating. The motorcycles from the sixties were made of steel, not the light weight aluminum used today. That bike weighed over nine hundred pounds and one slip could crush a person. Even as I said this I knew it was too late. The rear wheel of the motorcycle had reached the initial slope of the ramp, George, the older man, had grabbed the front left handlebar while his son held the left rear of the seat. I watched as the bike began to cant sharply to the right, falling away from the two men. I heard George yell at Andrew to get off, as he was losing his grip. I watched as the angle of the bike shifted dramatically to the right. Clearly they were losing control and if Andrew did not get off quickly he ran the risk of being crushed when the motorcycle landed on the ground. These events seemed to be happening as if in slow motion. I sensed more than saw Harridy dash forward to help. Even so, I knew he would be too late. I felt a sense of panic rise in me, and instinctively reached my hands toward the bike. As if doing so would help. As I reached out, I felt a sudden sense of calm overcome me. I watched mesmerized as the motorcycle, now at a forty degree angle, stopped falling. It was as if some unseen hand was holding it in mid-air. I watched as Andrew leaped off of the bike onto the ground then rolled out of danger. I saw Harridy also move away from the suspended bike. To my amazement, the motorcycle seemed to right itself. It rolled easily down the ramp and onto the street. George grabbed the handlebar and immediately placed the kickstand down. It wasn't until later that I realized George and his son had instinctively moved out of the way when the bike began to fall and that the bike had not been supported by anyone as it rolled down the ramp. With the motorcycle now safely on the ground, I felt myself wavering. My knees wobbled and I began to fall. Fortunately, Rhodes and my wife caught me before I fell. "What happened?"

Mary, her face pale, looked at Rhodes and then at me. Even though she had witnessed the other weird events as had the others, she was at a loss to explain what had happened. "You don't know?" She nodded at Rhodes and indicated he should help her ease me into a sitting position on the ground. "Stay here. I'll get a towel."

Rhodes motioned for her to wait and reached into his pocket. He removed a small handkerchief and handed it to her. "Use this. It's just a nosebleed." Rhodes glanced in Harridy's direction as if looking for him to confirm the events he had just witnessed. Unless his imagination had been working overtime, Reynolds could now add telekinesis to his list of powers. "Good work Harridy. You probably saved Andrews life." Rhodes knew Harridy had not been responsible, but needed Harridy to confirm it. This was one of those times when a camera would have been good to have on hand. Unbeknownst to him, the entire sequence of events had been captured on film.

The van's interior was cramped with surveillance equipment. A tri-pod with a high resolution video camera sat on the floor, its lens pointed out the darkened rear panel windows. Randy Mosser, freelance surveillance technician, had spent the morning watching football when the Homeland Security Office had called with this one day assignment. Times being what they were, he didn't need the job, but decided at the last minute that maintaining a good working relationship with the big boys could pay dividends in the future. As he sat working on a crossword puzzle, he had glanced up when he heard the red headed guy yell something about losing his grip. Randy sat mouth agape and watched the events unfold. Even as he watched, his brain told him he didn't see what he thought he had seen. He scrambled into the rear of the van and hit the rewind button on the video unit. After two minutes, he hit the play button and watched as the scene was re-enacted. He hadn't imagined it. That motorcycle should have fallen yet didn't. It seemed as if it had been offloaded without help from anyone nearby. What made the scene even more surreal was the video image clearly showed a whitish looking streak between his mark and the motorcycle. Excitedly he removed his cell phone and pressed the speed dial option for the local Homeland Security Office.

# Chapter 28

## **Homeland Security Office.**

*T*he conference room table was cluttered with files and papers. Costa sat at the end farthest from the door. This allowed him to observe the activities taking place in the computer console area or the "pit" as they referred to it. After he had left the hospital, he and Ryan had joined the rest of the team in the formal debriefing process mandated by procedures. While Costa did not understand the technical aspects of what Ryan had said, the gist of it was that there was a slim probability that the magnetic anomaly or disturbance could be attributed to the positional relationships of the super-conductors Wong had mentioned. Theoretically, such a relationship could generate an electrical charge of a magnitude great enough to create the disturbance seen, the lack of evidence suggested that was not the case. In the end, his opinion was that the cause of the disturbance was still unknown. From Costa's perspective, the only good news was that Ryan was convinced the disturbance was not the result of a weapons grade EMP discharge. However, Costa still had a lingering apprehension that something was happening that he could not explain. Something he sensed, more than knew, involved Reynolds. The rest of the de-briefing went as expected and the meeting was about to adjourn when he received a call from the Loyola Medical Center Chief of Security John Larsen. Larsen reported that the patient Reynolds had signed himself out of the hospital. Of greater interest was the fact there was no evidence of bandages or signs of the trauma that had placed him there in the first place. Costa had been shot and knew well the body did not recover so quickly and these events only reinforced his growing suspicions about Reynolds. He decided to follow his instincts and requested Buchannon take steps to place Reynolds under "boot" surveillance. While the agency had many means at its disposal to track Reynolds, using a "free-lance" operator was far more cost efficient than the expensive satellite resources. According to Buchannon, the "operator" had successfully set up surveillance near the Reynolds home only minutes before Reynolds had arrived along with his wife and son.

Ryan sat across the table, closed his file, and glanced at his watch. As he had not eaten since the previous evening his stomach had been grumbling for the past half hour. He looked in the direction of Costa and finally decided to broach the subject. "Can I buy you an early dinner? My flight to Washington doesn't leave for another three hours and I'm starving." Ryan wasn't enamored with the idea of having dinner with Costa but knew it was his only choice.

Costa looked up from his files. "Sure just give me a minute to secure these files." He liked Ryan, but at the same time knew they were at opposite ends of the social spectrum. Given a good reason, he would happily have declined the offer. As he turned toward the file cabinet, he was stopped by the insistent ringing of the telephone. Costa replaced the files on the table with one hand and picked up the phone with the other. "Costa here." Costa listened to the voice on the other end of the phone. "Are you sure?" He hesitated and again looked in Ryan's direction. "Okay, bring them up. I'll tell him. Thanks!" Costa replaced the phone in its cradle with a look of consternation on his face. "Well Doctor it would appear that dinner and for that matter your flight will need to wait." He paused before he continued. "That was the Regional Director. It seems there has been another "disturbance". The charts are being brought up as we speak." Costa looked at Ryan, only a little pleased by the expression of incredulity on his face.

Ryan was clearly surprised and a little dismayed but simply nodded. "Were they able to pinpoint the source? Was it the hospital again?" If it was and they could show that the super-conductors were in operation, it may be enough to validate Wong's theory.

Costa smiled. "Yes, they were able to triangulate the position of the disturbance. And no, it was not at the hospital." Costa grinned to himself. His instincts were once again right. "This disturbance took place about twenty-five miles from here." Costa paused and knew how his words would affect Ryan. It came from the residence of a certain Mr. Reynolds." As he said this, Costa punched the intercom switch on the phone. "Jim, send a team to Reynolds's address. I need him detained." Costa paused, and then added. "And Jim, keep it low profile if you can." The last thing Costa wanted was another media event, at least until they had something concrete to work with.

Buchannon simply responded, his voice devoid of emotion. "Yes sir I'll take care of it personally." Buchannon was silent for a moment then added. "Sir, Mosser is on the other line and I think you need to hear what he has to say."

Costa hesitated before he responded. "He's our local surveillance guy, right?"

"Yes sir. And according to what he is telling me he has some interesting video for us to review." Buchannon was already making arrangements for the video to be fed into the system. "It should be available in about two minutes."

Costa looked at Ryan quizzically. "Thanks Tom. We'll be looking for it. In the meantime have Mosser stay with Reynolds until you have him in custody." Costa punched the button and disconnected the call. He looked at Ryan. "Buchannon said there is a video feed we need to see." As he moved to the computer console, Costa keyed his access code and selected the file listed as "Mosser feed". The file had been edited to show only the last five minutes of the feed. That five minutes of video left both Costa and Ryan speechless.

Ryan was still trying to understand what he had seen and sat quietly, staring at the screen. Surely there had to be an explanation. It simply wasn't possible for the laws of physics to be broken as the video had shown. He had always scoffed at the scientists who pursued the line of thinking that humans had enhanced capabilities, but now he wasn't so sure. A thought suddenly occurred to him. He looked at Costa and debated whether to ask. "Costa, is there a time stamp on that feed?"

Costa understood immediately where Ryan was going, replayed the video. The date and timestamp were clearly visible in the lower right corner of the screen. Costa picked up the phone and punched in the number of the Director's office. "Sally? This is Costa. Could you look at the magnetic chart data and see if there is a timestamp for the disturbance? There is. Good, what is it? Okay understood. Thanks Sally. No I will speak with him later. Thanks. Goodbye." Costa replaced the phone before turning to Ryan. "The disturbance occurred at roughly five thirty our time." The time on the video feed had said five-thirty pm.

# Chapter 29

## <u>Reynolds Home.</u>

*A*s I sat on the porch steps, I leaned my head back in an effort to stop the nosebleed; my mind replayed the events of the past few minutes. I knew I had somehow used my mind, or my energy, or something else to keep the bike from falling. I also knew that the others were suspicious and that I had been responsible. Strangely, with the exception of a look of amazement on Rhode's face, the others did not appear surprised at all. Rhodes was now standing in front of me and seemed at a loss for words. I looked at him and smiled. "So, you're Rhodes! I have read your columns and articles for years and I don't mind telling you I am an ardent admirer of your work."

Rhodes, as usual, uncomfortable with praise, blushed slightly and extended his hand. "Let me formally introduce myself. Yes, I am Rhodes, but let's dispense with the formalities. "Why don't you just call me Hal or Harold?" Rhodes paused. "And you must be William Reynolds. From what I've heard, you have had an eventful day." Rhodes stopped, not wanting to push the issue too quickly.

I smiled. "Call me Bill. And yes, it has been interesting to say the least." I looked at Mary who hovered over me like a mother hen. "You've met my wife Mary and son Andrew?"

As he nodded Rhodes glanced at Andrew and Harridy who were in the process of wheeling the motorcycle into the garage. "Yes, I had that pleasure earlier today at the hospital." Rhodes returned his gaze to me. "He seems like a good kid. You should be proud."

I laughed at this. "Oh he has his moments."

Mary heard this and slapped her husband. "Stop that, you know damn well he's a good kid." She looked at Rhodes and added. "Pay no attention to him. He's as proud of Andrew as a father could be. And you should see how he dotes on our other son Eric." She

180

didn't say it, but she was concerned that Eric had not come home yet. Surely he must have gotten her message, cryptic as it was. Mary looked at Andrew who had emerged from the garage. "Andrew while you're in there would you get the grill and bring it around back." She hesitated then added. "Please?" Returning her attention to Rhodes and Harridy she added. "I didn't have time to cook anything special and I don't want to go out to dinner given his condition, so I thought we might grill up some burger and brats. I also picked up some fresh sweet corn if you like corn on the cob."

Harridy and Rhodes nodded almost in unison. "That would be great." Harridy laughed then added. "Is there anything I can do to help?"

Mary nodded, and then slapped me on the back. "Yes! You can escort this scoundrel out back and see that he doesn't get into any more trouble." She laughed then added. "I'll bring some iced beer out so you boys can sit and talk." This said, she climbed the stairs and entered the house.

Harridy reached down and grasped me by one arm while he grabbed Harold by the other. "You heard her boys, let's go." Andrew carried the grill past them and laughed. "Are you arresting him officer?"

Harridy smiled. "Not yet. Just playing escort." He walked between the two as they made their way around the bushes toward the backyard. As he had not eaten, the prospect of burgers and brats sounded good.

The rear deck was an immense two tiered and very expensive affair. The primary deck at twenty by thirty feet descended eight stairs to another sixteen by twenty foot second deck which then extended in a semi circle around the now closed swimming pool. I uncovered the patio chair, removed the winter cover, and set it aside. Harridy and Rhodes did the same for their respective chairs. The pungent smell of lighter fluid wafted in the air as Andrew lit the charcoal. Mary descended the stairs with three bottles of beer, the condensation beads slowly dripping from the bottles. Although it was September, the evening was mild. The earlier rain clouds had dissipated and the sky, although clear was beginning to melt into the grey of early evening. I took the offered bottle. I removed the twist off cap and raised it in a

181

salute. "Here's to the end of a memorable day and to new friends." I waited as Harridy and Rhodes raised their bottles and tapped mine before taking the first sip. I placed my bottle on the table and leaned back in my chair. I was vaguely aware that my unwanted companions still hovered nearby. It was evident they were going to stick close to me regardless of where I went. I focused my attention on Rhodes. His "Seven" and "Three" were like bookends on either side of him. His "Seven" appeared anxious and advised Rhodes to talk about Angelina. I looked at Rhodes and said. "Tell me about Angelina." Inwardly, I smiled at the look of confusion on his face.

Rhodes glanced at Harridy with a look that spoke volumes. "How do you know Angelina?" Harridy was right! This guy could either read minds or knew more about him than he had originally portrayed.

I looked at Rhodes and smiled. "She is your wife?" When I said this, Christie and Jonathan stopped talking and crowded forward to listen to the conversation. I continued. "And she is ill?" Rhodes thoughts were crystal clear to me, even without his "Seven's" input. I knew in that moment my abilities were becoming second nature to me.

Rhodes was shaken by the conversation but nodded. "Yes, she is my wife and yes, she is very ill." He paused then asked. "How did you know?" Since Angelina had been diagnosed, Rhodes had made an effort to keep the knowledge within a tight circle of friends, and Reynolds was not part of that circle. Maybe Harridy had mentioned it to him and just didn't want him to know he had done so.

I smiled at this thought. "No, Harridy didn't mention you or your wife to me." I hesitated then added. "As you may have figured out by now, I seem to have acquired some strange abilities. Apparently one of them is the ability to read other peoples thoughts." I glanced at his "Seven" and was gratified to see the look of surprise on his face. I re-focused my attention on Rhodes. "And you want me to help Angelina."

Rhodes with his mind reeling merely nodded. "Can you?" He had only half believed what Harridy had told to him on the drive over. He was quickly becoming a believer.

As I sat there pondering Rhodes question, I remembered the events that had taken place earlier in the day with Wong. I also remembered the reaction of Jonathan and Christie when my "Three" replayed the event. Both had been concerned with the impact felt in the non-physical realm. In fact, Jonathan had implied that while the disturbance had not upset the fundamental dynamics, it had caused some sort of disruption. I looked at Jonathan and Christie who still stood close to me. Although I knew both had agendas of their own, I was equally sure they had far more experience in these types of matters than I. Minimally they had a better understanding of the potential impact on the dynamics, dynamics I was only now beginning to understand. In spite of my reservations I decided to ask for their input. "What do you two think?" I watched as Harridy and Rhodes exchanged looks. I had again verbalized my thoughts and they thought I was asking them. I raised my hand palm outward and told them. "I'm sorry, I wasn't asking you. I was asking someone else." Harridy and Rhodes, their faces portraying confusion, looked around but of course there was nobody else there.

Jonathan was the first to speak. "I would suggest that you should not use your powers until you understand them better." What he did not say was until "he" understood them better. Jonathan had sensed Arinons concern and was sure Arinon would not want this power to be used under any circumstance.

Christie listened as Jonathan gave his advice and noted it was posed as a suggestion. Not surprisingly, she took the opposing viewpoint. "I suggest you should help if you can. And, I might add, while you can. You don't know how long you will be able to use these powers" She paused then added. "It's entirely possible that when your cranial pressure is relieved, you may lose these new abilities. You should do something good while you can." While she didn't know Eldred's thoughts on the issue, she was sure that taking a position opposite to Arinons camp was always the safer approach.

I was not surprised they had taken opposing positions and had anticipated them doing so. I also knew that before this was over, I was going to make it a point to better understand their roles and their goals. "What affect will it have on the "dynamics" you were concerned with earlier?" As neither had brought this up I decided asking directly was the best course of action.

Christie nodded then replied. "While it may be disruptive to the natural energy flow, I do not think it would be powerful enough to change the underlying dynamics." She looked at Jonathan and asked him. "Can we agree on that point?"

Jonathan shook his head in agreement. "As much as it pains me, yes, I agree with that assessment." The agreement that bound the two groups and which dictated the do's and don'ts precluded the use of outright deception, otherwise known as forthright lying. Subtle deception was of course permitted, like not telling the whole truth. But when asked directly, they were obligated to tell the truth.

Harridy sat quietly watching Reynolds's face. Reynolds seemed to be having some sort of non-verbal conversation with the night air. He did not want to interrupt and sat patiently sipping his beer, with the smell of cooking hamburgers on the evening breeze. Harridy glanced at Rhodes, whose full attention was now on Reynolds. It was obvious Rhodes now fully believed Reynolds could help Angelina. Harridy could only hope his faith was not being misplaced. A slight movement in the shadows caught Harridys eye. His sense of awareness, finely tuned after thirty years of police-work, came to the forefront. Someone, or something, was stealthily approaching them. Harridy glanced toward the line of trees bordering the yard on the other side of the porch and was sure he saw another shadow move slightly. Harridy slowly reached out his foot and tapped Rhodes in an effort to get his attention. He leaned forward as if to tie his shoe and removed the .38 revolver from his ankle holster. At the same, time he whispered to Rhodes. "Get Andrew and Mrs. Reynolds into the house. I think we have company." Harridy waited as Rhodes rose from his chair and climbed the stairs to the upper landing.

"Mary, could I use your bathroom?" Rhodes had not seen anything to suggest they were in danger, but trusted Harridys instincts and would do as requested.

Mary was busy turning the burgers and gestured to the door. "Of course, there's one just off the kitchen."

Rhodes nodded. "Thanks, but I really think you and Andrew should show me where it is." Rhodes caught her eye and nodded his head imperceptibly. "Now!" If she didn't catch this hint, he would grab her and pull her inside.

Fortunately, Andrew had understood. He took his mother's

arm and guided her toward the door. "Okay mom, let's show the city slicker how to find a country bathroom." He looked over his shoulder at his father and Harridy who had successfully palmed the gun in his hand. Andrew was torn and desperately wanted to join his father.

Rhodes reached out and opened the screen door to the kitchen to allow Mary and Andrew to enter before him. His efforts were interrupted by the presence of a man in a dark suit who stood in the doorway holding a nine millimeter pistol. Rhodes recognized Buchannon immediately. "What are you doing? You have no right to be here and certainly no right to enter a private home without cause." Rhodes was well known in the journalistic circles for his staunch opposition to the administration's "Patriot" Act. In his opinion this, single piece of legislation had stripped away any true rights the American citizens thought they had. Now his worst assessment was being played out and he was part of the play.

Harridy, his muscles taut in anticipation, was not surprised when two black clothed security officers vaulted over the porch railing. He had raised his gun at the first sight of movement and was now forced to lower it if only to prevent Reynolds from being caught in a cross fire. "What is the meaning of this? Why are you bothering these people? They have not broken any laws, have they?" Harridy was furious and at the same time ashamed. These were his fellow law enforcement brothers, men sworn to uphold the rights of citizens. Not trample them.

Buchannon stood at the top of the stairs and nodded in the direction of one of the black suited officers. "Take his weapon." Buchannon looked at Harridy, then turned to Rhodes and said. "Well, if it isn't Harold Rhodes! What are you doing here?" Buchannon smiled to himself. He had read many of Rhodes stinging articles and was enjoying this moment immensely. "Looks like you'll be able to give a first hand "realistic account" this time." He paused then added. "Be sure to mention how efficient we were."

Rhodes shook his head. "You can be sure of it. I will also mention the pending lawsuit as well. What gives you the right to barge into a private home, and I am of course going to assume you don't have a warrant." Rhodes knew he was wasting his time. The revised Patriot Act allowed any law enforcement group to bypass the legal niceties as long as doing so was part of a legitimate investigation. "Now what! Are you going to arrest all of us? That might be a little hard to justify, don't you think?" While he knew they had the power to arrest them, Rhodes also knew they would think twice before doing so. Arresting him would result in some very embarrassing journalistic fallout and he was equally sure Harridys service and reputation would also give them pause.

Buchannon smiled. "Sorry Harold. No story there. No! We just want to have a more detailed discussion with Mr. Reynolds." Costa's orders were clear. Simply bring Reynolds into custody. The others would be collected later if necessary.

As I stood watching and listening, I could feel the warmth of anger rising within me. Aside from the obvious danger presented to my family, I was also offended by the brutal assault on what I had perceived as my rights as a citizen. I looked in the direction of the black clad officer who was holding Harridy at bay, his gun cocked. Based upon the thoughts emanating from him, he was willing to use it. I visualized the officer throwing his gun down onto the deck floor and raising his hands in surrender. Almost immediately the events I had visualized transpired. The figure dropped his weapon and raised his hands as if to surrender. Using the same technique, I focused my thoughts on the other figure and on Buchannon as well, with equal results.

Harridy stood and watched as the events unfolded. He did not know what had happened, only that the tables had somehow been turned on the Homeland Security Officers. He reached down and picked up the weapon at his feet and made sure to place it into a safe mode before he placed it gently on the table in front of him. He looked at me and nodded. "I suppose you're responsible for this?" For the first time Harridy was beginning to fear his new friend, or the power his friend seemed to possess.

I nodded. "Yes it would appear I am." I turned to Buchannon. "Did it ever occur to you that I would have come willingly? That you did not need to jeopardize my family and friends." I looked at Rhodes, whose face glistened with sweat in spite of the evening chill. "Bring her to me tomorrow at three o'clock. Bring her to where you first met my wife." I was sure the cryptic nature of my words would not be understood except by my family, Rhodes and Harridy. "Do you understand?"

Rhodes shook his head. "I understand and thank you." He was also beginning to fear me yet at the same time grudgingly admired my willingness to fight back.

I smiled at Rhodes and nodded, then looked at Buchannon. "I'm ready to go when you are. I assume you will leave my family out of this?" I knew this would be interpreted correctly for what it was, a veiled threat. He had witnessed what I was capable of I knew he had no choice but to agree.

Buchannon nodded, although he had been angered and more than a little surprised by what had transpired. He knew his options were limited to one. "Agreed." This said he motioned for the black clad officers to take me into custody.

As I stood and watched the officer's approach, I had the sensation of lightheadedness associated with fainting. The last thing I remembered was the two officers reaching for me as they tried to place some type of plastic handcuffs on me. The events which followed, while not known to me at the time, were told to me later by my son Andrew. According to him, as soon as the officers took my arms, I simply vanished and left them holding nothing but air.

# Chapter 30

## **On the Line.**

*T*he sensation of being light headed began to subside. I was again able to focus my senses. It was obvious I was in a new place. A place I can only describe as grey. In every direction, all I could see was the color grey. Equally important was the realization that for the first time since this ordeal began, my companions were not evident. Even Jonathan and Christie, who seemed to be able to follow me wherever I went, were gone. As I looked at my new surroundings, I was amazed to see I stood on what appeared to be a path. I walked to the edge of the path and looked down. The sight below was absolutely mind boggling. I could see the porch where I had been standing only moments earlier. Harridy, Rhodes, my wife and son still stood as I last saw them. The black clad officers and the one Rhodes had called Buchannon, were also standing as I left them. The look on their faces was, to coin a term, "priceless". A voice came from behind me and interrupted my moment of amusement.

"Amazing isn't it?"

I turned around and found myself facing a seemingly spectral being. The shape was dressed in what looked to be a grey robe. I laughed to myself. Given the events of the past fourteen hours, I was not surprised to find myself in yet another aspect of what was turning out to be a new definition of reality. I glanced again at the scene below me before answering this new acquaintance. "Yes it is. Where am I now?" It was evident this was something completely new. In the earlier separation my physical being had remained in the physical world and only my non-physical self had interacted in the other realm. In this case, it was clear that my full being had in some way changed realms. "And where are my companions?" Strangely, I somehow missed them.

The grey robed figure laughed. The newcomer's lack of surprise and resigned acceptance to this new reality was amusing to her. "You are in the area we call the between."

I turned again to the scene below. "So this is the between? Where are the others?" Based upon the description of the between state given during my earlier visit with my "Seven" and of course the Hall of Understanding I had expected to find tormented essences and their "Sevens", none of which were apparent.

The grey figure laughed again. She read my mind and understood immediately the confusion. "No. You don't understand. This is not the same as the "between state" described in the "Hall of Understanding", this is the state of between." She sensed that I still did not grasp the significance and added. "The "between state" you are referring to, is a state of being where the essence has separated from the physical body but has not yet been recycled. That "between state" can be thought of as a "state of being", not a place. This is a place, a place between." Rena motioned for Reynolds to follow her. She led him to the opposite side of the path. "Look." She pointed at what appeared at first to be an empty space.

I looked in the direction she was pointing and saw nothing. "Look at what?"

She smiled. "Exactly!" Rena waited before adding. "This is the other side of the physical realm."

My mind reeled as I tried unsuccessfully to grasp the nuance of the statement. "I'm sorry, I don't understand."

The grey figure smiled. "You are familiar with the concept of balance, are you not?" After a moment of hesitation she continued. "Given that there are two opposing conditions, there logically must be a point where the two come together. This is that place." The figure paused, and then added. "Between the two, lies the one. This is the one." After another moment of silence she added. "Think of this place as your sanctuary, a place where you are safe and unreachable." She paused then added. "Your companions, as you call them, cannot come here."

As I stood digesting this new information, I had the sense that I already knew this place existed. Logically, I had to know, or I would not have come here. Unless of course, I didn't come here, but was brought here. "And who are you? Let me guess, you're the caretaker of this place. Do you have a name? How did I get here? Did you bring me here?"

Once again the figure just laughed. "Slow down! No. I am not the caretaker of this place. I, like you, have come here seeking sanctuary. As for my name, well, I have been called many things. To Arinons group I am known as Croatoan. Eldred simply refers to me as an independent." The figure paused then added. "My birth name was Rena."

I heard the note of sadness on this last statement and knew there was much more to know. "Rena, that's a pretty name. If it's all right with you, I will also call you Rena." Her smile told me that would be acceptable. "How did I get here? Did you bring me here?"

Rena shook her head. "No I didn't bring you here. You came on your own. More than likely, it was an instinctive reaction, or for lack of a better term, an act of self preservation."

"I don't understand. Until a moment ago I did not even know this place existed. How would I know to come here?" Even as I said this I wondered to myself if this was also one of the "powers" I had recently acquired.

Rena was silent for a moment, she looked at the newcomer, unlike herself, he was a hybrid, yet if that was so, how had he obtained the use of the power once only possessed by pure humans. Was it possible Arinon had finally succeeded in creating one who could penetrate the sanctuary? Finally she spoke. "Did Arinon send you?" She knew of the agreement. She knew as well, neither Arinons nor Eldred's group could avoid answering direct questions truthfully. The trick was to phrase the question in such a manner that there was no ambiguity.

Surprised by the question I looked at her. "Who is Arinon? I've never heard of anyone by that name." I had met a Jonathan, a Christie, an Eldred, and several others but no one called Arinon.

Rena gasped audibly. Could this be true? Was it possible this one was here of his own volition? There was only one way to know for certain. Slowly she reached out and grasped me by the hand. "Relax this will not hurt."

I felt her hand take mine and had the urge to step away. At the same time I could feel a slight rhythmic pulsing as if a low voltage energy passed from her to me. The sensation was not unpleasant and I resisted the urge. Within seconds, I found myself swaying to the rhythm of the pulse. I was aware of a presence in my mind that appeared to be searching my memories. A moment later she removed her hand and I found myself wishing she had not.

Rena was confused. Her mind probe of the newcomer had left her with more questions than answers. He was telling the truth about not knowing Arinon. He did, however know of Eldred and as well knew some of Arinons group. She had also determined that his support unit, also part of Arinons system, had become disassociated from him. He was, for all practical purposes, like her, an independent. "What is your name?"

Deciding to be coy, I replied. "I have been called many things. My wife calls me dear, my children call me dad, but my birth name is Bill." Judging from her reaction, I knew she had not caught this wry attempt at humor. "Why don't you call me "Bill" or "Reynolds"."

Rena smiled. "I will call you Reynolds. I like the sound of it." Even though her mind reading had convinced her he was not an emissary from Arinon, she was still uncomfortable treating him as an equal. In despite of his apparent independence, he was still after all a hybrid. She had watched the hybrids for these many thousands of years and knew well what motivated them. Now, to have one with full possession of the powers was a frightening thought. "Again I welcome you to the sanctuary."

This was the third time Rena had called this a sanctuary. A sanctuary from what I wondered. "Who are you?" I paused then added. "I mean aside from being one called Rena. Where are you from? And what do you mean by sanctuary?"

Without hesitation, Rena replied. "I am the last of my kind, the last pure human." She wasn't joking, although there had been other survivors of the "event". Most had through the ages succumbed to the futility of their condition, or as in the case of her sister, been killed by the hybrids. While it was possible others still existed, she had not seen any evidence of them for almost five hundred years. "As for where I am from, I am from here, the same as you." She paused before adding. "This is a place accessible only to pure humans. The others of whom you spoke cannot come here."

As she seemed willing to share her thoughts freely I pressed the issue. "What do you mean by "pure human"? Does that make me a pure human as well?" Somehow I knew the answer even before I asked the question.

Rena paused before answering. "No. You're what I call a hybrid human." She knew not to say more until she better understood this newcomer.

"What do you mean by hybrid?" I was only now becoming aware of the differences between us. She was not as tall as I, her eyes had an oblong aspect to them, and her fingers were longer and seemed to have a thin membrane of webbing between them.

Rena read these thoughts and smiled. "In the beginning, humans did not require the use of a support unit to survive in the physical world. This did not happen until after the "event". So you and the six billion people on the planet are all hybrids." She paused then added. "However, you are the first hybrid to have found a way to survive without a support unit, more than likely because you are reacquiring the powers originally only possessed by the pure humans."

I did not like the direction the conversation appeared to going, so I decided to change the subject. "How long have you been here?"

"I have been coming here off and on since I was a child. However I came here for good four hundred of your years ago, just after my sister was killed." The memory of that day still haunted her. Her sister, Reba older by a year, had been ambushed by the hybrids while gathering berries for dinner. Although she had possessed the power to fend off any known threat she was powerless to stop an attack from ambush. The musket ball pierced her chest and knocked her down. Before she had time to direct her healing power to the wound, her attackers were upon her. They immediately cut off her head, preventing her from focusing her thoughts enough to escape. Rena had sensed the loss immediately and went in search of her sister. She came upon her lifeless body, hung unceremoniously on a wooded stake at the gate of the hybrids' settlement. That was first and last time she had ever focused her power in anger. An anger so great it caused the earth to tremble. Every hybrid within the village died where they were standing, their bodies burned until even their ashes had been consumed. That was the day she had come to the "between place" for the final time, swearing to never again enter the physical world.

I was amazed by this revelation and asked the next obvious question. "How old are you? Are you immortal?" If she had already here four-hundred years, I could only imagine her true age.

Rena, thoughts of her sister fading, looked intently at Reynolds. "No we are not immortal. Quite the contrary. While in the physical realm we are as fragile as any hybrid. Here, on the other hand, time does not exist, and the effects of the physical world are minimal. I have been coming here since before the "event". By your definition of time, that occurred roughly twelve thousand years ago." She was probably off by a few centuries but decided that level of accuracy was not required.

I was shocked, given the events I had already experienced this day. A thousand years would not have surprised me, but twelve thousand years! Since the age modern man began! A sudden thought occurred to me. Was it possible the "event" Rena had referred to coincided with the introduction of what the anthropologists referred to as modern man? "This event, can you tell me more about it?"

Rena again nodded her head, her eyes gazing into the grayness of the room. "That is the day when the great lightening took away the powers we humans needed to survive." She remembered the day well. It was the first time she had come to the sanctuary without cause and her sister Reba had accompanied her. Since that day she had come to the conclusion that being in the sanctuary when the event took place was the only reason she, and a few others, had not been adversely affected.

I was fascinated and pressed the issue. "How is it you were able to retain your powers?" I wondered how many others like her still existed.

Rena's eyes refocused on Reynolds. "My sister and I, as well as a few dozen others around the world were here, in the sanctuary, when the event occurred." She paused then added. "Because this place is the "between place", and the event was of a physical nature, it did not affect us." She did not add the details of the event she had surmised in the thousands of years since. He would need to learn about them for himself.

"How have you been able to survive? Haven't you needed water or food?" According to what she had said, the last time she left the sanctuary was over four-hundred years earlier.

Rena laughed at this question, although the thought of once again collecting and eating wild berries did evoke strong memories of her childhood. "As I said, in this place, time and physical needs do not exist."

I sat there and thought of what Rena had said. I began to wonder why and how these powers had come to me. "Tell me about these powers. What are they? Where do they come from?"

Rena shrugged. "I know what they are, but not where they come from. I also know that they still reside in every human, even in hybrids. You are evidence of that." She paused before she continued. "The powers as you call them have always been a part of the human experience. These powers allowed us to live in the physical world in spite of our fragile biological condition. Our ability to heal one another, the ability to communicate without language, the ability to move objects with a mere thought, and as you can see, to be able to move ourselves, or other physical matter between the realms, allowed us to live virtually free of fear." She paused then added. "I will tell you one more thing, and you must listen very carefully, heed my warning carefully." She paused then continued. "The powers you possess are dangerous, to you and to all you hold dear. Do not use them unless absolutely necessary."

I was confused and looked at her. I remembered how these powers had already changed Wong's life. Surely that was a good use of the power. "But why? I could use this power to help the world! To make it a better place! What is the danger in that?"

She read my thoughts about Wong and immediately responded. "When you healed Wong, you were not in control of the process. The energy you transferred to him was not moderated in any way. As a result, you may have given him more than just healthy legs. Fortunately, the duration of your contact with him was very short and with luck that, will limit his abilities. Even so, his abilities are growing just as yours are. In fact, as you know, he is already becoming cognizant of the "others". Am I right?"

"And why is that a bad thing?" To my way of thinking that wasn't bad.

Rena shrugged. "How well do you know Wong? What motivates him? How will he use these powers?" Rena hesitated, and in a softer tone added. "In the hands of the wrong person these powers could be used in ways that could seriously impact the course of events for the entire planet." She had witnessed this firsthand and knew there was truth in what she had said. She knew with certainty the "hybrids" had not yet evolved to the point where these powers would not be abused.

I had becoming uncomfortable with what she had said. After all I had promised Rhodes I would help Angelina. "Is there no way to use the power, yet limit the scope?"

Rena looked thoughtful for a moment. "I told you there were others who escaped the great "event". Some of them, who felt as you do, decided to return to the physical realm. They hoped to reinstate the power into the people, just as you may have done to Wong. Unfortunately by that time the hybrids were fully under the control of Arinons group. To have given them these powers would have been the same as giving them to Arinon. Most returned immediately to this sanctuary. A few were convinced by the interlopers they could best help restore their kind by helping them guide the affairs of the hybrids. In any case, one or two did manage to pass on portions of the power to a few hybrids. In the process, they found that the degree and type of power could be limited by using their minds. In other words, if "they" mentally limited the scope to a specific purpose, only that power was passed on. So yes, it is possible to limit the "scope" as you put it, but, if you are unable to control it, the consequences could be severe. It would be better to not use the power at all."

I was frustrated and could not help voicing my thoughts. "What good are these powers if I cannot use them? Surely they could be used for some good."

Rena shrugged indifferently. "You will cither heed my warning or you will not." She paused then added. "If you wish to pursue this path, it would be wise for you to better understand what you are up against. To that end I would ask you do two things."

"What two things?" I had grown frustrated but knew her

wisdom came from more years and experience than I could even fathom.

"First, return to the Hall of Knowledge, review the event data rings with Eldred and his group. You should understand what has happened in your history and to your kind." She could only hope this knowledge would help him understand the danger of inadvertently passing the power to the wrong kind. "Second, after you learned what has been, ask Eldred to show you what is to come."

I was surprised by her knowledge of Eldred and the data rings. I wondered if she was also capable of going there. "Tell me about this Arinon, what does he want?" I paused then added. "You know about Eldred and the data rings? I thought he was one of the "bad guys", yet you trust him?" My sense was that Rena considered both Eldred and Arinon to be "outsiders". This thought had been conveyed to me when she scanned my thoughts earlier.

Rena smiled. "Of the two, Eldred is more of a supporter than is Arinon. He will help you, but you would be wise to keep your plans to yourself. As for Arinon, I can only say that you are fortunate to be free of your support unit. It means that none of the usual pathways to your thoughts are available to him." She paused, then as an afterthought added. "You would do well to also remember that while you are in the physical world you are subject to the same dangers as any human. You can be harmed or even killed. Your powers can protect you from known threats, but not from threats you cannot see." She hoped this last would serve to reinforce the dangers I would face.

I was shocked by this revelation and could not help asking. "How? I thought you said they could not reach me here? Additionally I did not think they could directly interfere with the physical realm without violating their "agreement"."

Rena, who had watched the saga unfold for ten millennia, was aware of the agreement. She knew that Arinon would be in violation of the agreement if he directly interfered in the hybrid's affairs. Even so, he had managed to do so indirectly, and in often subtle ways. This he had done through the manipulation of the systems and established social conditions he had developed over the long history of time. "That is true and until now there has never been an instance of direct interference. However, actions taken by other hybrids in response to

events can be just as dangerous. And I might add, far more subtle."
Throughout the thousands of years she had witnessed such subtlety
many times, most recently with the killing of Mahatma Ghandi and
others who had challenged the existing order. "In order for you to
return to the non-physical realm, your biological being must remain in
the physical realm, otherwise the balance will not be maintained.
During this time your body is unprotected and susceptible to harm.
Without your support unit to maintain it your physical being would be
the same as if it were dead." Rena saw the look on Reynolds's face.
"It's not really dead, just waiting for you to return to it. Make sure it
is protected while you are away from it. But you would do well to
make sure your protection is not provided by another hybrid.
Understand that while you are in the physical world, Arinon can and
will use his support unit network to find you. Your only hope is to go
someplace where you will not be recognized, perhaps into seclusion.
Even the support units of your family are tools to him."

"But why would Arinon want to find me? I have done nothing
wrong." The prospect of being a target in this cosmic tug of war
angered me.

"You are threat to his plans." She paused then added. "After
you have reviewed the event rings, ask Eldred to show you the "black"
ring. Perhaps that will help you to better understand what is at stake
here." She paused then added. "After you have done these things,
return here, and we will talk more." She could have easily answered
all of his questions, but there were some things he needed to find out
for himself.

"How do I get back here?" I wasn't sure how I got here in the
first place let alone how to find my way back.

Rena smiled. "Just picture me, or this place in your mind. If
you do so, you will brought here, just like anywhere else for that
matter. If you want to go anywhere in the physical or non-physical
realm, just visualize it and you will go there. If you wish to return to
the Hall of Knowledge just think of being there." She paused, and
wanted to add one last piece of information, but not giving too much
away in the process. "Remember, thoughts are causes, and causes
have effects. Your mind is the key. It always has been, and always
will be." She silently hoped he would understand the true meaning of

her words. Time of course would tell. "Now close your eyes and think of where you want to be. And remember; do not use your powers until we have spoken again."

I did as instructed. I closed my eyes and mentally visualized my rear porch. In spite of Rena's warning, I was going to make sure my family was safe. The "Hall of Knowledge" would have to wait.

Rena smiled to herself. She was tuned to his thoughts so she knew where he was going. She would have been disappointed had he gone anywhere else.

# Chapter 31

# **Hall of Understanding.**

$A$rinon listened silently as Jonathan and Thomas updated Peter on the most recent events. Peter had already known most of this by virtue of the support units of the Bios involved. It was now evident beyond any doubt that Reynolds had somehow been able to gain access to the powers once possessed only by pure humans. When he had vanished, Reynolds had demonstrated that he also possessed the one ability for which Arinon had no answer. Arinon knew of the sanctuary, the place where the two became one. And more importantly, it was a place beyond the reach of his network, a place where he could not go. Arinon had often wondered if other "independents" had sought refuge there as well. He remembered "Croatoan" and how she had simply vanished. Was she still there?

Peter listened as Jonathan described the events leading up to Reynolds's sudden disappearance. He found it especially interesting when Jonathan described the conversation with Wong about seeing "others". This confirmed an earlier report from Wong's "Seven". He had made a mental note to follow-up with Wong's "Seven". If Wong was acquiring this ability, was he also developing the other powers? Peter was frustrated and more than a little worried. He had made the mistake of assuming Reynolds's abilities were limited to the telepathic and healing powers. His mistake became evident when Reynolds had used his telekinetic power to upright the motorcycle. Reynolds's subsequent use of the teleportation power had removed any doubts Peter fostered that he was a threat. Just the fact Reynolds had these powers made him a threat to his plans, add to this the potential to awaken the powers in others made him doubly so. Peter now knew without question that Reynolds would have to be removed. As he looked Jonathan and Thomas, he shook his head. "There is nothing that can be done until he re-surfaces." Peter glanced at Thomas. "You return to your duties in the Hall, I will send for you if I need your services further." He looked at Jonathan. "I want you to go to Eldred, tell him Arinon and I would like to meet with him." He paused then added. "Soon!"

Jonathan nodded. He had been as surprised as Peter when Reynolds demonstrated his powers. Unlike Peter however, the source of his surprise lay in the realization that the stories he had heard were true. He had heard there were beings like this, but had never witnessed one firsthand. He had only half believed they ever existed. Now as he watched Peter's reaction, he felt his first pang of fear. What was Peter afraid of? Was it possible this power Reynolds had was stronger than that possessed by Arinon? "I will leave immediately." Jonathan turned to leave, only to be stopped by the voice of Arinon.

Arinon, his voice subdued, asked. "What is the status of Reynolds's support unit?"

Jonathan stopped and turned to face Arinon. "They are on standby, waiting for Reynolds to re-appear." When Reynolds had vanished, his support unit had been left alone. Just as he, Thomas and Christie had been. The fact they were not immediately presented to the evaluation process meant Reynolds was still alive and consequently their duties were not completed.

Arinon smiled an almost sardonic smile. He knew the support unit would never again be attached to Reynolds. More importantly, the memory records they protected could not be accessed. This was unfortunate, as his memories of people, places and thoughts would have been invaluable tools to help find him. The unit was in a state of limbo, they could not be re-assigned until after the evaluation process, a process that in this case would never take place. "Have them return to the Hall of Understanding." At least they could be used to support that process until this issue was resolved.

Peter waved for Jonathan to leave. To Arinon he said. "I have already made arrangements for them to return." Peter had come to the same conclusion as had Arinon, that Reynolds's memory records could prove valuable in finding him. However, unlike Arinon, he was not going to give up so easily. The records could still be accessed if

Eldred agreed. Hence, the request for the meeting, he had sent to Jonathan to arrange. If they could convince Eldred that the need for a viable support unit outweighed the protocol requirement of Bio agreement, Eldred might approve the special dispensation, allowing the records to be opened, and evaluated. That would make them available to his group. Peter was counting on Eldred's understanding of the longer term implication of losing a support unit, in effect, the possible ending of a familial strand.

Arinon waited until Jonathan ha left the room before he turned to Peter. "I thought you had an operation underway to stop this?" Arinon was not pleased by these recent events.

Peter shrugged. "I did and for that matter still do." Until the moment Reynolds had vanished, his plan had been flawless. The first part of the plan was to have the analyst at the observatory mark the magnetic anomaly chart as a potential threat. Since this was a normal part of his duties, it would not be questioned during the Bio's evaluation. Part two of the plan was to get the appropriate response from the security agencies. They had also responded as anticipated and had sent a team to contain the threat. Fear, it seemed, was still the greatest tool at his disposal, just as it had been since the beginning of this enterprise. The third element of the plan had a higher degree of risk. This was a two part activity that involved an unsuspecting fuel truck driver and a teenager who was to make an erroneous telephone call to the driver's cellular phone. The plan was to have the teenager make the call while the truck was exiting an off-ramp of the highway. The truck driver who would be momentarily distracted would have lost control of his vehicle, and crash his truck into the government's security vehicle, killing all parties involved. Because the cellular caller did not know the truck driver or the victims there would be no direct linkage found during the evaluation process. Unfortunately Reynolds's vanishing act had effectively nullified the plan. When the truck did crash it was into a van carrying evening worshipper's home from church, obviously Reynolds was not among the victims. Still, Peter was satisfied knowing Reynolds would soon become a person of interest to the Security agencies. And while Peter's own network was effective, it was limited to the extent that Reynolds would only be recognized by support units of Bios who knew him. Having the security agencies publish his picture would introduce his face to other support units, who otherwise would not have known him. Peter was sure that unless Reynolds stayed in the sanctuary, he would eventually be found. And his planning group would rectify the situation.

Arinon did not know the details of Peter's plan, nor did he want to. Through the long expanse of time, Peter had proven to be quite adept at making problems disappear. Eldred had full confidence this situation would end the same. Still, he had a foreboding sense of pending disaster. A feeling in his gut told him this episode was different, and far more dangerous to his plans than any they had encountered in the past. There had been independents in the past and dealing with them, usually came down to simply identifying and trapping them. This had always been easily accomplished due to their innocent natures. This Reynolds was a different sort altogether. As a mature hybrid, and one with the residue of countless lifetimes, he understood the nuances and dynamics of deception and that made him very dangerous. Arinon re-focused his attention on Peter. "Why did you send Jonathan to arrange a meeting with Eldred?"

Peter shrugged. "If we can convince Eldred to open Reynolds's memory records, it may be easier to find him." He was quite certain they would find him without the records, but having access to the memory records would certainly make things easier and more expedient. Peter did not voice this thought, but sensed time was going to become a critical factor in the near future.

Arinon nodded. "I would not get my hopes up if I we're you. Eldred will know your true purpose." Arinon did not share Peter's view that Eldred would consider the ending of a strand as more important than the maintenance of the security protocols. "Besides, that information will only be helpful if Reynolds leaves the sanctuary. If he stays there you will never reach him."

Peter grinned. "We should be that lucky. If Reynolds stays in the sanctuary he is no longer a threat to us." Peter knew Reynolds would not stay in the sanctuary. His family and friends in the physical world would bring him back, and if his current plan worked he would make certain of it.

Arinon saw the grin on Peter's face and understood its meaning immediately. "You're running another operation aren't you?" He could only guess what Peter was up to. "What is it? What are you doing?"

Peter smiled. "I am setting a trap for him. I am using his family to get him to come out of the sanctuary." This plan, already in motion, was devilishly simple. The security agency had followed standard procedures and had taken Reynolds's wife and son into custody. Peter was sure that Reynolds would try to find them and when he did, Peter would have a fix on him. His planning group was already designing the plan's next, and hopefully, final steps.

As he shook his head, Arinon marveled at Peter's treachery. "Just make sure nothing happens to them. Eldred will suspect we were behind it and we can't risk that." Arinon knew his advice was unnecessary, but voiced it anyway. Even one instance of proof was all Eldred would need to shut their operation down permanently. After this discussion, Arinon left Peter to his own devices.

# Chapter 32

## <u>Reynolds Home.</u>

*T*he porch was dark, as was the house. The grill, although cold, still held the burgers and brats Mary had been cooking. Although it was still early evening, moonlight provided sufficient illumination for me to find the "fake rock" in the myriad of rocks surrounding the flower garden. This "fake rock" contained the emergency key to the house. Years before the boys had shown a penchant to forget their keys and on more than one occasion Mary had to leave work early to open the house for them. The "fake rock" provided a different solution. I twisted the top half of the rock which opened to a cavity which contained the key, allowing the key to fall into my hand. I climbed the stairs and had the fleeting thought that it would have been easier to visualize myself in my living room instead of on the porch. At the same time I rationalized the decision, telling myself that I had not expected to find an empty porch. While I was concerned about the absence of my wife and son, I knew that if Harridy and Rhodes were with them they would be safe. I opened the door and entered the darkened kitchen. I flipped the light switch on, and almost as quickly off again. The thought occurred to me the Homeland Security people probably had the house under surveillance. I made my way through the dark rooms and allowed my hands to slide along the wall to maintain my direction. I entered the bathroom and closed the door before I turned on the light. As this room did not have windows, I knew the light would not be seen. I sat on the toilet with my head in my hands and realized for the first time I was again alone. I had half expected my "Seven" and of course Jonathan and Christie to show up. More than likely, their connection with me was lost when I went to the sanctuary. I remembered what Rena had said about Arinon using his support unit network to find me, and knew as soon as I met someone who recognized me, my companions would return. Then, the only way to lose them again would be to return to the sanctuary, I was beginning to understand why Rena called it a sanctuary. As I sat there thinking of Rena, I wondered why she had chosen to stay in the safety of the sanctuary. She clearly possessed the same powers I had so recently inherited, and understood the powers could be used to change the course of history, yet she has chosen to not act. Was she afraid? According to what she had said, her sister had been killed by what she had called the hybrids, was that why? Even as I thought this, I knew that wasn't the case. She did not fear death, she was waiting for something else, but what? And who were Eldred and Arinon? Based upon what I had already learned, I knew they were opposites in this saga, but not equals, Eldred clearly had some power over Arinon, but what did they want? What were their goals? More importantly, why did Arinon fear me? I had never met Arinon and had only met Eldred for a brief moment. But in that moment I did not sense that he had feared me, so much as had tolerated me. And while it was clear that Jonathan was part of Arinons group, on which side did Christie belong? And what of this agreement? What was it? Why did it exist at all? And what role was I to play? Fourteen hours earlier I was just a normal guy doing normal stuff. Now I seemed to be the center of cosmic attention. Attention I was beginning to dislike immensely. What about my family? Where were they? It was obvious they were being used as pawns in this game, although without the protection of the powers. An idea began to form in my mind. Rena had said that my mind was the key. That I had the ability to go anywhere I wanted. All I had to do was visualize it. I wondered if this applied to people as well. Could I visualize a person instead of a place? And would I then be teleported to them? There was only one way to find out. I reached into my pocket and removed my wallet. The wallet contained pictures of my family. I opened the picture section and selected a picture of my youngest son Eric. The picture was a year old and was one of Eric holding aloft a twenty-two inch walleye he had caught the summer before. I focused my thoughts on him and mentally wished to be with him. Almost immediately, I found myself standing in a bowling alley. On the lane in front of me I saw my son Eric, bowling ball poised in his backswing. While I was ecstatic that the plan had worked, and not wanting to risk being recognized, I immediately closed my eyes and focused my mind again, this time on a picture of Mary. When I reopened them I found myself standing in a glass enclosed room, Mary, Andrew, Rhodes and Harridy sat around a table, with Costa and Buchannon on either side of them, Ryan, the guy from Washington, to Costa's left.

Costa was the first to see me. His surprise was sufficient to stop him in mid-sentence, leaving his last word a mere syllable. When Buchannon saw me he instinctively reached beneath his coat and removed his firearm. I saw this movement and at the same time sensed his thoughts, without hesitation I sent him the mental message to point the barrel of the gun to his own forehead. I was not surprised to see him do so. I looked at Harrridy who sat with a confused expression on his face. "I think you had better take that before he hurts himself."

Harridy did as I requested. He took the gun from Buchannon and he tossed it to the floor where it collided gently with the wall. Ryan and the others simply stared, unsure as to what they had seen.

I looked at Costa who had by now regained his composure. "Why have you taken my family and friends into custody?" I could hear my own voice and was surprised at the casual tone of it.

Costa smiled. This was even better than he had hoped for. His attempt's to gather information as to Reynolds's possible whereabouts had been getting him nowhere. Now here, a mere few feet away, his target had presented himself. "They are not in custody. We only wanted to talk with them. They are free to go whenever they wish." Technically, this wasn't exactly true. They had been detained as material witnesses to an event he had not yet figured out how to describe. It was certainly not a crime, and as yet, unrelated to any terrorist activities that could be proven.

I nodded in the direction of Harridy. "Is that true? Can you leave whenever you wish?" I had sensed Costa's thoughts and knew he would not allow them to leave so easily.

Harridy stood and faced Costa. "I guess so. And since that is the case. I am leaving right now. Andrew and Mary will join me, I'm sure." He continued to watch Costa's face, before adding. "Of course we will need transportation."

I turned to Rhodes and asked. "I assume you want to leave as well?" I had the fleeting thought of Rena's final words to me. "Your mind is the key." I had an idea on how to solve the transportation issue.

Rhodes stood and adjusted his coat in a manner to suggest he had also had enough of the Homeland Security conference room. "Yes, I am ready to go."

I turned back to Costa and put what I hoped would sound like a steely tone into my voice. "Do not bother my family again. Nor for that matter Harridy or Rhodes as well." I paused trying to gauge his reaction then added. "I have done nothing wrong, nor have they. But you need to understand I will do whatever is necessary to protect them." I looked at Buchannon then added. "You have only seen the surface of what I can do. Don't force me take it to the next level." This said I turned to Harridy, Rhodes and my family. I stretched out my hands and instructed them. "Join hands." I watched as they did so, hoping what I was attempting would work. I closed my eyes and visualized us standing on the rear porch of my house. When I re-opened my eyes the evening shade of darkness surrounded us. The grill stood waiting, a sentinel guarding the remains of our dinner. I smiled to myself then looked at Mary. "What about those burgers?"

# Chapter 33

## Homeland Security Office.

Costa watched as Buchannon picked up his weapon. He was having difficulty absorbing what his mind told him had just happened. Earlier, when Buchannon had reported that Reynolds had simply vanished into thin air, he'd had reservations. He was convinced the events Buchannon described were the result of some form of mass hallucination, perhaps even hypnosis. Now after witnessing firsthand the same phenomenon, and as well, having observed a manifestation of the physical powers on Buchannons weapon, he was less skeptical. Of one thing he was certain. Whatever means Reynolds had employed, they were far beyond his agency's abilities to understand, let alone cope with. Costa turned to Ryan. "Well, Doctor. What is your official assessment?"

Ryan shook his head in disbelief. "It isn't possible." Every bit of knowledge and his years of training screamed at him that what he had witnessed could not have happened. The immutable laws of physics, the very cornerstone of all science, were being violated almost at Reynolds's whim.

Costa smiled. "Dr. Ryan, I think your assessment may be wrong." What had started as a simple, almost routine investigation, had quickly transformed itself into perhaps the greatest asset, or greatest threat, his country had ever faced. A thought occurred to him. Costa looked again at Ryan. "Dr. Ryan, I wonder if you would mind contacting the scientists tracking these anomalies. Find out if they observed the same magnetic effects when our friends disappeared." Costa hoped this would be the case. If Reynolds's disappearance had caused an observable anomaly, perhaps it was possible they would be able to track him by his actions. "In the meantime, I will contact the Director and bring him up to speed on what has happened." Costa turned to Buchannon. "Jim, I want you to start working on a BOLO for Reynolds." BOLO was an acronym meaning. "Be on the Look out". The BOLO would automatically be sent to every law enforcement agency in the country. If Reynolds were to be stopped for any reason, his name and face would be known. "And while you're at it, put him on the international watch list as well." If Reynolds tried to purchase travel tickets or used his credit cards for any reason they would know, if he tried to enter through immigration of any country, he would also be flagged as a person of interest to the intelligence communities and they would be notified. Inwardly Costa knew it was a waste of time. Based upon what he had just seen, he was sure Reynolds wouldn't need tickets or Immigration to get wherever he wanted to go. Still, they could get lucky.

Buchannon nodded. "How do you want him listed?" Every BOLO required a reason and the watch list would require a threat level assessment. Both would dictate the appropriate action to be taken if Reynolds was found.

Costa shrugged. "For the BOLO list as "detain without force." On the watch list as "advise only, take no action". Costa did not have the authority to approve release of the BOLO or to add a person to the watch list, but he was sure the action would be approved once he updated the Director. "Jim, just prepare them, don't post them until after we have approval."

Buchannon understood the politics involved. "I'll have it for you when you need it, boss."

Ryan had overheard the conversation and looked at Costa. "Why are you doing that? Reynolds has not broken any laws, and you have no tangible evidence to suggest he is a threat to national security." Ryan hesitated before he added. "At a minimum, you are violating his constitutional rights, and, I might add, breaking the law." As a scientist, Ryan was by nature sensitive to the unwarranted oversight of government types, and although he was a government employee, he also considered himself an average citizen. And as such, was outraged at the thought his rights could be violated so easily.

Costa jerked his head up from the file before him. "Reynolds just broke into this office and assisted four detainees to escape. By my way of thinking, that is at least two federal offenses. And of course, there is the matter of obstructing a federally authorized investigation. So yes, Doctor, I have every justification to take these actions." Costa again looked at the file. "Besides, I would think you of all people would want access to Reynolds, if only to understand how he is doing whatever he is doing." He did not add his thoughts about the potential Reynolds's abilities had for security purposes.

Costa picked up the phone and punched in the number for the Director's office. "Sally, this is Costa, is he in?" Costa listened for a moment then said. "Yes, please tell him he is needed in the fishbowl." The fishbowl was the nickname they had given the conference room. He continued. "Yes it is very important. Okay thanks Sally, I owe you one." Costa looked at the receiver then replaced it in its cradle. "The Director will be here in a few minutes.

Director Ross was not your average career politician. He had spent twenty years working for NCIS, the military version of the FBI. Then another nine years had been spent as a field agent in the National Security Agency. When the Homeland Security Agency was formed he had been selected to head up the mid-west regional operations. While the majority of his time was spent serving the bureaucratic needs of the operation, he still felt a kinship to the operatives in the field, and as such made himself available to them without reservation. Earlier in the day, he had been notified of Washington's concerns related to the magnetic anomaly and as a result had authorized Costa and his team to investigate. Since then, periodic updates from Costa and the science guy Ryan had given him the impression Washington's original threat assessment was unwarranted, impressions he had dutifully passed on to Washington. Now Costa was asking for his presence to review new information. He could only hope this new information did not significantly change the reports he had already sent. Ross descended the final stairway and turned left into the conference room. Costa and an agent he recognized as Buchannon sat facing each other across the conference room table. A taller man he assumed to be the scientist from Washington occupied the seat at the end of the table. Ross entered the room and approached Costa. "Hello Sam." Ross nodded to Buchannon before he turned to Ryan. "You must be Doctor Ryan." Ross extended his hand.

Ryan stood and took the offered hand. "Yes, Tom Ryan. Please call me Tom." Ryan silently assessed the Director. He was not what he had expected. Ross was not a big man by any stretch of the imagination. His balding head and half glasses gave him a grandfatherly look.

Ross smiled. "Fine, please call me George." Ross turned to Costa. "Okay Sam, what's up? I assume this is about that magnetic anomaly thing?"

Costa nodded. "Yes sir it is."

Ross nodded. "I see. So there is a threat level we should be concerned about? I thought your assessment and that of Doctor Ryan was there was no valid threat. What's changed?" He was already thinking of the fallout from Washington.

Costa shrugged. "Our original assessment was, and is still valid. There is nothing to suggest the anomaly was in any way related to terrorist activities." Costa hesitated before adding. "However, other circumstances have come to light which I think you will find interesting."

Ross peered over his glasses. For Costa to request his presence he knew these new circumstances were important. "What circumstances?"

Ryan interrupted. "Sir, If you would take a seat we will give you a complete update." This said Ryan proceeded to describe the events that had transpired, starting with the team's original physical assessment and even their "instinctive sense" that led to the follow-up meeting with Reynolds at the Medical Center. Ryan watched the Directors face as he watched the video taken by Mosser at Reynolds home.

Ross was amazed at the scene which he had just witnessed and looked at Ryan. "How is that possible? That motorcycle righted itself and rolled off the ramp when nobody was near it. And what was that whitish streak?"

Costa smiled. He had expected this response from Ross and was not disappointed. "There's more." Costa then went on to describe the events that took place on the rear porch of Reynolds's home. He nodded in Buchannons direction. "Buck was there and will attest that this happened just I have described it."

Ross was clearly shaken by this new revelation and looked first at Buchannon then again at Costa. "I mean no offense to your team, but what you are describing is impossible." Although based upon what he had seen with the motorcycle he wasn't so sure.

Costa nodded. "I thought you might feel that way sir." Costa nodded to Buchannon. "I think perhaps you should see this." All conference rooms, including the fishbowl, had been constructed with audio and visual surveillance features. The events which had taken place when Reynolds had appeared and subsequently disappeared had been dutifully recorded. That was the evidence Buchannon now displayed.

Ross watched the screen as the images unfolded. As he sat in his chair, his back became rigid as he saw Buchannon placed the barrel of his gun to own his forehead. He listened as Reynolds questioned Costa then two other men. One he recognized as the reporter Rhodes. Reynolds's final warning to Buchannon left him with a sense of fear that Reynolds was more powerful than what he had already demonstrated. The final moments of the video shocked him even more. The entire group had simply vanished.

The room was silent except for the low humming of the overhead projection unit as its cooling fans cycled. Ross was stunned and struggled to categorize what he had seen told and seen. He turned to Costa. "Who else knows of this?"

Costa looked thoughtfully at the file lying on the table before him. He had expected this question and had already prepared the list. "Aside from those present, and Reynolds's group, only three others. Two of our operatives and a freelancer named Mosser." Costa hesitated then added. "Mosser only knows about the motorcycle. It was his video you saw. And yes, it has been confiscated."

Ross nodded pensively. "Good, let's keep this close to the vest for now. In fact, it might be best for you to also bring Mosser under control as well. What do we know about this guy Reynolds? And who is the other man with him?" Ross knew Rhodes and knew as well he could be "managed", although not without his personal involvement.

Costa looked again at the file. "Sergeant Thomas Harridy, Illinois State Police. As for Reynolds, the preliminary background check indicated he is just an average guy, no criminal record, and no known ties to activist groups of any type." Costa paused then added. "We are in the process of running a deeper scan, but quite frankly, I don't think we will find anything."

Ross looked at his watch. "Okay, let me know what you find. In the meantime, I want you to do a few other things. First contact Rhode's editor. Nothing of his is to be published without first going through this office. Second, arrange for Harridy to be transferred to this command. And last, I think we should put out a BOLO on Reynolds."

Costa smiled. "I thought you might. I asked Buchannon to generate one and as well to add him to the watch list." Costa was thoughtful for a moment then said. "Rhodes and his editor will consider this as an act of censorship. What if they disagree?"

Ross shook his head. "Don't worry about that, I will handle it if there is an issue. Now what status did you put on the BOLO and the watch list?" Ross would authorize them but would also make sure they were controlled.

Buchannon slid the two papers across the table. "On the BOLO we listed as "detain without force" and on the watch list "to advise only"."

"Change the BOLO to "advise and observe only". The watch list is okay. Is there anything else we can do to track him?"

Ryan spoke quietly. "Yes, I think there is. It appears that each time he uses his power there is a corresponding and detectable effect to the magnetic flow fields. I checked with the NSA scientists and they did confirm anomalies were detected at the same time as the events we observed. More importantly they were able to triangulate Reynolds's position each time."

Ross looked at Ryan. "Doctor, it would appear you and I are going to Washington this evening." He looked at Costa. "Sam, make a duplicate of everything. Your team reports, your personal reports, and especially the visual evidence. I will be taking the originals with me to Washington. You make sure the duplicates are secured here." Ross hoped making copies would ensure the evidence would not be lost forever, either due to some catastrophe, or worse, into the black hole of Washington's intelligence archives. Ross turned to Ryan. "Doctor I assume you will be ready in an hour?" It would take an hour for their private plane to be readied.

Ryan nodded, then leaned over and lifted his as yet unpacked travel bag. "I'm way ahead of you. "

Ross smiled. "Good see you downstairs in ten minutes." With a final nod to Costa and Buchannon he strode from conference room.

# Chapter 34

## Rear Porch Reynolds Home.

$M$ary looked at her husband with a look of incredulity. "You're crazy! You know that?" Throughout this long and stressful day, she had experienced virtually every emotion a person could have had. She had watched as unknown events had unfolded. Events, that had left her baffled, and to a very large extent afraid. She feared for her husband, her son and of course herself. Now, after all of these strange events, the one person she needed to help her understand, to come to grips with what was happening, could only think of food! "Well dear, I suggest if you want to eat you order something and have it delivered."

I looked at her and smiled. After thirty years of marriage, I could tell she was not in the mood for my humor. I also knew she had interpreted my response correctly. She knew I was worried, if only because joking had always been my response to stressful situations. "I'm sorry dear, you're right of course. But I am hungry and I suspect so is everybody else. "I'll order a couple of pizzas and have them delivered." After a moment of thought I added. "That is, if everybody wants pizza." I looked at Andrew, Harridy and Rhodes who nodded in unison.

Andrew watched his mother. He sensed her level of frustration and knew she was afraid. It was evident that whatever had happened to his father had in some way placed them in danger. And while he was sure he could handle it, he was not as sure about his mother. He looked at his father and said. "I'll order them and have them delivered." He paused then added. "I assume the regular will be alright?" Throughout his childhood, pizza had been a once a week treat. As such, the size and toppings were already pre-defined. He turned to Harridy and Rhodes. "I hope pepperoni and sausage is good for you?"

Rhodes looked at Harridy, who shrugged. "That's fine with me." Rhodes grinned. "Pepperoni and Sausage it is then."

Andrew nodded and picked up the telephone. "It will take about an hour. In the meantime, I think you have some explaining to do." This last comment was directed at me.

I watched as Andrew spoke into the telephone. I knew they wanted answers, as would I if the circumstances were reversed. But where do I start? Should I simply start at the beginning? Should I just relate to them the events as they happened? If I did, would it somehow place them in greater jeopardy? I knew I owed them an explanation, especially Harridy and Rhodes as their lives were also being affected, and I was sure, not in a positive way.

Andrew returned to the dining room. He pulled a chair out and motioned for his mother to sit. He motioned for Rhodes and Harridy to do likewise. He waited until they were seated before he took his own chair. "Okay dad, let's hear it."

As I sat there, I could feel their eyes watching my every movement. Whatever hopes I had fostered about avoiding this vanished. "I don't know where to start or how to begin. It's all so bizarre." I knew that even with a full explanation they could not possibly understand, or for that matter, believe what I said.

Harridy watched Reynolds's face. After years of interviewing suspects, he had learned to gauge facial expressions and to translate them into thoughts. He looked at Rhodes sure that he had developed similar skills as a reporter. Harridy returned his gaze to me. "Perhaps you should start at the beginning, just tell us what happened." He hesitated then added. "If you don't mind, Rhode's and I will take notes and ask questions that might help." This process, although arduous, would hopefully provide a chronological sequence to the events. From this he hoped they would be able to develop a logical picture of what had happened.

I shook my head in agreement. "Okay, but promise you won't have me committed after we're done." I said this half-jokingly, but knew there was a real possibility they might think that was the best thing to do.

Rhodes smiled. "Based upon what just happened, I can assure

you, I for one wouldn't even think of that." He looked at me then added. "I do hope you're going to explain how you did that little trick as well." As he had stood in the conference room, he had been unsure why Reynolds wanted them to join hands. Then when he found himself on the rear porch seconds later, he knew he had somehow been teleported. There was no doubt some power had been called upon and I was the key. No, institutionalizing him would not even be considered.

I looked at Rhodes. I could hear his thought as clearly as if they had been my own. He could be trusted, of that I was sure. "Alright, I'll try." I looked at Mary and Andrew, then leaned back in my chair and began to recite what had happened to me, beginning with the attempted robbery that morning.

"I remember voices. When I opened my eyes I could see I was in some sort of medical facility. I remember hearing the Doctor talking with the nurses, something about my vital signs, and there were other voices as well. Voices not so much heard as thought." I stopped and knew the statement did not adequately convey what I was saying. "You see, I could hear the doctor and nurses with my ears, but these others were different. It was as if they were in my mind." I watching as Rhodes and Harridy made notations in their respective notebooks. "I remember looking around trying to find where the voices were coming from. Eventually I saw them standing at the end of the bed looking at me. I remember thinking it was strange that the Doctor, a guy named Turner, and the nurses didn't seem to know they were there. I remember sitting up and asking them who they were." I paused, unsure how to convey to them that during the process of sitting, I had the sensation of passing through the Doctor, as if he wasn't there.

Harridy glanced up from his notes. "How many of them were there? Did they answer you?"

I shook my head. "There were two, and no, not at first. But based upon their reaction, I knew they had heard me."

Harridy made another notation and nodded. "What happened then?"

I closed my eyes and tried to recall the picture of the scene in my mind. "I remember getting off the bed and walking over to them.

I think it was at this point that I glanced back and saw myself still lying on the bed. Turner was stitching up my head. As you can imagine, it really shook me up. I thought I had died and was having one of the "near death experiences" you read about. I remember thinking the Doctor would not still be working on me if I was dead, and I could see that the monitors all seemed to be working. I could see my pulse and blood pressure readings. They appeared normal. I asked again who they were, even asked what they were doing in my room. They still did not answer me. They didn't need to, I could hear their thoughts as if I was part of their conversation. They were discussing my being able to see and hear them. It was apparent they were unsure of how, or if, they should respond to me.

Harridy placed his pencil down then asked. "Did they ever talk directly to you?"

I nodded. "Yes. The smaller of the two convinced the other one they had no choice, that my ability to hear them and converse with them could not be ignored, if only because it was becoming a distraction. I also remember them thinking that whatever I had seen or heard would go away when I returned to consciousness. In any case, yes, they finally responded to me."

Rhodes was clearly excited and interrupted. "Are you saying you actually had an "out of body experience"? That you saw angels?" In most instances of "near death experiences" people had reported being met by either an angel, or a loved one from their past, one who escorted them "into the light". "Did they tell you who they were?"

I looked at Rhodes, his thoughts had betrayed him. He was thinking of his beloved Angelina and I could see in his mind his relief that her belief in a better place had not been misplaced. Inwardly, I was distressed. I knew the words I was about to say would dash his preconceived perceptions and thus his hopes, for a moment I considered ending the discussion. Only the need to explain to my wife and son prevented me from doing so. "Yes, they told me they were my companions. They told me they were responsible for my well being. What's more, they told me that they were only two of the six that were supporting me. I now refer to them my "support unit"." I paused and looked directly into Rhodes' eyes. "I also thought of them as Angels, and in some ways I guess they are. But they're not what we think of angels."

Rhodes placed his pen on the table. "I don't understand. What do you mean they are not angels?" His euphoric moment now seemed a distant memory.

I reached out and patted his arm. "I know this is not what you want to hear, but you asked me to tell you what happened and I am. This is just a small part of it." I paused then added. "I truly am sorry if what I say hurts you in any way."

Harridy knew he needed to re-focus the conversation and interrupted. "You said this "team" or "support unit" has six members, what do they do? Who are they? Where do they come from?"

I thought of my own struggle to understand their roles and remembered how it did not really make sense to me until I had understood the dual nature of our being. As I had learned from this lesson, I decided the best approach would be to "paint the background" before I introduced the characters and their roles. "To answer this, you need to understand the true nature of our being." I paused, before continuing. "Everything that exists consists of two fundamental aspects. It doesn't matter if it is a piece of physical reality or just a thought. This fundamental duality must exist or nothing can exist." I laughed at the thought that even "nothing" required a corresponding "something" for it to exist. I continued. "You cannot have light without dark. Life cannot exist in the absence of death. The concepts of love and hate are by their nature opposites. So you see in all things an inherent duality must exist. Given this duality is a pre-requisite, you begin to realize that in order for physical matter to exist, there must also be a corresponding non-physical counterpart, or a state of non-matter." I stopped and looked to see if they comprehended what I had said. "If you understand this, then you will understand when I say that "we" human beings also have two aspects to our reality. One is physical, what the support units refer to as our Bio, and a corresponding non-physical aspect which they refer to as our "Essence". Are you still with me?"

Andrew had been listening but now nodded. "You mean our soul?"

I shrugged. "I am sure it is called many things, but yes, I guess that term could apply. But for the sake of this conversation, I will refer to it as our Essence."

Andrew shrugged his shoulders. "Okay. So this "support unit", these six companions are our "Essence"?" He hesitated then added. "And everyone has a support unit?"

"No, and Yes. No they are not our "Essence". They are more like caretakers of our combined being. And yes, each of us has a support unit made up of the six elements. Each of the six members of a support unit serves a different role or function, but all serve the purpose of maintaining us throughout our many lives."

Rhodes picked up immediately on the many lives statement. "I don't understand. You said many lives. Does that mean reincarnation is real?"

I nodded to him. "Yes, but that discussion can wait until we fully understand the support units and their roles. I will describe the team members and their roles as they were explained to me." I hesitated then added. "Some are clear, others are a bit ambiguous. First, each support unit has one they call "Two". From what I understand, "Two" is that part of us which maintains our physical body, or I should say, ensures the functions of our physical body are performed without our conscious knowledge. Things like keeping the heart going, digesting food etc. Because "Two" does this, we do not need to worry about it." Are you still with me?"

Harridy completed his notation and glanced up. "Two"? Don't they have names?"

I smiled and remembered that I had asked the same question of my "Seven". "No just numbers. Then there is "Three", who can be best described as our memory recorder, it is "Three's" job is to record everything that happens to us, and for that matter, our every thought, even our feelings. It is by this method that our memory process works. According to "Three", every event and thought has an associated feeling. Therefore, when the event or thought is recorded, the attached feelings are included. As a result, when a similar situation arises, the memory function recalls not only the event, but also the associated feeling. Because of this recall process we can learn from our mistakes. A good example would be if you burned yourself with a match. That is an event, and the associated feeling is pain. The next time you light a match, the memory of the event and the associated feeling is recalled, and hopefully you are careful. These memories are stored throughout your life in such a way that until the moment of evaluation, only your support unit has access to them." As soon as I mentioned the evaluation process, I knew Rhodes would ask about it and he did not disappoint me.

"What evaluation process?" Rhode's knew many philosophies claimed that at the end of a life, all memories are reviewed to determine whether a person was worthy. However, after much thought, he had concluded that such claims were nothing more than a form of social control. Now he was not so sure.

I shook my head. "Yes, there is an evaluation process. We'll talk more about it in a little while. For the purpose of this discussion it's important to know that your support unit's "Three" maintains these records or memories." I stopped then continued. "After your "Three", there is one called, you guessed it, "Four". Your "Four" is what can be described as your creative self. This is one of those I do not fully understand. This role was explained to me this way. Your "Four" works with your "Two" and "Three" to help find solutions to meet your needs. From what I could gather, it works something like this. "Your "Two" determines the body requires a green leafy vegetable, your "Three" recalls your memories of a green leafy vegetable (hopefully one you like). Your "Four" then helps figure out a way to get that green leafy vegetable. I think your "Six" is also part of this process to the extent it may suggest alternative green leafy vegetables if you cannot find the one you want." I paused and thought through the example I had given. Satisfied, I continued. "Your "Five" is the one I find most interesting. Your "Five" can be described as your internal doctor. This is the one responsible for keeping your body healthy. If you have a cold, it is you're "Five" who sends the required histamines and red blood cells to make you feel better. If your arterial walls begin to crack or break down, it is you're "Five" who directs the cholesterol to the trouble spot, to seal the wall before it ruptures. In a nutshell your "Five" is your resident doctor."

Andrew interrupted. "If we have an internal Doctor, why do people die?"

I thought on this before answering, especially as I could sense Rhode's thoughts. "As the body grows older, its ability to produce the

221

ingredients the "Five" requires diminishes and eventually your "Five" cannot meet the demands and is overwhelmed. I would also add that we often make "Five's" job more difficult by abusing our bodies by doing things which detract from his ability to heal."

Mary pounced on the opportunity. "You mean like smoking?" She had been after me to quit smoking for over twenty years. Even now, two heart attacks later. I still had the habit.

I smiled and knew I had finally given her the ammunition she needed. "Yes dear, smoking is one of many such possibilities. Even induced stress can be considered a detractor." The thought occurred to me that I had not had or for that matter felt the need for a cigarette the entire day. Maybe my newfound power had come with a good side affect. "Our next member is "Six". "Six" is that part of your consciousness they call the scientist in you. More specifically, it is that part of you that draws relational knowledge together. This was explained to me as "intuition". We have all had moments where we "knew" something but could not rationalize how we knew. That is your "Six" at work. In the case of the leafy vegetable your "Six" may have said "broccoli is green" and suggested it as a substitute for the green peas your memory suggested. And the last member of your support unit is called "Seven". You might want to think of your "Seven" as the team leader, or more precisely, their spokesman. It is "Seven" who most often converses with you, who try's to guide you, the one who brings all of the data from the others together and delivers the message to you." I paused then smiled. "If you remember those old cartoons of the little angel sitting on your shoulder whispering in your ear, you might begin to understand the role of your "Seven". I think it also important to note that your, "Seven" does not, and cannot, make decisions for you. He might "suggest" you take a course of action, but in the end, it is your decision, not his. And yes, before you ask, there is a counterpart to your "Seven". They are called "Sleepers". I paused and looked at each of them. "Any questions before I move on?" With the exception of Harridy, whose face was completely passive, the others simply looked overwhelmed.

Harridy placed his notebook aside, looked at Rhodes then turned to face me. "The support unit you have described appears to be dedicated to maintaining the Biological aspect. Who or what maintains the non-physical side? The "Essence" as you called it."

222

"Good question. The direct answer is that while the physical body or "Bio" unit functions, the Essence resides within it. Therefore, your support unit also maintains your "Essence" by default. And just as the physical body recycles, so does the "Essence"." I noticed the look on Rhode's face, and sensed his thoughts. I knew further explanation was needed. "If you recall, earlier I spoke of a condition called duality. We understand there is a physical aspect, the Bio, and a non-physical aspect called the "Essence"." I stopped talking for a moment then said. "What I am about to tell you will seem like convoluted logic, and quite frankly, on the surface it is, but once you understand it, I think you will agree it cannot be denied. When you think in terms of balance, or in this case the pre-requisite of duality, you begin to understand that the two sides are diametrically opposite. By that I mean if one side equals "you can" then logically the other side must equal "you cannot". If one side equals "you must", its corresponding opposite is "you must not"." I paused again, unsure if they understood. "When our physical body completes its natural cycle, it "must" become something other than what it is. Because its physical nature is biologically based, we know it will decay, and eventually transform itself into another aspect of the physical reality. If only a nutrient for the soil. This satisfies the "MUST" side of the equation. Given the pre-requisite of balance, it stands to reason that the opposing side, the non-physical "Essence" "MUST NOT" change. The "Essence" therefore begins a new cycle without being changed."

The ringing of the doorbell broke the silence. Mary, for one, was glad. While she had been able to keep up with most of the conversation, this most recent dissertation would require more thought. She glanced at Andrew and wondered if he understood. The excited, knowing look on his face provided the answer. He seemed to understand. She smiled to herself. She shouldn't be surprised he was after all his father's son. He evidently possessed the same brilliant mind. Mary stood. "That would be the pizza. While I'm getting it, would one of you rocket scientists get the plates and silverware?"

Andrew laughed. "I'll get them." He was excited. He had listened to what his father had said and at many levels had understood. Still he knew he was missing a connection somewhere. Nothing his father had said to this point explained the power he had demonstrated earlier.

The pizza was still steaming when the boxes were opened. The smell of pepperoni and the glistening of the oil on the round pepperoni slices served only to excite my already excited taste buds. It was soon obvious I was not the only one whose taste buds were working overtime. "This is excellent." I shoveled another piece into my mouth. I had not known how hungry I was.

Rhodes looked at his notes. Between Harridy and himself, they had created a summary statement of what I had said. His pizza, lying untouched on the plate in front of him, grew cold. He looked at me and tried to decide whether it would be impolite to interrupt my meal. "Let me understand what you just said. You said that this state of duality or balance exists in all things, that for something to exist it must have an equal state of non-existence. Yet in saying this, it appears to be fundamentally illogical."

I glanced at Rhodes, curious to know where this was going. While I could easily have just extracted it from his mind, I wanted to hear how he would pose his question. "What part of it is illogical?"

Rhodes looked again at his notes before he replied. "You said every condition requires an opposite. You stated that duality and balance is a pre-requisite to all that exists, even in concepts and in thoughts." Rhodes paused then said. "If that is true doesn't it stand to reason that even the concept of the "pre-requisite of duality" also requires an opposing condition? Shouldn't there be a state where this pre-requisite of duality is not required?"

I sat there and thought of Rhodes' question. More specifically, I wondered why I had not thought of it. Had I done so, I could have asked Thomas when I had the chance. I rephrased the question in my mind. If the "pre-requisite of duality" is required, there should be a state where the "pre-requisite of duality" is not required. What is the opposing position of duality? A statement made by Rena flashed across my mind. "Between the two lies the one". Of course! The state of duality existed and its opposing position had to be the state of singularity where the two sides came together. I smiled at Rhodes. "That is a very astute question, and the answer is yes. To require that balance exist in all things, even thoughts, and since the concept of balance is an idea, then it follows that there must be a corresponding condition where balance is not required. And that condition does exist. It is the state of singularity. This singular state can be best described as that point where the two opposing sides meet." This revelation caused me to mentally re-assess what I thought I had understood. It occurred to me that when I visited the sanctuary I was there as a whole being, my physical and non-physical aspects still combined. Yet earlier in the Hall of Understanding and the Hall of Knowledge, my physical self had remained in the physical realm. I was beginning to understand Rena's warning about finding a secure place for my physical self when I returned to the Hall of Knowledge.

Rhodes made an adjustment to his notes then nodded that he understood. "Were you able to find out where these support units came from? You said they were caretakers, not the essence itself."

I had been seeking that answer since the first conversation with my "Seven". As yet I had not found the answer, only more questions. "No, when I asked them, they said they didn't know. They only knew they were performing the functions they had always performed. My "Seven" thought I might find the answer in the Hall of Understanding so he brought me there. And although I learned a great deal while I was there, I came no closer to getting an answer."

Rhodes made another notation in his book, as did Harridy. "Tell me about this "Hall of Understanding." Rhodes smiled. "It sounds like somewhere we should go right about now."

I looked at Mary and Andrew before I answered. "Earlier, I said the Essence and the Bio remain together until the Bio can no longer support itself. At the point where the Bio's cycle is completed, the "Essence" leaves it and goes through some sort of evaluation process. It is then re-cycled into a new body or Bio unit." I hesitated before continuing. "That is the normal process. In this process, the support unit has adequate time to prepare the Bio and Essence for the inevitable separation. Because they are prepared, the transition into the re-cycling process is easy. However, this normal process is sometimes not possible. There are times when the Essence and Bio separate without adequate time to prepare." I paused and looked at Harridy. "I'm sure in your line of work you can attest to that. Sometimes when the Essence and Bio are separated prematurely, the Essence has difficulty adjusting to the separation and as a result finds itself "stuck" between the physical world and the evaluation process.

They call this the "Between state". They cannot move on until they accept their separation. The Hall of Understanding is a place where they can go to get help with the transition."

Andrew grinned. "Are you saying they're ghosts?" He was remembering the stories he had read of ghosts haunting people and places. He had even spent a few nights in the Resurrection Cemetery, hoping to see resurrection Mary.

I could feel Mary's glare as I answered him. "Yeah, I guess that's possible. It certainly fits the circumstances." I didn't add that based upon the other events of the day, it would not have surprised me at all.

Harridy noticed the glare Mary had given to her husband and decided it would be best to change the subject. He turned to me and posed the next question. "What happened next?"

I turned back to Harridy, grateful for the timely interruption. "After I left the "Hall of Understanding" I returned to my support unit. That was just before I woke up, and as you know, gave Doctor Wong a jolt."

Rhodes put his pen on the table, his notebook now filled with scribbled notes. "You said earlier that every person has a support unit. You also said you spoke to yours while in this out of body experience. Can you still speak with them?"

I smiled at this question. While my own support unit was gone, his, as well as that of the others, were present. "No, I have become separated from them." I paused then added. "But yours is here, as are Harridys and theirs." I nodded in the direction of my wife and son. I had the fleeting thought that the others, Jonathan, Christie and Thomas were not there. Maybe Rena was wrong. Perhaps Arinons support unit network didn't work as she thought. Of course, maybe it did and they simply hadn't arrived yet.

Rhodes glanced quickly around. "You can see them?"

I nodded. "Yes, and hear them as well. For instance, right now your "Seven" is telling you this isn't possible." I grinned. "And Harridys just told him to test me. He suggested Harridy should ask me to tell him what he was thinking. His thought was to drop his pencil on the floor."

Harridy heard what I said and looked at Rhodes. "I was just

thinking of dropping my pencil to see if he would know what I was thinking. But I thought that up by myself." At least he thought he did. Was it possible the suggestion was given to him?

Rhodes was stunned. "Is that how you've been able to know things that other people were thinking?" While it wasn't telepathy in total, it certainly covered half of the requirement.

I nodded. "And what's more, they can hear me as well. And through them, I can send suggestions to you. So yes, I have the complete telepathy package as you put it."

Rhodes grinned to himself. He had only thought about the half requirement and Reynolds had indeed picked up on it. "That's amazing. Do you know what you could do with this ability? One thing is for certain, I'll never play poker with you."

I nodded then took a piece of paper, and with Rhode's pen, wrote five words. "Andrew, go to the bathroom." I folded the paper and slid it across the table to Harridy who silently read it and smiled. I focused on Andrew's "Seven" and conveyed the thought that a trip to the bathroom was required.

Andrew, although intrigued by the conversation, had the sensation that he need desperately to go to the bathroom. As he stood, he addressed the group. "If you will excuse me, I need a bathroom break."

Harridy slid the note to Rhodes, who after having read it, began to laugh aloud. "Okay, I believe you."

Harridy, equally impressed, changed the subject back to the Hospital. "What happened with Wong?"

Andrew returned from the bathroom and took his seat. "What did I miss?" When he had gotten to in the bathroom, his urgent need had miraculously disappeared. He hurried back, not wanting to miss anything.

Harridy laughed. "Nothing, we were about to talk about Wong." Harridy liked this kid, he was different than most of the delinquents he had dealt with.

Rhodes, still summarizing his notes, looked across at me. "Before we move on, we should summarize what we know so far." He looked at Harridy who nodded his agreement.

Rhodes nodded. "So far we have established that somehow

while you were incapacitated, you had some sort of out of body experience. During this time you met your support unit. This support unit is comprised of six separate beings who collectively maintain your physical, and by default, your non-physical being. This group is lead by one they refer to as "Seven", and it is this "Seven" who interacts with you and tries to guide you." Rhodes paused. "Have I missed anything?"

I shook my head. "No so far you're doing fine."

Rhodes looked at Harridy who nodded his agreement. "Good. Furthermore, you said part of this group's responsibility is to maintain the "memory records" which are used to help them maintain your existence while you are here, and that these records are also used during some kind of evaluation process that precedes the reincarnation of your "Essence"."

"Yes that is true." I was amazed that Rhodes was able to quantify the information so succinctly, especially since his notes appeared to be nothing more than a jumble of lines scribbled haphazardly across the pages of his notebook.

Rhodes paused before he continued. "And this "support group" gave you the power to read minds and use suggestions to make other people do as you wish." This was the critical question Rhodes had wanted answered.

I looked at the table before I responded. I knew my support unit was not responsible for my new abilities. Their initial surprise at my being able to see and talk with them was evidence of that. "No. They did not give me this "power" as you call it. In fact I'm positive they wish I didn't have it."

Rhodes smiled. He had suspected this but needed to ask in case he was wrong. "Where do you think this power is coming from? Is it possible it is coming from whoever manages the support units?" While Reynolds had never directly mentioned any hierarchal structure, one could be inferred if the culmination of the support unit's activities was a higher level process of reincarnation.

I remembered Rena saying these powers were innate to every human, even within what she called the hybrids. "I don't think the powers are coming from anywhere, I suspect they are already within us, just not accessible." Somehow, the trauma I had endured had in some way awakened or re-connected me with these powers. I wondered to myself if they would go away once my body overcame the effects of the trauma. "And yes, I believe there is a hierarchal structure in the non-physical realm." As I had read his thoughts on this issue, I felt the need to answer him. "Earlier, I told you I went to a place they called the "Hall of Understanding. While I was there, I met others. One of them, the one called Jonathan indicated he needed to get approval for me to be there. While I waited, he assigned what he called an "associate" to accompany me. Based upon this, I think there were at least four levels of organization. My support unit is one. Whoever Jonathan needed to get approval from is two, his associate would be the third, and of course himself." I paused and watched as Rhodes made notations in his book "I also met one of the "Sleepers", so perhaps even a fifth level, although based upon their reaction to her, I believe she represents yet another major group. One I had not yet met. Her name was "Christie"."

Harridy had already circled the word "Sleepers" as one of his follow-up questions. "Who are these "Sleepers"? How do they fit into this?"

I decided the best analogy was the one I had given earlier. "Do you remember earlier I described a cartoon where the little angel sat on one shoulder giving advice? Well the same cartoon had a corresponding devil sitting on the other shoulder, naturally giving different advice. While I do not necessarily think these are angels and devils, I think the concept probably fits. According to what my "Seven" told me, they are called "Sleepers" because it is while we are sleeping that they are most capable of influencing our thoughts. Who knows, perhaps while we our dream. In any case, he considers them as a threat to us. He used terms like misleading, deceptive, manipulative and dangerous when he described them."

Harridy nodded. "But what do they want? Why are they a threat?"

I shook my head. "I don't know. According to my "Seven", the "Sleeper's" goals are the same as those of the support units, only their methods are different." I hesitated, unsure if I should continue. "I met some of them, and quite frankly I'm not convinced they are a threat, or if they are, that they are the greatest threat." It wasn't

Christie's group that Rena had warned me about.

Harridy looked thoughtfully at me. After years of questioning suspects, he sensed, more than knew he wasn't getting all of the facts. He looked at Rhodes and shrugged his shoulders. "Are you ready to move on?"

Rhodes also felt there was more but decided not to push the issue. "Yes, that's probably a good idea." He made a mental note to re-visit this "Sleeper" issue at another time.

Harridy turned to face me. "What happened with Doctor Wong? Did you somehow heal him?"

I thought back to that moment when I first come out of my sleep or coma, whatever it was. "All I remember is that I woke up and saw the Doctors, and of course Andrew and her." I gestured in the direction of Mary. "The next thing I knew, I was back with my support unit, once again viewing everything from a third person perspective." I paused then continued. "It was while I was with them that I found out what had happened to Wong."

Rhodes interrupted. "You were able to read the nurse's mind and that's how you knew about her daughter." Rhode's had already figured that out from the earlier discussion but still wanted to confirm he was correct.

I nodded. Yes, I also heard Blake's "Five" tell his "Seven" about                    his                    heart                    condition."

Andrew had witnessed firsthand what had happened in the hospital room interrupted. "But how did you heal him?" He had seen what he thought was flash of lightening just before Brangeel came between Wong and his father.

"I don't know. I remember feeling some kind of energy when he touched me, almost like static electricity."

"What happened then?" Harridy made another notation in his book.

"As I said, I returned to my support unit." I didn't think I needed to add I had reverted back to a comatose or unconscious state.

"How did your support unit react to what happened?" Rhodes asked this question hoping to positively determine if the support unit played a greater role than he had been told.

I remembered the look of shock on my "Seven" and "Threes"

faces. They had been as surprised as I was. "They were surprised. In fact, they were speechless." I hesitated then added. "And they weren't the only ones. Evidently whatever happened with Wong created some sort of disturbance in the non-physical realm as well. Jonathan, Thomas and Christie showed up almost immediately and wanted to know what had happened."

Rhodes heard a new name and asked. "Who is Thomas? Is he another "Sleeper?"

I realized I had not yet mentioned Thomas. "Do you remember I told you about going to the "Hall of Understanding"?

Rhodes shook his head. "Yes."

I nodded. "Do you remember I said that Jonathan left me with an "associate" while he spoke with his superiors?"

Rhodes again nodded his head. "Yes."

"That associate was Thomas. It was he who explained to me the natural cycle and the purpose and nature of the "Hall of Understanding"."

Harridy again attempted to direct the conversation. "What did they want to know?"

"They wanted to know what had happened. That was when my "Three" played back the memory recorder so they could see for themselves."

Harridy made another notation then asked. "How did they react when they saw it? Were they also surprised?"

"Yes, surprised and I think scared." I paused and tried to recollect my thoughts at the time. "More specifically, Jonathan was scared. I got the sense Christie was more excited than scared."

Rhodes interrupted. "Why do you think they were scared or excited?" If Jonathan was in fact scared, and the other one, Christie was excited, it meant the event had a different meaning for each of them.

"I don't know. Christie said something about my being the "one". I don't know what she meant because she closed her thoughts to me. Jonathan, on the other hand, was thinking he needed to report the event to someone, but I don't know who."

Harridy decided to press the matter further. "What happened next?"

I thought for a moment and tried to relive in my mind the sequence of events. "I think that was when Christie suggested I visit the "Hall of Knowledge". She told me it might be possible to get the answers to my questions there."

"What questions?" Harridy also wanted to know more about the "Hall of Knowledge" but decided understanding what motivated me took precedence.

I shrugged my shoulders, at this point even I didn't know. What had started out as a simple question of "why" had been transformed into a long list of other questions. "When I first came into contact with my "support unit", I couldn't accept that our reality was nothing more than a great recycling process. I wanted to understand why, to what end. Equally important, I wanted to know where they had come from, why they did what they did. When Christie suggested I might find the answers in the "Hall of Knowledge", I jumped at the chance." I thought for a moment then added. "In hindsight, I think she suggested this as a means to keep me from returning to this realm."

Rhodes was excited. First a Hall of Understanding", now, a "Hall of Knowledge", he had read of a mythical place where the supposed "Akashic records, records of all memories" were kept, was this that place? "Tell me about this "Hall of Knowledge""

Because I had already read Rhodes thoughts, I knew I would be able to validate at least one of his beliefs. "Do you remember the memory records that are maintained by the support units "Three"?"

Rhodes nodded his head. "Yes, they are used during the evaluation process, right?"

I nodded. "Yes they are. After the evaluation process, they are sent to this place where they are stored in the form of a "data ring". The "Hall of Knowledge" appears to be some sort of a library, only instead of books they use data rings."

Rhodes sat quietly and contemplated what I had said. "You mean the memories of every person who ever lived are there?" Rhodes grinned to himself. As a reporter, the thought of that type of information made his mouth water. To be able to look at historical events through the memories of the people involved had a tantalizing aspect to it.

I smiled. As I knew his thoughts, I decided to feed his desire. "Yes, every memory of every person ever evaluated is there. What's more, while I was there, I saw others like us who were accessing the records."

Rhodes dropped his pen. "You mean people like you and me? How do they do it? Do you know?"

I laughed aloud. His reaction was what I had expected. "Yes, people like you and me. As for how, I don't know for sure, but they told me some manage to get there through meditation, others through the use of drugs, and still others are brought there by the "Sleepers"." I wasn't sure how much knowledge these people actually retained when they returned to their conscious selves, and decided not to bring the subject up.

Rhodes was clearly excited and pressed for more details. "How does the process work? I mean, how do you to access these records, or "data rings", these memories?" He had already decided to revisit the whole concept of meditation. If there was a way to get there he was going to try.

"You access the data by simply touching the data ring. When you touch the data ring, you are instantly brought into the memory record at a time corresponding to that point in time of the person's life." I paused and realized I had not yet explained the circular purpose of the ring. "To understand this you would need to understand the concept of the natural cycle."

Rhodes was not to be put off. "Natural cycle? You mean the cycle of life?" In his studies he had read of the concept. It was one of the concepts he believed to be correct, if only because it was immediately apparent in all of nature, and of course conceptually in the human experience.

I saw the look of confusion on Andrew's face and decided an explanation was in order. "Yes, you could call it the "cycle of life"." I turned to Andrew. "In all that exists there is a natural sequence of events. The sequence starts with a point of creation or birth. It has a growth phase, a decay phase, and eventually a death phase. You can see it throughout the natural world. Some cycles are long and some are short. The cycle of a flower is relatively short. In the spring, it is created and blossoms, through the summer it continues to live but is already beginning to decay, and eventually in the fall its cycle ends. Humans also have a cycle beginning with birth, growth through adulthood, old age and of course death. Do you understand?"

Andrew nodded his head. "Yes, but what about a tree? It also follows the same cyclic pattern as the flower but in the winter it doesn't die."

I smiled. Andrew had always had the ability to take the question to the next level. "You're right, the tree does follow the same cyclic pattern as the flower, and yes it has the ability to repeat the cycle year after year. This brings me to the next point. When a cycle is completed, a new cycle begins. In the case of the tree, that new cycle begins again in the spring. In the case of a human, the new cycle is in another form, if only as a nutrient for the soil. But a new cycle none the less." I turned back to Rhodes. "The "data ring" follows the same sequencing. The bottom of the ring near the six o'clock position is the beginning point of the person's life, as you move clockwise up the ring you are following his life cycle. Therefore, where you touch the data ring dictates the point in the life cycle of the person. Obviously, all preceding memories are then available for review. Do you understand?"

Rhodes nodded his head. "Conceptually yes, but how does the actual process work? And is that all you can do? View one ring at a time?" To his way of thinking the process should be more interactive.

"I don't fully understand the mechanical aspects either, but I was shown that it is possible the "jump" to a different data ring, or person's memories while you are viewing the memories of another." I went on to describe my adventure into my brother's data ring.

Harridy again tried to re-focus the direction of the discussion. "What happened next?"

I grinned at the expression of dismay on Rhodes face. It was obvious he wanted to discuss the memory rings in greater detail. I mentally sent him a message to tell him we could do so at another time. I looked at Harridy. "Other than meeting a guy named "Eldred" nothing else happened. I returned to my support unit, and eventually came back here. That was when I woke up and you were there.

Harridy made a notation in his notebook. "Who is "Eldred"?"

I thought for a moment before I answered. "Initially, I thought he was, for lack of a better term, the "Head Librarian". But by his demeanor, and the way the others like Christie and Thomas reacted to him, I now think he is one of the leaders. Leader of what I don't know, but he is definitely more than just the custodian of the data rings." I remembered the look of awe on Thomas's face, and as well, Eldred's warm greeting of Christie. It was evident they knew each other. I wondered if they were on the same team. "According to what Rena told me, Eldred is less of a threat than Arinon. But she didn't seem to fully trust either of them."

Harridy sat back in his chair. Reynolds kept adding new faces to the scenario. This only reinforced his thought that he was not telling all he knew. "Who is Rena? And for that matter, who is Arinon?"

The image of Rena formed in my mind. "Do you remember earlier this evening when I vanished?"

Harridy nodded. "Yes."

"When I vanished, I went to a new place, a place that exists between the physical and non-physical realms. While I was there, another being who called herself "Rena" appeared. She claims to be the last "pure human". She also claims to be at least twelve thousand years old. She also possesses the same powers as the ones I now have. In fact, it was she who told me that these powers reside in all humans." I paused then added. "She also warned me to not use the powers, that they were dangerous."

"Twelve thousand years? How is that possible? And what do you mean "pure human", aren't we all humans?" The look of disbelief was evident on Harridys face.

I looked at Harridy. In many ways I shared his skepticism. But at the same time, I had no reason or evidence to dispute her claims. "I know it's hard to believe, and quite frankly, I'm not sure I do. But at the same time she did know things. She knew of Eldred and this guy Arinon, and clearly she possesses and understands these powers. As for what a "pure human" is your guess is as good as mine, but she did refer to me as a hybrid, so I'm guessing that something happened in the early times that made us different."

Harridy shook his head, obviously still struggling to understand. "But if she has these powers, and she has been here for twelve thousand years, why is she hiding? What is she hiding from?" To his way of thinking, she could have used her powers to do something, although he couldn't fathom what that something was.

"I don't know, but she did tell me that there were others like her who had tried unsuccessfully to come back. I got the sense they were hunted down and killed, in spite of their abilities." Rena's reference to unseen threats flashed through my mind. Perhaps that explained why she stayed in the sanctuary. "She did say that she was the last. Perhaps she stays there to keep her kind alive. I really don't know."

Rhodes interrupted. "How would using these powers be dangerous?" The thought had occurred to him that I might be hedging on my agreement to help Angelina.

I looked at Rhode's. As I had read his thoughts earlier I understood his true motive for asking. "I don't know the full extent of the risks, but, she did ask me what would happen if a person abused the power." I thought for a minute and remembered a comment Rhodes had made earlier. "Earlier you said you wouldn't play poker with me. Why?"

Rhodes laughed. "Obviously you would know what cards I had and even if I had you beat, you could simply plant the suggestion that I should fold or I would lose." As he said this he was beginning to understand the danger I had been referring to. "So you think an unscrupulous person would abuse these powers and that's why they are dangerous?"

I shook my head in agreement. "Yes, I think that was what Rena was saying, and I have to agree. But I also got the sense that the greater danger was not in how the powers are used, but more that the powers can be easily passed on if not properly controlled."

Harridy heard this and as he sat up, his back became rigid. "You mean when you use this power you risk passing the power to another person? Let's use Wong for an example. You healed him. Does that mean he can now heal others the same way?" For the first time during the discussion Harridy was afraid. The thought that the average criminal could have the ability to mentally disarm, or even control the thoughts of a police officer had left him with a knot in his stomach.

As I read Harridys thoughts, I recognized and agreed with his fear. "I don't know about Wong, whether he will be able to heal people with this power or not. When I healed him, I had no control over the power and don't actually know how much I passed to him, but Rena thinks because the duration of our contact was very short, it's unlikely it passed to him. Although according to Rena, it wasn't so much passing the power on to him, it's more a case where I might have re-activated the powers already residing within him."

Harridy nodded. "So when you used your power to disarm the Homeland Security people you may have passed or re-awakened that ability in them?"

"No, I don't think so. There was no physical contact with them."

Andrew looked up. "Wait a minute, you said physical contact right?"

"Yes. Why?" I knew where he was going with this question.

"When we joined hands and you brought us here we made physical contact. Does that mean we now have the power of teleportation?" Andrew was excited at the prospect.

I smiled. "No. Sorry to disappoint you. Rena told me how to control the power in such a way that I would not inadvertently pass it on." I grinned to myself at Andrew's obvious disappointment.

Rhodes lifted his eyes. "So you can control these powers?" His hopes were again restored that Angelina would be helped.

I looked at Rhodes and smiled. "Yes, Harold, I can still help Angelina." I hesitated and realized I had again made a promise I might not be able to keep. "Harold, I can only promise you that if I still have the power tomorrow, I will help. But you need to know there is a possibility that between now and then, I could lose it." I was also thinking of Rena's warning about Arinon wanting to find and destroy me. Obviously, my promise to Rhodes meant nothing if that happened.

Harridy again looked at his notes. "What about this Arinon character? Who is he and where does he fit in?"

I shrugged my shoulders. "I've never met him. In fact, until Rena mentioned him, I didn't even know he existed." I paused then added. "If I read between the lines of what Rena said, I suspect he is in charge of the support units. Other than that, I don't know." I decided it would be wise to not reference Rena's warnings about him.

Harridy sensed the discussion was almost over and decided to summarize his observations. "Okay, let's summarize what we know." He paused and waited until he had everyone's attention. Harridy reached over and took Rhodes notebook and removed a page. He placed the sheet of paper in the center of the table and drew a circle on it. Then he used the edge of the pizza box for a ruler. He drew a line through the center of the circle from top to bottom. "According to what you have said, we have two aspects of reality. One is physical, and one is non-physical." He wrote the word physical on the right hand side and the word non-physical on the left. "On this side we have us, humans." He wrote the word "humans" on the right side and circled it. "And on this side we have the "support units" as you call them." He wrote the initials SU on the left side of the sphere, and again drew a circle around it." According to what you have described, we know the support units are in some way connected to the humans." Harridy carefully drew a "squiggly" line between the two circles. "Then we have a place called the "Hall of Understanding". I assume that is on the non-Physical side?" Harridy paused and looked at me for affirmation.

I nodded. "Yes it is." I watched as Harridy wrote the words on the lower side of the left sphere then drew a box around the words. Evidently, the box shape was going to be used to delineate a place.

Harridy continued. "Then there is another place, again I assume on the non-physical side called the "Hall of Knowledge"." He wrote the words, this time on the upper half of the left side of the sphere, and again drew a box around them. "Now, if I understood you correctly, Jonathan and his associate Thomas can be linked to this box." Harridy pointed at the HU box.

I nodded again. "Yes that's correct." I was beginning to see where Harridy was going with this exercise.

Harridy wrote the initials J and K next to the HU box and again circled each. "Then we have "Christie". Where does she fit into this?" Harridy suspected she was linked to the HK box but wanted to see if I thought the same.

I pointed at the HK box. I don't know for sure, but I think she is linked to that one." Aside from my sense that she already knew Eldred, my assumption was also based upon Jonathan's reaction to her when she first appeared at the "Hall of Understanding". It made sense that she would be in a position opposite that of Jonathan and Thomas.

Harridy nodded then wrote her name beside the box HK and again drew a circle around the word. "And this guy Eldred is obviously also in this box." Harridy wrote "Eldred" next to the HK box as well.

"Yes, I think that is correct. You can also add the names Anne and Franklin to that box." I wasn't sure if I had mentioned them, but knew they were part of the HK box.

Harridy dutifully wrote and circled the names and wondered to himself who they were.

As I watched him write the names and circle them, I read his thoughts and replied. "I think they are the same as Christie. Lets call them what they do, "Sleepers"."

Harridy nodded. He had already deduced they were the "Sleepers". "Okay, who are we missing?"

Rhodes immediately replied. "Rena." He was curious to see where I would place her on the diagram.

"I think she goes here." I pointed at the line separating the two sides of the sphere.

Harridy looked at me then asked. "On the line?"

I smiled to myself and remembered Rena's cryptic description of the Sanctuary. *Between the two lies the one.* "Yes on the line." I watched as Harridy wrote her name and also circled it.

I had a sudden thought that it would be appropriate for Harridy to also link her name to the circle marked "humans". After all, she did say we possessed the same powers even though we were hybrids. "Harridy, I think you should draw a line between her and the humans as well."

Harridy nodded, and drew another "squiggly" line connecting the circles. "Now we have this guy Arinon. Where does he fit in?" He suspected Arinon would be linked to the HU box.

I shrugged. "I don't know I've never met him. But based upon what Rena said, he would probably be opposite Eldred, so he must be assigned to this one." I pointed at the HU box.

Harridy smiled. "I thought so." He wrote Arinon next to the HU box and circled it. "Are we missing anything?"

Andrew looked at the drawing and was amazed the picture had so easily been brought into focus based on the result of an hour's discussion. "What about these powers? Where do they fit in?"

Harridy shook his head. "Yes, we can't forget them." Harridy looked at me. "What do you think?"

I pointed at the word "human", seemingly alone on the right side of the paper. "Obviously there. According to Rena, all humans possess the powers." I paused then pointed at Rena's name. "And I think we can assume there."

Harridy wrote the word "power" next to the circled words "Rena" and "humans". He then drew a triangle around the words. Harridy looked again at me and gestured at the left side of the page. "These others don't have the powers?"

I thought for a moment before I answered. "No, in fact this group," I pointed at the HU box and Arinons group of names. "Seem to fear the power. And this group." I pointed at the HK box and Eldred's group. "Were excited by it."

Harridy drew a line from the HU and HK boxes to the triangles that contained the word "power". On the line from the HU box he wrote "fears" and on the other he wrote "does not fear". "Can we all agree to this?"

I watched as everyone nodded in agreement. "Should we add the Homeland Security guys to the diagram?" To my way of thinking, they were my greatest immediate threat.

Harridy shrugged. "We can if you want, but I think if anything, they are also just pawns in a much larger game." Harridy had already deduced that the controls used in the physical world were in someway created at the behest of the other side. If he was correct in his assessment, the diagram would need a lot more space.

Rhodes had used this same process as a reporter and knew the next step to take. "Okay, based upon this diagram what can we infer?" He paused and waited to see if anyone wanted to make a first attempt. Nobody spoke and he continued. "I'll start. It seems to me that this "power" is the only element common to all of the groups." He paused then continued his thought. "One group has it." He pointed at the human linkage. "One group fears it." He pointed at the HU group. "And one group is excited by it." He pointed at the HK group.

Harridy nodded his agreement. "So what we need to figure out is why they feel that way." He sensed Rhodes was correct. The power was the key to understanding the larger picture. Harridy looked at me then asked. "Was there anything they said that might help us?"

I leaned back in my chair and closed my eyes. I mentally replayed the events and conversations of the day. Nothing my "Seven" or for that matter Thomas had said, had anything to do with the power. I vaguely remembered that Christie and Jonathan had taken opposing positions as to whether Wong should walk immediately, or whether he should wait, I dismissed this since it did not reference in any way the actual power. The only time I could remember speaking about the power directly, was the moment on the rear porch when I had asked Jonathan and Christie if I should use the power to help Angelina. I remember Jonathan had advised me not to use it. And of course, Christie took an opposite position. I remembered as well they had agreed that the use of the power would be somehow disruptive to the dynamics of the non-physical realm, but it would not be significant. "I can't think of anything. There is no doubt they know about the power, and I think Christie knows more than Jonathan, but neither of them said anything useful."

Harridy was disappointed. He had hoped I could give them some clue. "Okay let me summarize what we know. "First, we have a "person", who possesses the power to heal, use telepathy, telekinesis, and of course teleportation. Second, said "person", by virtue of his actions today, is without a doubt a person of interest to the government. Third, based upon what he has told us, there appear to be at least two other distinct groups also interested in him. Groups, I might add, who we know very little about, especially their motives." Harridy hesitated, then as an afterthought added. "I think we can safely assume that at least one, if not both of these other groups should be considered as a threat as well. Fourth, by virtue of our involvement with this "person" I suspect we are also going to be affected in some way."

I looked at Mary then at Andrew, I knew what Harridy had said was true, because of me they were in danger. "I looked at Harridy, what do you think the Security guys will do? Are they going to come back and take them again?"

Harridy clasped his hands together, placing them on the table in front of him. "I think for now they are probably safe." He smiled then added. "You sent them quite a message tonight, and I doubt they will take it lightly. No, I don't think they will do much more than keep them under surveillance." He paused then added. "At least until they get new orders." Harridy continued. "I'm more concerned about these other groups, without knowing their agenda's it impossible to know if, or how much, of a threat they are. Let alone what is really happening in the larger sense."

I had already decided to focus my efforts on finding out who they were, and what they wanted. Who knows, perhaps during the process I might even find my answers. "I agree with you. We need to know more about them." I hesitated then added. "And I'm the only one who can." I looked at Mary and added. "I will be going away for awhile, someplace safe, where nobody will recognize me. While I am there, I will return to the "Hall of Knowledge". It's possible what we need to know can be found in the data rings."

Mary, her eyes beginning to well up with tears, grabbed my arm. "I don't want you to go. What happens if they catch you? They might hurt you or worse."

I instinctively patted her arm, a subconscious attempt to reassure her. "Actually, based upon what we know, I don't think they can hurt me. I say this because their realm is non-physical and while I am there, so am I. No dear, I will be perfectly safe." I did not add the greater concern lay in the fact that while my non-physical being was there, my physical being had to be here in the physical realm, and as such could be harmed. And although their supposed agreement disallowed direct interference in the physical realm, I wasn't foolish enough to think they couldn't find a way if they really wanted to.

Andrew was obviously upset and jumped from his seat. "You said you could use your power to awaken the power in others. I think you should do that to me. I want to go with you." Yet even as he said it, he knew I would disagree.

I smiled at Andrew. "I figured you would say that, but the answer is no. You need stay here with your mother and brother."

With each passing moment, my appreciation for the man he had become was reaching new heights. "Trust me when I say that I will be fine, they cannot hurt me there."

I nodded at Rhodes. "Remember our appointment, tomorrow, three o'clock." I turned to Harridy. "Will you watch out for my family?"

Harridy nodded his head. "I'll do my best."

"Thanks. Hopefully someday I can repay you." After I said this, I went in search of my passport. While I knew I could use my teleportation power to bypass Immigration. I would need it to check into the hotel.

# Chapter 35

## Hall of Knowledge

$A$rinon, with Peter standing behind him, stood and faced his old enemy. He was upset and Peter was even more so. The meeting with Eldred had not gone as Peter had hoped. Eldred had, as Arinon had said he would, refused to allow the Reynolds memory records to be opened. Now to make matters worse, Eldred was in the process of issuing even more devastating news.

Eldred smiled inwardly. He had expected Arinon and Peter to request this special dispensation. He also knew the true motivation for the request. It was evident to him that Reynolds sudden disappearance had affected Arinons group just as it had his own. Neither knew where he was, and both sides needed to find him, although for different reasons.

Eldred turned to face Arinon. He knew his next statement would not be well received, especially by Peter. "Before you go, I would also suggest you to tread very carefully in this matter. I have already advised the evaluation center to forward the memory records of any person related in any way to Reynolds. I can assure you they will be scrutinized carefully." While Eldred knew the full extent of Peter's treachery could not be known within individual memory records, he was delivering the message that the records would be set aside for further review. As other memory records of Bios related to Reynolds were acquired, they would also be scrutinized within the context of the earlier memory records. Eventually the plot, if there was one, would become evident and Eldred would have what he needed to end this charade. He watched Peter's face and by the change in his countenance, knew he his assessment was correct. Peter did have an operation underway to stop Reynolds.

Arinon was not surprised that Eldred refused their initial

request. However he was surprised by Eldred's warning. Clearly the plans Peter had underway would need to be stopped quickly. Arinon looked at Eldred, feigning surprise and replied. "That's fine. We are only trying to protect him." He paused before adding. "As I'm sure you are." He knew Eldred wanted Reynolds as much as he did. In the end, he suspected it would boil down to Reynolds making his own decision as to which side he would support.

Eldred smiled. "Good, as long as we understand each other." He nodded to Peter and turned his back to his protagonists, a clear signal that the meeting was over.

# Chapter 36

## <u>Dusit Laguna Hotel. Phuket, Thailand.</u>

*W*hen I opened my eyes, I found myself standing in front of the large white sign at the entrance to the Dusit Laguna Hotel. Years before, I had visited Thailand for business purposes and stayed for two weeks in this idyllic setting. Two years before, this place had been virtually destroyed by a Tsunami and I often wondered if it had been rebuilt. It obviously had been and the beauty of the place was once again restored. I walked slowly toward the reception center and main lobby, the fragrance of the tropical flowers wafted in the air and relieved some of the tension I was feeling. I found myself wondering if my old room, a corner room with a balcony facing the open sea on one side and a small lagoon on the other, was available. I approached the main desk and presented my passport and credit card to the beautiful Thai clerk. "I would like to check in."

The desk clerk, whose name tag said Kia, took the passport and punched my name into the computer. "Do you have a reservation sir?"

I didn't but had hoped since was their off-season a room would be available. "No, actually I don't. I am staying at another hotel in town for business, and thought I would spend a week of vacation when the meeting is over. I was a guest here before and decided to move to this hotel." I smiled at her and hoped my explanation would be accepted. "Do you think you can find a room for me? This is my favorite vacation spot."

Kia nodded. "I'm sure we will be able to accommodate you Mr. Reynolds. Do you have a preference of rooms? Smoking or non-smoking?"

"Either will work."

Smiling she continued. "Lagoon side or sea side?"

I smiled at her in an effort to convey my gratitude for her

efforts. "Actually is room one-one-eight available?" This was my old room.

The clerk keyed the numbers into the computer and nodded. "Yes sir, it is available for the next week. How long do you plan to stay?"

I nodded. "A week of vacation time is all I have." I knew I would not be there a full week but would deal with that issue later. I also suspected Kia's "Seven" who would not recognize may face, would eventually recognize my name and pass it on to Arinon. No this stay would be very short.

A few more keystrokes and the room was mine. Kia took my credit card and scanned the magnetic strip. This process only validated the card, the actual billing activity would not take place until I checked out. Still, I wondered if the validation process would be enough for anyone trying to find me. I didn't have a choice. It was a risk I would have to take.

Kia handed the card and passport to me. "Were all set Mr. Reynolds, we have you in room one-one-eight for one week. Do you have luggage?"

I shook my head. "No, it's still at my other hotel. I will bring it later."

"Yes sir, of course." Kia smiled and handed the magnetic keycard to me. "If you will just wait a moment, I will have someone show you to your room."

I took the keycard and shook my head. "That will not be necessary I remember how to get there." I paused then added. "I might lie down for a few hours. Would you give me a wake up call for five am?" This would be three pm in the states, the time I needed to meet Rhodes.

Kia nodded and entered a command into the computer. "Five am, no problem sir. The restaurant doesn't open until seven am but there is a coffee maker in your room and a fruit basket as well." She thought it was strange that I wasn't returning to my other hotel, but had long ago decided westerners were by their nature already strange, so she didn't question it.

I walked to the rear of the lobby and descended a wide set of flagstone stairs which led down to the pool. The path split into three separate paths. I took the left path and crossed a grassy area. I passed a tropical garden and small stream filled with colorful coy fish. Fifty meters beyond the stream was the corner room one-one-eight. I inserted the keycard, and pushed open the door and walked into the air-conditioned room. I placed the do not disturb sign on the outside door handle and closed the door, careful to set the security bar into its locked position. I knew from long experience that the do not disturb sign would be faithfully honored and I would not be disturbed.

The layout of room was as I remembered it, although it lacked the moldy smell so often evident in the tropics. Instead, there was a faint odor of new construction, no doubt the byproduct of the rebuilding effort after the tsunami. I opened the small cupboard I knew held the coffee maker and after filling it with water I pressed the "on" button. I was finally going to get that cup of coffee I had stopped for at the rest area for.

The afternoon sun slowly encroached its way through the small forest of trees that stood between my balcony and the beach. As I sat drinking my coffee I thought of the diagram Harridy had developed. Based upon the diagram and as well my conversation with Rena, it was clear there were opposing forces at work behind the scenes. Forces whose agendas I needed to understand. I remembered Rena's suggestion that I should return to the "Hall of Knowledge" and that I should allow Eldred to show me the event rings. And a ring she called the "black ring", whatever that was. I picked up my now empty coffee cup and re-entered the room. I knew that if I returned to the "Hall of Knowledge, I would have to leave my physical body behind. The thought of doing so was not peril. The last time, my support unit had still been with me, and my "Seven" made sure I returned safely. Now with my support unit gone, I could only hope the arranged wake-up call would be enough to bring me back. Of one thing I was certain. If I really wanted to understand what was happening, it was a risk I had to take. I kicked off my shoes and lay down on the bed. I closed my eyes and tried to recall the image of the sea of data rings.

# Chapter 37

## Headquarters Office of Homeland Security, Washington D.C.

*This* room, situated the equivalent of eleven stories underground, was not monitored by audio or video methods. In fact, access to the room was reserved for only the highest security clearances, and even then, the parties involved were escorted to the room by a number of innocuous routes. Were you to ask any one of them how they got there, or for that matter where the room was, none would have been able to tell you. A series of tables arranged in the shape of a horseshoe faced a cinematic size projection screen. The podium behind which Ross now stood sat to the lower right of the screen. His now completed presentation had provided a chronological profile of the day's events, beginning with a review of the magnetic anomaly charts and ending with the disappearance of Reynolds and his friends. Two hours earlier Ross had contacted the OHS Director and had managed to convince him to issue a Category One request. A Category One request, used only for emergencies, resulted in a process whereby the participants who now occupied the chairs before him were rounded up and brought to this room. Needless to say, in making the request, Ross had gone far out on a limb. And in the process he had brought his boss along for the ride. If the assembled group believed the Category One level request was unwarranted, it would certainly be a career ending event for him personally. And to a certain extent, for his boss as well. Now, as he had concluded the presentation and saw the look on their faces, he knew he was safe.

Secretary of Defense Samuel Sheppard was the first to speak. "Thank you Director Ross." Sheppard leaned back into his chair. What he had just seen and heard had excited and at the same time had frightened him. He sensed more than knew the others had similar

249

feelings. He glanced in the direction of Archibald Winston, the British liaison and then at Helmut Schmidt, Winston's counterpart from Germany. Had he known the nature of the presentation he would have taken steps to exclude them from the proceedings. It was now too late and the proverbial cat was out of the bag. Sheppard stood and made his way to the podium. He nodded to Ross, who promptly took a seat. He turned to face the six men seated at the table. "Well gentlemen. How do we proceed?" By posing this as an opened ended question, he had hoped someone else would take the lead. Admiral Kinsey represented the Joints Chiefs of Staff and did not disappoint him. Kinsey, as expected, had already envisioned Reynolds and his abilities as a potential threat. It was obvious Reynolds had the ability to read minds, and to even influence them. In Kinsey's line of work such a capability was invaluable. He also knew others from the various agencies had similar thoughts. Kinsey looked at Ross, who sat next to Ryan. "You said he can read minds and even influence them, is that correct?"

Ross glanced at the file on the table in front of him before he responded. "I don't know about reading minds. We are deducing that he can." There was no firm evidence to support this, but the consensus of his team was that he could. "However, we know with certainty he can influence the thoughts of others." That evidence was solid. The officers involved with the attempted detention process on Reynolds's porch, along with Buchannons sworn statement, and Reynolds actions caught on video in the conference room, made that fact incontrovertible.

Kinsey nodded. As he turned back toward Sheppard, he decided to take the imitative. "Even if that is all he can do, and the evidence suggests it is not, I think we should take the steps necessary to contain this." He hesitated and knew his next statement would be met with disfavor. "I propose my organization take the lead in this matter. We'll take full responsibility for him." He paused then added. "Of course, we will make sure each of you are periodically briefed on our findings."

Fleming, Director of the CIA was the first to react. He looked at Kinsey before he turned to Sheppard. "While I appreciate Admiral Kinsey's willingness to take the lead in this matter, I think the resources within the intelligence community are better equipped to

250

handle it." Fleming paused before he added. "I would also propose that the future use of whatever skills Reynolds has would serve a far greater service from an intelligence gathering perspective than merely a military tool." The ability Reynolds had displayed to appear and disappear at will potentially opened avenues for the intelligence gathering community that even the administratively restricted Secretary of Defense should be able to see.

Winston and Schmidt, almost in unison, immediately objected to both Kinsey's and Fleming's positions. Winston nodded at Schmidt to indicate he would take the lead in the discussion. "We understand Reynolds is an American, and as such you think he is your domain, but I must say that we." He gestured in Schmidt's direction. "Insist he should be considered as a person of interest globally and should therefore be managed with global considerations in mind."

Sheppard nodded. "And what "Global" organization might that be?" He had expected this recommendation and as well their next answer.

Schmidt stood a pensive look on his face. "I would suggest Interpol or maybe the UN security committee." While neither met his personal preference, nor the preference of his country, he knew it was better than having Reynolds as purely an American asset.

Ryan sat and listened. He once again found himself getting angry. These people spoke of Reynolds as a tool, or an asset, to be used as they saw fit, not as an individual who had the supposed rights afforded by the constitution of the United States. Ryan glanced at Sheppard and at the same time closed his file and tapped it on the table.

Sheppard and the others heard this sound of the file edge echo off the table surface. This had temporarily interrupted the dialog. Sheppard looked at Ryan. "Is there something you wish to add, Doctor?" He anticipated that Ryan would offer the scientific communities' resources for Reynolds and was surprised to not receive it.

Ryan stood and slowly scanned the faces of the men sitting before him. "I was just thinking to myself how ludicrous this sounds. You have apparently forgotten that Reynolds is a person, not an object. And I might add a person with individual rights. From what I have heard I suspect those rights are about to be taken from him." Ryan paused and tool time to assess the reaction to his words. "Tell me, what are you going to do if Reynolds refuses to cooperate with you? What then?"

Sheppard shook his head. He was not so naive to think that Reynolds actually had a choice. Still, since his position was politically based, he understood his decision in the matter would reflect on the administration that had appointed him. He was equally confident the President, if pressed, would support the use of Reynolds's abilities. Voluntarily if possible, but involuntarily if needed. He turned to Ryan, then back again to the other members. "Reynolds is an American citizen and his rights will not be violated." He stopped and looked at Winston and Schmidt. "As an American citizen, he will not be used in a global capacity without his consent. In fact, he will not be used in any way without his consent." This last comment was directed to the American participants. Sheppard looked again at Ryan. "I hope this satisfies your concerns, Doctor." He smiled at Ryan's nod of assent. "However, I will authorize this group to find and at least ask Reynolds for his cooperation." Sheppard didn't need to express this. Every agency in the room, including the foreign agencies was going to find Reynolds, with or without authorization.

Ryan understood what was happening, and knew as well regardless of what he thought, Reynolds would be found, and would either become part of their solution, or part of the problem. In either case, his rights as a citizen would not protect him. The sound of Ross's beeper interrupted his thoughts.

Ross looked at his beeper and saw the agency code for emergency. He looked at Sheppard, who pointed at a complicated looking telephone on the table. Ross picked up the phone and dialed the office number. Buchannons voice was audibly flat, no doubt the result of the encryption technology used, advised him they had received an alert based upon the watch list. Ross quickly jotted down the information and disconnected the call. He returned to his seat and passed the message to his boss, who in turn passed it on to Sheppard.

Sheppard glanced at the note, before returning his attention to the group. "For now, I want Hershmeir and Fleming to take the lead on this issue." Hershmeir was the FBI Director and was responsible for all domestic activities. Fleming, as the Director of CIA operations, would coordinate all international efforts." Sheppard hesitated, and tool a moment to assess the faces of the other participants. "No actions, I repeat, no actions are authorized." He looked in the direction of Winston and Schmidt, a look of resolution on his face. "I remind you that Reynolds is an American citizen, and as such, any attempt made to detain him will not be well received." Sheppard reached down and pressed a button on the podium console. The sound of the door bolts as they disengaged let the group know the meeting was adjourned. He looked at Hershmeir and Fleming. "I would like a word with you two before you leave." He looked at Ryan and Ross then added. "You should stay as well.

Sheppard waited until the room was empty except for those he requested stay. He handed Ross's note to Fleming who glanced at it before he returned his attention to Sheppard. "It would appear we got a hit on the watch list. Reynolds's credit card company reported activity in Phuket, Thailand." He looked at Ross and Ryan and asked. "How is it possible for Reynolds to be in Thailand? According to your report he was in your office three hours ago." Sheppard had recently returned from a defense summit held in Singapore and was well aware of the travel time to that part of the world. It was simply not possible for Reynolds to get there in three hours.

Ryan smiled. This confirmed his assessment the power Reynolds had used to disappear was some form of teleportation. He wondered if the science guys had observed two magnetic anomalies. The first where Reynolds had departed from, and the second in the area where he had arrived. In this case, Thailand. Ryan looked at Sheppard. "I suspect Reynolds went there hoping to avoid being detained." Ryan saw the look of disbelief on Sheppard's face and added. "If what I suspect is true he can go virtually anywhere he wants. Although quite frankly I don't know why he selected Thailand, he could have simply gone to Canada or Mexico just as easily."

Fleming looked thoughtfully at Ryan. He also wondered why Reynolds had gone to Thailand. It was an area where anti-American sentiment had been prevalent since the 1991 invasion of Iraq. Was it possible Reynolds was part of an anti-American group? Fleming the CIA Director looked at Hershmeir then back to Sheppard. "We have local assets there. How do you want to proceed?" Fleming knew the assets in place were sufficient to complete any type operation. "Do you want us to bring him back or" He allowed the "or" to remain suspended in space.

Ryan looked at Fleming. "Or what?"

Sheppard sensed the Doctor's concern and shook his head. "No, I think for now we should just put some eyes on him. If you can tie him to something larger we can take appropriate actions as needed."

Fleming nodded. "I understand completely. Surveillance only." With a nod he motioned for Hershmeir to accompany him. Fleming turned and strode through the door where their military escorts patiently waited.

Sheppard looked at Ryan and Ross. "Doctor, I think maybe you should prepare yourself for the possibility that Reynolds may not actually possess the rights you think he does. I think it might also be prudent for you to realize our "allies" do not necessarily recognize those rights either. Personally I think it would be better for Reynolds to agree to work with us versus them." Sheppard hesitated then added. "But make no mistake about it Doctor Ryan, there were people in this room who would view Reynolds as a serious threat if he decided not to cooperate." This said Sheppard motioned for them to join their escorts as well.

# Chapter 38

# Hall of Understanding.

*R*ena had been correct, I opened my eyes and the sea of rings had appeared before me. I could see small clusters of seeming spectral beings dispersed throughout the room. The door through which Eldred had appeared earlier was directly in front of me. I had only taken a few steps when Anne almost magically appeared. I watched as she approached. Her radiant smile assured me I was welcome.

"Welcome back. We've been waiting for you." Anne raised her hand in a gesture to follow her. "Eldred said you would return and is anxious to meet with you again." She walked beside me, her hand on my elbow as she gently guided me towards the arched doorway.

I wondered how Eldred could know I would return. I looked at her. "So he is expecting me?" I felt a sense of relief in knowing I would be welcome.

Anne nodded. "Oh yes, and the others are anxious to meet you as well." The council had been assembled the moment I had appeared.

"Others? What others? Do you mean Christie and Franklin?" I had hoped they would be here, especially Christie. My instincts told me she would play a large role in helping me understand what was really going on.

"She means the council." Eldred's voice interrupted before Anne could respond. "But yes, if you wish, I can ask Christie to join us as well." Eldred extended his hand, a wry smile on his face. "Welcome back. I assume you are here to find the answers to your questions."

I took the offered hand and nodded. "Thank you for allowing me to return. And yes, I am here to find answers." I paused then added. "As you might imagine, my list of questions has grown since I last saw you. But I'm sure you can help me find the answers."

Eldred smiled. "We will do our best, of course." In their earlier meeting he had only suspected that I had possessed the powers. Now, with his suspicions proven to be fact, he knew gaining my trust and support was essential. "I assume you will want to pick up where you left off last time you were here?"

I shrugged. "Is that the best way to find the answers?" I had already concluded the endless jumping back in time from memory ring to memory ring would be cumbersome and a potentially fruitless process. I remembered Franklin's reference to a higher level set of "event" rings, and although I suspected those data rings would logically reflect "events" deemed important based upon someone else's perception of importance, they might be enough to provide answers to my questions. "Franklin said there is another set of data rings maintained at a higher level which are based upon significant events. Would I be able to find my answers in them?"

Eldred nodded, inwardly ecstatic. "With appropriate guidance, yes, I believe the answers you seek can be found within them." He had hoped I would follow this path. "Those event rings are maintained by a group of experts in human affairs. That is the council I referred to earlier. They are assembled and I have asked them to guide you, and to answer any questions you may have." Eldred turned and looked at me. "If there are questions which are not answered to your satisfaction, remember them. You can ask me later."

As I followed Eldred, I had the distinct feeling I was being manipulated. Anne's comment about the others being anxious to meet me, and the obviously planned assembly of this "council", had me wondering if the entire process was being choreographed. If so, I wondered why, and for what purpose. I followed Eldred into yet another room and found myself before a small group of people. A projection screen, similar to the one I had used to enter my brothers data ring, sat beside a row of golden data rings. It occurred to me that the golden color was probably used to keep them separate from the silver individual memory rings. I listened as Eldred introduced the group.

Eldred pointed at a young woman. "This is Joan. Joan is what you would call a sociologist. Beside her is James our historian. To his left Henry, our geologist, and as you requested, Christie." Eldred turned and looked at me. "Each of them is an expert in his field and I am sure they can answer any questions you might have." He paused then added. "I would suggest that you allow them to guide you, understand and learn from them and ask questions if you like. But above all you must believe we are all here to help you. We will not withhold information and will answer any direct questions you have truthfully." I watched as Eldred turned away and left the room.

An awkward silence followed Eldred's departure. Finally Christie stepped forward, took my hand and led me closer to the group. Christie looked at me with a smile on her face. "Do you have any questions before we begin?" She would have been surprised if I did not.

I nodded to her and gestured toward the row of golden rings. "Tell me about these rings. I understand they represent significant events, but I am unclear as to what defines significance."

Christie nodded. "Good question." She paused as if thinking of the best way to answer. "Perhaps it would be best to review a few of the basic concepts before we begin." Christie glanced at the group. "As you know there is a natural cycle which applies to all aspects of reality. It is important for you to understand that this cycle applies not only to the physical reality." She gestured at Henry who shook his head in agreement. "But also in the social and historical processes." Christie stopped and looked at me. "You do remember the natural cycle, don't you?"

I nodded to indicate I did. "Yes, of course. It begins with creation, processes through the growth and decay phases, and eventually ends." I hesitated then continued. "And yes, I understand that the end results in a new beginning." I had the sense of where she was going with this line of thinking but decided not to interrupt.

Joan, the sociologist, picked up where Christie left off. "These event rings are a record of the changes affecting your people. In terms of social development, you might think of them as a series of events which resulted in changes to the consciousness of man." After a moment of hesitation, she continued. "The same approach is used to assess the key historical and geological events which affected the course of human development." Joan turned to face me. "Is that clear enough?"

At a conceptual level I understood the approach they were using, but I still struggled to understand what constituted a change. Perhaps it would become clear as we reviewed the event rings. "Where is the baseline information derived from?" I suspected it was an output of the individual data rings but decided to ask rather than assume.

James, the historian, confirmed my assumption. "As you know, an evaluation process takes place each time a Bio cycle is completed. During this evaluation process, every memory of the Bio's life is reviewed. Our representatives at the evaluation identify data rings of interest which are then sent to us for further analysis." He looked thoughtful for a moment before he continued. "Seldom is an event defined by a single memory ring, because Bio cycles complete at different times, new information sometimes changes the perceptions made from earlier rings, in fact more often than not, significant events are defined in hindsight based upon many data rings. We have research teams who continuously review past data rings relative to new information. You may have seen some of them on your way in."

I looked at Christie and shrugged my shoulders. "I think I understand the basics, but I still wonder what constitutes a significant event."

Joan, as if on cue, stepped forward. "In some instances, an event was defined by a technical change which altered the living conditions, or behavior of the people. However, as a general rule, most of the events are based upon predominant behavioral changes common across the population. For example, the move from the hunter-gatherer society to one of an agricultural society did not mean the hunter-gather societies disappeared. They were simply no longer the predominant social structure." She paused, a thoughtful look on her face. "Before we get to the event rings I think it would be good to understand the fundamental nature of your kind." She paused and knew that her next words would impact my overall perspective of the event rings. "Humans have a saying that is most appropriate for this discussion. "To understand the purpose of a thing, you must first understand its nature." Joan looked directly at me before she continued. "The nature or natural condition of a human is biologically based. As such, humans have basic needs which must be satisfied if they are to survive. It is this effort to satisfy the basic needs which
258

often dictate their behavior. It is also important to realize that the basic needs are hierarchal, starting with those most essential for survival. And as one level of need is met, a higher level need becomes the new focus. By the same token, if a previously achieved level is not maintained, there will be a recession of thought and behavior, until it is again realized. Let me illustrate. To survive, humans require food and water. That is the first and most definitive need. If this need for food and water is satisfied, a second level need becomes predominant. This is the need for shelter and security. Above this level is the need for fellowship or community, and finally, the highest level, the need to control, to have power over their existence." Joan stopped then added. "As we review the events leading to your social development, this hierarchy applies not only to a single human, but also at a community level. As James will attest, your history is replete with examples of the buildup and breakdown of communities based upon this hierarchy of needs."

I nodded to indicate my understanding. From my studies of history, I already knew the significance of what Joan had said. Social and historical development had always been a progressive and regressive process. Fortunately, the lessons learned during the progressive cycles were not completely forgotten and were carried forward, this allowed continued social evolution to continue in spite of intermittent regressive cycles. "Let's get started."

Joan nodded, then stepped forward and selected a data ring from the rear of the long line of rings. She placed the ring in into the projection unit and stepped away from the screen. I watched as an image came into focus. I saw as a small group of people dressed in animal skins, as they slowly encircled an unsuspecting prey. Their weapons consisted of sharpened sticks, and in one instance, a large rock. Their prey, a small boar, rooted at the base of a tree, using its short tusks to dislodge the bark. I watched as the group tightened their circle, finally pouncing on the boar, stabbing and clubbing it. A flash of movement to the left of the small group caught my eye. Another group stepped out of the bushes and stood facing the first group. This new group, larger than the first, was led by a large man who boldly stepped forward and seized the boar. The leader of the smaller group, unwilling to relinquish the kill, slashed out at this newcomer with his stick. The large man parried the blow with one hand, and brought his

259

own club down savagely on his attacker's head killing him instantly. After a moment of hesitation, the smaller group picked up the body of their now dead leader, and fell into line behind the larger group. I watched as the now larger group left the forest and made its way to a river where they followed the river bank until it came to a clearing. In the center of the clearing, a fire was burned brightly. A woman of significant stature stood before the fire, a sharpened stick held at the ready. I could see the heads of women and children peering over the edge of shallow pits which they obviously called home. Joan stepped forward and pressed a button on the projection unit. Immediately the image disappeared. She turned to face me and knew I would have questions. "What I just showed you was our first major social event." She smiled at the evident look of confusion on my face. "What you just saw was unique for several reasons. It was the first memory record that showed two groups assimilating into one. And secondly, it was the first record to show any attempt to change living conditions." She paused then added. "You see, until this time, humans had never accepted outsiders into their groups. And until now they had never attempted to create any form of shelter. Generally they simply took advantage of the natural protection areas like caves or trees."

I looked at her. "So if I understand you correctly, this was the first community?" I had always pictured a community as something more defined. "Why did they take the body of the dead guy?"

Joan laughed. "Yes and No. They were hunter-gatherers and what you saw was probably a short-term living condition. But, it was the first attempt to modify the environment to satisfy a need." She paused then added. "And they took his body for food."

I nodded. I was not surprised that he would be consumed as a food. It was suspected that early humans were cannibalistic. "How long ago was that?" Based upon my own studies, I had anticipated a response in the thirty to forty thousand year range. Her response startled me.

Joan looked at James who appeared to be mentally calculating. He looked at her and said. "Ten thousand five hundred years ago." James smiled then added. "Of course, that is only a rough estimate."

I mentally translated the time frame James had given. In current terms, this equated to 8500 BC. Yet I knew scientists had determined that Homo-Sapiens had existed at least thirty thousand years earlier. "Is that the earliest memory record you have?"

Joan shook her head. "No, there are older records. But again, these are "significant event" data rings, and what you saw was the first socially relevant event that impacted the future development of your kind." She paused and looked at Henry. "I think Henry has data rings of a geological nature that predate these social events. Is that right Henry?"

Henry nodded his head in agreement. "Yes, yes of course." He tilted his head upward as if contemplating where to begin. "I think the earliest record available would be another thousand years older. Would you like to see it?"

I shook my head. "No that's okay, I was just curious." I paused then turned back to Joan. "So your earliest record is roughly eleven-thousand-five hundred years old?" I watched as she looked at James for a time equation. He nodded his head in agreement before she replied. "Yes, that would be approximately correct. But from a sociologist's perspective, before this event humans existed in an extended period of darkness. They lived in clans or family structures, and were purely nomadic and followed the food supply. The worldwide population was so small, just under two million. In fact it was rare for two clans to meet within a single lifetime." She stopped. An afterthought came to her. "The only thing of social value during this dark time was that the population was growing."

"I see." I glanced at the long row of golden rings then looked at Joan and asked. "Based upon what you have shown me, can I assume you plan to walk me through every step of the social evolution? Or is there to be a focus on the really influential changes only?" I knew by asking this I ran the risk of missing key pieces of information, but knew as well time was a factor and the line of event rings seemed endless.

Joan, with a look of dismay and obvious disappointment on her face, shook her head. "Of course, I will focus on the larger events." She selected a new ring, one a little closer from the end of the line. She inserted the ring into the projector and stepped back as the image unfolded.

I looked at the screen and saw small structures made of stone and sealed with dried mud. The eyes which captured this scene obviously did so from a high vantage point, perhaps a hill. As I watched, the view slowly shifted. In the distance, I could see alternating fields of green and gold. Hundreds of people dotted the fields and from the activity, it was evident they were in the process of harvesting crops. The view shifted again, this time to a high walled area beyond the cluster of primitive huts. Within the wall, smaller groups of people were performing various functions. One group, the largest, consisted of middle-aged women. Each knelt before a flat stone and used a round stone to grind the crop into a usable grain. Younger children, perhaps seven or eight years old, provided a continuous supply of the raw materials. Older women were formed in a circle and stood watch over even smaller children. Three buildings stood inside the wall. The largest appeared to have two levels. The lower level was large and was built of stone and mud, then buried with dirt a meter thick. Atop this lower structure a second smaller building stood. The size difference resulted in the formation of a balcony, which surrounded the upper building. I saw the shapes of several men and a woman standing on the balcony, their attention fixed on the activity in the fields. The largest figure, a head taller than any of the others, looked vaguely familiar to me. Were it not for his long silver beard, I would have sworn he was the same "larger man" from the earlier data ring. The view shifted again, this time to the right. In the distance I saw a line of thirty or more men approaching from the forested hills. Each carried a spear or club and interspersed along the line, groups of two or four men carried their fresh kill. I watched as the line of men wound their way toward the village. The view shifted again to the left and I saw the field workers also begin to make their way toward the village, baskets and bundles of crop carried with obvious care. The men guarding the lower entrance to the high walled area uncrossed their bronze or copper tipped spears and stepped aside to allow the workers to bring the harvested crop inside the walled enclosure. As each worker exited the enclosure, he was given a small loaf of what looked like bread. Upon receipt of the bread each lifted his eyes upward, toward the people on the balcony. My view again returned to the group descending from the hills. The group approached the enclosure and stopped thirty feet from the walled entrance. The men carrying the fresh meat stepped forward and lowered their burden to the ground, before rejoining the main body of the group. After a few minutes, the figures I saw on the balcony appeared and approached the group. Two of them lifted the meat as if trying to gauge its weight. One of them raised his hand to show three fingers to the tall figure. I watched as the larger figure turned to the leader of the hunting group and raised his hand with three fingers raised. With a nod of his head the hunter accepted the offer and watched as three baskets of crushed grain were placed on the ground beside the meat. Joan stood and again shut off the projector. "This memory record is representative of a social development that was taking place in most parts of the world. The communities you spoke of earlier now exist, and equally important a rudimentary form of social cooperation and trade was beginning to take place. From my perspective as a sociologist, the division of labor, and the payment for work, is a most significant development. And needless to say, the trade between the groups implies a state of peaceful coexistence." She anticipated my next question and looked at James who promptly said. "Ten-thousand years ago. And just as a point of reference, the world's population is approaching five million."

I looked at James before I returned my focus to Joan. "How is this possible? In a mere five hundred years they moved from being nomadic primitive hunter gatherers, to a society with fixed structures, trade and agriculture?" My instincts told me there had to be other factors involved. I mentally chastised myself for asking Joan to skip the "lesser" social events. "When and how did they develop the agricultural knowledge and what about those spears? They had either copper or bronze tips on them."

Joan smiled the smile of vindication. "If you would like, we can regress and view other data rings. I'm sure the answers are there."

I thought about this suggestion and tried to weigh the possible knowledge against the long line of rings yet to be viewed. "No, perhaps later, if there is time. What about that tall guy? Is he is their leader, or King? He looked identical to the person we saw in the earlier data ring." As I said this, I saw a flash of dismay in Joan's eyes. I knew I had struck a sensitive nerve.

Joan glanced quickly at James before she returned her gaze to me. "Based upon the rest of this person's memory record, yes, he was their leader. As for being the same man as in the earlier record, I'm sure you're mistaken. Perhaps he is one of his descendants." She knew that she would need to be more careful. She hoped the next data ring would be from some other part of the world. Yet even as she thought this, she knew there was no way to avoid similar observations from those as well. The interlopers had played a key role in the human development and would continue to appear over and over again, for at least the next five thousand years. For a brief moment, she considered skipping the next five thousand years, but dismissed the thought immediately. She knew the leap in social change could not be explained easily, she would just have to take her chances and hope for the best.

The next ring Joan selected appeared to be a continuation of the preceding one, an assumption soon proven wrong. The viewer, whose eyes originally recorded the memory, appeared to be in a crouched position, behind a large boulder. Below him, arrayed on the floor of the valley, were campfires of what could only be a migratory force. The camp had been set up in a semi-circle with the river protecting its flanks. Small herds of goats and sheep were afforded the most protected position, in the center of the crescent. Tents of various sizes, constructed of animal skins, formed a circle around the herds. Men carrying shiny tipped spears patrolled the outer perimeter of the encampment. The view shifted again, this time to his rear. The sight of what seemed like hundreds of men, armed with clubs and spears, left no doubt as to their intentions. I watched as they surged forward toward the camp. Within a short period of time they overpowered the patrols, and entered the center of the camp. The survivors clustered together, now surrounded by the attacking force. Women and children were quickly separated from the men, who knelt with their hands held above their heads. The circle of men from the attacking force separated creating an avenue through which a woman with bright red hair approached. A young boy lying on a litter carried by four men followed her. At a gesture of her hand the men placed the litter holding the boy on the ground. I watched as the surviving men were brought before the boy one at a time. As each approached, the boy looked at each of them. He occasionally pointed and then looked toward the woman. Each time the man was taken aside and his hands were tied. Those not selected by the boy, mostly very young or very

264

old were permitted to rejoin the women and children. When the segregation process was complete, the woman turned to face the bound and frightened men. She removed a small knife from her belt its copper colored blade glinting in the evening light. She walked behind the line of kneeling men stopping at each only long enough to draw the blade slowly across their throats.

Joan stood and removed the data ring from the projector. "This event ring is indicative of a major shift in the area of social development. Until this time, communities tended to remain self sufficient and isolated from one another. However, as the population grew, it became necessary for them to expand their resource base. In general terms, this expansion was achieved as small groups splintered from the main body, and formed smaller settlements. Such was the case in this instance. What made this event significant was the implication of centralized ownership. Even though smaller splinter communities were being developed, there was a recognition that they still belonged to the larger group. In a sense it was the first multi-community nation."

I was confused. "I don't understand. Are you saying they killed their own people?"

Joan looked at me with a puzzled look on her face. "No. Of course not." She realized the source of my confusion and added. "The group you saw by the river was a group of migrating settlers, but not from the same tribe or community as their attackers. According to the individual memory record, that group had come from the north to find a place to settle. Unfortunately, during this migration, they attacked and destroyed several small communities which did belong to the indigenous population. The young boy on the litter survived one such attack, and as you saw, was able to identify those responsible."

"What became of the rest of the people?" I was thinking of the women and children who appeared to have been spared.

Joan shrugged her shoulders. "I don't know. More than likely they were taken as slaves or perhaps they were simply accepted into the community." She paused and looked again at James. "Can you date this event?"

James dutifully nodded his head. "Nine-thousand years ago." He looked at me with a smile and added. "In your terms, that would be 7000 BC." James paused then added. "In the thousand years since the last event ring, the world's population had doubled to ten million. As a result we are beginning to see various cultures coming into contact on a more frequent basis. As you will soon see, the interaction between cultures will result in a major shift in the social environment, one which will become the foundation for most future historical events."

I looked at Joan then turned back to James. "I don't understand what social shift or change are you referring to?"

Joan placed a new ring into the projection unit, but did not turn it on. She turned in my direction and replied. "Let's take a moment to review what we have seen until now." She hesitated as if formulating her thoughts. "In the first event ring, we saw two significant changes in the human condition. The first was when we saw humans accept outsiders into their group, and the second was their attempt to modify the environment to satisfy a need. In effect, this marked the end of one cycle and the beginning of a new one. The new cycle resulted in the establishment of the first fixed communities. We saw that the communities had developed into an agriculturally based society, where the people shared in the work for the common good. We also saw divisions of labor, and if you recall, a willingness to trade or barter with another group." She paused then continued. "What is important to realize is that the social structure was not hierarchal at this time, but rather consisted of two basic types. There were the hunter-gathers and farmers."

I thought back to the event ring she had referred to and wondered if the figures on the balcony didn't represent a hierarchal structure. I posed the question to my host. "What about the people on the balcony? It seemed to me they were the leaders. And if that were the case, weren't there really two classes of people?" The image of the tall figure making the decision on the amount of grain to trade came to mind.

Joan nodded her agreement. "Every group, even the hunter-gathers, had a central figure, or what you might think of as the "Alpha-male". However, from the individual memory records that we reviewed, it appears that this was the communal role he was given by his peers. The records did not indicate he was expected or took advantage of his position. His share of food was the same as any other person and he apparently assumed the same risks as did the others." Joan paused then continued. "The last event ring was significant because it implied a centralized sense of responsibility for the well being of smaller communities existed. It was evident the splinter communities were viewed as extensions of the larger community, and as such, an attack on them was viewed as an attack on the overall community. As you saw, a large force was deployed to address the issue. "What you did not see was the effect this deployment had on the overall well-being of the community. While these men were out playing soldier the fields were not attended to properly, and the resulting loss of harvested grain meant less trade for meat. The result of this was the hunter-gathers had little if any grain. The winter months that followed were especially difficult. The farmers went in search of their own meat, and in doing so encroached on the lands of the hunter-gathers. At the same time the hunter-gathers began to raid the grain stores of smaller communities. And as you might expect, both populations began to develop independent military forces." Joan looked at me and tried to gauge my understanding of what she was saying. "From a social perspective, we now have for the first time, a group whose sole reason for existence is the protection of the community. In the space of a short year, society had evolved into a hierarchal structure consisting of three classes of people. The leader we spoke of earlier now became, for lack of a better term, the "King". The military force became an independent class, the third and lowest level consisted of the general population."

I was beginning to understand the "social shift" James had alluded to. "But was this development forced on the people?"

Joan shrugged. "Perhaps by the circumstances, I suspect the average person did not look forward to leaving their families and homes to fight. After all, they were farmers, not soldiers. So I think the prospect of having others who were trained to fight, had a certain appeal for them." She paused then added. "Remember the hierarchy of needs? The community had food and shelter. Their new goal was safety and security and this military force seemed to provide this for them. And let's not forget that as an individual, you were exposed to less risk." Joan walked to the projection unit and paused one last time to look at me. "Are you ready to continue?"

I nodded and wondered to myself what this ring would show. "I'm ready when you are."

Joan started the projection and I watched as the screen came into focus. I had the sensation of a gentle rocking motion and could see the dim outline of a shoreline to my left. The eyes through which I watched followed the shoreline and focused on what looked like a small city of tents. I could see shadowy figures huddled around small fires eating, what I assumed was breakfast. Other figures, closer to the tents, were setting their wares out as if preparing for a market to open. I felt the rocking sensation subside, and knew I was being held in fixed position, as other boats passed on the right. The boats were similar in construction but varied in size. The decks consisted of small saplings tied together by bundles of reeds with animal skins covering them. The largest boat held three men, each of whom used a long pole to propel their craft through the water. The deck was piled high with what looked like pottery. My own deck, much smaller, held two baskets of fish. I watched as one by one the boats made landfall. Soldiers with long spears met each boat and appeared to barter their services. As each transaction was concluded, one of the soldiers took the agreed payment to what could only be their commander. The commander then dispatched the required number of soldiers, who returned to the boat and helped the boaters bring their wares to the market. When it was our turn to land, the bartering process was short lived. I watched as my benefactor handed two fish to the soldiers. After obtaining the necessary approval and the soldiers lifted the baskets, and he was led to the market area. Joan stopped the projection and removed the ring. I watched as she returned the ring to the line of rings. I was confused as to the relevance of the scene I had just witnessed. As if sensing my confusion, Joan smiled. "As you can see, the military force we spoke of earlier appears to have developed a second source of income." She paused before she added. "Actually, the soldiers in this scene are what you now call mercenaries. They are not actually part of any army. You see, earlier James said there was an increase in the interaction between the different major societies. These interactions occurred most often in the area of trading. The tent city you saw was one such trading area which existed between the communities. A kind of no-mans land. As neither community had ownership and responsibility for keeping the peace, it therefore became a high risk area. Small groups of soldiers such as the one you saw here provided safety in exchange for goods." She looked in the direction of James before she added. "Over time, these mercenary groups grew in number and strength. In the future, they would be instrumental in the development of the civilizations your historians are familiar with. But for our purposes it marks a point in social evolution where a non-community based power comes into play."

James stood up and approached the projector. He punched a button and the screen came alive with the image of a two dimensional map of the earth. The map was dotted with what looked to be a dozen or more bull's-eye targets. Multiple targets were evident on every major continent, but the heaviest concentration appeared in what we now call the Mediterranean area. James pointed at this area which showed several of the targets in close proximity to each other, but as yet not merging. "Think of the center of the circles as major population centers. As you might expect they are clustered near the major fresh water areas." James hesitated before continuing. "As the population grew and additional resources were needed, they began to expand outward." James pointed at the concentric rings. "Eventually this expansion process will result in the meeting of these larger cultures. When this happens, their ability to continue expanding without resistance will come to an end. Without the ability to expand, the concept of resource scarcity will come into play. How humans react to this resource scarcity issue will forever change the landscape of human history and obviously social behavior." James shut off the projection before adding. "This data ring is from six thousand years ago, or roughly 4000 BC. The global population has doubled and is approaching twenty million people." He paused then added. "In keeping with your request to highlight only the high level changes, we are not showing you specific details of important, but less significant developments. But I will mention a few. At this point we are beginning to see the creation of large bricked cities as well as art and rudimentary written languages."

As I listened to James, it occurred to me that in all of the data rings we had viewed, there was no evidence of a religious nature. I had thought that even in the most primitive times, man had ascribed their well being to some power greater than themselves. Now after viewing five thousand years of human development, I saw nothing to support this thought. I looked at Joan and posed the question to her. "Tell me about their religious beliefs. I assume they had them."

Joan looked at me and nodded. She had wondered when this question would come up. "Since the beginning humans have been motivated by fear and of course, the need food and water. As small nomadic groups of hunter-gathers, they placed little significance in anything beyond their own abilities. If one of them died, it was simply accepted, and as you saw earlier, the dead were often a food source. As communities were developed and their primary need for sustenance was satisfied, their focus began to shift to safety and security. Invariably the leader of the community became their first recognized power. At first this leader was not afforded any special qualities, but so long as the community prospered the people accepted their leadership and decisions. It wasn't until after the formation of familial leadership structures, and the creation of the military class, that the common person began to ascribe special qualities to the leadership. So, in a sense, the first "Gods" by default became the Royal leadership. The military became the means by which the rulers were able to maintain control over the primary and younger communities. Much the same as the police do in your society. This change from communal consensus to communal acceptance of royal edict also set the stage for the further classification of the peoples, but more importantly for the first time communal equality ceased to exist. Even so, the majority of the people accepted these changes because they believed that as long as they protected their leaders, they would continue to prosper and be safe." Joan hesitated then added. "Keep in mind that at this time the expansion process we spoke of earlier was well underway. In fact, many of the newer "splinter" communities became powerful within their own rights and the original community had to find a way to ensure they would remain loyal, and although the military provided them one method, they realized that a military approach would only succeed for as long as they maintained a superior numerical or technological advantage. They also realized that the use of force, although potentially effective, would alienate the population and in doing so create other problems. What they needed was another avenue; one that would appeal to the collective consciousness of the people, and at the same time, be viewed as beyond the control of the ruler. To satisfy this need, a new class developed. This new class was

270

placed between the royal family, the military and ob course the lowest class, the general population. It was not long before this group became the sole voice of the royal family. This group of priests began by associating untold power to the royal families, powers which by design took advantage of the fears of the common man. Given their role in the hierarchy the priests soon became the sole access to the royal family, and it was not long before they began to require "offerings" as the price for their representation. The royal families, as active participants of this sham also acquired wealth and stature did not interfere."

James interrupted Joan in an attempt to provide further clarification. "Keep in mind that at this time the major civilizations had yet come into contact with each other. As a result, the people had little reason to question the validity of the divine merits defined by the priests." He paused then added. "Eventually the various cultures did clash, and in the process, kingdoms were overthrown, old religions were replaced by the religious beliefs held by the conquerors. However, as each civilization succumbed and the faces of the "gods" changed, the average person began to realize that men were not gods. Nevertheless, for a thousand years the "need" for a god or gods had been ingrained into the human consciousness. To fill this vacuum, the priests created new gods. Gods who by their nature existed beyond the physical realm, gods even the royal families were subservient to, and of course gods still only accessible through the priests." James grinned in the direction of Joan then added. "From a purely historical perspective, this single change in consciousness had a greater impact on human development and history than any other event that would follow, even to this day and age. From this point forward, any would be ruler had to accept the "god" or in some cases, "gods" of the people if they wished to rule. And with few exceptions these gods were unknowable to the average person without the guidance of the priests." James chuckled aloud. "This "arrangement" was the first known instance where the true power was prescribed to one group, but was actually held by another. In many ways this "model" continues to this day, only a fool believes that the elected or appointed leaders actually make the decisions. I personally find it ironic, that what the rulers initially created to control their people, had now become the tool by which the people now controlled the rulers."

As I listened to James describe of the origin of religion I was thinking of the early civilizations I had studied, scholars had determined that the Pharaohs of the early Egyptian dynasties were viewed as "Gods" by their people. A concept now usurped by the version of reality presented by James. As if reading my thoughts James smiled before continuing. "The changes in consciousness I am referring to took place over thousands of years, and in fact still continue today. The early great civilizations like the Egyptians did view their Pharaoh as a god. This is consistent with my earlier statements when I said the early "gods" were the ruling families. However as the centuries passed that perception changed just as I described. In fact, during the later dynasties the Pharaohs not only considered themselves as less than gods, they devoted much of their time and effort to appeasing the gods to ensure when they died they would then "become" one with the gods. As you know these efforts were clearly documented in the pyramids and tombs, and equally well documented was the role of the various priests who provided guidance to the Pharaohs'. So you see the process even then was as I have described. But we are getting ahead of ourselves. Historically speaking this was a time in human development when a model process is being developed which civilizations would follow and are still following today. But there are still one or two significant social events that must be considered before we can fully understand the historical events. Joan will take us through them then we can revisit the historical perspective." That said James nodded to Joan to continue.

Joan nodded at James before returning her attention to me. "Before we go on lets recap what has happened so far. In the preceding five thousand years we have observed several critical social changes. We saw a change from nomadic hunters to agricultural communities; the living conditions from caves and holes in the ground to structures of stone and mud and even brick and mortar, we saw the development of primitive technology in the form of farming implements and metal weapons, even boats made of reeds, we saw structured, cooperative communal activity and even inter-community interactions in the bartering or trading of goods. We watched as the communities grew and expanded into other communities, we saw the development of ruling elite families and of a military class, and lastly, as James indicated a new class of religious leadership. Over the next fifteen hundred years we will continue to see more of the same, but in many respects different. Whereas at this point the communities are still fairly remote from each other, they were developing an awareness of each others by virtue of their trading activities. As the communities continue to grow towards each other and the military asserts control of the trading routes the "no-mans" land became smaller. The rogue groups like the mercenaries we saw earlier were unable to subsist without the goods provided them from their "protection" services. They began to prey on the traders and some began to sell their allegiance to the larger communities. Regardless, the end result was that over the next fifteen millennia the different factions will found themselves in a continuous state of war, warfare that in the end resulted in significant technological advancements in weaponry and as one would expect a consolidation of the many communities into even larger groups, what you might call nation states. The early Egyptian Dynasties James spoke of earlier would be prime example of this consolidation process. This next data ring is of a time after this consolidation process, as you will see tremendous strides have been taken from a technological perspective, unfortunately you will also see the chasm between the elite and the common person has grown larger as well." Joan turned away from me and inserted the ring into the projection unit. The image presented to me was of a high brick walled city viewed from a distance. The landscape was in a word beautiful, lush green fields extended to the right as far as I could see, to my left a large lake or perhaps a sea, extended to the horizon, peaks of a distant mountain range provided the backdrop. An obviously well traveled road separated the two scenes. I watched as a caravan of traders made their way along the road toward the gate of the walled city. A herd of goats tended by two small boys led the procession. Older men followed, leading donkeys also heavily laded goods. As the column neared the gates soldiers bearing shields and wearing long curved swords formed a semi-circle blocking entrance to the gate, another soldier standing in a chariot held a long spear while the driver struggled to hold the two horses in bay. Atop the city walls I could see more soldiers bearing bows with arrows at the ready, face the now stopped column. This standoff continued until a man large man dressed in bright orange ceremonial clothes made his way through the soldiers and stood facing the newcomers. While I could not hear what was being said it was soon evident the newcomers were expected to pay an entry fee. The man dressed in orange looked vaguely familiar to me, and I watched as he made his way slowly through the goats selecting several which the soldiers immediately segregated from the herd. As the man approached the older men I watched as they unloaded their donkeys and laid their packs open on the ground. After several moments of discussion the man leading the donkeys handed the lead rope of one of the animals to a soldier and watched as the animal was led away. The remaining men slowly repacked their wares and fell back into line before entering the city. The man who had given his donkey turned away and began his slow trek away from the city, even at this distance I could see his shoulders slumped in obvious dismay. The image disappeared as Joan removed the data ring.

I watched as Joan returned the data ring to the line. "What was the significance of that?" I placed special emphasis on the word significance.

Turning she smiled at me. "On the surface it probably appeared insignificant to you, but, from a sociologists viewpoint there were several items of importance." She paused before continuing. "What you witnessed was not unique to this place, by now many large city states or perhaps more appropriately small empires exist. You may have noticed the armament was significantly more advanced than earlier and the tactics used by the soldiers were well rehearsed. This alone represents a major social shift, but the real shift is in the thinking process of the people. Until now people had been free to trade or barter their goods without having to pay any form of tax. And while it is true they often traded their goods for services, like the protection we saw earlier, they were not in any way required to do so, in this instance the group was required to pay before being allowed to enter the city. The soldiers' being present as they were also speaks volumes about the social environment." Joan stopped obviously expecting a response. Receiving none she continued. "Let me put this to you another way, suppose you have just been paid for your work and on the way to the store a group of policemen approached you and demanded you pay them before they would allow your family to buy groceries. How would you feel?"

I smiled at this simple analogy, in my life the robbery was much more subtle, the "powers" did not need to stop me; they had

274

taken their portion long before I saw the first nickel. "We all pay taxes, it is the price you pay to maintain the various services society requires." Although I detested pay taxes I understood the need for them.

Joan laughed. "Good then you understand why this was a significant event. Until now any form of taxation was non-existent, even the priests were dependent upon "donations" to survive. When communities were smaller there was no such thing as individual goods, the entire output of the community was considered the property of the community, the food and livestock, in fact, any product was shared equally by the all members of the community. And as you saw earlier, if there was a surplus it was often bartered for other goods the community required. In this instance the goods were not "owned" by a community but by an individual, this alone is a significant step in social development. The next social implication was the apparent acceptance of this taxation process. In earlier times any attempt to take something from a person as they did here, would have resulted in a pitched battle, yet this group simply accepted this as normal."

I thought of what Joan was saying and had to agree this seemingly inconsequential event, did represent a significant change in the social fabric, for the first time a third-party had represented the use of force, in an apparently legal manner, to take possession of another mans goods. And from what Joan had said this practice was now prevalent throughout the civilized world. "But why did they only tax that one man? Wouldn't it have made more sense to tax each man equally?"

Joan nodded her head in agreement. "It's difficult to say what the motivation was, but the individual data rings did indicate that the taxing authority viewed this as a tax on the group, in other words the proportion taken was the tax levied for the entire group, it just so happened that the goods taken, belonged to the one man. The others merely benefited from his loss." She paused, a wry smile on her face. "I would like to think the others in some way made it up to him, but more than likely they did not. And I'm sure when he returned to his village the local priests told him it was divine retribution for failing to donate to them."

I mulled over the implications of what I had seen, as a student

275

of history I understood that inappropriate taxation of the people was a significant source of dissatisfaction, more often than not, it was a major contributor to social unrest and often changes in leadership. I looked at James and asked. "Can you date this event?"

James nodded before replying. "Roughly 5000 years ago or roughly 3000 BC, and before you ask the population of the world has grown significantly, it is approaching 50 million. Unfortunately that number is going drop rather dramatically soon, and as Joan can attest, some of the social advances we have seen will regress for awhile."

I looked at James trying to digest what he had said. "Why is the population going to drop dramatically?"

Henry until now listening quietly spoke. "It was around this time that the earth suffered a series of major geological upheavals." He rose and approached the projection unit, he punched a button on the control panel and the same two dimensional map of the earth appeared suspended in mid-air. Using his finger as a pointer Henry pointed at the area north-east of the Mediterranean Sea, north of the Caspian Sea. "This area had been glaciated for the past ten thousand years, it began to melt and de-glaciate at an accelerated rate approximately seven thousand years ago, during this de-glaciating process the pressure on the earths crust diminished to the point where the internal pressure from several deep volcanoes began to surpass the downward pressure of the crust, when it reached critical point, a series of eruption took place with sufficient force to fully de-glaciate the remaining ice. The water from the ice combined with the Tsunami effects from the tectonic plate shifts caused massive tidal waves which extended worldwide." Henry moved his hands in a circular motion around the area on the globe where the greatest number of concentric circles lay. As you know many of the main population centers were on or near the shorelines of the seas or rivers, consequently the flooding that took place was catastrophic and took many lives. To make matters worse, the smoke from the volcanic eruptions blackened the atmosphere, which prevented the sunlight from fully penetrating the atmosphere and this resulted in a global cooling that lasted for five hundred of years. The effect on human civilization was tremendous. Except for those in the remotest of areas, mankind once again found itself trying to satisfy their most basic needs." Henry pushed the button to extinguish the hologram. "According to our best estimates

276

the global population after these events dropped to under thirty-million people."

Joan stood again and thanked Henry for his analysis. She looked at me her expression conveyed the sadness she was feeling. "Of all the time I have watched your kind, this was the hardest for me. Thousands of years of social change was undone in a mere moments, fortunately not all of the knowledge gained through the earlier times was not lost. A few of the greatest city-states survived and one or two were unaffected, perhaps even gained from the events." She hesitated before adding. "Gradually the survivors began to rebuild, and over time, some even regained their former levels of development, but most again became nomadic and spent the next millennia searching for a new home. In both instances, the collective consciousness of your kind retained the knowledge of that time. In point of fact, some of your newer religions reference that time as the point of a new beginning for the world."

I understood what she was saying, stories of a great flood were told by many religions of the world. The stories of Gilgamesh and of Noah, stories in Japan and even in the Mayan's folklore made reference to a great flood. "Yes that's true. Perhaps there was some truth to those stories after all." I looked at James and asked. "Where does that place us on the timeline?"

James glanced at Henry before responding. "My best estimate is between 4500 and 4800 years ago." He paused before adding. "About 2800 BC." James looked at Joan before again speaking to me. "From a social perspective I am not aware of any other major changes during the next 1700 years, however from the historical perspective, this was a time of significant change." He again looked in Joan's direction. "Would you agree with me?"

Joan shook her head indicating her disagreement. "No, as a matter of fact, one of the most important social changes occurred around this time." She waited until James had regained his seat before continuing. "After three thousand years of religious indoctrination humans had become dependent on having a god or gods in some instances. And as we have already discussed the early religions in most instances had many gods and deities to worship, we suspect this was because of the dichotomous nature of your reality. In this time period however, a movement began that fostered the idea of a single god, one who was above all lesser gods or beings which they referred to as Angels. These early Zoroastrian books became to a large degree the foundation of many of the religious beliefs held even now. While there would still be many civilizations which worshipped multiple deities, the seed of this social epiphany stayed with your kind. I am sure we will discuss it in greater detail later, but you should know that it was during this time that this monotheistic movement began." Joan nodded to James before taking her seat. "The next significant event with social implications will not occur for another 1700 years, during this time history is a better descriptor of the development of your kind."

I was struggling to understand the significance of what Joan had said, and decided to press the issue. I looked at Joan, ignoring James for the moment. "I don't understand what makes the introduction of monotheism so significant."

Joan nodded slowly before answering. "Until the introduction of this concept the "Gods" were the exclusive domain of the ruling elite. All other people had been created to serve the needs of this elite group. The fundamental precept of the monotheistic concept was that this "one" god cared for every person regardless of their status, further it planted the seed of self-determination into the consciousness of the average person." Joan hesitated before adding. "As you might imagine this philosophical change of perspective was not well received by political and of course the various religions. In point of fact, as time will show, this new concept would become the foundation of many of your current religious beliefs."

James approached the data rings. After selecting one from the center of the line he turned to face me. "Before starting, let me provide you some background information. As Henry told you the past several hundred years have been difficult for the majority of the world's population, but not all. Most notably the Egyptians of the early dynasties survived the cataclysmic events with a significant portion of their infra-structure intact. As you might imagine, they quickly became the most powerful and socially developed group on their continent. In fact, it was during this time the two Egypt's became fully united under Menes the Great. Their advances in architecture, art and religion combined with a consistent ruling family afforded them

278

centuries of prosperity and growth. The pyramids found in the Valley of the Kings are a testament to their ingenuity and wealth during this time. I think it is safe to say they were the elite civilization in an otherwise primitive time for humans. As the longest lasting and most successful kingdom before and since their model of government and the associated hierarchal structures were emulated by all future kingdoms and empires for the next 4000 years. And yes, before you say it, I know there were exceptions. The Greeks ill-fated attempt at democracy and even the early Roman States tried new models based upon a consensus and electoral approach, but even they, invariably de-evolved back to this model of a ruling elite. This Egyptian model was the benchmark against which every civilization was compared. None have come close to the longevity of the Egyptian Dynasties and I doubt if any ever will." James paused allowing his words to sink in. "However this is not to say they did not have problems, remnants of other displaced civilizations began to encroach on the waterways and lands claimed by the Egypt. Nomadic tribes displaced for hundreds of years sought refuge on both sides of the Egyptian domain. Over time a few even developed sufficiently enough to challenge the Egyptians outright, and at least two eventually contributed to the downfall of this mighty empire around 300 BC."

While I listened to this dissertation by James my mind still contemplated Joan's commentary about monotheism. I knew the historical significance of the Egyptian Dynasties and of the developmental impact it had on the history of mankind. At the same time I knew the issue of individualism had a much greater impact on human social development than any historical event, even the Egyptians. This change in consciousness had survived the thousands of years of history James spoke of in spite of severe opposition by the powers. "Before you start the data ring I have a question." I looked in Joan's direction. "What happened to the monotheistic idea? How did it survive during this time?"

Joan smiled at James before turning her attention to me. "The people who fostered the idea were severely impacted by the flood Henry spoke of. They became one of the groups who wandered for hundreds of years searching for a new home. Unfortunately every time they thought they found a place and began to settle, the controlling power of the area, especially the priests of the local religions demanded they pay homage and worship their gods. As their religion was founded on the belief there was only one true god, they of course refused. In most cases they were persecuted and forced to flee, and to continue their search for a home." Joan paused before adding. Eventually they did settle, often in areas of significant trading and commerce."

"Why in areas of trading and commerce?" I thought I knew the answer but posed the question anyway.

"Areas of trading and commerce by their nature are focal points where peoples from different lands and different belief systems could co-exist without being persecuted, areas where religious tolerance prevailed."

James as if on cue added. "What Joan says is true. Trade was an important part of every major civilization. As such, the Pharaohs and Kings tended to overlook these trading areas in their application of their forced belief systems. In fact, the single greatest tribe subscribing to this monotheistic philosophy settled in a seaport trading settlement in the region northwest of what you now call Syria. And as Joan will soon show you, they made another great contribution to social change which is prevalent even today."

As I watched James reach for the projector the thought occurred to me that I was not going to get the answers I sought by continuing this process. While the data rings and the subsequent conversations were fascinating I was no closer to my original objective. I raised my hand and gestured for James to stop. Standing I turned to face the group. "This has been very helpful and I certainly appreciate your assistance, but quite frankly I do not think I will get the answers to my questions from this process."

Eldred's voice emanating from the doorway interrupted my dialog. With a nod in the direction of the council he approached me. Even now his demeanor was one of sincere interest. "Have you not found what you were seeking?"

I turned to face him. "No I haven't." I raised my hand in the direction of the group and added. "Don't misunderstand me they have done a fine job presenting the information. I just don't feel more of the same will answer my questions."

Eldred held his gaze steady on my face, his smile not wavering in the least. "Are you sure the problem is with the information? Or is it possible you have not yet grasped the true significance of what they have shown you?" He paused then in a softer tone added. "Perhaps you are right maybe this isn't the best approach. Perhaps we start with your questions and allow the answers to dictate the next step. What is your first question?"

This change in tactics surprised me and it took a moment before I could mentally list my questions in the order I felt most significant. Finally I spoke. "My first question has not changed. What is the ultimate goal of this process?"

Eldred nodded before replying. "The answer also has not changed the purpose or goal is the continuation of your kind."

His answer, obvious as it was, still left much to be desired. "But to what end? When does it stop?"

Joan stepped forward, glancing briefly at Eldred before turning to me. "After all of these data rings have you not understood that the natural cycle applies to all things? You have watched cycle after cycle start and end, with each ending we saw a new beginning, usually at a higher level of development, hunter-gathers became communities, communities became kingdoms, kingdoms became empires, from a social control perspective we saw the strongest become the leader only to be replaced by leadership accepted by the population, we saw the actual control pass from the recognized leadership into the hands of priests and those representing divine influences. In Henry's demonstration we even saw the earth regenerate its cycle, an event I might add humans were lucky to survive. Had we continued the review process you would have witnessed many more social and historical cycles started and completed, yet through each, you would have seen your kind continue to move forward, to eventually become what they are today. Given the prevalence of this natural cycle in all aspects until now, do you really think there is no cycle for your species as a whole?"

Eldred raised his hand gesturing for Joan to stop. The look he gave her was clearly one of displeasure. "I asked this group to advise you, to help you understand the critical social and historical events that have led to the reality your kind currently live in. Based upon the data rings you have reviewed, I know there are at least two critical points not yet discussed, two points you must know if you truly want to understand. Are you willing to listen to them?" Eldred's steady gaze carried an unspoken challenge.

The sincerity in his voice made me question the wisdom of stopping the process as I did. Was it true the answers were being given and I was refusing to see them? I looked at Eldred. "What are the two critical points? Can we review them through discussion or do we need to use the data rings?" At this point I preferred the discussion approach.

Eldred smiled. "Whichever method you're most comfortable with will be fine." He found it interesting that humans fell into three basic groups when it came to learning, group one was purely visual, group two preferred written media and the final group, the more difficult of the three, was audio based, evidently Reynolds was from this group.

"I prefer open discussion if it's okay." I turned to Joan and James. "I'm sorry if I was rude, perhaps we can continue. What is this next significant event?"

Joan again stood, glancing briefly at Eldred before answering. "Before we discuss this next point I think it best to re-visit the hierarchy of needs. If you recall the lowest level was the need for sustenance, for food and water, and as we have demonstrated, this need has for the most part been satisfied, the next level was the need for safety and security, again for the most part the established societies have achieved this as well, the third was for a sense of community or belonging, and in many ways this is a byproduct of the first two levels. The final level is the need to exercise control over ones own destiny. This need is, as you might imagine, in a constant state of fluctuation. In our scenarios this level was initially achieved by the communal leadership or royal families; they assumed the role of ensuring the well-being of their communities. With the advent of the military and the subsequent development of the "religious class" this control became a "shared" responsibility. As time passed we saw a gradual shift of actual control into the hands of the priests and religious castes. This shift allowed them to maintain control regardless of changes to the ruling elite or the military leadership." Joan looked directly at me. "Do you follow me so far?"

I nodded that I did. "Yes, so far."

Joan continued. "About 3000 years ago or roughly 1000 BC on your timeline, a new component began to affect this control equation. This new component took place in the ancient trading seaport city of Lydia and forever changed the way trading took place. Remember until now all trading had been in the form of bartering. If you had three goats and you needed three sacks of grain, you needed to find someone with three sacks of grain who wanted three goats. If you were not able to find such a person, more often than not, you did not find your grain and ended up keeping your three goats. It was here during this timeframe that the first inter-mediate form of currency was introduced. I will describe the process. In this new process you brought your three goats to the market and traded them to a broker for "currency", of course a small commission was charged by the broker who now took possession of your three goats. In exchange he guaranteed your currency would be accepted as an exchange by other traders for grain. Similarly the man with three baskets of grain also exchanged his product for currency. Each of you can now use this currency to buy the product you need. In this way trading became easier and certainly more efficient. Although you generally ended up buying your grain from the same broker it was also possible for you to use your currency to buy from other sellers for other goods. They in turn used the currency to buy items and before long economies were born. The point is this. This revolutionary idea of currency added a new dimension to the concept of control. A new class of people emerged almost overnight. The brokers or middlemen became, for lack of a better term, the first "non-profit adding class" to the population. But of greater importance is the fact that, for the first time, wealth and power became intricately linked. Even today the concept of rich versus poor is measured in terms of currency." Joan paused as if trying to gauge my understanding of the significance of this change.

James picked up where Joan left off. "The first currencies were made of gold and sometime silver. Primarily because they were one of the few available metals malleable enough to be easily produced, and while gold had always sought after for its intrinsic decorative value, this new process quickly elevated it to being a commodity with a defined purpose. This "currency" concept soon led to the development of the weight and measure systems used to assess the value of gold in terms of how many gold coins could be made. Gold and silver became the most sought after commodity of the time. Wealth or I should say the definition of wealth was now measurable in something other than how many goats one owned."

I nodded in agreement, there was no doubt in my mind the development of currency was one of the key building blocks of our society, and although gold and silver had since lost their standing to other "conceptual" standards, the relationship of wealth to power still remained. "So if I understand you correctly the highest level of the hierarchy has a new dimension, one related to wealth."

Eldred shook his head in agreement. "Yes, you understand correctly. And you can be sure this new dimension was not overlooked by the royalty or for that matter the religious leaders of the time. It was not long before they began to assess taxes and request offerings in currency instead of chickens, goats and grain." He smiled a sardonic smile before continuing. "The churches of that time, just as now became quite rich and often "loaned" the money to the king exchange for "favors", in fact over the next 2000 years churches often funded expansionary expeditions under the banner of various kings and nations to further their own agendas."

"What was the other significant event you spoke of?" I looked again at Joan.

Joan again referenced an earlier conversation. "You recall our earlier discussion on monotheism?"

I nodded that I did.

She continued. "This is an extension of that discussion." She pursed her lips as if searching for the correct words. "By this time the concept of divine power or powers had been ingrained into the consciousness of men. As already discussed these divine qualities were initially ascribed to the ruling families, and when that proved untenable, other "non-physical" deities were created. Given the duality of your reality it was not unusual to have multiple deities prescribed by the priests, deities who by default were opposing to each other. Eventually as religions came and went the people began to question the validity of the priests and what they represented. It was at this time that the concept of a single divine god, or Supreme Being, was put forth. This new "God" was different than the gods of the other religions; this god was not just for the royalty or the privileged, it was for every person regardless of social status. For the first time every person could know "God" and didn't take long before this new concept grabbed the imagination of the people, even in the face of strenuous efforts by the existing religions to repress it, the concept prevailed. Eventually it managed to gain prominence and the old religions fell by the wayside, over the next thousand years this "new" religion became a power within its own right. Power that often crossed and superseded even that of established kingdoms or nations, more than one kingdom would fall victim to the churches vagaries and abuse of power. Without getting into timelines and historical points of reference, suffice it to say that this new church became the single greatest political force in the world. Even today the power of this organization to affect the daily lives of people throughout the world is unimaginable."

I watched as James resumed his seat, Eldred stood watching me his normally smiling face, now wore a frown. I gazed at Christie who had been silent during the entire process. Her face also portrayed a look of expectation. I wondered to myself what were they expecting. I turned back to face Eldred. "Why have you shown me this? You knew this information would not answer my questions."

Eldred, his smile returning, chuckled. "But we have given you the answer, the ultimate goal as you put it, IS to ensure the continuation of your kind." He looked at the others before continuing. "During your earlier visit to this Hall you commented that nothing had changed. I hope now, after having viewed this history, you will agree that your kind have undergone many changes."

As I listened to what Eldred was saying, I fought the urge to scream at him, to tell him he was wrong. Yes it was true the human condition had changed, that the social and historical changes we reviewed, and many more we had not, did take place, but I also knew these changes were nothing more than the same cycles repeating themselves, empires changed, the technology changed but in reality it was just more of the same. I looked at Christie but directed my comments at Eldred. "When I first came here I did so because I wanted to understand the reason for my existence, I already understood the concepts of duality and balance, of harmony and even

285

accepted the process of evaluation and re-incarnation. My simple question was why? What was the purpose? And now after all of this, your answer is still to "ensure the continuation of my kind"." I paused taking the time to fix my gaze on each of them before going on. "If this is true then I think we have wasted our time, and it is probably best if I leave." As I turned to leave Eldred placed his hand on my shoulder.

"Before you leave can I ask you a question?" He hesitated before adding. "Please?"

I looked again at Eldred, curious to know what he would ask. "Ask your question."

"Why did you come here?" In an undertone I was sure could only be heard by myself he added. "Set aside your disbelief for a moment and assume I have told you the truth, would you go back satisfied?"

His question, innocuous as it was, had the desired affect. In my frustration, I had lost sight of the other reasons for my quest. There were other questions of equal, perhaps even greater importance that I had not yet asked. I thought of the diagram Harridy had drawn, and my resolution to find out who Eldred's and Arinon really were, and the roles they played in this drama. I thought of Rena in her sanctuary of solitude, her words came back to me. "Understand what has happened, what is to come, and finally ask Eldred to show you the "black" ring." I looked at Eldred whose demeanor held a look of expectation. "You're right, perhaps I am overreacting." I hesitated before adding. "It's not that I don't believe you, I just find it disheartening to think this endless loop of re-incarnations has no purpose."

Eldred raised his hand to stop me. "Perhaps you are failing to understand the benefits of that process." He glanced at the others who were also listening intently. "What you say may be true at an individual level but at the specie level the benefits should be clear. The billions of individual cycles have resulted in the evolution of the greater cycle of your specie. Consider for a moment what you have seen. For 8000 years bio's cycles have started and completed, yet the Bio unit itself has not really changed. As you look at the larger picture, you realize each generation has in some way advanced the condition of the specie as a whole. James showed you even the cycle of the greatest of all human civilizations came to an end. And they were not alone, hundreds if not thousands of smaller Empires and Countries have done the same since. Just in your lifetime you have witnessed the ending of one of the most powerful countries in your world, and yet even in its ending you saw the birth of numerous smaller, but still new nations just beginning their cycles. From a social perspective your kind have gone through an untold number of cycles, power and leadership once held by the strongest, was replaced by leaders accepted by the community, they were eventually shared power or were supplanted with the advent of an organized military, the military were subsequently usurped by the esoteric efforts of religion. And now in your time, even their control is waning, succumbing to the power of economics." He paused briefly then added. "The concept of the natural cycle has held true in every aspect or circumstance you can imagine."

The obvious sincerity with which Eldred spoke tempered my feelings of frustration. He was right, when viewed in the perspective he had presented it, it made much more sense to me. "So what happens next? What does the future hold?"

Eldred's face, a moment earlier relaxed, immediately clouded. "The future has not yet been written." He glanced at the council before adding. "However based upon the past, it is predictable." He gestured toward the council. "Joan can tell you with virtual certainty what will transpire from a social perspective, as can James from the historical perspective. I know Henry has been closely monitoring the geo-physical dynamics of the earth, and no doubt has a few predictions of his own. And I can tell you from my own perspective that a significant change is coming and quickly."

I was taken back by this straightforward and clear response. The urgency with which Eldred spoke, only served to reinforce his words. "You say the future has not yet been written, and yet you imply these "changes" are inevitable?"

Eldred nodded. "Some are inevitable and will occur, and I might add in fewer years than you have fingers, others could be delayed, even avoided if steps are taken quickly." He paused allowing his words to register. "Joan indicated earlier that your specie is not exempt from the natural cycle and it's true, the cycle you have been in for the last 8000 years has almost run its course, your kind have experienced the initial phase, the development phase, and to your credit I might add, you have achieved the pinnacle of technological advancement in many area's, but as with every cycle, you have also experienced social, economic and geo-physical decay, so yes it is inevitable that the cycle will end. The only question that remains to be answered is what will the next cycle bring, and of course, how painful will its birth be."

I was shaken by Eldred's candor, and although at a certain level I knew his words were true, the optimist in me held fast to the belief we would pull ourselves from the edge of the abyss, when the time came. "I think you underestimate us. I would think after all these thousands of years, you would have learned that we are a very resourceful people? It's true we have stumbled, but we always found a way to survive."

Eldred walked slowly toward the window overlooking the room containing the sea of data rings. His words, although softly spoken, echoed across the room. "There is a change coming about which your kind knows nothing, and still other changes that you have been are aware of for some time, but have chosen to ignore. In those cases you still have time to react, but only a focused and determined global effort will allow you to avert them. And to be quite frank, the social issues separating your kind make such a global effort, improbable at best." He turned to face me. "And that is where you come in."

"Me?" I had a sense of where Eldred would go with this. My newly acquired abilities had changed the equation and this council's effort to educate me was only a prelude to something else. Eldred wanted something from me of that I was certain. "I don't understand. What do I have to do with it?"

Eldred turned to face me his facial expression one of sadness. "When you first came here you said it was to gain an understanding of the true purpose of this process. I then asked you what you would do with this knowledge, and you replied." He hesitated before adding. "AND I QUOTE. "I don't know, I guess that would depend on the knowledge, and I suppose, what I could do with it". Do you remember

288

that?"

I nodded that I did.

Eldred continued. "Well, you will never have a better opportunity than now." After a momentary pause he continued. "We have shown you the data rings which reflect how your specie has evolved from a social and historical perspective, and as I said, there are changes coming, changes you alone have the ability to affect. What remains to be seen, is whether you want to."

"What makes you think I can affect anything? I am just one person?"

"A forest fire can start from a single spark." Christie, until now silent, had approached me from behind. "You can be that spark. You can prepare you're kind for the changes Eldred referred to." Christie gestured in the direction of the council. "The evidence presented by Joan, James and Henry is overwhelming, the fact is, your world is in a death spiral, disparities between the classes of people are getting larger not smaller. Political and social unrest, terrorist attacks, biological and nuclear weapons, the destruction of the eco-system combined with the loss of your support units does not leave one with a confident feeling for the future."

As I listened to this litany of future woes I almost missed the final comment about losing the support units. "I don't understand why would we lose the support units?" Was this the change Eldred had referred to when he said a change was coming about which we had no knowledge?

As if he had read my thoughts Eldred nodded. "It's true, in just a few years the support units which have maintained your kind for the last 9000 years will be withdrawn."

"Withdrawn? Why? I don't understand. What will happen to the people when they lose their support units?" Although I seemed capable of existing without my support unit, I wondered if that would be the case for everyone.

Eldred, once again looking out the window shrugged. "I cannot say for certain what will happen to them, we believe they have become biologically self sufficient and even if the expected event does not occur they could survive." He paused before adding. "As for why they are being removed, I can only say that is what was agreed to in the beginning."

The conversation reminded me of the questions I had originally come to find answers for, perhaps this was the opportunity to do so. "Is that what you meant when you said our cycle was coming to an end?"

Eldred nodded. "Partially yes, but again, if we are correct, your kind should continue to exist." He turned to again face me. "But unless we can eliminate some of the other issues, it may only be for a short time."

"And you think I can help with those other issues?"

"Yes I do, in fact, I do not just think you can, I know you can."

While I did not share his conviction, I knew if I could make a difference, I would try. At the same time, I knew I would never have a better opportunity to get my questions answered. I looked at Christie before turning to Eldred. "How important is this to you? Is it important enough for you to tell me the truth about what is really going on?"

Christie, hearing my question, immediately came to Eldred's defense. Her face adopted a pinkish hue. "How dare you insinuate we have not told you the truth? Everything Eldred and the others have said is true."

Eldred laughed and held his hands up as if defending himself from a blow. "Christie! It's okay. He's right. We have not told him what he really wants to know."

Christie still upset glared at me. "We didn't lie about anything."

Eldred took her hands, placing himself between us. "He never said we lied. He simply knows we have not told him everything we could." He turned to face me again. "You asked how important this is to me, or us." He glanced in the direction of the council. "To be quite honest with you it is not as important to us as it is to you and your kind. Regardless of what happens we will be here." He hesitated before adding. "However, that being said, I will also tell you it IS important to us, if only because our every thought and action for the past 9000 years has been ensure your people survive." Eldred looked again at Christie before again looking at me. "What is it you want to know?"

I looked at Christie knowing my response would further anger her. "I want the truth. I want to know who you are, who they really are." I gestured at the council. "I want to know who the support units are, where they came from, why they are here and why they are leaving." I paused then added. "And I want to know about this "agreement", but more than anything I want to know WHY!"

Eldred looked at me a look of resignation on his face. He had known at some point he would face these questions, although not here, and certainly not to a Bio. "Are you sure you want to know? If I tell you what you want to know will you work with us? Or is there something else you want?"

"Yes there is." I remembered Rena telling me to view the "Black ring" whatever that was. "I want to see the "Black ring."

The expression on Eldred's face could not be mistaken for anything but what it really was. Shock! There was only one way I could know about the "Black ring". Aside from himself and Arinon only Rena had ever viewed that ring, and he was certain Arinon would never have told him about the ring. But "Rena"? He had not seen her in over 400 years and had thought she had passed on, obviously he was mistaken. "How do you know about the "Black ring"?"

Unsure if I should mention Rena I decided not to answer. "Does it matter? I know of it, and want to see it. Are you willing to answer my questions and show me the ring?" It was time to find out how important this really was to him.

The room was silent, I looked at the faces of the council and of Christie, it occurred to me they did not about the "Black ring" either. I looked at Eldred waiting for him to respond.

"Very well, I will show you the "Black ring"." He turned to the council. "I will show all of you."

I noticed he had not answered me on the other questions. "And what of the other questions I asked?"

With a look of resignation he nodded. "When we review the data ring they will also be answered, if not I will answer you directly."

My gratification was short lived. I heard of a loud ringing and at the same time had the now familiar feeling of being pulled away, the Hall of Knowledge faded

# Chapter 39

# Dusit Laguna, Phuket, Thailand.

$C$hang Pong Low, although Malaysian by birth, had spent the first twenty-nine years of his life living in Singapore, after completing his studies at the Singapore Institute and serving his pre-requisite two years in the Singapore Air force, he spent another five in the SDF, the Singapore Defense Force. Now, three years later, at the age of thirty-two he was the sole proprietor of a popular tourist bar in Phuket Thailand. At least on paper he was the sole proprietor, the reality was much different, financing for his business venture had come from the American CIA. In return for this financing, and a healthy monthly bonus, he provided local support to the American Embassy on low level issues. His team, all locals, had also been recruited by the CIA and placed under his direct control. To maintain their "cover" and following orders, he gave them jobs in his club, and paid them as real employees, and sometimes "under-the-table" bonuses when additional work was performed. Tonight was one of those additional work nights. The evening before the US Embassy's junior information officer had entered the club for an evening drink. As he drank his "Tiger" beer he used his pen to doodle on a few bar napkins, the bartender having been alerted by CP, pocketed the napkins while cleaning away the empty bottle and glass. CP took the napkins and proceeded to reconstruct the jigsaw puzzle of napkins following the number sequence he found on the corner of each. Combined the four napkins outlined the "job" his team needed to complete.

Eight hours later sitting in the lobby of the Dusit Laguna Hotel he was pondering why his team had been assigned to watch the tourist "Reynolds" in room one-one-eight. His team of four, along with himself, had covertly positioned themselves to maintain a visual of Reynolds's room door, and as well the room's patio door. A third member sat in a vehicle outside the gated entrance to the hotel, and a fourth bobbed in a small boat off-shore, using night vision binoculars to continually scan the beach area. Their orders were clear, maintain surveillance, but do not approach. A clicking sound from his earpiece broke into his reverie, three clicks, the signal sequence assigned to the operator in the parked car. He stood and walked slowly toward the balcony, out of the sight of the bored, but well paid, desk clerk. He removed his cell phone and keyed in the numeric code creating an open channel, almost immediately his contact responded. "Four men are approaching on foot." He hesitated then added. "They are pretending to be drunk." He had seen enough drunks to know they were faking.

CP casually stepped behind a pillar yet still maintained a clear view of the entrance and lobby. "Okay I see them." CP didn't need to alert the others, he knew they had been tuned in and had heard every word. He watched as the newcomer's "staggered" across the reception hall and approached the desk, based upon their dress and accents he knew they were German, the newness of their luggage and the ease with which they were handled indicated they were empty, clearly they were not tourists. Two clicks on the earpiece indicated the agent with eyes on the room door had also seen something. He listened quietly as the voice came through the earpiece. "There are two more down at the edge of the lagoon and their armed." A moment of silence followed before he added. "I see another team approaching from the beach." This was immediately confirmed by the operative in the boat. Cp turned slowly to face the beach. That placed two of them at his back, obviously not a good situation, to minimize his profile he sat on one of the lounge chairs, he hoped doing so would place him below the railing, and out of sight from the beach. It was becoming clear his team would be in trouble soon. Following established protocol for surveillance jobs they did not risk carrying weapons. If the newcomers were interested in his "mark", his team didn't stand a chance. Careful to not raise his voice CP asked. "Are they stationary or moving?" The response was cryptic. "Stationary, looks like they are just eyes." A moment later the voice said. "Sir, I think they're Chinese." CP turned his attention back to the reception area. The four newcomers were checking in. Nervous glances in his direction by the desk clerk told him they were asking questions about Reynolds. It was obvious they were professionals, their body language and movements were too precise, and even while pretending to be drunk, it was evident they were trying to assess the immediate area. CP looked at his watch, it read 2:30 am, unless the desk clerk gave them the information, there was no way they could know Reynolds's room number, they would need to get a direct visual before they acted. He hoped that would allow him enough time to contact Stiles. He watched as the four men left the lobby before dialing the "special" telephone number to the American Embassy.

John Stiles, aka Junior Information Officer for the American Embassy had just retired for the night. His position in the CIA Far East office was well hidden, and he hoped it remained that way, his predecessor had not been as diligent, and his body washed up in a remote lagoon three months earlier.. A light knock on his door followed by the face of the duty officer, brought him instantly back to the waking world. "Sir, you have an encrypted call from Bluebird." Bluebird was the name given to the surveillance team for that guy Reynolds. The evening before the home office had sent an urgent message about Reynolds with specific instructions to get "eyes" on him quickly, but it also stressed he was to take no further actions without obtaining clearance. Stiles, bathrobe flapping in his wake, followed the duty officer to the communications room. He lifted the handset and turned away from the duty officer before speaking. "Stile's here." He listened quietly as Bluebird spoke. Finally he spoke. "Maintain mission directive, I will get back to you on "six clicks". This said he disconnected. He turned to the duty officer instructing him. "Get Fleming for me, level three priority." Stiles waited while the connection was made to Langley, three transfers later they found Fleming. Stiles took the handset from the duty officer and motioned for him to leave the room. He didn't know why the Germans and Chinese were interested in Reynolds, but he did know his team didn't stand a chance if they moved on the target. Without undue ceremony he described the situation to Fleming who quietly listened. After a brief moment of silence Fleming authorized Stiles to bring a second, "prepared" team into the mission. His revised mission directive was to protect the target until arrangements could be made to "recover" him. The newly authorized team was to be of sufficient force, to insure the opposition would think twice before making an attempt on Reynolds. Fleming was obviously counting on the Germans and the Chinese not wanting to risk creating an international incident with the United States or with Thailand. Fleming advised him efforts would be undertaken with the State Department to coordinate Reynolds's extraction, hopefully with the assistance of the Thai government.

# Chapter 40

## Room 128, Dusit Laguna Hotel, Phuket, Thailand.

*I* opened my eyes to a room which was still dark. The only illumination came from the soft blue light of the digital clock which said it was 3:00 o'clock. It wasn't five o'clock as I requested, why was I here? I sensed I was not alone and a movement to my right confirmed it, more movement on my left, had they somehow found me? I reached for the lamp only to be stopped by a familiar voice.

"I wouldn't turn that on if I were you."

A second voice, this from my left and equally familiar, concurred. "I agree."

The voices which I knew belonged to my "Seven" and my "Three" surprised me. I figured they would catch up with me, but thought it wouldn't be until I met with Rhodes, since they had heard me make the commitment to meet him. "How did you find me? And why shouldn't I turn the light on?"

"Seven's" reply came in the form of a short laugh, followed by his soft words. "Well its like this, we have been with you for over fifty years, we probably know you better than you know yourself, we just figured it out." He did not add this was their fourth stop of the search. "You can't hide from us, we know you too well."

"So you brought me back?" The thought suddenly occurred to me that Arinon had sent them. "Can I assume then that your boss knows where I am as well? Is that why I should leave the lights off?"

"Seven", his voice adopting a more serious tone replied. "If your referring to Arinon, the answer is no, and just for the record he is not our boss." He paused before continuing. "You should leave the light off so the ones watching you will think you are still sleeping.

And no, we didn't bring you back your cell phone ringing did that."

I instinctively reached into my pants pocket and retrieved my phone. The flashing envelope on the backlit screen indicated I had a new text message. I left the bed and slowly made my way to the bathroom using the cell phone screen to guide me, hoping to avoid banging my knees into the furniture. After closing the door I turned the light on and read the cryptic text message. "DO NOT LEAVE THE ROOM", it was signed by somebody named Stiles. The rest of "Sevens" statement finally registered in my brain. I turned to face him, "Three" as always stood beside him. "What did you mean the ones watching my room? Who's watching?" The text message made a little more sense now.

"Seven" shrugged. "I don't know, but we passed them on the way in, there are eight that we saw, and I would assume probably more." He smiled and added. "And you should know that at least half of them are armed."

I glanced at "Three" who was busy recording the conversation. How could they have found me so quickly, it must have been when I used my credit card to register into the hotel? I glanced at my watch, it was still set for Chicago time and read 3:00 pm, my meeting with Rhode's was still two hours away. For a brief moment I wondered if I would be alive long enough to make the meeting, and quickly dismissed the thought, unless I had lost my teleportation power, the "watchers" would not even see me, my thoughts returned to the text message, who was Stiles? "So why are you here? Why did you come back?"

"Seven" shrugged. "Well technically speaking we are still responsible for you."

"Three" gave him a reproving look before looking at me. "We missed you, and yes we are still responsible for you." In spite of her transparent features I swore she blushed. She continued. "And to tell the truth we were kind of sent back" Then as if reading my thoughts she added. "No not by Arinon, we spent time in the Hall of Understanding and saw a number of other "Sevens", they had heard through the grapevine about us, or I should say you and were curious. They said they had heard this was their last cycle and you were the reason why." I could feel her eyes on me as if trying to gauge my response to her words.

I was surprised at her words but tried not to show it. "I don't understand, what did they mean I was responsible?"

"Three" looked at her counterpart before answering. "Nobody knows, we were hoping you could tell us." Meeting with other "Seven's" in the Hall of Understanding had been a rare treat for them, while they were in the physical realm the Bio's electro-magnetic fields prevented contact with other support units, and even in the Hall of Understanding it was rare as the "Seven's" usually departed as soon as their charges did. For some reason this wasn't the case this time. That in itself was a strong indicator that changes were coming. She heard a few mention that they had heard this would be the last cycle, but when she pressed them for details, none were forthcoming. The closest thing to an answer she received came from Thomas who said during his studies he had found obscure references to a cyclic timeline.

As I listened to her Eldred's statement about the support units being withdrawn came back to me. I had the fleeting thought that, as with every organization, the internal "grapevine" appeared to work here as well, and was obviously equally accurate. I looked at my companions realizing again how much our relationship had changed, when I first encountered them they could read my thoughts as easily as I could theirs, now, based upon their expectant looks, I knew they had not picked up my thoughts of Eldred and his comments. "I don't know what to tell you, if I have a role to play, I am not aware of it." I hesitated before adding. "I just left the Hall of Knowledge and I think Eldred was on the verge of showing me the answers to my questions."

"Seven" glanced at "Three" before turning to me. "And you think Eldred can be trusted?" Once again his ingrained distrust of the "Sleepers" was foremost in his mind. "You cannot trust them, even Eldred."

I looked at him withholding the urge to challenge his statement, perhaps he was right, it was possible that what they had told me and shown to me was false, perhaps serving a purpose I did not understand. By the same token, they were answers, something I was not receiving from "Seven". "Unless you can tell me what I need to know, I have to go back there."

The downcast expression on "Sevens" face provided the

answer. I continued. "Eldred told me things that I need to understand, things that affect my people and I suspect." I looked at "Three" and added. "You."

"Three" stopped recording and looked at me. "Me! What did he say?"

I shrugged. "Not enough for me to want to comment on, that's why I need to go back. But if I had to guess I would say your friends may be correct, this may be your last cycle." A sudden the thought occurred to me, why not take "Three" back to the Hall with me, her skills at recording would be invaluable, at the same time perhaps she would gain the knowledge I knew they were seeking. I looked at "Seven" wondering if I should ask. "I'm going back and I want to take "Three" with me. She can record everything that happens." I paused then added. "As my "Seven" you can access my memory records even before the evaluation process, right?"

"Seven" shook his head. "Yes I have access to them." He smiled at the thought of having the knowledge so long denied them, and reveled at the irony of acquiring the knowledge from their historic "enemy", and because "Three" had recorded the information, there was no doubt it would be reviewed during the evaluation process, others like himself would see it, and the long held secrets would be revealed.. As enticing as the thought was, he also knew allowing "Three" to go would be a breach of conduct, the rules clearly stipulated the "Seven" and "Three" had to stay together with the Bio. Both could face serious consequences if the plan failed.

"Three" looked at him, the excitement on her face clearly evident. Although "Seven" could deny the request she had already decided to go. "I'm going."

"Seven nodded. "I will stay with your Bio and if necessary I will pull you back."

I laughed at this last comment. "Are you sure you can? The last time I checked, we were officially divorced, oops I mean separated." It didn't really matter. If my ringing cell-phone brought me back, I was sure the wake up call from the desk would do the same. And unless my new "Watchers" intended to kill me, something I doubted since they wanted to use my skills, I would probably return if and when they touched me.

"Seven smiled. "That's right, I forgot." Then as an afterthought, added. "We're only separated!"

I turned to "Three". "I'm not sure if this will work, but we can try. Are you ready?" I reached out and took her hands, before closing my eyes and envisioning the Hall of Knowledge.

# Chapter 41

## Hall of Knowledge.

*E*ldred with Christie beside him stood looking out the observation window, Joan, James and Henry sat as they were when I left. My attempt to bring "Three" was obviously successful, as she stood to my right. Eldred turned to face me. "Welcome back." He scrutinized my new companion, before continuing. "I see you brought a guest." He nodded to "Three". "You're a recorder aren't you?"

"Three" nodded that she was. I could sense her discomfort and knew it was from being in such close proximity to her adversary of so many years.

Eldred smiled. "Relax your welcome here." He turned back to me. "Are you ready to continue?" Although his countenance still maintained a smile I could see concern in his eyes. I wondered what the cause was.

I looked at my "Three". "Are you ready to begin recording?" I heard a sharp intake of breath coming from Christie's direction and only peripherally caught Eldred gesture for her to relax.

"Three", still silent nodded that she was.

Eldred walked slowly toward the projection machine, he spoke as he walked. "What I am going to show you should answer many of your questions, but I'm sure not all, please stop me at any time if you need clarification, I will do my best to answer." He paused before adding. "What I am about to show you is the historical data record from our colonization ships. The data pre-dates the data rings you have seen so far. I suspect you're not going to like some of what you see, and that's understandable, but, before you pass judgment ask me about the circumstances, and then ask yourself what you would have done if faced with the same situations." This said he activated the projection unit.

I watched as a three dimension holographic image appeared. The image, obviously taken from a high orbit position, was of a planet rotating anti-clockwise around a sun. This planet, unlike the pictures of Earth I had seen, followed an almost but not quite, circular path as it journeyed around the sun, the elliptical path I knew to be earths orbit only slightly evident. The planet itself seemed different, the pole areas were as I expected, ice encrusted, but unlike my memories, the ice seemed to extend outward from both poles toward the planets equator, my rough estimation was only about forty percent of the surface was free of the ice. I recognized some of the ice-free land masses, but was surprised they were not where I expected to see them, one I knew to be Mexico appeared in the middle of the ice-free band, and significantly above the imaginary equatorial line, the tip of South America lay just below the equator, and another continent I assumed to be Antarctica was clearly visible. I raised my hand indicating I had a question. Eldred stopped the projection. "Is this the Earth?"

Eldred nodded. "Yes! This image was captured roughly 17,000 of your years ago."

"You said a colonization ship. Does that mean you came here to colonize our planet?" I was already feeling my blood pressure rise at the thought. "Where did you come from? And what gave you the right to colonize here?"

Eldred looked thoughtful for a moment before responding. "Twenty-five thousand of your years ago, a solar system known as the Adean system had a sun that became unstable, according to our calculations we were certain it would eventually go nova." He stopped speaking and asked. "You know what that means?"

"Yes it's going to explode."

Eldred nodded. "Close enough. The Adean scientists presented their findings to the governments of the systems twelve populated planets and were able to convince them to pool their resources into developing the technology needed to save some, and hopefully all of their people. Their efforts paid off to the extent they were able to build twenty-four ships, each capable of transporting a half million colonists." Eldred was silent for a moment as he recalled the difficulty in selecting the twelve million who would surely survive the cataclysm. "The ships were eventually dispatched and began their search for new planets to colonize, it was hoped that as each succeeded they would return to their home worlds and hopefully transport more people to the new worlds." He paused then continued. "Before you ask I should tell you that this colonization effort was well defined and not without rules. The pre-screening process was quite stringent and only the most qualified were selected. As a further condition each colonist was required to sign an agreement which stated they would abide by what we called the "Rules of Colonization and Conduct". While this may seem trivial to you, I can assure you we took it very seriously, the last thing we wanted was to survive at the expense of another civilization. The penalty for violating the rules is quite severe, up to and including death. The point is this. The rules were designed to insure that any planet chosen for colonization had to meet strict criteria before any colonization effort to place. In conjunction a smaller oversight group was created, whose role was to insure compliance to these strict rules. In addition to the twenty-four massive colonization ships four smaller ships called star-liners were created, unlike the slower colonization ships these were as you can guess by their name, capable of achieving light speed. My ship is one of those, when a colonization ship felt they had found a suitable planet, it was my responsibility to verify all of the established protocols and the pre-colonization conditions had been satisfied before allowing the colonization process to begin."

I was intrigued by what Eldred was saying. I like many others of my generation, had always believed humans were not alone in the universe, and had even entertained the thought that humans were somehow a byproduct of some colonization effort. "Are you saying we are not indigenous to this planet? That we came from this "Adean" system? Did the sun go nova?"

Eldred did not immediately reply, but instead spoke again of the colonization rules. "The first and most important rule, what we call our "Prime Directive" required us to bypass any planet where civilized life already existed. The second rule is a subset of this first one, if they found a planet where "life" exists, but no established civilization is evident, they were required to assess the potential impact on the indigenous life forms if colonization took place. If that analysis showed no impact, or a minimal impact, the planet could then be considered a candidate. In other words, they had to determine if the life forms could peacefully coexist, and that their colonization efforts would not adversely affect the life forms already there." Eldred looked at me wondering if I had understood the distinction he was making.

I understood the distinction and knew he was at the same time answering my earlier questions. "Can I assume we were in the second category?" How could that be? If humans existed when they arrived why did they decide to colonize? I decided to ask. "Why did you colonize if you knew we were here?"

Eldred shrugged his head before answering. "I was not here when Peter, the ships commander, and Arinon the colonization leader made the decision. However, as you will soon see, except for the decision to proceed without approval, I am not sure I can fault their initial decision. But were getting a little ahead of ourselves, shall we continue?" He turned the projection unit on and the rotating planet appeared again, Eldred clicked a button causing the image to "zoom" toward the planet. "It should be noted, and even I would have to stress, the scientists and crew of the colonization ship did follow every protocol as prescribed by the Rules of Colonization. They spent five hundred of your years in high orbit observing every facet of the planet, every form of life was analyzed and categorized, geo-physical analysis, electro-magnetic analysis's were completed in exacting detail, in fact the records show the level detail was sufficient to recreate them on the ship if necessary. And it is also important to note each assessment was completed with the specific intent of determining if any civilization or technology existed, anything at all to indicate they would be in violation of the "Prime Directive", and quite frankly none were found. Let me show you what they found as it pertains to your kind." Eldred continued the "zoom" until the scene was close enough to make out the distinct features of a jungle. "There in the upper right corner, do you see them?"

It took a moment but eventually I saw them, a small group of humans were picking berries and walking unhurriedly through the jungle. I counted ten adults and two children, they were naked and carried no tools or weapons, the children, chased each other laughing and playing, the adults seemed to not pay any attention to them at all. I looked at Eldred who was watching me closely. "Well there you are! Humans live here, why didn't you move on?"

304

Joan sat watching the images, as a sociologist she was mesmerized by the scene. She had heard of this data ring but had never actually watched it. She answered for Eldred. "It only means there were life forms, there is nothing to suggest intelligence or for that matter any form of civilization, there are no tools, weapons or for that matter clothes."

Eldred nodded to her before turning to me. He clicked another button on the projector and the planet receded again. He pressed another button and small red dots appeared giving the globe the measles. "Based upon the biological profiles of the humans we were able to use the ships computer to identify their locations, initially the intent was to make sure any colonization efforts would take place away from any highly populated areas. The ships computer calculated there were over a million humans spread across the habitable area of the planet. And as you can see there were no discernable high density areas that might indicate any form of centralization. The scientists and sociologists watched thousands of scenes such as the one you just saw for the next five hundred years, and not once found any form of social, political or technological coherencies." He hesitated then challenged me. "Now, put yourself in Arinons position for a moment. If you came upon a planet and found wild squirrels running around eating nuts and berries, would you consider that evidence of civilization?" He did not wait for a response. "Or if you saw birds building a nest would you call that civilization? Is a nest a structure? The point I am trying to make is this, in fairness to Arinon and the colonization team I cannot fault them for coming to the conclusion the planet met the initial requirements of the second rule. The second part of the rule was satisfied when they made the decision to colonize using only materials inherent to the natural environment."

I remembered Rena saying all humans had the inherent abilities I had so recently acquired, surely in all that time they had seen them as well, wouldn't that be considered a form of civilization? I looked toward Joan for the answer. "So your telling me these "humans" were not unique in any way, they possessed no skills that would qualify as civilized behavior? What about the fact they stayed together, isn't that communal evidence of civilization?"

A clouded look came over Eldred's features, it was evident my questions had triggered a memory in him. He looked at me and was silent for a moment before answering. "Have you ever watched a movie and afterward had someone say to you they thought a particular scene made them laugh, and try as you might, you could not recall the scene they spoke of? This is very similar to that, in hindsight, I would watch the video and see tiny clues I had not seen before, clues that in and of themselves were innocuous, but when put together over time, gave me a different understanding of what I was viewing. Yes, we observed anomalies; in fact, the clip we just saw had one. But quite frankly they did not fully recognize or appreciate the human capabilities until well after the colonization process was well underway."

I knew of what Eldred had referred to, I remembered watching a movie with my son, after the movie he was laughing about the words on a tombstone he saw in one of the scenes. I remembered the scene but did not recall the words. According to my son it was a funny play on words. "Here lies Les Moore, shot in the heart with a .44, alas, no less no more." I subsequently rented the movie, and sure enough, it was there. Still Eldred did not answer me about the communal aspect I had proposed. "What about the fact they were together, isn't that a form of community?"

Eldred nodded. "Perhaps, but consider this. If you went to a pool of water and saw a school of fish, would you consider them a community?" He paused then added. "Or if a flock of birds flew by, are they a community? What is the deciding factor? At that time our protocols defined civilization under the umbrella of technology."

Much as I hated to admit it, he was right. In all of the circumstances he had described I would have come to the same conclusion as Arinon. In fact, I was beginning to wonder if they were adversaries, so far Eldred had supported all of Arinons decisions. "You said in the video there was an anomaly, what was it?"

Eldred laughed. "I wondered if you would ask." He re-activated the video. "Watch closely the smaller of the two children."

I did and saw nothing significant. The child was chasing the other one and stopped only once to look at the adults. I didn't see anything."

Eldred nodded. "Watch again, however this time keep your eyes on the adults, just before the child looked at them." He started

306

the clip again.

I watched and sure enough just before the child looked at them, two of the adults had looked intently in the child's direction, but neither actually said anything. "I don't understand. What am I missing?"

Joan again stepped forward. "That's the point your trying to make isn't it? Something happened that you did not see, or know happened, until much later." She watched Eldred's face to see if she was right.

Eldred looked at me. "What Joan said is right on the mark. When you watched the adult, you did not see anything to indicate she had communicated with the child, yet the child's behavior clearly indicated a communication of some type had in fact taken place. It wasn't until much later we understood the dynamics of what had transpired; unfortunately by then it was too late. So yes, the humans did have skills or powers which manifested themselves in various ways, even before the colonization process began, but I am adamant that they were not enough to suggest any formal civilization existed."

"So what happened?"

Eldred continued. "The point of this discussion was to try to convey to you the events and the circumstances that transpired in the earliest time, a time thousands of years before I came became involved. I can show you in finite detail that hundreds of years of effort went into making sure the colonization of your world took place according to the guidelines set forth."

I didn't understand Eldred's obvious desire to defend the actions taken by others so many millennia before, in retrospect it really didn't matter, the fact was they colonized and somehow screwed something up. "What happened next?" I hoped my failure to agree with his justifications would be noted, and based upon the look of resignation I think it was.

Eldred returned his attention to the projector, the scene projected before me was in a word, amazing. The image, although still taken from high orbit was mind-boggling. Where before there had been only jungle, I now saw a large circular city under construction, channels of water surrounded the island cities high walls, I could see even higher secondary walls had been formed in the deeper waters of the ocean further protected the city. Boats made of reeds and some of wood traveled channels of this "developed" river most hugging the shoreline. Small flying craft could be seen taking off and landing from an elevated platform near the center of the city, as I watched a few heading directly toward the camera lens and eventually disappeared from sight under the ships bulk. Larger craft hovered near the farthest of the city walls, walls apparently still under construction, I watched as one slowly lowered a huge block of what looked like granite, atop another equally mammoth stone, workmen in grey suits wearing bubble shaped helmets could be seen guiding the block into an exact position. It didn't immediately register to me that there was nothing holding the suspended block. I watched as the block was finally positioned and the craft veered away heading toward what looked like a quarry several miles away. As if sensing my interest Eldred made the image "zoom in" again, this time bringing the quarry into view. Machines constructed of long spidery shaped girder legs with a box shaped seat at the top, were using some sort of cutting ray or beam to cut large blocks of granite from the earth, as each block reached the point of final separation, a craft like the one I saw earlier hovered over the newly cut block, finally lifting it when the final cut was made.

I looked at Eldred and motioned for him to stop the projection. "When was this? Where was it?" Images of the great pyramids and the Peruvian pyramids passed through my mind, had they built them as well?

In answer Eldred restarted the projector and pushed a few buttons, he stopped the image at the point where the land masses were still visible but not distinguishable in detail. "The site you just saw was here." He used his finger to point at an area I did not recognize. "However there are other sites under construction here, here and here." He pointed at the area I knew was modern day Iran and another I knew to be the northernmost tip of Antarctica. "And according to the glyphs on the screen this was approximately 15,000 years ago, or in your terms 13,000 BC." He paused then added. "Other sites are planned as well." He pointed at the area north of the equator in the area that looked like Mexico, and then at another site several thousand miles south, in what I knew to be Peru. "In the end there will be twelve major sites developed, one for each of the tribes that comprise the twelve planets of the Adean system." While Eldred did not approve of

308

this colonization strategy he knew other ships had done the same with varying degrees of success, besides at this point he had not yet arrived on this planet and had no input to the decisions.

I was awed by what I had seen. One of the greatest mysteries of our time was explaining how the ancient civilizations had been able to construct such massive structures. I looked at Eldred knowing well he understood my excitement. "How did they lift those blocks? And how did they cut them so precisely?"

Eldred shrugged as if to indicate it was nothing to brag about. "Cutting lasers, anti-gravitational machines."

It occurred to me I had not seen any humans in the last image, I wondered what had happened to them. "I didn't see any humans, were they there?"

Eldred nodded. "By now humans and Andeans' have become acquainted, and although most humans shied away, a few ventured near the work zones. But for the most part they avoided each other. Even at this point the Adeans were not actually living on the planet, each day they would leave the ship with their tools, and each night they would return, partly because the cities were not yet suitable for living, but to a greater extent to maintain the tools, as you can probably imagine they required constant recharging and of course maintenance that could not be provided by the portable maintenance pods. In any case the opportunity to interact did not present itself very often. But yes, the humans are doing fine. If you would like we can check in on them."

"I would like that." It wasn't that I distrusted what he said, but I was just curious if I could see a difference in them after their encounter with the colonialists.

Eldred pushed a button bringing a new image up. "Before starting I want you to know this is one of my favorite scenes." He looked at me. "If you recall earlier I said the understanding of human capabilities occurred after the colonization process was well underway, this is one of those moments, to my way of thinking this particular scene should have alerted Arinon, but he either missed it, or chose to ignore it. As you watch this, pay close attention to the adults, as the tiger approaches the child."

The scene, like the earlier one, took a few minutes to register in my mind. Unlike the previous scene the human figures, four men and two women were seated in a circle, it was raining and naked as they were, I expected they would be have sought shelter, however as the scene zoomed closer I was amazed to see them sitting in a circle in an open area, between them the area was completely dry, rivulets of water seemed to pour down around them as if directed by some invisible umbrella, a child ran playfully around the circle, small puddles exploded as he jumped in them, his skin was shiny with moisture, evidently he was enjoying the rain, a movement in the brush close to the boy caught my eye, and from the reaction of the adults theirs as well. The child running in circles was quickly approaching the bush and I knew when he got closer the now visible tiger would spring, the thought had barely passed through my mind, when the flash of stripes leapt at the child, I closed my eyes not wanting to watch the rest, only "Three" nudging me, made me look. The tiger appeared as if suspended in the air, one of the adults stood facing the beast with his hands raised, palms up, another, one of the women, raced toward the child and pulled him into the circle and out of harms way, the man holding the tiger at bay lowered his arms and I watched as the tiger was lowered gently to the ground, the tiger, upset at losing his meal, lunged at the man who again raised his hands, this time with palms facing the tiger, the tigers leap ended abruptly as if he had crashed into an invisible wall, but not before his claw had opened a gash on the mans forearm. I watched as the tiger tried again to get at the man and was again stopped by the unseen barrier, the other men joined their companion, two of them also lifted their arms, palms facing the tiger, I saw the fourth close his eyes and point at the beast. Within moments the tiger fell to the ground motionless, and clearly dead. Thinking this the end of the scene I turned to face Eldred who raised his hand and pointed at the image. I watched as the man with the open gash on his arm rejoined his companions, the boy unfazed by the incident stood by the tiger prodding it with his foot, I watched as the woman took the mans arm and covered the open wound with her hands, a glowing light seemed to emanate between them, moments later it stopped. The man turned to face the child, his arm completely healed, as he looked at the child I had the sense he was communicating, yet his mouth never moved, moments later the boy approached the man, who picked him up, and both simply vanished.

310

Eldred pushed a button which froze the image in place. "Of the millions of images recorded of your kind, this is the ONLY one where every power your kind possessed was used. There were others of course, singular events that led us to believe there was more to human than we thought, but not enough to make us pause and reconsider whether we should even be here, this one image, was clearly the most damning evidence challenging our right to be here." He looked out the observatory window before turning again to me. "I did not arrive on your world for another two thousand years after this image was recorded. But I know Arinon had viewed it, as did Peter the Ships commander, those are their glyphs." Eldred pointed at two small figures at the bottom of the image. "This single image convinced me without question that our definition of civilization was far too narrow, that just because "we" needed structures to reside in, tools to build with and other technology did not mean all species needed to do likewise. Clearly your kind had evolved to the purest state of evolution, it was not necessary for you to change your environment, to have social hierarchies or any other control mechanisms." He paused, a look of sadness on his face. "No, we were the less evolved, and too arrogant to see it."

I was beginning to understand the source of contention between Eldred and Arinons groups. "So you think Arinon saw this and simply chose to ignore it?"

"Eldred shrugged. "When I confronted Arinon with this image, he merely said he had not viewed it in the same manner as I. In any case, this is not the worst decision we need to review."

I looked at him, any doubts I held about his veracity were set aside, in my heart I knew his motivation was to help. The conversation with Rena about a catastrophic event came back to me. I looked at Eldred trying to decide if I should let him bring it up or if I should take the initiative. "You're referring to the "great event"?"

Eldred looked at me, a look of incredulity on his face. "Yes, but how did you know?"

"Does it really matter?" I hesitated then continued. "I don't know what happened or how, or for that matter why, but I do know it changed us, and I suspect not in a good way."

Eldred looked at the Black ring before answering. "There is so much more you need to see, but your right of course, we should focus on the key events." He looked in the direction of my "Three" before continuing. "We should start with the "why"." He looked briefly at the floor then began to speak. "As I told you the mission of the colonization ships was to find suitable worlds, to colonize them, and then to return to their home system and begin transporting others." He paused to turn the projection unit on before continuing. The image was again the original one. "When Arinons ship arrived at forty percent of the planets surface was habitable. And while the area would support a large contingent of our people Arinon knew it would not be enough. He challenged the scientists to find a way to increase this habitable area, and to do so without damaging the eco-system or undermining the colonization efforts already underway. The scientists had anticipated Arinons request and were already well on their way to providing a solution. Their proposed solution was quite innovative, and although radical in concept and monumental in scope, if properly executed was very low risk."

I motioned for Eldred to stop. "So you were here when this happened?"

"He shook his head. "No, I would not arrive for another two thousand years. I am speaking from what you might call a "post-mortem" analysis of the event. By the time I arrived, the plan had already been executed, and the subsequent events had already taken place." He paused before continuing. "The proposed plan was set into motion and actually went very well, that is until the final stages, when a series of unforeseen factors culminated in a catastrophic event with disastrous consequences, not the least of which was the near annihilation of your specie."

I wasn't sure how to interpret Eldred's obvious zeal in describing this dubious scientific achievement, throughout the human experience we had similar moments of technological triumphs, but always, always, there was a corresponding negative side affect, I smiled to myself as I mentally pictured Thomas describing the fundamental law of balance and of opposites. I focused my thoughts again on Eldred. "Okay, I understand the "why", can you help me understand "what" this solution or plan was?"

Eldred smiled. "I can try. How much do you know about

astrophysics and geo-magnetism?"

I laughed. "You better keep it simple." I had studied both in college, and had even tried to keep up with the latest and greatest minds in the thirty years since, but I was by no means literate on either subject.

Eldred turned again to the holographic projection, he pushed another button and the image changed to a model of the solar system. I watched in amazement as the planets performed their exotic dance around the sun. Eldred pointed at the earth. "This is a simulation of your world roughly 14,000 years ago, as you can see the earth's orbit is stable and the obliquity of the poles is very small, in fact less than one percent. It is this lack of obliquity which is creating the latitudinal zones as we see them." Eldred stopped looking to gauge my understanding. Evidently my face must have portrayed my confusion because he laughed out loud. "Okay, let's try this again." He changed the image to one of a spinning top, not unlike one I had as a child. "Assume you have a spinning top, if you were to draw a vertical line through the top and extending through the bottom, and another vertical line at a ninety degree angle to the first line you would have a representation of the true north and south poles, and of course the planets equator." I watched as he superimposed the line over the spinning top. "Now if you position yourself directly over the top most pole and look closely at the spinning top you will see the center point of the top is not maintaining its true position relative to the pole." I watched as the view shifted and I was seeing a bird eye view of the pole, as I focused on the spinning top it was clearly oscillating around the vertical line representing the true pole position. Eldred continued. "This oscillating effect is the result of the geo-dynamic forces generated by the planet's rotation, and of course the gravitational influences of the sun and other planets that comprise your system. In effect this "wobble" or what is termed "precession" is what determines how much the planets surface is presented to your sun, surface area defined as latitudinal zones. As you can see the oscillation effect is relatively small, your planet has very little "wobble" and as such, the latitudinal zones receiving the benefit of the sun is correspondingly small." He paused before adding. "Now watch what happens to the latitudinal zones as we increase the "wobble" or precession." I watched as he adjusted the horizontal line and subsequently the angle

313

of rotation of the top. Just as with my childhood toy, as the angle increased the top became less stable, and the north-south centerline oscillated in a wider yet still predictable circle. Eldred smiled knowing I understood what had happened. "Now look what happened to the latitudinal area receiving the suns rays." I looked where he was pointing and saw the area had almost doubled. Eldred shut the projection off and turned to face me. "That was their plan. A slight change in the "obliquity of the ecliptic" resulted in a significant increase in the "precession" or "wobble", which in turn increased the latitudinal area presented to the sun. And just as with your childhood toy, if the rotational forces can be maintained, you would still have a stable orbit." Eldred paused before continuing with the explanation. "This simulation is a corollary to what was happening on your planet 14000 years ago, because the "wobble" is so small, only a small portion of the planets surface is being effectively warmed by the sun." He stopped and pushed a button on the projector, the image reverted again to the one of the earth with the forty-percent climate zone. "Our scientists were able to develop a process where they could safely increase this "precession" or "wobble", yet still maintain the orbital integrity, if they were successful the result should have been, and was, a significant increase in the habitable area. However, that being said, the process was not without risk   If the rate of change was too dramatic, or too sudden, there was a slim possibility the orbital path of the planet would degrade and just as with your top, it would spin out of its orbit and into space, should that happened the corresponding gravitational effect would affect the orbital path of the other planets as well, at that point the stability of the entire system would be at risk. Obviously it was critical that the scientists maintain absolute control not only the degree of change in the obliquity, but equally important the rate of change. The degree of change calculated by the astronomers and geo-physicists needed to obtain maximum latitudinal exposure and still maintain the orbital integrity was determined to be a minimum of fifteen percent and a maximum of thirty percent." Eldred hesitated before adding. "So there you have it in the shortest and simplest version."

Strangely enough I understood what he had said. "So your scientists came up with the idea to change the "obliquity of the ecliptic" to increase the degree of "precession" thereby maximizing

314

the latitudinal surface area affected by the sun?" I was feeling proud of my technically presented summary, at least until he replied.

"Something like that yes."

I looked at the still spinning globe wondering how such a thing could be done. "Well I now know the "why" and the "what", I guess next is the "how?" and you should know soon after I will ask what went wrong."

Eldred nodded. "The "how" is a bit more complicated, but I'll try to keep it simple. The solution of "how" was fairly straightforward, at least conceptually; to get the desired amount of precession they would have to change the relationship of the planets "magnetic north" relative to "true north". You may recall in our "spinning top" simulation that as we increased the "angle" of rotation the "precession or "wobble" also increased. You also saw that even as the "precession" was increased we were still able to maintain an equidistant area of oscillation around the pole. The scientists knew that because the dynamics of the universe are inherently balanced, and in many ways behaved like a pendulum, once the desired angle of change was achieved an inherent balance would be automatically maintained. However their simulation also showed that due to gravitational and rotational forces this "new magnetic north" would try to regress to its true state and would eventually come back to "true north", and furthermore the closer it got to "true north", the rate of change would accelerate, because of this the scientists had to factor in this rate of change to determine how far from "true north" they needed to move the "new magnetic north", their goal was provide enough time for the areas to be colonized and artificial methods developed to keep it that way." Eldred stopped, his finger still pointing at the image of the globe now rotating with a more distinct wobble, yet still maintaining a stable orbit. "The scientists determined the obliquity goal needed to be fifteen degrees offset from "true north". This would translate into an increase in the "precession" from less than one half degree to just over a full degree. If successful the habitable area would be increased from forty to eighty percent. The simulation model also indicated the maximum rate of change in the obliquity should not exceed one degree per trial." He stopped. "So that is the "how"." Then almost as an after thought he added. "Or perhaps I should say part of the "how"."

As I listened to Eldred I realized how technologically primitive we were relative to them. To even contemplate what he was suggesting was at best theoretical, to actually contemplated, beyond even that. I looked at Eldred shaking my head in disbelief. "Is your race so advanced that you can actually do this? Even if the plan was a good one, how could you possibly change the axial plane of a planet this size?"

Eldred shrugged. "I'm not saying there weren't issues, in fact there were two major concerns that had to addressed, the first, and the more difficult was developing a workable process to actually affect the change in a controlled manner, the second issue and equally important was how to insure the rate of change was well controlled. If you recall your basic trigonometry, this type of undertaking would require a multi-dimensional monitoring process, and while our current orbiting vantage point allowed for two of the dimensions, a third was needed for absolute control. And logically this third aspect needed to be from the planets surface for proper triangulation. And when you factor in the rotational aspects it was clear more than one planet based observation base would be needed, in point of fact the final plan involved six of them." Seeing the look of confusion on my face he added. "Think of it as an airplane, there are three control considerations which affect flight, the pitch, the roll and the yaw. This is very similar, from our orbiting position we can easily monitor the "pitch", or north to south changes, we can also monitor the "yaw", or east-west changes, but it is not possible for us to assess the third aspect of "roll". For that we needed to have ground-based observatory's that used fixed star positions, in that manner we could assess rotational roll. Again, monitoring all three aspects was critical to the issue of control. And because of the curvature of the earth, we need to insure that regardless of which "side" of the planet was prevalent during the operation, we would have this basic trigonometric data. The plan was put into motion and for the next 500 years the ground based observatories were built." Eldred clicked the projection button and a familiar image of the Egyptian Sphinx came into view, the great pyramids could be seen in the background, although all were still under construction.

Seeing the Sphinx I stopped Eldred. "You built that?"

Eldred nodded. "Yes, it was necessary to have a baseline

directional point of reference, that way we could make sure the Pyramids were properly aligned." He laughed. "That's right! In spite of all the evidence your scientists still believe the Egyptians built it."

Not wanting to miss the opportunity I decided to ask about the other great pyramids archeologists and scientists have been arguing over for years. "You said six sites like this were needed. Where are the other sites located?"

In answer Eldred changed the image to one of a two dimensional map. Using a remote he highlighted six other areas. "This is the one we just saw, there is another here." He pointed at the area that today would be of the coast of Japan." Here." He pointed at the Bolivian area I knew as Lake Titicaca, and then another in the Andes of Peru. "Another was built above the equator here." He pointed at the area I recognized as Mexico, but the northern hemisphere Mexico much closer to the Artic. "And here." He pointed at a location between the coast of Africa and the coast of South America.

I was not surprised, every area he pointed to contained as yet unexplained monuments of mammoth proportion, monuments which have baffled our best scientific minds for centuries. As an afterthought I decided to ask him about my favorite ancient mystery. "I don't suppose you can tell me about the "Nazca" lines can you?"

Eldred laughed again, this time a deep throaty laugh. "You mean these?" He again adjusted the image and the shape of the monkey came into view, followed by the snake and the rest of the odd figures. He looked at me his face now solemn. "This was one of our greatest achievements, even greater than the giant "heads" you found in South America." He paused then, with a twinkle in his eye added. "In fact the Nazca lines as you call them, won the contest for being the most creative, and I might add, made the stonecutters very angry."

I looked at him. It took a few second before his words fully registered. "You mean its only art? It doesn't have any other function?"

Eldred, obviously pleased with himself, nodded. "Yes that's all it was, you see after thousands of years of labor, the workers decided to have a competition to see who could create the best art, the stone cutters immediately set about cutting and carving huge edifices, often using each other as subjects, the lifters, those who piloted the various craft didn't appear to be doing anything, well when the contest ended the stone cutters proudly demonstrated their works, confident they had won. You can imagine their surprise when the award was given to the pilots." Eldred, seeing I did not understand what he was talking about added. "The pilots, using their anti-gravitational equipment created the images you see here, and did so without setting a foot on the ground."

"What did they win?"

Eldred smiled. "First choice of the settlement they wanted to live in, remember until now, no actual settlement had taken place."

I looked again at the image of the figures; somehow it was a letdown from my predefined notions of their purpose. I turned to Eldred. "Lets get back to the "how" question."

Eldred pushed the button and the image of the Giza strip re-appeared. "As I said the Sphinx was placed first, its sole purpose was to provide the baseline for the placement of all of the pyramids in all of the sites. The actual pyramid location and positioning was by design relative to what you call the four cardinal points, and based upon the "East" line defined by the Sphinx. This placement would allow us to gauge the degree of "roll", if any occurred during the process. The same baseline was used for all of the sites."

I held up my hand. "Just to make sure I understand what you said. All of the pyramids in all of the sites were positioned relative to this Sphinx?"

He nodded. "Yes! The Sphinx was the baseline for all of them. You see the Sphinx was located facing due east and in perfect alignment to the rising sun on the vernal equinox, in fact, if one were to draw a line through it and continue it around the world, you would in effect have defined the true equator, similar to the ninety-degree line we super-imposed on the spinning top earlier. From this line, the location of the pyramids was defined relative to the four cardinal points representing the four solstices. The original offset from north to south of the existing "magnetic north" could then be defined, and subsequently the degree of "obliquity of the poles". As we increase the offset we needed to insure that the shadow created by the setting sun fell in a straight line through the edges of the larger pyramids."

He changed the image to an overhead view of the site. "As you can see the smaller pyramid is offset relative to the other two, and for a reason. When the line of the descending suns shadow line comes into contact with the small pyramid it would indicate the "precession" goal had been achieved. Using this site design the same method could be used for all of the sites. In other words, regardless of the time the process was undertaken, it was possible to determine if the angle change of the "magnetic north", and at the same time determine if we had imparted any "twist" or "roll" on the planet."

I watched as Eldred turned the projection off. While I did not fully comprehend the scientific principles supporting what he said, I understood the overall purpose of the land-based sites. He turned to face me. "As I said earlier, there were actually two issues that concerned the scientists, the first, as I just showed you was addressed by creating the six land-based observation sites, the other major issue dealt with the mechanics of the actual process required to physically move "magnetic north" away from "true north". To accomplish this, the scientists came up with another creative solution. Again using model simulations they were able to demonstrate it was possible to affect the axial shift by modulating the planets existing magnetic fields while at the same time applying a polar "reaction" at the two poles."

I shook my head. "You lost me, how is any of that even possible?" I remembered my studies and knew the magnetic fields generated by the earth's rotation were integrally associated with the gravitational forces. Consequently any attempt to modulate the magnetic fields, would by default translate into gravitational disturbances as well. I had visions of people and things flying off the planet. Was this what had happened?

Eldred shrugged, I sensed my inability to grasp the scientific nuances left him struggling with how to convey his answers. Finally he said. "Are your familiar with magnet fields and their properties?"

While I thought I understood the basics, I decided that relative to him, I probably knew very little. "A little, I know opposites attract and like repels."

Eldred nodded. "It a good starting point. Now if what you said is true what would happen if I brought a positively charged magnet near another positively charged magnet?"

Without hesitation I answered. "They would repel each other."

He smiled. "Yes they would. Now let's create an example." He turned on the projection unit and after pressing a few buttons presented the image of a sphere, the north and south poles were represented by a red vertical line. He inserted another green line slightly offset from the red one. "The red line is what we will call "true north", and the green line represents "magnetic north", as you can see they offset is very small, in the neighborhood of three degree's. Now as you know our scientists want to increase the angle of the degree between these two lines, correct?"

I shook my head to indicate I understood.

"Good. Now, if we were to present a positively charged magnet field on the right side of "true north" What would happen?"

I watched as he placed a series of pointed wavy lines at the top right of the sphere, the arrows pointed to the left in the direction of the green line. He paused evidently waiting for me to respond.

"I would imagine it would be repelled." I was beginning to understand where he was going with the simulation.

He nodded. "Correct, the source of the charge would have to be of a greater mass than the planet in order for the planets "magnetic north" to move, if it is not, the source of the new charge would be repelled. Now, What would happen if you also applied a negatively charged magnetic field on the lower left "south magnetic pole" I watched as he again assigned the pointed wavy lines at the bottom of the sphere, with the points facing right at the lower end of the green line. "It would also be repelled for the same reason correct?"

I nodded in agreement. Eldred continued. "So what we know is the larger mass would stay relative and the smaller mass would be repelled. So the immediate issue for the scientists was how to create or simulate a source with greater mass than the globe, OR, to reduce the effective forces generated by the mass of the planet. If they could do this they would be able to "nudge" the "magnetic north" and "magnetic south" using polar reactions.

I looked at him. "I'm going to assume they found a way or we wouldn't be having this conversation?"

"Yes! Yes they did, and it was rather innovative. The simulation model told them if they could decrease the gravitational

320

influences in the equatorial regions at the same time they attempted the polar reactions, the mass of the planet could be reduced enough to shift the magnetic poles."

I shook my head in disbelief. "Are you telling me they manipulated the gravitational pull of the planet? How is that possible without tearing the planet apart?"

Eldred looked pensive, to answer the question correctly he would need to describe the as yet undiscovered relationship between electro-magnetic forces and gravitational forces, such a discovery would forever change the technological landscape for humans, clearly violation of their "Prime Directive". Finally arriving at a compromised approach he responded. "To fully understand the actual mechanics involved would require more time than you or I have." He paused then added. "I can assure you it would take more than the few remaining years left in your cycle."

Not to be put off so easily I decided to ask for a simple overview. "I probably wouldn't understand it if you told me. But is there a simple version?"

Eldred shrugged. "Gravity is affected by magnetic field densities and variations, or more specifically electro-magnetic field density. Positively charged electrons generate energy which in turns generates acceleration, this in combination with mass, generates gravity." He paused before continuing. "And as you know from your visit to the Hall of Understanding all aspects have a corresponding opposite, which in this instance could be loosely defined as negatively charged particles. So if you could reduce the positive particles and increase the negative ones you could theoretically affect the gravitational influences." He hesitated looking upward as if searching for a simple corollary. "Let's try this for an example. Suppose you had a ball and you wanted to roll the ball, it would require more force to turn the ball on a flat surface, than if it were bobbing in a pot of water, correct?"

What he said made sense even to my non-scientific mind. "Yes it would have more buoyancy. So you're saying the earth is like the ball on the flat surface?"

"Yes exactly. And if they could reduce the gravitational effect it would be like the ball in the pot of water."

"I see, and you're saying you have he technology to do that?"

Eldred smiled. "Do you recall in and earlier image you saw one of our craft lifting a large block of granite without any visible means of support?"

I nodded. "Yeah I was going to ask you about that."

"Well, the principles used to do that, are not unlike what the scientists had in mind for this process. That craft uses a negatively charged wide area energy beam to disrupt the electro-magnetic field density in the area around the block. With the positive energy disrupted the gravitational forces are reduced by a factor of ten, perhaps more. As such the block which might weigh a hundred tons might then weigh as little as ten tons, in fact if they were to use the full energy available they could conceivably reduce the lifting weight as low as a hundred pounds. The block is then lifted using a tractor beam and as you saw transported to the site where it is needed."

"So that little ship could create enough of a negative charge to change the planets gravitational pull?"

Eldred laughed. "No of course not, but a line of ships placed at the equator where the gravitational pull is weakest, when your moon is at its Perigee, could create and maintain enough of a electro-magnetic disruption for the few seconds needed to initiate the "Polar reaction", and keep in mind were are talking seconds not minutes or hours."

I could picture the scene he described and while I did not know "how" they would create the positive and negative energy forces needed to create the pole reaction, I knew they could do it. "So what happened? What went wrong?"

Eldred held up his hands as if asking me to slow down. "There are a few more details you should know before we talk about that. First the process could only be completed once per year, when you moon is at its closest point to the earth, its perigee, doing so maximizes the gravitational influences generated by the moon! Second if you recall the model indicated each trail should not exceed one degree per attempt. Which means this process was going to take a minimum of fifteen attempts before the goal was reached. I'm telling you this because I want you to understand the efforts that were taken to monitor these changes. The scientists calculated each trial would require a minimum of ten of your seconds. After each trial a period of eleven months would pass before the moon again reached its minimum orbit from earth, in the intervening time EVERY facet of your environment and of course the area of habitable area was analyzed, if there was any suggestion at all of a problem the project would have been abandoned."

"Okay, I understand that, so what happened?" Eldred's desire to justify their decisions while important to him meant little to me. In the end, it meant nothing.

Without a word Eldred continued. Turning on the projection unit he selected the image of the earth again, the "habitable area" was significantly larger, as was the degree of "obliquity around the poles". "Every test went exactly as planned, and as you can see the area now habitable, is significantly larger, at this point fourteen of the fifteen trials had been completed and they were initiating the final one."

I watched as the line of ships began emitting their negatively charged beams around the equator, the water beneath many of them began to rise as if being sucked up a line of giant straws, almost simultaneously I saw two beams being directed at the two areas I assumed were the magnetic poles. I was expected to see movement of some type but was unprepared for what I saw. In less time than it took to blink, the entire crust of the earth shifted from right to left in a downward twisting motion, the beams immediately disappeared, as did the line of small ship's now hidden beneath a sky I could only describe as coal black, with fiery red streaks. I turned to Eldred. "What happened?"

His face solemn, he turned the projection off. "The simple answer is the Lithosphere or crust of your planet shifted, as for why? I can say the subsequent analysis found two major contributing factors. The first, and one the scientists had not factored into the process, had to do with the affect of the gravity from the Sun. As I said earlier the gravitational relationship of every planet has an affect on every other planet in the system, the scientists had calculated correctly, that the changes we imparted to earths gravity, for the time of ten seconds would not adversely affect the stability of the other planets. However what they failed to consider was the fact that Venus would be in transit at the moment they began the last trial."

I looked at him. I had no idea what he meant. "Venus in

transit, what's does that mean?"

Eldred activated the projection unit again, this time selecting a view of the solar system. I watched as the planets circled around the sun. Eldred pointed at what I knew was Earths neighbor Venus. "At the moment the trail began, Venus began an orbital transit which placed it between the Earth and the Sun. For the ten seconds of the trial, the gravitational influence of the Sun on the Earth were measurably lower, this change in the gravity was not factored into the equation of the trial, the increased "loss" of gravity meant the force of the directed polarity beams was too great, and as a result the energy beams pushed the poles almost twice the trial limit. The second unforeseen factor is related to other changes which took place within the core of the planet. After fourteen trials the surface area of the planet had become de-glaciated enough so that internal volcanic pressures resulted in multiple eruptions, these in turn caused several major earthquakes, the subsequent shifting of the tectonic plates in the western Pacific and Indian oceans created tidal waves and of course a serious imbalance of the land-water mass. The combined effect of these factors resulted in a slippage of the crust by approximate thirty degrees east to southwest. Subsequent surveys indicated the actual displacement was over two-thousand of your miles." He pointed at the area I knew as the Mexican landmass. "If you recall from the earlier image, this area used to be here." He pointed at the area I knew would someday be New York State. He pointed at the tip of South America. "Before the event this area was just south of the equator, and our main settlement was here." He pointed at the area between South America and Antarctica. "This is now at the new South Pole." He shut the projection off before turning to once again face me.

Shocked by the suddenness of the change, I struggled for something to say. In literally seconds the entire face of the planet had been transformed. I stared at the area where a moment before the image had been visible. Finally I asked. "What happened to the people?" I hesitated then added. "Both of our peoples."

Eldred, still visibly upset at what had transpired took another moment before answering. "At the time, we had already begun moving the colonists into the settlements; as a result of this tragedy we lost 72% of our original number, some 360,000 plus another 20,000 of our crew. The affect on the humans far exceeded that. He again activated the projection unit. The image was similar to the one that had reflected the red dots, I knew were the humans. In the earlier image the red dots had given the image the "measles", this one could only be described as a bad case of acne. Eldred shook his head. "The earlier population was close to a million humans, and that was three thousand years ago, since that time the population had grown only slightly, to a little over a million. After this event the revised population estimate was just over 200,000." He paused before adding. "And I'm afraid that wasn't the worst of it." That said he again changed the image.

I watched as a new image came into focus. The scene left me speechless. Whereas in the earlier scenes the humans seemed to be healthy, this scene could not have been more opposite. Every human I saw, regardless of age, seemed to be sick or dying. I watched as a wild dog or perhaps it was a wolf, dragged a dead carcass into the brush, the few children I saw were crying, running to every adult they saw, only to be pushed away. The powers they had once controlled were no longer evident. I watched as two figures emerged from the jungle, one I immediately recognized as "Rena", and based upon their likeness I knew the other was the sister she told me about. As I watched Rena placed her hands on the bleeding leg of one of the children, the light told me the child was being healed. I glanced at Joan who had risen and walked toward the projection, Christie stood by her side, I could see both had tears on their cheeks, I turned to find "Three" who had stopped documenting, she also stared at the scene. Mercifully Eldred stopped the projection.

The room was silent for several minutes before Eldred spoke. "There are no words to describe the rage I felt the first time I saw these images, and quite frankly still feel today."

Still visualizing the image in my mind, I did not hear myself asking. "What happened to them?"

Eldred lowered his hands and turned to face me. "In all the time we studied your kind we were never able to determine the source of the powers they possessed. There was nothing of a biological nature that could account for them. After this event we made the connection. Your people were intricately linked to the pulse or vibrations of your world. The powers they possessed originated with

325

their interaction with the currents of the planets electro-magnetic properties; unbeknownst to us the modifications we made to the magnetic pole axis severed your people from the source. We were able to confirm by placing a few of the survivors into a lab constructed to exactly match the pre-event electro-magnetic properties of the planet. Almost immediately their health returned, as did the other powers they had possessed." He stopped as if thinking how to say his next words. "Fortunately we only allowed two subjects in that lab, as their strength and abilities returned, they immediately "phased out" or disappeared as you saw them do in the earlier image, we subsequently found them back on the planet, but they were dead."

It was only then that I grasped the nuances of what Eldred had said. "You brought humans to the ship?"

Eldred shook his head. "I am still a thousand years away, but yes, Arinon did. After the event he issued orders to the remaining crew and colonists instructing them to use all available resources to find and bring back every live human they could find. When they returned only 144,000 humans had been found, and they were immediately placed in stasis to keep them alive."

I raised my hands and gestured for him to stop. "You mean ninety percent of the humans were killed? Did any survive and retain their powers? What about those two we saw healing the child, did they die? And what do you mean placed into stasis?"

"Yes, sadly the majority of humans did perish, either during the event, or soon after, as for survivors, yes there were a few that we knew of who retained their powers, they had been in the "between" place when the event occurred, and the physical event did could not affect them, and stasis is a form of suspended animation, similar to your cryogenics, but without the cold." Seeing my look of confusion he laughed. "That's right we never talked about that did we. The event took place in 10000 BC, by now the colonists had been involved with your planet for almost 7000 years, if you also consider the expedition searched the galaxy for an additional 8000 of your years before finding this planet, you have to wonder how they could still be alive."

I hadn't thought it, and now as he talked about it, I realized how often I should have questioned it. Almost sheepishly I replied.

"No, it never occurred to me to ask. But now that you mention it, how did they live that long."

Eldred activated the projection and after making several adjustments the image of a large asteroid began to form. "This is the colonization ship. The image you are seeing is from my star-liner when I first arrived."

I watched as the Asteroid grew larger, it didn't look like a ship but it was certainly massive. "Why does it look like that and how big is it?"

Eldred laughed. It looks like that as a defensive measure, the colonization ships did not have weapons, so their only protection is disguise, after all who wants to shoot at a rock? As for its size, let just say that one of your entire major cities could easily fit inside it."

His comments about shooting at a rock intrigued me. "Are you saying there are others out there?"

He nodded. "Yes many and some are very dangerous. Now watch this." He pointed at the image.

As I watched the lower section of the asteroid seemed to break away revealing a hollow cavern into which the star-liner entered. Moments later I felt a jolt as the "door" locked back into position. I watched as the figures I knew to be Eldred with Christie, now dressed in a blue tunic, exited the ship and walked toward something that looked like elevators. I was curious to know how the image was being captured. "How is it I can see you, is someone following with a recorder?"

Christie having sat quietly for the entire time spoke up. "Every person and every action is captured by the automatic recording system aboard the ship."

As I watched the elevator stopped and the two stepped out. I could see behind them a cavernous area. Row upon row of cylindrical shapes extended as far as I could see, above each cylinder a small round orb glowed and pulsed. "What is this place?"

Christie smiled. "Those are what we call Regeneration pods, or as Eldred call's them Stasis tubes. This deck alone contains just over 100,000 of them, and there are five other decks as well. Each pod is connected to the ships core computer. The computer monitors them and makes any needed adjustments to insure they are functioning properly.   Each pod was specifically configured to its owner's physiology, and while they are in stasis, the pod is used to regenerate their biological unit to its original configuration."

I looked at her unsure if I understood what she had said. "You mean the pod actually regenerates the biological tissue?"

She nodded. "Oh yes. In fact, the pod not only regenerates new tissue and cells, it can also "recreate" the owner back to its original condition when it was first programmed." She paused then added. "When the colonist or crew member first came aboard they entered the pod and allowed the computer to develop a matrix of their physiology. That matrix was uploaded to the ships main computer and in pod's local memory as well. Whenever the owner enters the pod, the system automatically compares their current physiology to that matrix, and while the owner is in stasis, the pod regenerates the body to bring him or her back to the original configuration. In fact every ship from the smallest shuttle craft, to the largest transport, has at least one pod, and in some cases, as many as twenty pods, this way should an accident occur while they are away from their pod they can be placed into stasis immediately, and their matrix downloaded from the central computer to the pod."

It sounded strangely like cloning to me. "So they are cloned? Wouldn't that damage their minds?"

Eldred pointed at the glowing orb's which hung above each pod.   "Excellent question and the answer is yes after repeated regenerations it would damage their minds. That glowing orb you see is in fact the mind or consciousness of the occupant, one of the first actions taken is to place the occupant into a deep sleep, what we call stasis, most of the energy or consciousness of the person is then transferred into that orb. I say most because a small amount of the life force is still required by the biological unit to provide proper mapping when it is returned." He hesitated before adding. "I would not call them clones at least by your definition of a clone. They are still the same person, just "repaired"."

I looked at the glowing orbs. "How long can they stay in their pods?"

Eldred shrugged. "Indefinitely, the ones you see here have been in stasis for over ten thousand your years. There really is no time limit. However, once out of stasis there is a requirement that they return for regeneration once every six of your months. A complete regeneration process takes about a month to complete, so effectively the colonists could be available for ten out of every twelve months."

Curious I asked. "Why every six months? Would being out longer make them sick or something?"

Eldred glanced at Christie before answering. "One of the conditions of being accepted as a colonist was their agreement to wait to have children until their mission was completed. You must remember their mission was to find a home for the people still waiting on the home worlds. They also understood that because of these pods, they would still be able to have children in the future if they chose to do so. In any case, by requiring them to return for regeneration every six months we also insured if a pregnancy did develop, it would be terminated when the occupant was returned to its original matrix."

I wasn't sure how I felt about this process, but for the first time started to appreciate the sacrifices they were making to help their people. Perhaps under different circumstances I would have been proud to know them. I looked at the endless row of pods and couldn't help but notice many did not have a glowing orb. I gestured at one and asked Christie. "Is that one empty?"

Christie followed my gaze and was silent for a moment. "Yes, there are many empty pods, as you know over 70% of our people were lost during the event that so badly affected your people."

I looked at Eldred who still stood staring at the projected image. "You said Arinon brought my people here, can I ask why?"

In response Eldred shut off the image. "Because they were dying, and the only way to save them was to put them into stasis. According to the records, the pods were easily adapted for you physiology."

"Why were they dying? Didn't the ones who survived get better as they adjusted to not having their powers?"

He shook his head. "No they were dying, most from sickness, some at the hands of predators and even a few from starvation." He paused then added. "If you stop to really think about the powers they lost, you realize they are completely dysfunctional without them. Before the loss of their power they never got sick, their own

329

physiology could heal itself, cells regenerated automatically, and in fact, they often their collective power in the healing process, they had no need for clothing to keep warm because they could simply recreate their functional environment to protect themselves from inclement weather or cold. Predators were only an issue if they were caught by surprise, and of course, they could avoid known dangers by simply disappearing. When you take those powers away, especially the self healing, they are no longer immune to diseases, they could no longer communicate with each other or for that matter protect themselves. So yes, they were either dying or going to die."

I guess I should have been grateful but couldn't bring myself to say it. If they had not attempted the ill-fated experiment there would have been no need to thank them. "How long were they here?"

"The records indicate five hundred years. It took that long for the scientists to figure out what to do with them."

"What did they do? Are the support units part of that solution?" I looked at my "Three" who had stopped recording and was listening intently.

Eldred nodded. "Yes the support units were an integral part of Arinons solution. The humans were in stasis, and could not be returned until the scientists found a way to help them cope with their reality, both biologically and mentally. And while the humans had a spark or essence of their own it did not operate in the same way as that of the Andeans'. In any case, the scientists eventually found a way to re-engineer the consciousness from the Adean's, and to merge it with the humans." Eldred stopped speaking when he saw the expression on "Three's" face. He raised his hands indicating she should listen to the rest of his explanation. "When I say re-engineer the consciousness I do not mean they changed the Adeans, indeed every colonist currently in stasis, could be revived today, and they would probably not even notice a difference. In any case, the scientists developed a method whereby they could take a very small piece of an Adeans consciousness and to re-engineer or re-configure it so that it could be merged with the essence and bio of the humans. It would remain separate from the human essence, but would still be able to interact with the Biological unit and help support it. This re-engineering aspect came in two forms, the first was to allow it to be emptied of its own knowledge, and the second was a re-configuration so it could be merged with the humans and be of functional use. They knew it was not possible to "give back" all the humans had lost, but they tried to provide the facets of the human condition that the powers would have if they had been retained. There were five aspects addressed, beginning with the need to support the bio's natural functions, that as you know is the responsibility of the units "Two", the next critical process was to provide a method of learning and retaining knowledge, this was the original intent of the "Three". The next aspect dealt with helping the bio units use the memories recorded and retained by the "Three", hopefully helping them develop solutions to issues, like what is a good food versus a bad food. The "Four", or what you refer to as the creative self, helped draw on these memories in future decision making about food. And then there was "Five", while the scientists could not duplicate the human's ability to heal themselves, they did provide a surrogate process where, within limits, the body could regenerate itself. You're "Six" or what you refer to as your scientist, was an attempt to allow the humans to stay tuned to their physical senses and to translate them into thoughts or ideas. Then of course there is the "Seven", you can think of him as their leader. "Seven's the one that makes sure this re-engineered team works as a cohesive group, "Sevens" is also the one who communicates with the host or Bio. The humans or hybrids as they were now called, armed with these new tools were relocated back to the planet. Almost immediately they began to have problems. Because their nature was biologically based and quite fragile, they were no longer immune from the physical sensations like hunger or pain or death, and unlike their previous time when even the smallest was as strong as the largest, they now found the smallest could be exploited, the stronger hybrids learned to live at the expense of the weaker ones, this introduced the first true social separation of the specie, and even worse introduced them to their greatest enemy, fear. Then as if to satisfy the scientist's curiosity they began to procreate, in the eyes of the scientists this was the true determining factor as to whether their re-engineering process was successful. Fortunately the new humans were born with the same support structure the parents had. To further complicate matters the interlopers became involved and began to manipulate the hybrids for their own purposes."

I stopped him, wondering what interlopers were. "You said interlopers, who are they? Are they the humans who survived with their powers?"

Eldred looked at Christie before replying. "When Arinon told the colonists he planned to use a piece of their consciousness to support the humans, a few refused, not many, only about two-hundred. Arinon became angry and ordered Peter; the ships commander to arrest them for mutiny, Peter did as he was told and placed the prisoners in the custody of his chief navigator and second in command whose name was Maruk. However, unbeknownst to Peter, Maruk shared the sentiments of his prisoners, and consequently helped engineer their, and his own escape, using one of the transport ships. In spite of the still turbulent eco-system the ship made it safely to the planet and it was some time before it was eventually located and retrieved, the emergency pod units or portable re-generation units Christy referenced earlier had been removed, and the interlopers as we now called them, had been dispersed themselves to all parts of the planet."

Eldred activated the projector and an image of the two hundred escapees appeared, as I scanned the faces I immediately saw the face of the large man and the redheaded woman from the earlier images from the village. I glanced at Joan who I sensed also recognized them. "Aren't they the ones we saw earlier?" I paused then added. "They can't be, that was at least two thousand years after this."

Christie shook her head. "Yes that's Maruk and the redhead beside him is his wife. And yes, if they had a regeneration pod its possible they would still be alive two thousand years later."

I looked at the pictures again. The significance of what Christie had said was setting in. "Are you telling me they could still be alive today?"

Eldred raised his hand as if trying to defuse the conversation. "No, that would not be possible for several reasons. First the emergency pods or regeneration units used a crystal based power source. This means they would have a limited number of regenerations available before their power crystals would be exhausted. At best, they could have been used perhaps thirty to fifty times without being recharged. Even if the interlopers waited seventy years between regenerations it could only last for two or three thousand years. Even if they relied on just partial regenerations it would only extend their usefulness by perhaps another two thousand years, no, I think it is safe to say the original interlopers are now dead." He decided not mention the fact that many of the early conflicts between humans were the result of one interloper trying to take possession of the pod of another, thereby increasing his own lifespan.

Joan, free now to discuss the interlopers joined the discussion. "From a sociologists viewpoint the interlopers ended up becoming critical enablers in uniting the humans and moving them forward from hunter gatherer's, to agriculturally based communities. It would be wise to remember that unlike the support units Eldred described, the interlopers returned to the planet with their full knowledge and skill's intact, knowledge that included such things as farming, metal working, architecture and obviously skills like mathematics, astrology and physics, and although the use of this knowledge was inhibited by the available tools, they still managed to become the focal points and leaders of the humans." She looked at me before adding. "It's no coincidence the earliest "god's" were these same leaders, I mean, put yourself in the shoes of a human, you watch your leaders grow old and then instead of dying they miraculously become young again, over and over again for thousand of years."

I had already come to the conclusions Joan was trying to express. I raised my hands to silence her. I turned to Eldred. "Why did Arinon even make this effort? Wouldn't it have been easier for him to just let the humans die? With them out of the way he could simply begin the colonization process again."

Eldred had been expecting this question and knew the rest of the saga had to be told. "Earlier I mentioned the "Rules of Colonization" every colonist's was required to commit to, there were more rules than just the two or three we have already referenced. There were also conditional rules, which were to be applied if the first and second rules were not properly adhered to. In the case of the "Prime Directive" the process was clearly defined. The guilty parties were to be immediately returned to the home world for trial and possible sentencing. The second rule however was a bit more subjective, if you recall this second rule involved the decision of

333

whether colonizing was appropriate in terms of being able to peacefully co-existence with the existing life forms. Do you remember that?"

I shook my head that I did. "Yes I remember, that was the case with this world."

He nodded. "Correct. Now if for any reason, time revealed the decision to colonize was not appropriate, the colonists were obligated to leave the planet immediately. Failure to do so would leave them open to penalties similar to those of the rule one violations. Additionally, if during the process of colonization the decision were proven to be correct, but subsequently, as in this case was proven to be harmful to the life forms or the eco-system the colonists were required to take all available measures to restore the planet and life-forms, and when this was done they were required to leave the planet. So to answer your question, Arinon and the colonists were in fact following the rules of colonization. They were attempting to restore the humans to their homes"

I thought of his response and realized for the first time that I now understood the roles of all of the groups except Eldred's. The role of the pure humans, while still an open issue to me, provided the basis for all that had transpired, the role support units, the hybrids and even Arinons group had all been clarified. Only the role of Eldred and his group remained a mystery. "How long will Arinons group support this "recovery" process?"

Eldred looked out the observation window. I could sense he was struggling to find the right words. Finally he turned to me. "Earlier I told you my role was to oversee the colonization process, to insure the "Rules of Colonization" were followed, our intent then and even now, has always been to make sure we protect worlds like yours." He paused before continuing. "One of my responsibilities is to assess if violations have occurred and to take appropriate actions if needed. In this case I can say with full confidence that Arinon and the colonists did NOT violate any rule, in fact they have clearly demonstrated that they have taken extraordinary measures to insure they followed every rule to the letter. Their initial classification of this world as a category two was appropriate given the information they had collected, the subsequent decision that they could colonize and peacefully co-exist without harming the planet or the life forms it contained was also correct, every step taken during this now questionable planetary experiment process was meticulously thought out and supported by appropriate scientific analysis and modeling, and now even after the event all of the steps taken were correct as well, every effort was made to restore the planet and life forms. So in summary I cannot find fault according to the "Rules." He obviously sensed my objections to what he was saying and held up his hands to indicate he was not done talking. "While I personally think there were times and sufficient evidence to suggest Arinon should have departed this planet long ago, the interpretation of the evidence is subjective at best. So in the final analysis the only issue remaining is what happens next. And again if I follow the "Rules of Colonization" I can tell you that the rules also allow further colonization of this world, if in the determination of the overseer all efforts to restore it have been exhausted and nothing more could have been done."

I was shocked by this revelation. Was that why the support units were being removed? So that Arinon and his colonists could again move in and take over. "So you've made your decision? You think everything that could be done has been, that by removing the support units, we will either survive or die?"

Eldred nodded. "I guess in the final analysis that is the determining factor, but before you say any more please hear me out, there are factors you have not been told yet." He looked at me waiting for me to respond. I didn't I just stared at him. "After I arrived here and reviewed all of the evidence I met with Arinon to discuss what had happened and what he should do. During this discussion I invited the scientists to also present their findings, the data that showed the "hybrid humans" still possessed the powers they had lost during the field modulation experiment, that they had only been separated from it. What's more, the scientists were confident that based upon the results of the lab process with the first two humans, once the magnetic poles regressed and corrected themselves by point zero-three-seven degrees, humans will once again be able to connect with their lost powers, they presented data that the observed rate of regression has been stable at point-zero-zero-three degrees per century. At that rate they projected it would require twelve thousand years from the time of the initial separation until it will be achieved. That time is in eight years, or in the calendar year using the Common Era, in 2012. The scientists are ninety-two percent confident when this date arrives, humans will once again regain their lost powers. So yes, in eight years all support units will be returned to their true owners aboard the colonization ship."

I thought of what he was saying, could it be true? "What happens if it doesn't work? Will we die without the support units?"

He shrugged. "We don't know. We believe the biological immunities your kind has developed will protect you from diseases, and we know you are capable of thinking and of protecting yourselves, all the things you could not do as new hybrids. And quite frankly we don't really know what will happen to the Bio's without their "Fives", the cell regeneration process is not something you do yourself, the capability either exists or it does not." Eldred paused, a look of concern on his face. "The questions you ask are valid and I will not lie to you, there is an eight percent chance your powers will not return, but to be frank, I am equally concerned that they will. You know your kind and have also witnessed first hand the powers of which I speak, tell me how will people react to these reacquired powers?"

I remembered Rena's concerns about my accidentally passing the powers to others, clearly she believed the hybrids would not use them wisely, I shared her view, even with the best intentions they would be misused. It dawned on me that Eldred's group was looking to me to find a way to change the mindset of the people before they reacquired their powers. I looked at Eldred and the council who sat waiting for my response. "I don't know but I suspect it would be used just like every other power we have managed to develop. I take it that is what this is all about?" I gestured toward the group behind him.

Eldred nodded. "Yes! That's what this is about."

"So your ship is still out there?" I gestured in an upward direction. I would have thought with our new telescopes and shuttle flights we would have discovered it by now.

"Eldred laughed as if he had read my mind. "Yes it's there. It's in orbit at the outer reaches of your solar system, using your scientific terms it is eighty AU's from here, forty AU's beyond what you call Pluto."

I smiled at his reaction. "What is an AU?"

Eldred nodded. "Astronomical unit, each unit is about ninety-three million miles, so roughly translated our ship is seven billion miles from here, to give you an example, consider this, your planet requires one year to complete a single revolution around the sun, our ship make one revolution every six-hundred-nineteen years."

The numbers Eldred used were overwhelming. While I could not imagine it, I knew that anything over a billion was a lot. I looked at him. "And it's coming here in eight years to get the support units?"

"Yes, in eight years the ships orbit will coincide with a planetary alignment which will allow the ship to approach from deep space with the least gravitational effect from the planets." He paused then added with a grin on his face. "Maruk actually left this information for humans to learn in several of the temples on your world. The Mayan civilization who were descended from Maruks tribe, figured this out a thousand years ago."

I looked at Eldred, for the first time I began to appreciate the pressures he must be feeling. "I have one more question before I leave."

He nodded. "Yes I know. You want to know about the "Agreement" don't you?"

I shook my head. "That's right, based upon everything you have said I can't understand why one would be required."

"Do you remember a moment ago I told you that the colonization effort could resume if, after all Arinons best efforts, your people did not survive."

I nodded that I did.

Eldred continued. "Early in the process I asked my group to monitor the progress of your people to see if there was more that could be done. What they reported was shocking, they were convinced that Arinon was using his connections with the support units to find and destroy the original pure humans that were left. To support their allegations they presented the memory records of the hybrids involved. When I confronted Arinon he did not deny it, and in fact, tried to justify the action as a necessary one to protect the hybrids. I did not believe him, and personally felt he was eliminating them because as long as the pure humans existed Arinon would not be allowed to resume colonization. This led me to believe that the second part of his plan was to create the environment where the hybrids would eventually destroy themselves, in doing so removing Arinons last obstacle. At this point I was left with a dilemma, if I removed the support units from the planet, the hybrids would surely die, especially since the support units were the only thing keeping them alive. But, if I left them, Arinon could use them to destroy the hybrids and unless I could prove he was responsible, he would resume the colonization efforts. I decided the only possible solution was to forbid Arinon or any of his group to intervene or directly influence the hybrids. I told him from that moment on my group would be diligent in assessing his group's involvement in human affairs, furthermore, if any provable evidence was found of their involvement the opportunity of re-colonization would no longer be an option for them. To support this monitoring effort I asked my group to develop a process that would guarantee every interaction between the hybrid and the support unit could be evaluated. That as you may have figured out is the evaluation process."

I laughed when he said this. All this time humans including myself, had thought of the evaluation process was an assessment of their actions and behaviors, in reality it was an evaluation of Arinon and his group. "I take it you have not found anything?"

Eldred was quiet for a moment. "No, Arinon and Peter are very careful, but that does not mean they haven't been active. Think for a moment of your world and its people, there are chemical, nuclear and biological weapons that could kill off every human on your planet. Do you think they were really the result of human endeavors alone? I personally do not think so, throughout your human history events have occurred which logically should not have, ideas and technology developed which the circumstances of the time did not justify. But no! There has never been any concrete evidence of direct interference." Eldred hesitated then added. "And just for the record there have also been times when I suspect my own group." He looked at Christie when he said this. "May have "inadvertently" interfered. But I am equally sure those occasions were necessary to counter-act actions by Arinons group."

I looked at Christie and smiled. "Let me guess, you try to change things through peoples dreams and that's why they call you "Sleepers" right."

Christie shrugged. "You can't prove a thing."

I turned back to Eldred. "Why are you telling me this now? Aren't you interfering because of this?"

Eldred laughed. "Yes I suppose I am, and, should your bio cease to function within the next eight years, everything I have said will be open for review, and yes I would be in violation of our agreement with Arinon. The downside is I could no longer prevent his group from re-colonizing the planet." He looked at me before going on. "I am telling you this because I fear Arinon has a long standing operation underway which will result in the extinction of your people. Given he has only eight years left to complete it I am sure whatever it is, it will happen soon. If you look at the political and environmental situation of your kind, and add in a mix of extremely volatile weapons like the ones I mentioned earlier I am truly afraid your specie will not be around in eight years. Something or someone has to change this, and quite frankly you are the only one with the power to do so."

I looked at him. He was right about the situation and it was obvious changes would need to occur and quickly, but I did not share his belief that I was capable of effecting the required changes. "I think you give me more credit than I deserve, yes I have these powers, but what is power in the absence of knowledge? I wouldn't know where to begin."

Christie looked at Eldred who nodded to her. She turned to me. "Every person here wants to see your kind survive, I think I can speak for all of them when I say we will stand with you, we will help you as best we can. That is, if you will agree to trust us and work with us."

"Three" nudged my arm trying to get my attention. "I think I can speak for your entire support unit when I say we will also help you, we did not know what was happening and when the others see this." She nodded in the direction of her recorder. "They will agree to help as well."

I didn't know what to say. I looked at Joan, James and Henry who sat waiting for my response. Christie still stood next to Eldred, and I saw Anne and Franklin who had just entered the room. Finally I turned to Eldred and shrugged. "Six from Arinon and Six from your group, how ironic, my twelve disciples. I don't know what or how, but I will try." I turned to my "Three" and pointed at my watch. "It's time to go I have an appointment to keep."

Eldred stood a broad smile on his face. "I will be here if you need me." He turned to his group of six. "Don't leave his side and protect him."

I nodded and closed my eyes, my thoughts focused on returning to my body.

# Chapter 42

## Room 128, Dusit Laguna Hotel, Phuket, Thailand.

*T*he room was dark when I opened my eyes, "Seven" sat as I had left him, but jumped to his feet at the appearance of Christie and her comrades. "Three immediately intervened. She looked at "Seven" and said in a calm voice. "They are here to help us, relax."

I looked at the clock, five minutes until I was supposed to meet Rhodes. I turned to my "Seven", anything happening with our visitors?"

Seven shook his head. "Not yet, I went out earlier and overheard them talking, if you don't come out before seven o'clock, they will come for you."

I laughed. If all went well they will find an empty room. I turned to my new friends. "Are you ready?" I watched as they collectively shook their heads. "Good, I'll see you in Chicago." I closed my eyes and tried to picture the lobby of the Medical Center where I knew Rhodes had first met with my wife and son.

# Chapter 43

## <u>Loyola Medical Center.</u>

*T*he lobby was busy. People were entering and leaving, occasionally jostling each other but usually offering their apologies. I looked around and found Rhode's standing near a bank of elevators; Harridy was standing by his side. They saw me in the same instant and Rhode's began the trek across the floor. Harridy however stayed where he was standing.

Rhode's extended his hand. "I wasn't sure you would show up." He was surprised when Harridy showed up, especially after calling him an hour earlier to tell him the police were trying to find Reynolds, and to ask him to let Reynolds know.

I smiled and shook his hand. "I wouldn't miss it. Where is Angelina?" I could hear his "Seven" admonishing him for not giving me Harridys warning. I stopped and looked at him. "What warning?"

Rhode's looked at me. I could hear his thoughts as he questioned how I could know. "Harridy said to tell you the police are actively searching for you and that your coming here could place you in danger." His following thoughts were even more revealing; he was feeling ashamed for not telling me immediately.

I looked at Harridy who stood watching from his position by the elevator. I waved him over and watched as he approached. I extended my hand to the big man. "Hello Sergeant it's good to see you again." He was nervous, his "Seven" wanted him to tell me something but I couldn't exactly hear what.

Harridy took my hand before glancing nervously around. "You shouldn't be here, they are looking for you." He did not need to add that as a "newly appointed officer" of the Homeland Security Office he was obligated to take him into custody.

He didn't need to tell me, his thoughts told me. I looked at

342

him. "How are my wife and son?"

Harridy seemed surprised by the question. "They're fine. I put them at my summer cottage for now, they should be safe there, and your son Eric is there as well." He hated himself, the internal struggle he felt between doing his duty, and his friendship and personal thoughts about Reynolds was almost overwhelming.

I nodded. "Thanks I really appreciate your help." I paused then added. "You do what is in your heart Tom." I turned to Rhodes. "Where is Angelina?"

Rhodes grinned. "Wong's office, they waiting for us." He turned to lead the way.

I followed as Rhodes walked toward the elevator, Harridy walked beside me. I looked at him and smiled. "This should not take long, and then I will go away so you can relax."

Wong's office was empty save for himself and a middle aged, but still attractive woman I knew could only be Angelina. She was lying on a couch and did not look well. I looked at Wong who "walked" steadily toward me. I laughed at his "showing off". "Well Doc you're getting around pretty good for a cripple."

Wong laughed and gave me a hug. "Thank you again. If there is anything I can ever do to repay you just ask and it is yours."

Rhodes, his eyes on his wife, echoed Wong's sentiments. "You fix Angelina and I am also in your debt."

I turned to Angelina and took one of her hands. "Hello Angelina, my name is Bill. Do you know why I am here?" Her hand was cool almost cold, her "Seven" stood next to her, telling her I was here to help.

She raised her eyes and looked at me. "Yes, Harold said you could make me feel better." She paused then said. "Do you think you can?"

I sat on the chair next to her. "I'm going to try, but please understand this is my first time actually "trying" to do it and even I don't know what will happen." I hadn't given the "how" aspect any thought at all.

She smiled. "I don't think you can make me feel any worse. Please try."

I released her hand and turned to face the others. "Would you mind leaving us alone for a few minutes?" I watched as they slowly filed into the outer office, I walked over and closed the door behind them. I returned to the couch and sat in a chair by Angelina's side; taking her hands I raised her into a sitting position. I leaned forward in my chair and placed my hands on either side of her head. I felt her temples pulsing beneath my fingers. I closed my eyes and tried to visualize the energy was flowing from me into her, I felt a burning sensation in my chest and was relieved when I felt the warmth flowing through my arms into my hands into her head, even with my eyes closed I could see the light begin to emanate from where my hands came into contact with her. I felt pressure building in my head, a pressure which quickly turned into pain, the lights began to waver and flash like a strobe light from right to left behind my eyes, each time it approached me directly I felt discomfort, like looking into the beam of a strong flashlight. Moments passed and I felt my eyes open, a white blurry shape pulling away from me came into focus, a square tag with words written on it came into view, the words said "Dr. Turner".

His voice came to me as if from a distance. "How are you feeling?" He turned to the nurse. "Tell them they can come in."

I watched as the curtain moved and Mary with my son Andrew came into view.

Turner looked at me. "There's also a Sergeant from the State Police who would like to speak with you when you're feeling better."

Mary approached the bed and took my hand. "You gave us quite a scare, they said you were shot." Her eyes moved to my head. "The Doctor said your going to be all right and we can probably take you hope this afternoon. Doctor Brangeel is on his way here as well."

Andrew leaned over and said something to Mary. He smiled at me before grasping my arm and saying. "I'll be back soon. Sergeant Harridy is going to take me to get the truck."

Was it all really a dream?